THE ZION
COVENANT
BOOK 7

London Refrain

THE ZION COVENANT
BOOK 7

BODIE & BROCK THOENE

TYNDALE HOUSE PUBLISHERS, INC. • WHEATON, ILLINOIS

Visit Tyndale's exciting Web site at www.tyndale.com

TYNDALE is a registered trademark of Tyndale House Publishers, Inc.

Tyndale's quill logo is a trademark of Tyndale House Publishers, Inc.

The Zion Covenant series designed by Julie Chen
Designed by Dean H. Renninger

Edited by Ramona Cramer Tucker

Portions of *London Refrain* were printed in *The Twilight of Courage,* © 1994 by Bodie and Brock Thoene, by Thomas Nelson, Inc., Publishers under ISBN 0-7852-8196-7.

First printing of *London Refrain* by Tyndale House Publishers, Inc. in 2005.

Scripture quotations are taken from the *Holy Bible*, King James Version or the *Holy Bible*, New International Version® NIV® Copyright © 1973, 1978, 1984 by International Bible Society. Used by permission of Zondervan Publishing House. All rights reserved.

This novel is a work of fiction. Names, characters, places, and incidents either are the product of the authors' imaginations or are used fictitiously. Any resemblance to actual events, locales, organizations, or persons, living or dead, is entirely coincidental and beyond the intent of either the authors or publisher.

Library of Congress Cataloging-in-Publication Data

Thoene, Bodie, date.
   London refrain / Bodie & Brock Thoene.
     p. cm. — (The Zion covenant; bk. 7)
   ISBN-10: 1-4143-0358-0 (sc)
   ISBN-13: 978-1-4143-0358-1 (sc)
   1. Holocaust, Jewish (1939-1945)—Fiction. 2. London (England)—Fiction.
   I. Thoene, Brock, 1952- II. Title.
   PS3570.H46L66 2005
   813'.54—dc22   2004030812

Printed in the United States of America

11 10 09 08 07 06 05
7   6   5   4   3   2   1

London Refrain is a "Director's Cut,"
including portions of the Thoene Classic *The Twilight of Courage*
and thrilling, never-before-published scenes
with the characters you've come to know
and love through The Zion Covenant series.

THE FIRST TWO MONTHS OF WORLD WAR II

◌◌

1939
September 1—Nazi Germany invades Poland
September 3—England and France declare war on Germany
September 17—Soviets invade Poland
September 27—Warsaw falls

◌◌

October—"Phony War" begins

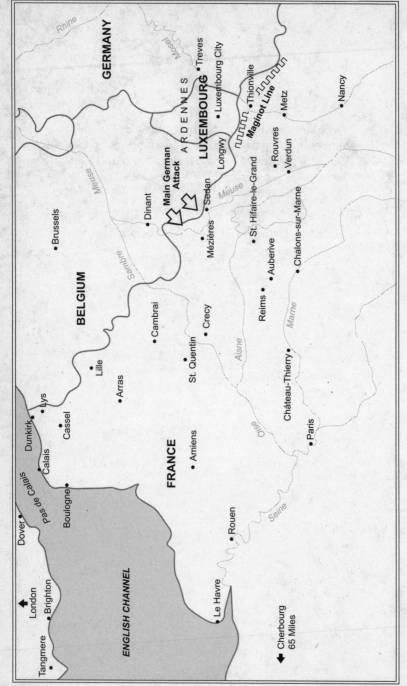

THE WESTERN FRONT

☆ THE ZION COVENANT SERIES

ENGLISH CHANNEL

London
Brighton
Tangmere
Dover
Pas de Calais
Calais
Dunkirk
Lys
Boulogne
Cassel
Arras
Lille
Le Havre
Rouen
Amiens
St. Quentin
Crecy
Cambrai
Paris
Seine
Oise
Aisne
Marne
Château-Thierry
Reims
Auberive
Chalons-sur-Marne
St. Hilaire-le-Grand
Mézières
Sambre
Dinant
Meuse
Meuse
Sedan
Main German Attack
Longwy
ARDENNES
Verdun
Rouvres
Metz
Maginot Line
Thionville
Nancy
Luxembourg City
LUXEMBOURG
Treves
Mosel
Rhine
GERMANY
BELGIUM
Brussels
FRANCE
Cherbourg
65 Miles

POLAND IN 1939

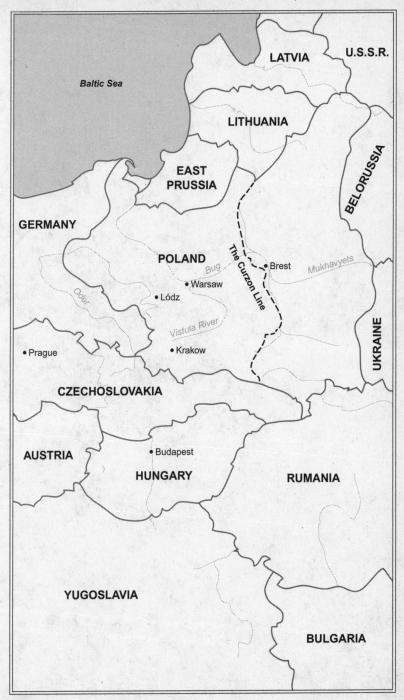

Baltic Sea

LATVIA

U.S.S.R.

LITHUANIA

BELORUSSIA

EAST PRUSSIA

GERMANY

POLAND

Bug

The Curzon Line

• Brest

Mukhavyets

• Warsaw

Oder

• Lódz

UKRAINE

Vistula River

• Prague

• Krakow

CZECHOSLOVAKIA

AUSTRIA

• Budapest

HUNGARY

RUMANIA

YUGOSLAVIA

BULGARIA

OLD CITY JERUSALEM
JUNE 12, 2004

The pastels of approaching dawn tinted the sky above Jerusalem. Morning seeped into the Old City house where Moshe and Rachel Sachar had once lived.

Sky Television, broadcast from America, had played all night as thirty-nine-year-old Shimon Sachar opened and sorted sympathy cards, meticulously cataloging donations like pottery shards on a dig.

At last, back aching, Shimon slouched in the leather wingback chair in his father's study. Stacks of unopened letters covered the top of Papa's old mahogany desk and spilled from mail sacks onto the floor. Donations to the Hebrew University School of Archaeology in memory of Shimon's father, Professor Moshe Sachar, had begun to flow in from all over Israel within hours of his death.

Scholarships created from the pennies of schoolchildren.

Papa would have been pleased to be remembered in such a way, Shimon thought.

Shimon ran his hand through his thatch of black, curly hair and stretched his long legs. He was exhausted but could not tear his eyes from the live broadcast of former President Ronald Reagan's sunset funeral half a world away in Simi Valley, California.

Familiar names and faces of former world leaders come to pay homage had flashed across the screen for days. Many of the great and near-great who attended the Reagan funeral had also been guests of Shimon's father and mother here in Jerusalem.

Shimon glanced over the long article that had been published in the *Jerusalem Post*.

*Moshe Sachar, archaeologist and scholar of the Dead Sea Scrolls,
whose life story could rival the plot of an international adventure
novel, died at his home in Old City Jerusalem. He was eighty-nine.*

*Israel mourns a sabra who worked with David Ben-Gurion and
Ezer Weitzman for the establishment of the state. He was also among
the foremost classical Hebrew linguists in the world. When the ancient Dead Sea Scrolls were discovered, beginning in 1947, Sachar's
role in verifying the scrolls' authenticity was so crucial that scholars
consider it the beginning of scroll scholarship.*

*"Moshe Sachar was literally working on one of the most important
Dead Sea Scrolls before anyone else was certain of their significance,"
said James McCurrey, a professor of Near Eastern Studies at Johns
Hopkins University in Baltimore, Maryland.*

*Presidents, prime ministers, professors, and researchers alike called
on the distinguished Hebrew archaeologist. Generals and journalists
traveled from around the world to shake the hand of Moshe Sachar,
the hero who commanded Old City defenders during the siege of Jerusalem in 1948. Professors and clerics made appointments to discuss
Torah with the gray-haired scholar. Professor Sachar was a popular
lecturer and teacher wherever he went, but especially here in Israel.
He drew large Israeli crowds who wanted to hear him speak classical
Hebrew because he pronounced it as it was intended to be spoken. It
was not only what he said but how he said it that was so beautiful.*

*Professor Sachar was preceded in death by his wife, Rachel. He is
survived by six sons, an adopted daughter who lives in America, and
twenty-two grandchildren.*

Shimon, youngest of the six sons, had his father's tall, lean, sun-
bronzed looks, as well as his high cheekbones, prominent nose, and
dark brown eyes. He'd also inherited his father's skill in the ancient language. Of all the boys, Shimon was most like his father. Everyone said
so. For that reason Moshe had seen to it that Shimon inherited other
things as well. Important things.

Transfixed by the pathos playing out on the television, Shimon
rubbed his hand wearily over the stubble of his curly black beard. Nancy
Reagan, frail and stoic, reached out to touch the American flag that covered her husband's coffin. She shook her head sadly and smiled wist-
fully. Perhaps some memory of better days passed through her mind.

It occurred to Shimon that an entire generation was rapidly passing
from the scene. How many were left who knew firsthand the cost of freedom?

Shimon rested his hand on the stack of over seventeen hundred

neatly typed manuscript pages. The original text—thousands of handwritten pages and letters by a dozen contributors—comprised the tale of
the early days of World War II and the miraculous survival of one Jewish
baby from Warsaw. The baby had been Shimon's uncle, Yacov Lubetkin.
The story of his rescue and the men and women who saved him was begun years before by Shimon's mother, Rachel. After her death the work
was carried on by close friends of Moshe and Rachel Sachar.

So many. Mac and Eva McGrath in London. Andre and Josephine
Chardon and Jerome Jardin in Paris. John and Elisa Murphy in America.
Lori and Jacob Kalner, and of course, Alfie Halder, right here in Israel.

Shimon and Moshe had edited the various letters, diaries, and ac-
counts together until now the full story was due to be published in three
volumes that were yet untitled. Papa had written on the title page *From
Warsaw to London, Paris, Dunkirk, Jerusalem: The Miracle behind the Survival of One Jewish Child.*

The title was miles too long, Shimon knew, but he left it just as Papa
had written it. The publishers would figure out something catchy, he
was sure.

Now there was only one thing left to do. Tonight Shimon would
carry the original handwritten documents of these witnesses through the
tunnels to the hidden chamber deep beneath the Temple Mount.

Alfie Halder, the ancient, barrel-chested gardener who had been part
of the Sachar family for over fifty years, entered bearing a tray of pastries
and a teapot. Halting in the doorway, Alfie squinted at the television.
"Shimon? Boy? All night you been up sorting mail and watching this.
Wasn't your papa's funeral enough for one week?"

"Papa would have stayed up."

"Did I tell you? Them American government people from Washington telephoned here to the house the day after your papa died. Asking
for your papa. Wanted him to come to Washington and read in Hebrew.
Read a Bible verse from Isaiah at Reagan's funeral. They hadn't heard
your papa died the same day as Reagan. I told them Professor Moshe
Sachar was dead and couldn't come read."

Shimon swallowed hard, feeling his father's absence. "Why aren't
you still in bed, Alfie?"

"I been to bed."

"Not even 5 AM. Too early for you to be up. You know what the doctor said. Your heart."

"My heart! I'll be with your papa and mama soon enough anyway.
Long as I'm still here, I didn't want you to feel lonesome. Just you and
me in this old house now." Alfie blinked at the empty chair behind the
desk where Papa had always presided.

Shimon suspected Alfie was the one feeling lonesome.

Shimon picked up a card and pretended to read it. "I'm okay. I want to see this to the end. History, you know? The end of an era. The end of a truly honorable life. So. Go back to bed."

Alfie shook his head ponderously. "I made tea. Reagan has a long funeral, eh? A whole week. I bet his wife's tired. Poor lady. Americans do things in a big way. You know your papa died almost the same moment as Reagan, and we buried him a day later. Now seven days of Shiva is finished. Mourning in Israel has to get over quick or nobody would get anything done. So, I brought you sweet rolls and Darjeeling tea like you like."

Without further comment Shimon nodded in acknowledgment and cleared a place for the tea tray amid the clutter.

Though Moshe's passing had been mourned by Israelis, his simple funeral had been virtually unnoticed by the rest of the world's media. And so for Shimon it was as though the fellow playing "Amazing Grace" on the bagpipes in distant California was also playing a farewell hymn for Papa.

Alfie, suddenly caught up by the scene, whispered, "You know your papa always liked this President Reagan. This American movie cowboy. This President. You know your mama and papa, they was friends with them. And Mrs. Thatcher, too. Your mama liked Mrs. Reagan a lot. Reagan and Mrs. Thatcher brung down the Wall, you know. The Wall in the city where I was born and lived until Hitler came. Berlin. Wasn't a wall there till after the war." Alfie gestured toward a display of photographs. "After that wall come down in Berlin, your papa and mama was invited to the White House for a party and spent the night. Your mama said when the Wall come down, it was like the war was finally over, you know?"

Shimon raised a finger in an effort to silence Alfie. But the old man did not seem to notice. "Amazing Grace" echoed over the Pacific valley and into the Old City Jerusalem study as Alfie chatted on and poured with a clatter of teapot against the cups. "Now, that Kennedy fellow? That president who everybody thought was wonderful because he said 'Ich bin ein Berliner'? Kennedy thought he was telling the world he was a citizen of Berlin, see? But his German wasn't no good. If you was raised in Berlin like me, you heard him say, 'I am a sweet roll.' That's what 'Ich bin ein Berliner' means in German: 'I am a sweet roll.' And so Kennedy did not bring down the Wall. Here. Eat. I brought you a nice Berliner for breakfast."

Thus was the wisdom of the world confounded by the simple, Shimon mused. He sipped his tea and ate his breakfast roll in the company of this gentle old man who had calmly survived wars and persecutions for eight decades. Alfie and those few cherished friends who had written their stories down on lined paper in spiral notebooks were among the last who could tell the tale.

Alfie stared at the open box that held reams of memories. It was the sort of container in which scraps of ancient documents were stored at the Hebrew University. "What you going to do with those? The letters? The papers? Your mama's notes about Warsaw? The others?"

"You know where they belong, Alfie. Papa and I had planned to take them to the vault together. It's Mama's story and the others', not his, but he wanted to find a special shelf to store them."

"Well, then. Yes. I suppose they belong there. Down there with the other great stories. Her handwriting. Lori's letters to Jacob. All the rest of them, too. A place of honor. Better than between the covers of a book. I always said so. When are we going?"

"You'll go with me then, since Papa can't."

"Turn off the TV, Shimon. It's almost sunset in California. We can lay these stories to rest at the same time they're playing 'Taps.' Yes. Get your jacket. I'll put the tea in a thermos. Pack some cheese and apples. I won't be a minute."

"Sure. Let's go." Shimon took one last long look at the stack of notebooks, sealed the box, and clicked the TV remote. The sounds of the bagpipe vanished.

1

Broken Promises

The full moon rose slowly over Jerusalem. British soldiers stood as watchmen on the massive walls surrounding the ancient city. Within that stone circle, Muslim, Jew, and Christian lived side by side in fragile and often shattered peace.

Tonight the spiked towers of minarets in the Muslim Quarter cast long shadows over the great arched rooftops of the churches crammed into the Christian Quarter and the synagogues of the Jewish Quarter. Around the holy shrines of three religions were clustered the vaulted souks, tiny shops, and crooked houses of each community, separated only by twisting alleyways or flights of worn stone steps. From the high perspective of the British guards manning the wall, the domed roofs looked like so many yarmulkes crowning the heads of the pious. The streets were deserted and iron grills covered the doorways of the empty souks, but in the moonlight and shifting shadows, the very stones of the Holy City seemed alive.

Rabbi Shlomo Lebowitz turned off the flame of the hissing Primus stove as the water for his tea came to a boil. In the winter the three-legged kerosene stove served both to cook the old man's meals and to warm the tiny, one-room flat he called home. But the days had been long and hot through August—too hot for him to heat even a cup of tea until long after the sun had gone down. This was the best time of day, the rabbi thought as he steeped the tea leaves and took two rough lumps of sugar from the jar on the shelf. Psalms, a calico cat and the old man's companion, looked on.

"So. We are both awake. It is the best time for an old man and a cat to think and study and pray. *Nu?*"

Heavy shutters were open wide. A cool sea breeze had finally drifted up the pass of Bab el Wad and slipped through the iron bars that covered

the window of the stone room. Blue light reflecting from the moon sup-
plemented the glow of a single beeswax candle that sputtered on a rough
wooden table.

The tea was strong and sweet. Rabbi Lebowitz sipped the steaming
brew gingerly as he sat down to reread the letter dated August 1, which
had arrived this afternoon from his daughter in Warsaw.

Propped against the stone wall was a gallery of photographs displaying the faces of his family. They smiled across the table at him: beautiful
Etta; her husband, Aaron; and the children—Rachel, David, Samuel,
and the baby, Yacov.

The old man had never met his grandchildren, but tonight as he read
the letter again, he was filled with the certain hope that soon they would
all be with him in Jerusalem. He would bounce the baby on his knee. He
would embrace the boys and touch the cheek of young Rachel, who was
the very image of Etta at the age of thirteen.

> *My dearest father,*
>
> *I know that the news you hear from Poland must be grim, but you must
> not worry. We are praying there will not be a war. The Polish
> government seems to be working out its differences with Germany.
> None of it affects us, except that there are many Jewish refugees now
> flooding into Warsaw from Czechoslovakia to escape the Nazis there.
> We have set up a soup kitchen to feed them all.*
>
> *Things are going well for us.*
>
> *We hope that soon our documents and visas will arrive so we may
> come home to Jerusalem. Aaron says he may send the children and
> me ahead, and then he will come later.*
>
> *I have had new photographs made. They will be ready in a few
> weeks. I will post them to you so you will not be surprised at how
> much the children have grown by the time you see us soon in
> Jerusalem!*

It was a good letter. Cheered, the old man lay down at last on the
groaning springs of his iron bed and dreamed of his grandchildren. . . .

The sweet dream lasted only until the morning, when news of the
German invasion of Poland reached the gates of Jerusalem.

SEPTEMBER 1, 1939

Hundreds of desperate people pushed and shouted at the gates of the
British Embassy in Warsaw, Poland. Twenty-two-year-old Eva

Weitzman waved her Czech passport and shouted in broken English at the British marines who had taken positions in the courtyard of the compound in case the iron gates were breached.

"I am Czech!" Eva shouted and stood tiptoe in an attempt to be heard above the din. "Please, political asylum . . . for me, please. I am Czech!"

Smoke from some bombed-out Warsaw building momentarily blocked the sun. Eva pushed her raven black hair under her hat and glanced fearfully at the sky. How long until the German Heinkels returned with a fresh load of bombs?

"I am Czech! Allow me into the compound! I beg!"

Her plea was drowned beneath the cries of hundreds of refugees who had fled their homelands as the Nazi storm surge swallowed nation after nation. The Republic of Czechoslovakia had been divided up and great swaths of Czech territory ceded to Germany in the fall of 1938. This travesty had been accomplished at a council of world leaders who met with Adolf Hitler in Munich. The council members included British prime minister Neville Chamberlain. Of course Beneš, the president of Czechoslovakia, had not been invited nor consulted when the Western powers granted Czech territory to Germany.

Eva, a Jewish schoolteacher on holiday in Warsaw, had escaped as the Nazis completed the occupation of the ceded areas of her homeland, which far exceeded the agreed-to boundaries. On the very day Chamberlain came before Parliament and presented Hitler's signature guaranteeing peace in exchange for the dismemberment of Czechoslovakia, the Gestapo had entered Eva's hometown and begun the customary pogroms. Eva's parents and brothers had not been heard from since October 10, 1938.

The government of Poland had granted Eva asylum and a work permit. She had survived by teaching refugee children in the basement of the Cathedral of St. John.

Now Eva Weitzman waved her passport at the stoic British soldiers. Surely they would understand and take pity! "Please! I am Czech! Refugee!"

An elderly man, well dressed, held tightly to the arm of his wife in the crush. He said to Eva, "We also are from Prague. Stranded here. If only the English would let us pass. Britain is not at war with Germany. We will be safe there."

Behind him a hatchet-faced, middle-aged Briton dressed in a business suit broke through the crowd. "I'm British. I say! Coming through. Coming through!" The fellow snaked through the crowd and, once at the barricade, flashed his British passport to the guard. A pedestrian gate set within larger iron bars of the vehicle entrance was unlocked. The

Englishman entered. Refugees, frantic and near panic, sought to storm the entry but were pushed back by rifle-wielding soldiers.

"Only British passports. Sorry. Sorry! Only those who carry a British passport. . . ."

Someone cursed in broken English and shouted, "Where is England? Where are the British planes? Are you not pledged to aid and defend Poland? Where is your army?"

As if on cue, the crowd roared a chorus of accusations against Great Britain's betrayal of their homelands. Eva heard a dozen languages, and yet it seemed all one thought, one voice.

The old woman remarked to her husband, "They do not care what happens to us as long as England is safe. It will take a miracle for us to leave Warsaw now, Papa."

He nodded. "A miracle. Yes. An English passport."

"Shall we return to the Bristol Hotel?" The woman was weary. Resigned. "These English will not give us refuge."

Eva frowned. Should she tell them that the Bristol Hotel had just been bombed? that it was a smoldering ruin? She did not speak. They would find out soon enough.

The man replied, "Yes. Yes, my dearest Bette. We'll go back to the hotel. We'll wait. Perhaps the English will send their army. Perhaps England will be our miracle."

To Eva's mind there seemed to be the acceptance of impending death in the old man's words.

"We shall rest and wait together, Bette." The old man picked up the small leather valise that contained their belongings. With difficulty the old couple retreated.

Eva swallowed hard, fighting the urge to weep. Stubbornly she brushed away the tears that escaped from the corners of her bright blue eyes. What would tears accomplish? Was she crying for the old couple? for her lost family? for herself? for the whole world? What good were human tears when free nations made pacts with the devil and refused to fight when every pact was broken? Eva and every other Jew in Hitler's path were doomed.

A miracle. *Oh, God!* Were there no miracles left in heaven and earth? Where was England? Where were French troops? The broken promises of governments had sealed the fate of millions!

ꔷꖕ

"So. It has come to this. Hitler promises peace in our time, and German planes drop bombs on Warsaw." Winston Churchill poured two brandies—one for himself and the other for American journalist John Murphy.

The lanky, boyish bureau chief of Trump European News Service in London declined the drink and shifted uneasily in the red-leather wingback chair in the British statesman's study. "You saw it coming, Winston. Spoke out for how many years?" Murphy frowned and looked out the window toward Westminster Cathedral, across from Churchill's London flat.

Churchill had met with Murphy dozens of times to discuss politics over the last two years. Churchill's articles had been published regularly in America through Murphy's news organization. Just as Churchill predicted, Hitler had devoured Europe, nation after nation, through diplomacy with weak leaders in the West. Churchill had always seen that war with Germany was inevitable unless Hitler was resisted. Murphy had made certain he consulted Winston Churchill about the content of news articles he had wired to America. The policies of negotiation and appeasement now were a proven disaster. In the end, Poland had been invaded; now the gaunt spectre of a larger war inexorably approached. The record was clear. Winston Churchill had never been wrong.

Churchill swirled the amber liquid and held the snifter to his nose. "Ah, Murphy, my friend. Being right for almost seven years about the intentions of Herr Hitler is poor consolation as Warsaw burns. And still England and France delay to come to Poland's aid!"

"What will you do?"

"I can only wait until Prime Minister Chamberlain calls me to join his government. The Admiralty. Until that moment I am still a private citizen."

"I'd say you're the man Hitler fears and hates more than any other in all the world," Murphy observed, "because you're the one man who has spoken the truth."

"A lone voice crying in the wilderness, I fear."

"Poland is proof you were speaking the truth."

"To hear the Nazi propaganda machine, you would suppose that twenty-five years ago the Great War began when Belgium invaded Germany. Peaceful Prussians minding their own business when suddenly the wicked Belgians, spurred on by England and the Jews, fell upon them. And then, just when they were about to win the war, the Jews stabbed them in the back and, armed with American might and President Woodrow Wilson's Fourteen Points, forced them to sign an armistice!"

Angered by the Nazi lies, Murphy drummed his fingers on the arm of the chair. "And so the Germans claim they are simply setting right the travesty of Jewish betrayal. With every act of aggression, they claim to be liberating other European nations."

"Such is history as it is taught in topsy-turvydom."

"The German press prints Hitler's lies, his claim that the Jews of Europe are the aggressors with a plan to take over all the world with Zionism. Jews, they say, are the betrayers, the reason there is no peace in the world. And the lie is believed. Not only in Germany but around the world," Murphy concluded.

Churchill nodded and sat down heavily behind his broad desk. He gazed pensively at the photo of Clementine, his wife. "So it has been throughout history when the powers of darkness possess humans."

So it was clear to Churchill, too, Murphy thought, that there was something more sinister at work in the world than mere human tyranny. Murphy himself was certain the battle was not merely against evil men but against ancient spiritual powers and unseen principalities whose daily bread was buttered with the blood of innocent victims. A chill coursed through Murphy as he thought of the drama of chaos and death now being played out in Warsaw.

After a long pause Churchill spoke quietly. "Clemmie is returning from France today. There are twenty thousand *known* organized German Nazis in England. The attempted destruction of St. Paul's Cathedral speaks for itself. There have been and still are Nazi plans for sabotage and murder here before France and England declare war in defense of Poland. Hitler recognizes me as his nemesis. I've called my former Scotland Yard detective out of retirement. Inspector Thompson is his name. I've told him to come along and bring his pistol with him." Churchill patted the pocket of his smoking jacket. "And I have a revolver of my own. While one of us sleeps, the other will watch. If they make further attempts on my life, or the life of my wife, they will not have a walkover."

The rotund politician stuck out his lower lip and cocked an eye at Murphy. "And you, young man? Your family represents everything the Nazis hate most. Your wife, Elisa . . . a German Jewess. Your baby girl?"

"Katie."

"Yes. Katie. And Charles and Louis, the boys you've taken into your home. The two sons of the anti-Nazi journalist Walter Kronenberger. Symbols of German defiance of the Third Reich. Do you carry a weapon for self-defense?"

Murphy blanched and shook his head. The images of how near they all had come to disaster recently were fresh in his mind. Their house in Red Lion Square had been destroyed. Elisa's niece, seventeen-year-old Lori Kalner, had been abducted and imprisoned by terrorists in the lantern tower of St. Paul's Cathedral. Discovered during the search for explosive charges set around the cathedral's dome, Lori was now safe in a suite at the Savoy Hotel with Elisa.

"Today all the children will leave for a farm in Wales with Elisa's mother, Anna Lindheim, and Lori Kalner's mother, Helen Ibsen. And there's a baby Lori has been caring for. Came to England on the Kindertransport. Alfie's his name. He's going with them to Wales."

"Wise. And your wife, Elisa? Will she go as well? And Lori Kalner?"

"Neither will leave London. Elisa says she'll stay here with me. As for Lori . . . it's Lori's husband, Jacob Kalner, you see. Jacob was working with Samuel Orde at the TENS News office in Warsaw when the Germans attacked. There's been no news from the staff. And then . . . you know Lori's father is Karl Ibsen. Evangelical Christian pastor in Germany. A resister. He was arrested by the Gestapo. If he's still alive he's in prison somewhere in Berlin, we think. There's been no word. Lori won't leave London until she hears what's become of Jacob. So two policemen are acting as bodyguards outside our suite at the Savoy."

"The nightstick of a London bobby won't stop der Führer's assassins." Churchill opened the top-right desk drawer and pulled out a heavy Colt .45 revolver in a shoulder holster, along with a small cardboard box of cartridges. "American made. I picked it up some years ago in New York. I find the shoulder holster uncomfortable. But you, young fellow. You're built like that American film star. What's his name? The tall one. His name . . . well, it will come to me. Keep it. My gift. My thanks."

Murphy's mouth curved in a half smile as he hefted the substantial weapon: top-of-the-line model, engraved with *Colt Shooting Master* on the left side of the six-inch barrel. With its heavy frame and prominent blade front sight, it had the look of something a cowboy would carry. "Well, then. Yes."

"Suits you. I thought as much the first time we met. It's recently cleaned. Loaded. Ready if you ever have need of it."

"Thanks. The most sensible gift I've ever gotten." Murphy thought of the movie *Stagecoach*, which had been playing to packed audiences at the Odeon Cinema in Leicester Square. He removed his baggy tweed suit coat and strapped on the shoulder holster. Donning the jacket he sat back, noting Churchill's pleased expression. "Parliament meets this afternoon. Will England declare war?" Murphy asked.

"It is my hope they'll be swift. Every passing hour without England's aid makes Poland's survival more improbable."

"Will you attend?"

"I'll wait here for the call. A declaration of war must not be delayed. But I fear it *will* be delayed once again. The Labour Party will still oppose our entry into the conflict. Even now. Even as Warsaw is bombed."

"It will hardly be noticed in America."

"Murphy, I am half American. My mother. I know the courage and resolve of your great people. And yet the voices of appeasement exist in your land as they do in England and France! Again and again politicians believed they could negotiate a peace. Negotiate with an evil tyrant. Now after everything Hitler demanded has been given to him, Poland is being attacked!"

Murphy put his hand to the Colt. If only right and wrong were as well-defined as the plot of a John Wayne Western. "The world is upside down, Winston. People believe the big lie. Politicians make speeches reciting what they think will get them elected. The people want peace so badly they don't care who dies as long as it isn't their son. Their brother. Their father. The pacifists in America will distort the truth just like the appeasers in England."

"America will delay taking action at her own peril." Churchill sighed and shook his ponderous head. There was silence for a long moment before he raised his gaze to command Murphy, "Young man, you must write a story to stir the blood of your American countrymen. Speak the truth! Tell them! The policy of appeasement is always fatal. Always. History teaches us. History is the schoolmaster. America cannot negotiate with evil men and expect to remain unscathed. Millions of innocents around the globe are doomed to slaughter because the Western nations looked the other way! In the end the powers of darkness will fix their gaze on America. The sons Americans hoped to save will perish because of spineless politicians. They lied and discussed when they might have united and put an end to the murderous tyrant and his minions. Write the story, Murphy! You have been called by God to this moment in history, for this purpose. If America does not join in the fight against evil now, she, too, will suffer."

2

An Uncertain Hour

It was steamy hot in the underground Victoria Station. The thin, diminuitive, harried-looking young man in the black raincoat instinctively touched the revolver in his pocket as he reached for a kerchief to mop beads of sweat from his neck.

Where was the train? Why was it taking so long to arrive?

Tweed cap pulled low over his brow, he glanced nervously over his shoulder, scanning faces in the waiting crowd. He hoped the train would arrive before the London police caught up with him. If they tried to arrest him here, he would at least take a few of them with him.

Kevin Miller and the other Irish recruits had failed in their missions of sabotage and assassination intended to be carried out against England before Germany invaded Poland. The primary target had been Winston Churchill, Hitler's most vocal opponent among the Western nations.

But Churchill was still alive. Just as the dome of St. Paul's Cathedral towered over the London skyline, Churchill towered over the English politicians who had given in to Hitler's every demand. That assassination attempt had failed. The Irish terrorist Allan Farrell, a master at constructing bombs, had plunged to his death from the dome of St. Paul's. Harvey Terrill, night-desk editor with Trump European News Service, had been arrested as the Irishman's accomplice and had died of a massive heart attack in his cell three hours later.

But had Terrill told Scotland Yard everything they wanted to know about the master plan? Did they know about Kevin Miller and the hundreds of Nazi agents active in Britain's National Socialist Party?

Kevin was uncertain what he should do now that months of planning had gone so terribly wrong. Should he attempt to get back to Germany and chance being arrested at the quay in Southampton? Would the Gestapo send further instructions to him by courier? a new plan for disposing of Churchill and the vocal opponents of the press who now clamored for England to declare war?

John Murphy, vehement anti-Nazi chief of TENS, was also at the top of the list of Gestapo targets. Beside his name were the names of his German-born Jewish wife and members of her family. All were refugees from the Third Reich.

But this morning Kevin had seen the policemen standing guard outside their suite at the Savoy. Elimination of John Murphy's family, a seemingly simple matter to accomplish in concept, had suddenly become difficult.

Silence the Reich's most vocal opposition! It was a direct order from Berlin to Nazi agents in England. Put an end to those whose voices and stories might somehow stir nations outside the expanding borders of the Reich to declare war!

The Gestapo's long assassination list also included members of the Western press, politicians, military men, Christian clergymen, Zionist Jews and their families.

Had Terrill talked to Scotland Yard about the plan? Had he told the English authorities that orders had been written personally by the German Führer? Kevin's freedom to act and the success of further covert operations in England depended on how much information the British authorities had.

It was too dangerous for Kevin to wait around his one-room flat to find out if his cover had been blown. Erich Bain would know what to do. Erich with his deck of playing cards and arrogant eyes smoldering with hatred of everything British. Erich would certainly have a plan.

Kevin Miller raised his chin as a blast of air from the tunnel preceded the arrival of the train. The doors hesitated, then slid open. Caught up in the crush of other passengers, Kevin boarded and slipped his hand into his pocket. He fingered the revolver. Its cold steel was a comfort in such an uncertain hour.

◎

Beneath the window of Elisa Lindheim-Murphy's suite at the Savoy Hotel, a crew of laborers dug slit trenches in the park along the embankment of the Thames River.

Lori Kalner, her wounded wrists bandaged from her stay in St. Paul's lantern tower, sat forlornly on the bed amongst a clutter of newspapers

with headlines declaring "Germany Invades Poland!" Misery! No word
from Warsaw! Where was Lori's young husband, Jacob?

The two women had not spoken more than a few cursory words in
hours. Food remained uneaten on the tray. The pot of tea was cold.

Now Elisa cleared her throat.

Lori, her shoulder-length blond hair disheveled and blue eyes red
from crying, looked up. "When will Murphy be back?"

"Soon, he said." Elisa studied the progress of the ditchdiggers as they
shoveled dirt carefully so as not to damage a bed of red rosebushes.

Lori lowered her chin once in acknowledgment. "Do you think England will declare war? Today?"

"Maybe Murphy will know more when he gets back."

"The British passports. For Alfie and Jacob. For the Jewish girl, Rachel. Did they get them, you think?"

Murphy had carried three forged British passports to Warsaw. Prevented from carrying them to the TENS office himself, he had sent them
by way of a taxi driver. Murphy had left the besieged city on the last
plane without ever knowing if the lifesaving documents were received.
Lori had asked the same question a hundred times since Murphy's return to London.

Elisa's answer was always the same. "Until we hear from Jacob and
Alfie, we have no way of knowing. They are in God's good hands, Lori.
We can only pray."

Lori nodded. "Yes, sorry. Oh, God, please."

Silence. The sound of spades drifted up from the park. A cockney
voice gave orders that forms for an antiaircraft gun must be set between
the beds of roses. A searchlight would be placed near the river in case
German bombers followed the course of the Thames in from the sea.

Elisa was relieved that the children would soon be safe on a farm in
Wales in case the bombing of London began.

Lori blurted, "They are British passports. What if Jacob got his British
passport, and then England comes into the war? Jacob will be thought to
be British. An enemy of the Germans. Not a neutral! Oh, Elisa. England
must not declare war before Jacob escapes from Poland!"

Elisa did not reply. She did not need to remind Lori that what was
taking place in Warsaw and London was much bigger than the life of one
young man. And yet all of Lori's world revolved around Jacob.

Lori gazed at the headline as if the words were a deadly disease. "Will
England declare war soon, Elisa?"

"The people of Poland are praying for help from England and
France, Lori. They are holding out now, praying that the English army
and the French army will come soon and help them fight."

"But do you think it will happen? With Jacob still in Poland some-where?" Lori blinked and gazed in horror at some picture her imagina-tion painted. "They say the Nazis are bombing Warsaw. What if Jacob is hurt? What if he is . . . ?" Lori dissolved into tears again.

Elisa went to her, embraced her. "Lori, your father would say you must pray. Trust Jesus in the storm, even though you can't see the shore. We are all in the same boat, and Jesus is in there with us! Isn't that what your father would say?"

Lori trembled. "But what if . . . first Papa and now Jacob! Oh, Elisa, why? Why?"

Elisa prayed silently, knowing that Lori did not expect an answer. She needed to grieve. To cry herself out. How often had Elisa done the same as the Nazis invaded one nation after another, and no one lifted a finger to stop them?

Yes, Lord! Why? There are so many. Not just Jacob. The children! There will be no more Kindertransport. No more kids arriving from the Reich. This means the end for so many, Lord. So many prayers rise to You today. So many beloved left behind in Vienna. Prague. Danzig. Now Warsaw. Lost to us for-ever. Unaccounted for. First Lori's father and now young Jacob . . . I have no answers for her! Please! Give us Your strength. Your grace to see us . . . and them . . . through.

⊘

Savoy Hotel
London, England

Dearest Jacob,

Though I do not know where you are or when you might read this letter, I must write to you as though you will memorize every word and your heart will be certain of my love. There is much I will not write about, but you must believe that someday soon I will be able to tell you every detail of the last few days.

England is full of foreigners who mean to do her ill. I have heard there are many thousands of Nazis here in London. Many intent on sabotage. Some I have met face-to-face, yet I believe that God will root them out and they will be defeated in the end.

We are far apart, but I think of you every waking minute as news pours in of Hitler's invasion of Poland. John Murphy returned from Warsaw, looking very haggard and exhausted. He told us how the Polish officer in customs stole Elisa's violin and yet allowed Murphy to send the violin case containing your passports by way of a messenger to the TENS office. We can only hope you received it and are, even now, with Alfie on your way from Warsaw to England.

We have decided to heed early evacuation warnings and send the children to stay in a farmhouse Uncle Theo rented in Wales. They will be in the care of Mother and Aunt Anna.

I will stay in London with Elisa and Murphy in case there is some word from you. You must not worry about me. We are staying at the Savoy Hotel, which is the only hotel in London made with steel beams and so is safe from bombs if Herr Hitler should turn his attention our way.

Next week we will move into the house on Prince Albert Road, across from Primrose Hill. A lovely place just a short walk to Regent's Park and the zoo. They are setting antiaircraft cannons in place at the top of Primrose Hill, where the view across the city is the most lovely. I would not mind standing watch in such a place and manning such a gun if war is declared. Elisa says we will be very safe in our little Georgian house.

I do pray you are safe and on your way to my arms, my darling!

Your loving wife,

Lori

The distant *crump* of artillery shells buoyed the hopes of the hundreds who waited outside the gates of the British Embassy in Warsaw.

Was this their miracle? Had England joined the fray? Was the Polish army bravely defending the homeland?

Eva Weitzman was grateful for the broad brim of her white hat. The afternoon heat was stifling in the crush of so many people. Several had fainted throughout the long hours. No one dared to leave their place in search of water for fear the Englishmen inside the compound would open the gates for one instant and allow the swarm of refugees to enter.

Hours passed miserably. Eva did not have a watch. Three times German Heinkels skimmed over Warsaw, dropping bombs and strafing the waterfront.

Where were the English? For that matter, where was the Polish air force?

Once again the roar of three German airplane engines issued warning of their imminent approach. Eva crouched low on the cobbled pavement and peered up past the brim of her hat at the swastika insignia on the wings.

Though exposed, the refugees supposed that no Nazi would dare to drop bombs on the British Embassy. This square of Polish pavement outside the British diplomatic fortress was closest to England and therefore seemed the safest place in all Warsaw.

The drone of planes receded toward the west. The stink of smoke, burning wood, and cordite filled the air.

An hour passed. The door of the embassy opened. An Englishman emerged and walked toward the crowd outside the barricade. He was dressed in a pin-striped suit. His shirt was crisp in spite of the heat. His tie was straight, shoes shined to impeccable brightness.

The clamor began again. Refugees made stateless by the policies of appeasement waved useless passports for nations that no longer existed. Brought to the doorstep of England when their homelands were absorbed by the Third Reich, they begged to be let in.

"Please. I am from Berlin!"

"I am Austrian!"

"I am Czech!"

"I am from Danzig!"

"Prague!"

"Vienna!"

"Munich! I am a refugee! Please. Take my son!"

The Englishman raised his arms, commanding silence. The uproar ceased. He began to speak. "In London Parliament is meeting on the matter."

A hiss of voices translated the Englishman's words into a dozen languages.

"Negotiations for peace continue," the Englishman said.

"What? What did he say?"

"Negotiations for peace?"

"Peace? The peace of the Republic of Czechoslovakia that was given to Hitler?"

"The peace of Vienna, where Jews were betrayed and arrested by tens of thousands?"

"Negotiating peace again with the Nazis, did this Englishman say?"

"They are negotiating with Hitler again?"

Betrayal of Poland by her British and French allies crackled like lightning in the air. Suddenly the silence of the crowd was shattered as pleas were renewed.

"Let us in! Save us! Please! Open the gates!"

The stolid Englishman instructed, "Return to your homes, all of you! You will be safer in your own homes."

"What did he say?"

"Return to our homes?"

"Safer in our homes?"

"My home was Vienna!"

"Munich!"

"Prague!"

"Danzig!"

Eva fluttered her Czech passport and howled with the others. A miracle! Where was England? Where was France? "*Go home,*" the fellow had said. There was no more home to go to.

"Please!" Eva begged in English. "I am Czech!"

Just then someone tapped her on the shoulder. A girl's voice said softly, "You dropped this."

Eva turned to see a young woman holding a passport with the crest of Great Britain emblazoned on the cover. "You dropped this," the teenaged girl said again. She was beautiful. Her expression radiated peace. She was tall. Inches taller than Eva. Slender. Shapely. Polish? No, Jewish. Long, dark hair framed a perfect oval face. Fair, flawless skin was smudged by smoke. Piercing cobalt blue eyes gazed at Eva through long lashes.

"No," Eva contradicted. "No, I didn't. It isn't mine."

"Yes, this is your passport. It is yours. I saw you drop it." The girl drew Eva to the side, opened the folder, and tapped the black-and-white identification photograph. "This is your picture. Can you not see it?"

Eva saw only that this was the girl's picture. Younger than Eva. Not Eva's photo. Although . . . there was indeed some resemblance between them. In black-and-white the similarity between the shape of their faces was uncanny.

Eva gasped. What was this young Polish Jewess doing? And why?

The girl clasped Eva's arm and shoved the document into her hands. "Please, take it. I mean it. It's yours."

Speechless, Eva stared blankly at her. "Who are you?"

The girl smiled into Eva's face. "I am my father's daughter. My mother's child. A sister to my brothers. They know me and love me as Rachel. God knows all the rest about me. About my family. Nothing else matters. But who are you, please?"

"Eva. Eva . . . Weitzman."

"Eva Weitzman. Good. You are also Jewish. I was hoping . . . hoping you would be. See, Eva? We could be sisters, you and I. We look enough alike, *nu*? They dressed me up like a goy for the photo. Your English passport photo. Yes, yours. They wrote down that I was twenty years old. The name is English on the paper. Julia Smith. English father. British. Czech mother. It's all there. So you will become Julia in my place. I must remain Rachel. I will remember you as Eva. Pray for you. Choose life,

Eva Weitzman. Go now to England and become Julia. My mother has written my grandfather a letter. Sent a photo of us, too. All there. I cannot leave my papa and mama, you see. My brothers. My heart would break, and I would die. Then all of this effort . . . this passport . . . would be a waste. So you, Eva, must take this British passport. Now go in. Live and be well. And remember those of us who are left behind."

Haunting eyes searched Eva's face. There was ethereal calm in the girl's smiling lips. Was Eva asleep? dreaming of a miracle? Was this young woman an angel?

Eva gaped at the passport photo. Julia Smith? A British citizen? *"Choose life!"*

When Eva raised her eyes, the girl had vanished into the crowd.

3

A Matter of When

Victoria Station was a five-minute walk from Winston Churchill's flat. Headlines of the London newspapers proclaimed that the Germans had bombed Warsaw and that the British parliament remained undecided as to a course of action.

The bulge of the weapon beneath Murphy's jacket was an ominous reminder of real, personal danger as he descended the steps of the tube station. The faces of the teeming crowds surging around him were grim. Few spoke. None smiled with the exception of young men of military age anticipating joining up and sharing glory on the battlefield.

At last it had come to this.

Murphy shuddered, though it was not cold.

Twenty thousand active and organized Nazis in England? He found himself evaluating every man and woman on the platform and wondering: Who among them favored a United States or Europe governed by the Third Reich? a world devoid of human beings with physical or mental disabilities? a society where there were no elderly? a culture where those of Jewish heritage were marked for genocide? a nation that separated children from parents, dictated schooling, rewarded betrayal of fathers and mothers by sons and daughters, condoned and practiced euthanasia and abortion? a government that arrested, imprisoned, and executed those who spoke out against legalized murder?

The unseen Evil that terrified children in the night had finally emerged from the closet. Perverting the constitutional laws of every nation it had swallowed, this Darkness would now devour all those who had been sleeping—all those who claimed the demons that possessed the body politic were only figments of childish imagination.

Yes, Evil was real and tangible! Now moral men and women would be required to fight for survival. For the survival of their right to worship in peace and freedom and to raise children their own way. Warsaw was burning. Soon London. Yes; it had come to this.

Murphy unconsciously put his hand on the checkered walnut grip of the handgun. He winced as a woman with two teenaged sons walked past him. Would her boys survive the folly of politicians?

Perhaps the last hope of humankind was Winston Churchill—and men like him—who had endured a decade of ridicule and obscurity for the sake of speaking the truth.

Murphy heard the roar of the approaching District Line train that would carry him to Embankment Station and the Savoy Hotel, where Elisa and Lori waited. He boarded the packed eastbound train, grabbed the leather strap, and looked back at the platform. How long would it be before every tube station in London was transformed into a bomb shelter?

It was no longer a question of *if*. It was only a matter of *when*.

⟨੭⟩

The planes of the German Luftwaffe skimmed low over the Jewish district of Warsaw, searching for victims to strafe. The streets of the city were deserted except for thirteen-year-old Rachel Lubetkin, daughter of Aaron Lubetkin, the beloved rabbi of Muranow. Happy now that she had given her British passport away, she walked slowly back toward the bomb shelter where her father and mother and three brothers waited. She walked in the center of the street so that bricks from bombed-out buildings did not block her way.

Papa had commanded her to leave Warsaw. Said she must take the English passport and make her way to Jerusalem, where she would live with Grandfather Lebowitz. *"Choose life!"* Papa had told her. But Rachel could not run away to safety unless her family came, too. She could not choose life for herself if it meant surviving in a world without Papa and Mama and David and Samuel and baby Yacov!

Surely Papa would understand. He would not chastise her for this disobedience. After all, it was love that had made her give the passport away. And wouldn't Mama be happy to see her again?

Smoke from burning buildings billowed up. The beautiful homes, cafés, shops, theatres, churches, and synagogues were obscured in a thick, sunless haze.

Rachel passed the sprawled bodies of three small children beneath the corpse of their mother. No doubt the woman died trying to shield them. In a strange contradiction, a canvas shopping bag—with a long loaf of bread sticking from the top, and a single cabbage—lay undamaged beside the tragic heap.

So this is what death looks like, Rachel thought, unafraid. A still-life painting of uneaten bread and a cabbage. Three children and a mother who would never come home from market.

Warsaw, often called the "Paris of Eastern Europe," was burning. The sounds of battle were far away. The engines of dive-bombers were sometimes louder and sometimes softer. When they climbed and dove, the pitch changed. Rachel knew this meant more bombs were falling somewhere.

No need of bread and cabbages now.

Bread forever uneaten.

Hunger pangs forever satisfied.

Rachel turned toward the cavernous doorway on Kozhla Street, onto the winding little lane where the animal market was. She passed beneath the familiar archway and through the smoke, stepping over a dead sheep and then over the body of Dolek, the milkman. The old man, mouth wide, gaped up at the sky. He was half buried beneath a mound of bricks.

Almost home! Mama! Papa! Almost . . . home!

☙

It took Kevin Miller's eyes a moment to adjust to the gloom of Erich Bain's one-room, ground-floor flat. The borough of Camden was dodgy even in broad daylight, but Erich's flat smelled like something had died in the walls. Littered with newspapers, it appeared to have been ransacked. Only the small round table was tidy. Erich's perpetual game of solitaire was laid out in front of him. The deck was blue.

Turkish cigarette dangling from his lower lip, Erich barely glanced up from his game when Kevin entered. "Well, well. The papers are filled with your failure, Kevin," Erich chided. Dark hair fell over the young man's broad, unlined forehead. Long legs in gray flannel trousers and large bare feet protruded from under the table. Erich did not invite Kevin to sit.

Kevin cleared his throat and blurted, "Terrill's dead. A heart attack, they say."

Harvey Terrill had worked for Trump European News Service—but all for the secret purpose of passing key information for the cause. Terrill had been good at his job. Now he was six feet under. The thought made Kevin shiver.

"They say that, do they?" Erich asked.

"What else?"

An enigmatic smile crept over Erich's face as he studied the deck.

"There are many ways for a man to die in jail. Heart failure is always the result of death."

"At least we don't have to worry about him spilling his guts."

"So many guts for Terrill to spill. Yes. All the mess buried with him."

"What do we do now?" Kevin wrung his hat in his hands.

"We?"

"Yes. I mean, what are the orders from Berlin?" Kevin asked.

"War against Poland. Soon England may declare war against the Reich. What do you suppose orders to be?"

Kevin inhaled the odor of mold and old cigarettes as he considered the question. "I'm not clear on it."

"Do you think war changes the Führer's objectives against those who are enemies of the Reich in England?" Erich turned up a jack of diamonds and slapped it down on the queen of clubs.

"Churchill may be out of reach now. He's got a bodyguard. If he joins the government, he'll be surrounded all the time."

Erich hesitated. His eyes narrowed. "The others? The American newsman? His Jewish wife? Her niece, Lori Ibsen?"

"Lori Kalner. She's married now."

"The Gestapo has taken a special interest. After all, she is the daughter of Karl Ibsen . . ."

"The Protestant pastor."

Erich smirked. "Or, should I say, the *late* Karl Ibsen?"

"He's dead?"

"Died for the Fatherland. All for a good cause, be assured." Erich winked.

"How do you know?"

Erich smiled and continued his game. "In the cards."

"And the American?"

"As vocal against the Reich in the American press as Churchill. An enemy of the Führer, to be sure. And his wife—Zionist. Do we not know of her involvement with the Underground? Smuggling refugees from the Reich?"

"So you're saying kill them? Is that what you're saying, Erich? They've got two bobbies outside their door at the Savoy. I saw them myself."

"Sounds simple enough. No doubt you'll find a way. Do they ever go out?"

"Never alone."

"Even so. On the streets after dark in the blackout? Or maybe an accidental bump in a crowd on the train platform?" Erich suggested. "Hard to put someone back together when they've fallen under the wheels of a train. Oh, I don't know. You'll find a way. I'm sure of it, Kevin. You've been so eager to advance the cause. Be creative."

Kevin bit his lip and nodded. "Sure. Yes. Of course."

"You're still with us?"

"Of course. Yes, I am. Only . . . I was hoping for something more specific, that's all. A plan like we had before."

Erich held up the ace of spades. "I'll let you know when something comes through. Meanwhile, solitaire is the game."

The interview was at an end. Kevin backed up a step. As Kevin turned to leave, Erich was still studying the playing cards.

4

Long, Dark Hours

The harried female clerk inside the British Embassy flipped through Eva Weitzman's passport. An identification card fell from the pages along with two envelopes.

Eva blinked at the ID card that declared in English and Polish that this was the press pass of Julia Smith, member of TENS, headquartered in London.

The clerk tucked the badge and the envelopes into the passport and returned it to Eva. "So. Julia Smith. Trump European."

"Yes. Julia Smith." Eva felt her cheeks color at the deception.

"No luggage allowed, I'm afraid. The shirt on your back."

"I have no luggage."

"Where are the rest of the TENS staff?"

Eva blinked dumbly at the passport. "Gone."

"What is your position with TENS? Reporter?"

"Interpreter." Eva frowned and bit her lip. Though she spoke several languages well enough to get by, she was fluent only in Czech and French. Her mastery of the English language was minimal. "I read Czech and Polish and French and German. Then speak into English. For the . . . gentlemen." This newfound ability to lie and be believed surprised her.

The official rubber stamp came down with a resounding *thud*. The clerk added Julia Smith to a long list of names and nodded toward a bench on the far wall of the crowded foyer. Six grim men waited, fidgeting like schoolboys beneath a large picture of the British monarch, George VI.

"Lucky you. Employed by an American news agency. You'll be leaving with those chaps. Mostly Americans. With the American convoy—Ambassador Biddle, a handful of foreign correspondents, and all the American Embassy staff. Wives with them. A few children as well. You're the only lady journalist in the pack."

"I am leaving? Leaving Warsaw, then? Yes?" Eva asked.

"That's the point, isn't it?"

"When?"

"An automobile from the American Embassy will pick you all up. Provided the Germans don't bomb the American automobiles, you should be home in London long before Parliament knows there's a little war going on here in Poland."

Eva hesitated. "I'm leaving? Just like that?"

The woman adjusted her spectacles and smiled. "Unless you want to stay here and take my place. I'll go to England instead of you and then I'll pretend to be you and . . ."

Eva blanched and clutched the passport to her heart. "Do I sit there among the . . . those gentlemen?"

"I don't know if I'd call them gentlemen." The clerk pointed to a sturdy, iron-jawed fellow sitting in an office chair apart from the rest. "That large, tousled-looking fellow there? The good-looking one with the long legs and the camera on his lap? Yes. There. The one in need of a haircut and a shave. And a good woman to press his shirts. Mac McGrath. Journalist. In your line of work. No gentleman, but a good fellow to stick by you in a pinch. Whatever automobile he's traveling in, ride with him. Uncanny luck, that fellow. Knows the Nazi minister of propaganda personally, I hear. Detests the German swine but still manages to get remarkable film from the Nazis for American cinema newsreels."

Eva nodded, not understanding most of what the processing clerk said. "I shall sit then? Beside him? Go with him?"

"You do that. Best of luck." The woman peered around Eva impatiently and summoned the next person in line.

Eva inched through the crowd of refugees toward the bench and the wooden office chair occupied by Mac McGrath. He did not rise as she approached. He did not offer her his seat. There was no place to sit but the floor. Right. He was no gentleman.

She clasped her hands behind her back and pretended to study the gilt-framed painting of the British monarch above his head. Long minutes passed as the crowd ebbed and flowed around her.

She removed the press pass and studied the photo. Her identity but not her. Yes. A miracle. The little priest from the Cathedral of St. John had told her before she left that he would pray for a miracle. Now here it was.

McGrath fixed his attention on the pass. He spoke to her. "So. You're with Trump European?"

"Yes."

"One of Murphy's Warsaw crew, are you?"

"Murphy," she repeated, hesitating a fraction too long. Murphy was someone in the news office in Warsaw? She thought it best to agree with Mac McGrath. "Yes. Murphy. Warsaw office. But he's not here."

First suspicion, then something like amusement flashed in Mac's eyes. "No. Murphy's gone, eh? Left Warsaw, did he?"

"Yes."

"Plan to meet up with him? The office in . . . Madrid?"

"Madrid. Yes. Yes."

"Quite a staff Murphy had here in Warsaw." Mac stood and offered her his seat. She did not move to take it. Did he intend to interrogate her? uncover her lies? trap her here in the chair and call the authorities to put her back outside on the streets of Warsaw? Mac lowered his voice and whispered in her ear. "How many of you kids were there? How many getting out?"

She shook her head vigorously in a silent plea that he not ask any more questions. She felt the color drain from her face. It was clear Mac McGrath knew something about her and the Trump European press pass that she did not know. Did he also know the identity of the young woman who had given her the passport? Eva's hands began to tremble. "Mac. I am . . . called . . . I am Julia Smith. By that name I am called. I will travel with you? They say you are a good fellow to travel along. Please. Don't tell them."

"Them? Sure. Oh! No. See? John Murphy and I are old friends. In Spain together during the civil war. You know Murphy's wife, Elisa?" Evidently her face must have turned ashen enough to alarm him. He took her arm. "Hey. Sit down."

A wave of exhaustion overwhelmed her. "Please. Yes . . . I'll sit down." She cradled her head in her hands and muttered softly in French, "*Mon Dieu!* Oh, God! So many! So many will not escape this place. And I? Why should I be so lucky?" She began to weep quietly.

Mac, clumsy at the first sign of tears, stooped down in front of the chair and pleaded, "Hey. Don't. Poor kid. You got a kerchief?"

"No. Nothing." Her eyes and nose streamed.

He plunged his hands into his pockets, searching for a handkerchief. Gum wrappers emerged. Loose change rattled. No luck. He shrugged and rubbed his nose. "Yeah. Sorry. Didn't mean to . . ." He crossed his arms and stuck out his lower lip. "When did you sleep last?"

"Two days. Maybe."

"Catch a few winks. I mean . . . sleep."

"Suppose they call for Julia Smith and I do not wake up?"

"Julia. Julia Smith. Sure. Look, I'll wake you when they call your name."

Savoy Hotel
London, England

Dearest Jacob,

I cannot sleep tonight for thinking of you, so I am writing again. Praying for you through the long, dark hours. The total blackout is now in effect. Headlights on taxis and all vehicles are covered by black paper with only tiny slits for light. Walking out at night will become a hazard. The city will be pitch-dark from sunset to dawn. Inside our hotel rooms heavy curtains have been hung over the windows to prevent light from escaping.

Somehow I feel as though a curtain covers my soul as well. I live in a blackout, waiting to hear some word from you. Hoping you are well out of reach of the Gestapo. There is no light without you, darling.

This evening Elisa and Murphy stepped out for a late bite of supper. The government has closed all theatres, picture houses, and other places of public entertainment for fear of terrorist activities. There is an uproar from the English public greater than any I've seen since we came here. There is no way for the English public to entertain themselves easily now that the curfew is in effect.

A romantic supper by candlelight is the best sort of evening out. Elisa and Murphy asked me to go along, of course, but I sensed they needed to steal a few hours alone. So I stayed here in the hotel and wished you were here with me.

We said farewell to Mother and Aunt Anna and the children at Paddington Station today. Very pitiful. Elisa kissed baby Katie's sweet face, and Katie smiled up at her, not knowing that instead of Elisa's milk, she would be dining now on the milk of a Welsh goat. Elisa wept quite a lot after the train pulled out. The train was not especially crowded with children, as we had expected. I suppose no one believes that the Nazis would dare to bomb London until they first demolish Poland. The news says that the Poles are fighting bravely and may yet turn back the raging tide.

I pray for you and Alfie with every thought and breath. Elisa *asks me if I would like to go out for a walk. "Yes," I tell her with my mouth. "That would be very nice." And inside my head my mind is raging, What if Jacob sends a wire? What if I miss a phone call?*

We walked for a long time along the Thames River. Elisa is certain now that England must declare war. But she says it is too late to save many we have left behind. I think of Papa. In prison somewhere in Berlin for preaching the gospel. What will become of him? There will be no hope for his release to the British or the American church. I feel today like my prayers are hitting the steel gray sky and crashing back to earth!

Preparations are being made for war everywhere. The Egyptian obelisk known as Cleopatra's Needle and the two stone lions are being covered with sandbags. Everywhere there is grass we see cockney gravediggers shoveling dirt to make slit trenches and grubby little boys in knee britches filling more sandbags with the dirt.

Where are you? That question plagues me. Are you safe? I can think of nothing else.

At least the children will all be safe.

I love you, my darling!

Lori

⊙⊙

The blackout curtains were drawn, the windows wide open, and all the lights extinguished. Even so, the bedroom of the hotel suite was hot. Not even a faint breeze stirred over London. The odor of the Thames River at low tide was strong and unpleasant.

Glenn Miller's orchestra music played softly over the British Broadcasting Company station as Elisa and Murphy drew their chairs nearer the windowsill. Murphy popped the tops of two bottles of Coke and passed one to Elisa.

"No ice." Murphy took a deep swig. "Hot Coke. Nobody would believe it back home. I miss ice."

"You Americans." Elisa held the warm glass bottle and wiped her brow. "Ice. Iced tea. Iced soda. Iced watermelon, you tell me. You don't know how to suffer."

He chuckled and reached for her hand. "No, I guess not. Back home there's more concern about which baseball teams will be playing in the World Series than . . ."

"As long as there's an ocean between New York and London, yes?"

Murphy's brow creased with concern. "'Fraid so."

They each sat alone in their thoughts for a while. The sounds of Lori's muffled sobs penetrated the wall between the rooms.

"What will happen, Murphy?" Elisa asked.

"I don't know." The Colt was within his reach. "But I want you and the kids to go to America."

"How do you say it? No . . . ice?"

"No dice."

"Either way, I won't leave you." Elisa's tone was firm, immovable.

"If Hitler ever figures out how unprepared the Brits are, there will be an invasion so fast—"

"I won't go."

"They could be goose-stepping through Piccadilly in two weeks."

"You know Lori will stay, too. She has no word of her father. Nothing from Jacob. Forget it, Murphy. I'm staying."

"I figured. Then there's only one thing left to say." He tapped his Coke bottle against hers with a resounding *clink*. "Rule Britannia."

♋

Sometime before midnight Eva awoke with a start. Had she missed the car from the American Embassy? She was slumped in the chair. Mac McGrath lay at her feet. He had stuffed his coat beneath her head as a pillow.

Those few hundred lucky enough to gain entry into the British Embassy now slept sprawled on floors, in corridors, and propped against walls.

Mac opened his eyes as Eva stirred. He sat up. "You okay?"

"I was afraid."

Mac exhaled loudly. "No. Still no car from the American Embassy."

"Do you think it will come?"

"Don't know. Maybe morning now."

"Is it safe for me to go to the loo?"

"Go. I'll guard the chair." Mac slipped into the precious seat as Eva picked her way across the dimly lit foyer into the ladies' room. Three stalls were all unoccupied. Eva stepped into the first, slid the bolt closed, and removed the passport. This was the first opportunity she'd had to privately examine the two envelopes tucked into the pages of the document.

The first contained fifty British pounds and the TENS press pass. Enough cash for travel, food, small bribes, and a ferry crossing to England.

The second, stamped and addressed to Rabbi Shlomo Lebowitz in Jerusalem, contained a message written on two pages of parchment, along with a black-and-white photo of four smiling children. Eva instantly recognized the clear eyes of the girl who had given her the passport. Rachel! Holding an infant, she smiled from between two young boys. On the back of the photo was written:

> To Grandfather Lebowitz
> With love from Rachel, Samuel, David, and baby Yacov
> July 14, 1939

Eva closed her eyes and moaned. *Why? Why? Why?* For a time she stared back at the beautiful children in the photograph. She grieved for them as she grieved for her own lost family.

Rachel. Why had Rachel given away the passport? Why had she not used it herself? With trembling fingers Eva opened the trifold parchment of the letter. Inscribed in ornate script, the message was written in a woman's handwriting:

> *September 1, 1939*
>
> *Written as the first air-raid sirens wail across Warsaw, announcing to us that war has finally come to Poland.*

The hand that recorded that terrible moment of history did not quake as bombs fell on Warsaw.

> *My dearest father,*
> *It is the hope of Aaron and I that when you see our darling Rachel's face there will be no need for me to tell you not to fear for us. We are not afraid. We are trusting our lives to the Almighty. We pray for . . .*

Eva gasped with surprise and the force of emotion that gripped her. *Oh, God! A brave mother of four. Her children trapped! Hopes that one would escape!* It all suddenly became very clear.

After a minute Eva glanced at the signature on the bottom of the second page.

> *My father, if we do not meet again on this earth, know I love you.*
> *Remember us only in happiness.*
> *Your loving daughter,*
> *Etta Lubetkin*

Refolding the parchment, Eva kissed the photo of Rachel and replaced it with the letter in the envelope. "I will not fail you, Etta Lubetkin," Eva whispered. "Brave Etta, I will make certain your father receives your letter. I will."

⏤⏤⏤ ⏤⏤⏤

The basement of the Jewish Community Center on Niksa Street was packed with Jews who lived in the neighborhood near Muranow Square. The atmosphere was stifling, but the insistent *crump* of distant artillery kept all but the most foolhardy from venturing out.

Who is winning? Rachel wondered. *The brave Polish army or the Nazis? Surely, Lord, you will help the Poles defend their homeland.*

Three blankets suspended by twine and wooden clothespins cordoned off the allotted living area of Rabbi Aaron Lubetkin's family. Rachel lay wide-awake, cramped and miserable between two of her brothers, David and Samuel. The boys tossed fretfully in their sleep. Baby Yacov slept with Papa and Mama, who sat with their backs against the wall and whispered to one another.

"Aaron, she meant well." Mama defended Rachel to Papa.

"My dear Etta. My love. Four children we have! Do you know what will happen if the Nazis enter Warsaw victorious? Etta, we might have had one child safe. Rachel might have gone to your father in Jerusalem. A chance, she had. One chance. Now this. She chooses to disobey? And at such a time? Peter Wallich, Jacob Kalner, the other Zionist Youth gone from Warsaw. Yet Rachel comes back. Why?" Papa was adamant.

Tears of confusion and shame stung Rachel's eyes as she lay in the dark and listened.

Papa had not spoken or come near her when Mama had run to embrace her. Mama had wept at the sight of her and asked again and again, *"Rachel! What have you done? Why have you come back?"*

How could Rachel explain? What could she say? Papa had commanded her to choose life. When Rachel attempted to describe the happy tragedy of a mother in the street embracing her little ones in death—all of them leaving this terrible world together—Mama had wept all the more and begged her to stop.

After supper the head of the soup kitchen had approached Papa with the request that Rachel be allowed to give a report to the defense committee of what she had seen and heard outside. Papa had refused permission.

The klezmer band played music, and the community sang songs that drowned out the sound of the war, but Rachel's evening had passed in uncomfortable silence.

Prayers were said. Each family went to its own little blanket cubicle. Lamps were extinguished. Babies cried. Lullabies were sung. A middle-aged couple had argued about whether they should stay in the basement and die from the heat and discomfort or go home to their own flat, where a bomb might fall on their heads. In the end they had decided that a bomb landing on their mattress at home would be more merciful. They had gathered their suitcases, stumbled over the others, and gone out into the night to see if their house was still standing. They had not come back.

It was very late; now only occasional whispers rippled through the refugees. Mama and Papa, barely audible, discussed Rachel's disobedience.

"A British passport. Like a miracle," Papa said. "There will come a time, Etta. Too soon people will kill for such a document. *Nu?*"

"Aaron, she didn't understand. Aaron! How can she know what it means?"

Rachel grieved that she had displeased Papa. Caused disagreement between Mama and Papa. Could he have meant he wanted Rachel to live and leave them behind to die? possibly never see them again? Did he not understand that her heart would have broken, and she would have died anyway?

Rachel sniffed and wiped hot tears with the back of her hand. She held her breath and tried so hard not to let them hear her crying in the dark. A gasp for air and then . . .

Silence.

Mama's voice, gentle. "Rachel?"

At first Rachel did not answer.

Then again, Mama, comforting. "Rachel? Are you awake, angel?"

Rachel's voice trembled. "Yes."

"What is it then?" Mama asked. "Bad dream?"

Rachel managed a reply. "Papa . . . Papa told us . . . he who saves a life, saves the universe. . . ."

Papa considered this a long moment. "So I did. This is why we sent you away with Peter. 'Choose life,' I said."

Rachel licked the salty tears from her lips and whispered hoarsely, desperately, "But . . . I *did* choose life, Papa. I did! But not my life. She is a Jewish girl! Her name is Eva Weitzman. She was all alone outside the embassy, wanting to get in. Praying for a miracle, I think. I saw it in her face. So I chose life. Just like you taught us, Papa. But not life for myself. I want to go where you and Mama go! I'm not alone like Eva is. And I'm not afraid! So I gave away my passport to her. So it's her life, not mine, oh, Papa . . ." She could not finish the explanation.

She did not need to.

Papa's deep voice, understanding, loving, forgiving her for coming back, called, "Come on then, my Rachel. Come sit beside your mother and me."

She crept over her sleeping brothers and fell into Papa's arms.

His voice quavered with emotion as he patted her back. "Rachel. There's my brave daughter. Was there ever a papa more proud of his daughter? A true daughter of Zion. A lioness we've raised, Etta! Was any man blessed with such a daughter as this? She shines like Queen Esther saving her people against the plots of evil Haman. Like Jael in the tent of the enemy. Very courageous! A mitzvah. Yes. To save the life of one Jew, she saves the universe. My Rachel! There now. Don't cry. The Almighty has written your sacrifice in His book. No more tears. A very righteous deed, Daughter! You did choose life. Only it is the life of another you have chosen, not your life. Yes, my Rachel. I see it now."

5

The Raging Tide

September 2, 1939

Dearest Lori:

I don't know when—or if—I'll be able to mail this letter to you, but
Captain Orde says I must keep a record of what happens to us . . . and
the only one I can think of who would care is you.

We are on board Herr Frankenmuth's fishing boat. When I say
we, I mean big Alfie Halder (and Werner-kitten, of course) and
me. There's also Captain Orde and Lucy Strasburg, baby Alfie's
mother. Peter Wallich is here, too, and twelve more of the Zionist
Young Pioneers.

Alfie says we're going to the Promised Land, and no one argues
with him . . . not even Herr Frankenmuth.

There is much about yesterday that is very confusing.

The Bristol Hotel was bombed. The Nazis are pounding
Warsaw into rubble, and we saw a ship just downstream from us take
a direct hit. There was a bright flash, a big waterspout, and then the
freighter just broke in two, like it had been split with an ax.

Everyone says the Polish air force is waiting to strike back with
a crushing blow, but I heard Captain Orde mutter that if they wait
much longer there won't be anything left of Warsaw to save.

Nazi planes strafed anything moving—boats on the water and
trains crammed with refugees trying to get out of the city. Our boat
was sheltered by a wooden shed and a garbage scow, so we stayed

undercover until evening. By then we had counted twelve air raids . . . and never saw a Polish plane.

Sparks from a burning dock landed on the roof of our refuge, setting it on fire. Herr Frankenmuth said we had to go, even if it wasn't yet fully dark.

He wanted to travel toward his home at Wyszkow, but Captain Orde said the bombed bridges and sunken ships probably blocked the river. Anyway, he said south was better. Everybody, even Herr Frankenmuth, listens to Samuel Orde, so we chugged south all night, just to get away from the bombing and the fires.

At dawn we were somewhere between Warsaw and Pulawy. We found a place where willows hang over the bank, and we tied up close to shore. We cut branches and tied them all over the boat's side and cabin to cover us. Now we're going to sleep, and we'll travel again tonight.

I miss you. When I close my eyes, I see you waving to me from the ship that took you to England . . . and I'm glad you're safe.

Pray that the English keep their promises and counterattack soon. Captain Orde says Hitler can't face the English and the French and the Poles all at once and that the war will stop.

Pray for that.

All my love always,

Jacob

Reports of German atrocities against Polish citizens were pouring in.

"Where is England?" begged the Polish government over the radio transmitters as Warsaw burned. *"Where is France?"*

On this evening of September 2, 1939, there was standing room only in the gallery of the House of Commons. The atmosphere was solemn—like the opening of a murder trial, Murphy thought as he leaned against the back wall and studied the political players on both sides of the aisle.

But whose trial was it? Hitler's? Everyone already knew he was guilty.

Perhaps the British prime minister, Neville Chamberlain, was before the bar tonight as an accomplice to the Nazi march across Europe by allowing slaughter without lifting a finger to oppose the tyrant. Yes, tonight, depending on what Chamberlain said, he would be judged either innocent or guilty in the court of history.

Murphy glanced at his watch. It was 7:35 when the clerks filed in. Two minutes later the Speaker of the House entered, and all was silence as the Honorable Members stood. It was a hostile, bitter silence as all eyes fixed on the arched portal where Prime Minister Chamberlain, the man who had sold out all Britain's allies to Hitler for the sake of peace at any price, entered at last. He was dressed all in black, as if he was in mourning. With Chamberlain was Mr. Greenwood, the deputy leader of the Opposition Party. Greenwood, dressed in a rumpled suit, looked particularly green tonight, Murphy noted.

Long prayers from the chaplain begged heaven for peace, wisdom, patience, and prudence. As Murphy listened, the words seemed more like the ineffectual lecture of a pacifist than a prayer. Yet clearly the sentiment of all England chafed against the men of the House of Commons who had sat back and watched Hitler break every political treaty he had made with Britain. At this very moment the German navy was bombarding the Polish barracks at the free port of Danzig. German Panzer divisions pushed ever nearer to Warsaw.

At last! Murphy thought as he looked around the room at the sullen expressions. The Members of Parliament were beginning to react to the disgust of the ordinary citizens of Great Britain. Surely, surely, Germany's latest act of aggression against Britain's Polish ally would mean war!

This evening all MPs appeared angry and dissatisfied as Prime Minister Chamberlain, gray and shaken, stood at the podium and shuffled his papers in preparation for his address.

Mr. Greenwood's eyes were fierce as he stared at the floor, not at the podium.

At 7:44, Chamberlain began to speak. He seemed ill. He spoke for only four minutes.

Murphy summed up the prime minister's speech to Parliament and the world in seven words: *A warning has been sent to Germany.*

Chamberlain sat down. The stillness was oppressive.

Could it be? No decision for Britain to assist their Polish ally had been reached. And France wanted more time. Britain waited for France? For France! Unbelievable! Once again Chamberlain vacillated.

The entire German air force was engaged against Poland. Bombing villages. Destroying factories. As the blitzkrieg flowed across the landscape, no one remained alive to tell the story!

Still Britain would not fulfill her obligation to help Poland! Britain waited on France. No ultimatum had been delivered to Hitler. No time limit set for Germany to withdraw from Polish territory. No agreement with the government of France on when they would make a joint announcement declaring war.

Faces in the gallery and on the floor reflected outrage. They were astounded. Stupefied. Flabbergasted. Infuriated.

Silence smoldered. A silence born of stunned fury.

Then Murphy heard the angry clearing of someone's throat. A voice bellowed from the floor: "Speak for England!"

Suddenly the room erupted with shared exasperation at months and years of Chamberlain's indecision and vacillation. Hands thumped loudly against the benches in protest.

Murphy mopped his forehead. He thought about Elisa and Lori. Wished they were here.

For five minutes the roaring continued:

"Speak for England!"

"What of British honor?"

"Is there to be another sellout? another Munich?"

But Murphy knew well enough that the indignation of Parliament had come too late. Too late for Poland. If only the voices had raised in unison to protest the politics of appeasement years ago. If only. Perhaps then, if powerful governments had stood up to Hitler, resisted him as the coward he truly was, perhaps this tragic night might have been averted.

At last Mr. Greenwood, the grim and rumpled Opposition Party leader, took the podium. His party cheered his rising. All well and good. No surprise there. What astounded Murphy was that Chamberlain's own party also cheered. Those who had supported Chamberlain through every misstep now rose to their feet in support of Greenwood.

MP Bob Boothby rumbled, "Now *you* speak for England!"

Greenwood blinked with amazement.

Murphy scribbled shorthand notes as Greenwood took up the soiled banner of British politics.

"I am gravely disturbed. A German act of aggression against Poland has begun and is ongoing even as we meet here. The moment that act of aggression took place, one of the most important treaties of modern times automatically came into operation: the British promise to come to Poland's aid! But where are we? Still debating what should be done. There are many of us on all sides of this House who view with the gravest concern that hours go by and news flows in of German bombing operations! And news today that German aggression becomes more intense! And I wonder. How long are we still to vacillate? The prime minister declares we wait upon France. Upon our allies. But I should have far preferred the prime minister to have been able to say to us and the world tonight, 'It is either peace or war. . . .'"

A rousing cry rose from the floor and the gallery. The cheer of approval was long and sustained. Greenwood, buoyed by the support, raised his hands to speak again.

"I would have preferred he tell us that there will be no more Nazi devices for dragging out what has been dragged out too long. The moment we look like we are weakening . . . at that moment the dictator knows we are beaten!" This was greeted by boos. Greenwood slammed his fist on the podium. "We are not beaten! We shall not be beaten! We cannot be beaten! But delay is dangerous. I cannot see Herr Hitler making any deal that he is not prepared to betray!"

The House of Commons rocked with the huzzahs of the Honorable Members.

Neville Chamberlain, tight-lipped, his weary eyes fixed on the tops of his shoes, appeared more exhausted by the ordeal than stirred by the demonstration.

In Murphy's years of covering British politics, he had never witnessed such unity and resolve. Both sides of the aisle hailed Greenwood to the rafters. If only Lori and Elisa could hear this. What joy! What renewal of hope there was in this display of righteous anger from men who might summon the power of their nation to action!

Murphy mopped his brow again and searched the faces of civilians packed in the gallery. There were at least twenty thousand Nazi sympathizers in England, Winston Churchill had said. Who among this crowd? Murphy wondered. No doubt there were spies here. Of course. Well then, perhaps they would relay a fierce and frightening message from England to Berlin.

Murphy was certain at that instant that it was only a matter of time before Chamberlain's government would fall. Chamberlain's flock of appeasement chickens had at last come home to roost.

Murphy believed Winston Churchill would be first in line to take up the sword for Britain when Chamberlain's government collapsed. Winston had not come tonight. There was no need. He had his finger on the pulse of his people. By now he had his bodyguard in place at his flat. Winston was not wrong when he decided to sleep with a gun beneath his pillow.

No doubt the Gestapo and the Nazi butchers of Berlin also realized that Churchill would be a very different opponent than Neville Chamberlain had been.

⁘

Savoy Hotel
London, England

Dearest Jacob,

Where are you, my darling? News from Poland is such chaos. Murphy haunts the TENS office when he is not covering the emergency political meetings being held to determine what England must do now that Poland is attacked.

So much has happened, and yet nothing has happened. Where do I begin? Still Prime Minister Chamberlain dithers. An ultimatum has been issued to Herr Hitler that he is a naughty boy and must stop blowing up Poland and killing Jews.

I doubt Hitler will listen.

But fear not; I am safe. Murphy carries a big cowboy gun beneath his coat. At night he tucks it beneath his pillow, as does Mr. Churchill. Two London policemen stand guard at our door, and Elisa and I dare not venture out without these gentlemen trailing us. I assume it is because of the threat of Nazi agents against us here in England. Papa being such a prominent Christian protestor against abortion and euthanasia in Germany has made silencing my voice in the West of possible interest to the Nazis.

Today Murphy helped me petition the American Embassy to help us find out from the German government which prison Papa is in and attempt to arrange for us to communicate with him. But the fellow at the embassy did not hold out much hope. He says there are thousands of people like me trying to get word about their loved ones still in the Reich.

Not knowing is the hardest part of all this, Jacob. I must force myself to focus on what I think is true—what Papa always taught me: Our lives are in the hands of a loving God. And yet. And yet, I wonder often how it is that, with God in charge, the world can be in such a mess.

My arms ache for you. My prayers for you to return to me never cease.

Good night, my dearest husband.

I love you,

Lori

6

They Shall Not Pass!

It was the third morning since the German army had flooded across the Polish frontiers. As yet, no help had come from either England or France.

Murphy sat between Elisa and Lori in Westminster Chapel, Buckingham Gate, London.

It had been clear the evening before that the temper of the House of Commons was for war. All the same, England gathered this morning to pray once more for peace.

Even the balcony of Westminster Chapel, parish of Reverend Martin Lloyd-Jones, was packed. There was no more room in the long pews. Men and women stood along the walls. Children, giddy with the prospect of an exciting war, sat in the aisle and in front of the pulpit.

Hymnbooks were opened, and the hall reverberated to the spiritual anthem of Martin Luther:

"A mighty fortress is our God,
A bulwark never failing. . . ."

It occurred to Murphy as he sang that this was a German hymn. He wondered how many voices in Germany were likewise raised in the same melody at this very instant. The image of men and women wearing swastika armbands as they belted out Luther's words made him fall silent, made him angry.

His sudden unhappiness must have shown. Elisa took his hand and gave him a chin-up look.

In spite of news from Poland, there remained a few Pacifists among them in Westminster Chapel this morning. Murphy could spot them, smug and fervent as they warbled. Their presence now, in the light of the damage their politics had done to the cause of putting a stop to Hitler's antics, added to his outrage. The Nazis might have been halted long ago, before the world had come to this moment. By allowing evil to eclipse central Europe unchecked, the shadow was about to fall across England and France as well.

As the organ boomed, a balding little man in a tweed coat too hot for the morning made his way through the throng. He was waving a yellow slip of paper, much as Chamberlain had waved the little document signed by Hitler that the prime minister had said promised "peace in our time."

The sexton climbed the steps to the pulpit and presented the message to Reverend Lloyd-Jones. The song continued. Second and third verses were sung as the minister silently reviewed the message, and the congregation watched his face reflect the content.

He stood as the music died away. Approaching the podium, he raised his hand and with a hard, piercing look said, "This message has just been broadcast by Prime Minister Chamberlain at 10 Downing Street." He drew a deep breath and began:

> *"This morning the British ambassador in Berlin handed the German government a final note stating that unless we heard from them by 11 o'clock this AM that they were prepared at once to withdraw their troops from Poland, a state of war would exist between us."*

Murphy tapped the crystal of his watch. It was 11:20.

> *"I have to tell you now that no such undertaking has been received, and consequently, this country is at war with Germany."*

A murmur rippled through the crowd. Here and there a few heads bowed. The shoulders of mothers with military-age sons shook.

Elisa grasped Murphy's hand. She put her arm around his waist and raised her chin defiantly. If Hitler were standing in front of her she would spit in his eye!

> *"You can imagine what a bitter blow it is to me that all my long struggle to win peace has failed. Germany will never give up force and*

> *can only be stopped by force. May God bless you all and may He defend the right, for it is evil things we shall be fighting—brute force, broken promises. I am certain right will prevail. "*

As the message ended, the prolonged, weird wailing of an air-raid siren pierced the air. Heads jerked up in realization that German bombers might be approaching the coast of England this very moment.

The congregation was dismissed. Men in uniform were instructed to report immediately to their posts. There was a general scramble to retrieve children, and the invitation was extended for everyone to make their way to the cellar beneath the church.

Murphy kissed Elisa good-bye. "I'll be at the office." Then, without a backward glance, he left the church just as the siren fell silent.

Outside, nothing seemed changed. Murphy stood on the steps and listened to the silence as if he was hearing it for the first time. Above him, on the cornice of the chapel, pigeons cooed and fluttered. He wanted to memorize the first minutes of conflict, to remember them forever. It seemed no different than the peace of an hour before, yet he sensed that from this hour his life would be irrevocably altered. He closed his eyes and conjured up images of screaming bombs falling on London, of rubble and ruin and the cries of the injured. . . . But when he opened his eyes again, there was only London, brick and stone and undisturbed tradition.

Just to his right the spires of Parliament rose in the cool, light, September morning air. He walked the long block and turned toward Victoria Embankment.

No German bombers had passed overhead as he reached the Thames. But as he strode along the embankment, thirty or forty silver barrage balloons slowly rose over the city, like a school of fish swimming the breezes above London. They held in place the nets used to protect the city from air attacks.

So this was war.

ೲ

The bells of the clock tower chimed twelve as the loudspeaker played "La Marseillaise," the French national anthem. After a respectful silence, the doors to the enormous dining hall of the upperclassmen of the Ecole de Cavalerie near Lys, France, burst open and fifteen hundred young cadets, ages twelve to seventeen, flooded into their places at the long tables.

Captain Paul Chardon stood at attention with six fellow instructors behind the head table as the commandant of the school, Colonel Michel Larousse, entered solemnly through a side door. His left sleeve was pinned up, due to his having lost an arm in the last war against

Germany. He carried a communiqué in his right hand. Standing for a long moment before ascending the platform to the head table, the colonel observed his young charges with the weary eyes of a man who knew what war would do to the youth of his nation.

From the high walls, portraits of the great soldiers of France also looked down on the boys. The emperor Napoleon and one of his favorite commanders, Marshal Ney, stared across the hall at General Petain, who had led French armies to victory in the Great War.

Many of the best and bravest leaders of the Republic had begun their education here in the Junior School at age five. They had progressed through the ranks and supped at these same long tables. In a dozen wars, brave comrades had gone from this place to die for France before they had a chance to grow up. Who remembered their names now?

Today the hall rang with laughter and boisterous conversation, just as it had for one hundred and fifty years. Paul Chardon glanced at Colonel Larousse and then at the cadets, dressed in the dark blue uniforms of the Cadre Bleu. It was as though the faces of past centuries gazed back at him. France was at war once again.

The tradition of the military school had been broken only once in the 1914–18 war, when German troops had threatened to overrun Armentieres and the vast estate where the Ecole had been founded by Napoleon in 1805.

At that terrible time the cry had risen: *"Ecole de Cavalerie! France éternel! Not one inch of ground will we surrender! Ils ne passeront pas!"*

Colonel Larousse cleared his throat and gave a nod to the bugler. The sharp flourish of the trumpet called the boys to attention: eyes forward, chests out, shoulders back.

"At ease." The colonel stood before a whining microphone. He cleared his throat.

Silence. Here was the news they had all been waiting for, praying for. Perhaps they could fight!

Colonel Larousse began. "I hold in my hand a communiqué from Paris." He held it up to the light. The portrait of General Petain seemed to be reading over his shoulder. "'Be it known . . . the recent attacks on our ally, the sovereign democratic nation of Poland, by the forces of Nazi Germany, violate all international laws and treaties. In view of this fact, this act of aggression is an act of war against the Republic of France. Therefore, the Republic of France is now at war with Germany.'"

There was a stirring of excitement among the cadets. Paul Chardon saw their half smiles, their winks, their delight at the prospect of putting into practice what they had learned in theory at the school.

Colonel Larousse likewise sensed their joy at the declaration. "All cadets under the age of thirteen will be evacuated to the South. . . . "

There rose a universal moan of misery among the twelve-year-olds. Winks and smirks and jabs to the ribs came from the older boys.

Larousse held up his hand for silence. "Those of the Cadre Bleu who are thirteen and older will remain at the school for the time being. We have nine hundred fine cavalry horses in our stables that will certainly be called to battle. It will be our duty to see that they pass into the hands of the Grand Armee in the most excellent condition and with the finest training. That will be our obligation as soldiers of the Republic and the future leaders of France."

When his speech ended, a great cheer rose among the older boys. The twelve-year-old cadets sat dejected, near tears. They were to be shipped off like the little boys. They were to miss all the excitement!

A group of cadets due to graduate to Officers School in the spring jumped up on their table and led the cheer: *"Vive la Ecole de Cavalerie! Vive la France! France èternel! They shall not pass!"*

Then "La Marseillaise" was sung and lunch cheerfully eaten, marking the beginning of the war for the Ecole de Cavalerie.

☙

Savoy Hotel
London, England

My dearest Jacob,

As I write this, I am in the basement of the Savoy Hotel. The air-raid sirens have sounded the warning across London. We were at the church of Martin Lloyd-Jones, an old pastor friend of my father, when the announcement was made. It seems that Chamberlain's suggestion that Hitler withdraw from Poland was rejected by the Nazis. War between Germany and England was therefore a fact.

Elisa and I walked back to the hotel because there were no cabs. Murphy hurried off to the news office to send a message to America. The Americans are all still asleep, Elisa tells me. They will get up on their Sunday morning and sip their coffee and read about what is happening here. They will go to church and sing their hymns and pray for peace. But will they know that there will be no peace unless they join us in a war against true Evil? Let's pray they care enough to help us here in England, because we will need it.

Where are you, my darling Jacob? Are you safe? Are you in a shelter somewhere? Have you escaped the Nazis? Do you fight at the side of the Poles?

Papa always taught that all things work together for the good of those who love God and are called according to His purpose. I admit only to you that I am having difficulty believing such a promise right now when there is no word from you. Sometimes it is very hard to believe God is hearing my prayers at all.

I love you,

Your wife,

Mrs. Jacob Kalner
Aka Lori

Dearest Lori:

We couldn't stay all day under the willow branches after all.

About noon we heard shouting on the opposite bank of the Vistula. I was the lookout, on my stomach on top of the pilothouse but buried in leaves. I saw men in some kind of uniform I didn't recognize pacing up and down and pointing toward us.

Captain Orde, who speaks more languages than I can count, said they were Ukrainian partisans wanting to take over southeastern Poland for themselves. He said they were doing the work of the Nazis and no friends of ours.

Suddenly he pushed my head down. A bullet whistled into the willows just above me.

A Ukrainian commander shouted that there was something there and then in Polish ordered us to come out and surrender.

Captain Orde told us to keep quiet and maybe they'd go away, but four or five shots hit the boat. One broke the glass of the pilothouse underneath me.

Herr Frankenmuth, who had been sleeping in the cabin, pulled out an old pistol and fired back at them three times.

The Ukrainians scattered, but Captain Orde heard their officer yelling for them to bring up the machine gun.

A cloud of choking blue smoke billowed from under our covering as Herr Frankenmuth's son, Hans, fired up the engine. Trailing fumes and shedding willow branches, we chugged away south. More shots hit the boat, but no one was hurt, except a boy named Aaron, who was cut by flying glass. Captain Orde stitched up a place in his shoulder and says he'll be fine.

We traveled south the rest of the day. We passed some villages during the night, but were afraid to stop. Once we were nearly run down by a tug towing a string of barges. He was running without lights, and Herr Frankenmuth barely got out of the way in time.

Now we're tied up under a ruined stone bridge that only reaches halfway across the river. Both banks are solid with brush, and it doesn't look like anyone's come here for centuries.

Today we had boiled potatoes for breakfast and dinner and no lunch.

Where is England? Where is France? Has the counteroffensive started yet?

Alfie says he sees a pillar of cloud by day and one of fire by night and not to worry.

All my love, always,

Jacob

7

Who Shall Live?

Rachel pretended not to listen as Papa and the young secular Jew discussed what was most feared in the Jewish Quarter of Warsaw.

Everyone in the shelter of the Jewish Community Center knew what it would mean if the English army did not come. If France delayed even one more day. If the weakening Polish defenses crumbled beneath the German ring of steel that now encircled Warsaw.

When bread ran out tomorrow.

"Yes. Our children." Papa agreed with the assessment of Herr Niemann, the director of Jewish Education. "Yes. It always is the most vulnerable who are the target of evil."

Niemann produced a message scrawled on a torn sheet of lined notebook paper. "Rabbi Lubetkin, it's from the priest of the Cathedral of St. John, Father Kopecky, you see? A good fellow. But they can't risk sheltering our boys."

"Circumcision. An easy way for the Nazis to prove one is a Jew, eh?"

"Dangerous. In Germany and Austria sheltering Jews is punishable by death. So the priest can't take the chance. So many children at risk. But our girls. Yes. He'll shelter two hundred girls under the age of twelve. Take them into the convent. *Nu?* Rabbi Lubetkin? He's offering protection for two hundred. It will mean survival if the Nazis are victorious."

Papa glanced toward the semicircle of nine- and ten-year-old boys and girls receiving instruction in mathematics. On the far side of the room, six-, seven-, and eight-year-olds were being taught Napoleonic history. There were many more girls than there were spaces at the Catholic church.

"How will we choose?" Papa said aloud to no one. Rachel knew it was a question he was asking God: Who will live, and who will probably die?

Niemann replied, "We must call a meeting. Speak to the parents. Some among the Orthodox will not want their daughters to live with the Christians. Those children also will be taken from the list. Some children cannot bear to leave their families. They will be removed from the list."

Papa glanced at Rachel and murmured, "No. We cannot make them go if they don't want to go."

"Precisely. So. Those who are left. Who want to go. Who can pass for Gentiles. I propose we draw lots."

Papa's large brown eyes brimmed with sorrow. "Yes, Niemann. It is a good plan. Send word to the priest. Send word we will have a meeting. Send him our thanks. Niemann, we must hurry."

⌘

The hazy September sky was brown from the dust that rose from the unpaved road. The caravan of cars from the American Embassy in Warsaw inched along the two-lane highway behind an unending stream of refugees in desperate retreat toward the safety of the Rumanian border.

Carts pulled by half-starved horses, handcarts, wagons, and even baby carriages were heaped with belongings. Polish soldiers, the survivors of divisions routed in the first assaults of the German war machine, abandoned their weapons and joined the retreat of the civilian population. Behind the column lay the smoldering remains of the towns and villages they had called home.

Character references sufficient for sainthood had been required for Mac McGrath to film the Polish front lines. Officers of the Polish General Staff knew as much about Robert "Mac" McGrath as his own mother did. Thirty-one years old. Graduate of USC. BA in photojournalism, specializing in cinematography. Now the American newsreel camerman for Movietone News.

His hard-won *cartes d'identite* gave the following facts:

> *5'11"*
> *182 lbs*
> *Brown hair*
> *Brown eyes*

Beneath the official stamp, his scowling photograph displayed rugged features . . . well, beat-up features, actually. A one-inch scar above his right eyebrow was the result of a sandlot football game in high school. His nose, bent slightly to the left, was a souvenir of a fistfight. These were only the most ordinary of details. Polish authorities had a thick file that included his grades from grammar school and the precise length of his appendectomy scar.

More to the point: He was escaping the slaughter in Poland in the company of Ambassador Biddle with nothing but the clothes on his back, his DeVry cinecamera, and a rucksack full of film that would bring the war home to one hundred million American theatre-goers.

There were eight staff cars in the American caravan. Each vehicle had the letters USA plainly painted on the roof. The lead car, containing Ambassador Anthony J. Biddle Jr. and his wife and daughter, flew the American flag. Secretaries, liaison officers, assistants, and intelligence personnel followed with assorted American and Polish citizens crammed into every spare inch. Under American diplomatic protection, the French ambassador to Poland, Leon Noel, occupied the last car with Mac McGrath. In the front passenger seat was a Polish Jew named Richard Lewinski, whom Mac assumed was connected with the embassy staff, and the woman pretending to be Julia Smith, a member of the TENS Warsaw office.

The fleeing diplomatic corps had already been strafed twice. American flags and clear identification seemed to make no difference to the pilots of the Messerschmidts, who had honed their techniques fighting for Fascism in the Spanish civil war.

Brakes groaned as the vehicles came to a complete standstill. The driver of the lead car leaned on the horn as the backs of the crowd pressed against the bumper. They were still thirty miles from the border of Rumania. In the distance Mac could clearly hear the even cadence of exploding bombs.

He lowered his window. The backseat of the French-made Renault filled instantly with choking dust. Mac watched with amusement as Lewinski pulled the straps of a gas mask over a shock of wildly unruly hair. Julia covered her face with her hands as though she could not bear to look.

Just outside the window was a weary young peasant woman with two young, filthy children perched in a wooden wheelbarrow. The woman's angry face, framed by a bright red scarf, considered Mac with resentment.

"Why are we stopped?" Ambassador Noel asked the woman.

She shrugged as if she would not answer, but then the question was relayed forward to a stooped old man who passed it on. When the reply returned five minutes later, the convoy still had not moved.

"The Nazis strafed the road. There are many dead and wounded and their belongings being moved out of the way," the woman reported with bland acceptance, acknowledging that the wounded would be left in the field beside the dead. "Two dead horses and an upturned cart block the road."

Mac chafed with impatience. The journey that should have taken only a few hours had stretched into several days. The driver cut the engine of the vehicle to save on precious fuel.

"Only thirty miles," Mac remarked. "We could walk faster than this."

The French ambassador eyed him patronizingly. "Impatient Americans." He jerked his thumb at the tangle of pedestrians. "No one is moving, Monsieur. Perhaps if you walk on the heads of the people you will arrive at the Rumanian border before me, but I cannot see any other way than that."

Mac looked for support from the occupants of the front seat, but the driver only shrugged. Lewinski, still wearing the gas mask, ignored the discussion completely. He was playing the child's game called cat's cradle with a loop of string. Julia, who had hardly spoken a word since the journey began, stared straight ahead.

Mac raised his hands in surrender, then retrieved his DeVry cine-camera and cranked the key wind. A moment later he swung out the side window and onto the bullet-riddled roof of the black Renault as the Frenchman shook his head in amusement.

From his high vantage point, Mac focused on the ragged sea of heads that stretched beyond the roofs of the eight official vehicles. Mac shot a few seconds of film and then walked forward, stepping from hood to trunk, until he reached the lead car of Ambassador Biddle.

Haggard and unshaven, Biddle sat up on the window frame to see what Mac was doing on top of the car.

"You're going to want a record of this, Ambassador." Mac captured on film the dead horses being dragged into the roadside ditch and the fifty human bodies laid out like rag dolls in a field of scattered baggage.

One hundred feet of film could capture only sixty seconds of action. Within the first five seconds of his shot Mac heard the distant buzzing of an airplane engine. By now he did not stop to wonder if the approaching craft was friend or foe. The mob of refugees stumbled off the road, leaving their bundles and plunging into the fields and ditches.

Mac stamped his foot hard on the metal roof. "Plane!" he yelled.

The doors of the vehicles were flung wide as men and women staff members poured out to join the headlong flight away from the road.

"Come on!" Biddle pounded the steel fender. "Get down!" He did not wait to see if Mac followed.

Mac remained rooted on the hood, following the undignified scramble of the lanky American ambassador with the camera as the lone Messerschmidt circled and released a burst of machine-gun fire. Handcarts were destroyed. Six stragglers fell to the ground.

From the ditch Biddle shouted Mac's name as the trail of bullets stitched two straight lines toward him. Through the lens Mac saw baggage erupt. Clothes and belongings whirled into the air. The screams of men and women blended into the roar of the engine.

The aircraft skimmed the road only a few feet off the ground.

"Get down!" Biddle cried.

Mac clearly caught the face of the pilot and the pinwheel cross of the swastika through the blur of the propeller. The guns stopped, but there was no doubt that Mac was still a target. The pilot nosed up only slightly, aiming to sever Mac's head with the prop.

Mac vaulted face-first into the ditch, a bare instant before the craft roared past. Then it climbed and disappeared over the crest of a hill.

Cradled against his chest, the DeVry had knocked the wind out of Mac but was itself unharmed. Mac had twenty seconds of new footage in the camera. There were fresh bullet holes in the American flag and the right front fender of Ambassador Biddle's car.

Mac sat up slowly as people climbed to their feet. Women searched for children lost in the scramble. Children cried for their mothers.

Six refugees lay dead in the road, including the peasant woman and her two children in the wheelbarrow. They were carried out of the way. Mac took his place in the rear vehicle across from the pale and shaken French ambassador and Julia Smith, who wept quietly. Workers completed the removal of the horses from the highway. Gradually the convoy began to creep forward again as an old man beside the road raised his hands and wept, pleading with the Blessed Virgin to save his family and Poland.

Mac considered that the old man might make it to Rumania if he hurried, but he doubted even the Blessed Virgin could save Poland now.

"Where is England?" Julia sobbed. "Why do they not come?"

∽

Dearest Lori:

We reached a little village called Zielna, just beyond Kasimierz. This is such an insignificant place it seems no one has any reason to attack it.

Captain Orde and Herr Frankenmuth agreed that we'd seen no signs of war or raiding parties for miles this far south of Warsaw, so we could go ashore in daylight for food and news.

We pooled our zlotys and found we had enough to buy fuel for the boat and bread and dried fish and more potatoes and even a sack of excellent apples, so the news about the provisions is all good.

But the other news is not.

We heard that England and France declared war on Germany . . . finally.

Some of the boys cheered and said, "Now Hitler'll run back to Germany with his tail between his legs." Some said, "Now we can go back to Warsaw."

Captain Orde snapped at them and told them to shut up. He then sat quiet, brooding, while Lucy held his right hand in both of hers.

Later, Captain Orde said, "What was Chamberlain thinking? Why wait so long? And where is France? Where are the French?"

The villagers here say that a Nazi army has cut the Danzig corridor in the north and that another army is slashing across central Poland toward Warsaw. Then they speak confidently of the valiant Polish horse cavalry turning back the Nazis . . . the Nazis with their tanks and their artillery and their dive-bombers!

And Lori, I must tell you that other news closer to us is even worse.

Here at Zielna we met refugees fleeing north from Krakow. They say a Nazi army has invaded south Poland from Slovakia and is moving rapidly. If they reach the place where the San River joins the Vistula we could be trapped between their advance and their supply line.

There is nothing else for us to do but turn around and go back toward Warsaw after all.

Captain Orde says he's working on another plan.

Alfie says through the blackest night the Red Sea will open for us.

It's good I know you're already praying for us . . . we need it.

All my love always,

Jacob

∾ᏩᎧᏮ∾

"Julia." Mac McGrath spoke the name that was on Eva Weitzman's passport. "Julia?" he said again.

It was difficult for Eva to answer to the strange new name. Instead she studied the faces of children in the photograph. The girl, Rachel, who had given her the document, smiled serenely at her. Shame, born of surviving when others died, stung Eva.

"Julia." Mac placed his index finger gently on the edge of the photo.
She glanced up. "Me? Julia . . . yes."

"Yes, you. You've been staring at the picture for the last one hundred miles."

"I have." She was aware that Richard Lewinski was staring at her. His lips turned up in an amused grin. "One hundred miles. Is that all? Yes, I suppose I have."

Mac crossed his arms and settled in. "So. We have a few miles to go. We should get to know one another."

Lewinski snorted and opened a book of Russian poetry.

Mac glared at the strange man with the wild red hair. "Well, some of us might like to have a conversation with other passengers."

Lewinski seemed not to hear.

Eva tucked the photo back in her passport. "Mr. McGrath, I've been rude. I'm sorry."

Mac leaned closer to her. "Call me Mac. And I'll call you . . . Julia? Okay?"

"My family calls me Eva." She admitted this one fragment of truth.

"Eva then. Listen . . . Eva . . . I mean . . . are they family? In the picture, I mean. The girl looks so much like you. A sister?"

Eva nodded once. "Family. Yes."

"Where are they?"

"Warsaw. Still there."

"I'm sorry." His expression confirmed his pity. "You know? I am."

"Thank you."

"You want to talk about them? Your family. Would it help?"

"No. It won't help. Nothing will help."

For a long time he said nothing more.

Eva looked out the window as they sped past a broad field of tall sunflowers. "What sort of farmer would plant sunflowers?"

Mac followed her gaze. "You know sunflowers. They always follow the sun. Turn their faces to the light."

"I didn't know."

"Yes. Look. Four o'clock in the afternoon. The afternoon sun. Just there. Now look at the flowers. All facing west."

It was true. A fact Eva had never noticed before. "Looking west for England to come save Poland, yes?"

Mac smiled sadly. "Foolish. Foolish sunflowers, I'm afraid."

It was in that moment Eva decided she could like this rumpled young American. He was an anachronism. A knight fighting against the Nazis with a camera. A cowboy shooting at bandits from the window of

an American Embassy automobile tearing away from the disaster of Poland. Yes. She could like such a fellow easily.

"How long?" Eva asked.

"A matter of time." He was speaking of the fall of Poland. She was
asking another question.

"No. I mean, how long until we are away from here? Until we reach
England? your friend, John Murphy?"

"We'll be driving the long way around. Through countries we hardly
heard of. More like a couple weeks than days." He fumbled in the pocket
of his jacket and pulled out a deck of cards. "So, Julia. Or Eva. Mind if I
call you Eva? Care for a game of gin?"

"I don't know how to play."

"There's time. I'll teach you. Lots of time to learn."

8

An Opportunity Will Present Itself

The London *Times* was splashed with reports of Poland's collapse under the Nazi blitzkrieg. Kevin Miller, seated in the lobby of the Savoy Hotel, scanned the editorial pages as he waited for his quarry to emerge from the bank of lifts.

Playwright George Bernard Shaw had written a scathing opinion piece protesting the British government's closure of theatres and places of public entertainment. Kevin was certain that such inane English concerns in the face of Poland's desperate cries for assistance was proof that the Reich would soon prevail. No doubt every Nazi in Germany, from the Führer down to the lowliest member of the Hitler Youth, was rejoicing that the British bickered about canceled West End theatre performances even as the great concert halls of Warsaw burned.

Kevin checked his wristwatch against the clock above the reception desk. For four days running, Kevin had sat in the lobby to take note of the comings and goings of Elisa Murphy and Lori Kalner. The pattern had been the same each day. At 8:40 Elisa and Lori had emerged from the lift in the company of two London bobbies. Elisa, violin case in hand, caught the number four bus to the BBC. Lori caught the number six to Fleet Street, where she worked part time at the TENS office. Such predictable patterns of activity made the elimination of Lori Kalner and Elisa Murphy inevitable.

Perhaps a shove sending one or both under the wheels of an approaching bus. Or a plunge off the platform as a subway train pulled into a tube station.

Kevin was certain the opportunity would present itself. One day the bodyguard would look away at just the right moment. The success of Kevin's assignment simply required patience.

Savoy Hotel
London, England

Dearest Jacob,

Where are you now? The same sun shines down on you as shines on me. At night you must look up at the same stars I see. I sense you are alive. I believe it. And yet another day has passed, and still there is no word from you.

I am desperate.

The train stations are crowded now with children being evacuated to the country. Mother writes that every day the little villages of Wales sound more and more like suburbs of London. Cockney and London public school students all mingle together in churches to be chosen by local residents who will board them. For how long? Mother wonders.

Meanwhile Aunt Anna and Mother are doing very well with all our children. The babies are content. There is no electricity or indoor plumbing, so the boys count the farm cottage as highest adventure.

Elisa is working every day playing at the BBC. It helps her not to grieve so terribly for Katie and Charles and Louis. The conductor managed to find her an adequate violin. It is nothing like the Guarnerius that was stolen from Murphy in Warsaw, but Elisa could make any fiddle sound lovely.

As for me, I have decided to volunteer to work with the Home Guard for any duty they need. After a day of instruction in the use of gas masks, I helped train civilians in how to put the things on. All this took place at the Savoy Theatre, which is quite far underground and a lovely little theatre. George Bernard Shaw wrote a letter to the Times, deploring the fact that Gilbert and Sullivan operettas have now been replaced by the drama of gas-mask scenarios.

We have only the news of the BBC and the newspapers to tell us what is happening. Today they report that the Polish army is holding out very well against the Nazis. Murphy believes soon the government will come to see reason, and the picture houses will be opened again . . . at least to show newsreels and civil-defense training films.

*I feel very brave today. I am hopeful that the good news we read
about Poland will strengthen our resolve. Soon England must send
troops to help, and then perhaps it will all be over by Christmas.*

*I pray I will hear from you soon. Your safety is the only thing
that makes me tremble inside.*

I love you,

Lori

⌇

Two hundred Jewish girls under twelve years of age were at last selected
from the thousands of children in the Jewish Quarter of Warsaw to go to
the great cathedral.

The parting of children from mothers and fathers was accomplished
with grief that rivaled that of the exile from Jerusalem in AD 70, when
children were sold as slaves while their parents were massacred.

Rachel Lubetkin, a letter in her pocket, found her best friend, Mikka
Najinski, among the refugees. Even at the age of twelve, Mikka was a
poet and a singer. Thin, wiry, blond and green-eyed, she was the daughter of a dentist. The silver braces on her teeth added to the illusion that
she was anything but Jewish. Mikka could pass for a Gentile as long as
she did not speak Yiddish. Her tearful father had just finished warning
her that she must only speak Polish to the Poles and German to the Germans if they came. And she must never, *never* let any of them know who
she was.

Mikka had a pitiful little bundle of belongings at her feet. Her diary
poked out from the top. She clutched a worn-out, wool-stuffed brown
dog she had slept with for as long as Rachel had known her. Stroking her
cheek with the dog's long ear, Mikka wept and murmured pitifully that
the dog was the only one who would speak to her from now on.

Poor little Mikka.

Rachel went to her and embraced her in farewell.

"Who will sing to me at night?" Mikka asked. "Who will listen to my
poems and say they are wonderful if you aren't there? The goyim don't
know Yiddish!"

"Listen, Mikka, and remember." Rachel cupped Mikka's chin in her
hand and sang to her softly,

> "Ven, mentsh, bist yung,
> When you are young,
> Iz groys dayn shvung,
> Your spirit's strong. . . . "

Mikka sang along tentatively, her voice quavering with emotion:

"When your old age draws near
The past then reappears,
We question what occurred.
How little we observed—
Just yesterday my childish voice was heard."

Solemnly Rachel instructed her, "You must not forget. It is written that the ink of the scribe is as precious to the Lord as the blood of the martyrs. Mikka, you must live and write our story down."

"I won't forget, Rachel. I won't."

"No. I know you won't forget. Listen, Mikka, there is something important you must do for me, *nu*?"

"Anything."

Rachel pressed an envelope into Mikka's hand. "You must give this to Father Kopecky when you see him. Tell him it is from the rabbi's daughter. Tell him it is my prayer, the prayer of the rabbi's daughter. And ask him to offer my prayer to God on the altar of his sanctuary. Will you do that for me, Mikka?"

Mikka looked at the paper as though it might burn her. "If you say so." She held the thing to her heart.

"You must promise me, Mikka. In the hands of the priest. We have been such friends, you and I."

"Oh! Yes. Yes, Rachel, my friend. How can I go and leave you behind? Please come with us! You are the rabbi's only daughter. You must come!"

Rachel lifted her chin. "Mikka, you are only twelve. You are small. I am over thirteen. I have had my bat mitzvah. I am the rabbi's daughter, and so I must stay and help with all the little ones who cannot go, *nu*? I am a woman of Israel and so will stay and help."

"I will look for you, Rachel. I will! Next year in Jerusalem!"

"Next year . . . in Jerusalem!"

Mikka clung to Rachel, sobbed against her shoulder for a few last moments, and then it was time to leave.

9

The End of the Line

After days of almost uncontested gains, part of the German onslaught was in danger of grinding to a halt. The resistance of the Polish troops on the road to Lodz was unexpectedly fierce. Captain Horst von Bockman, leading the 3rd platoon of motorcycle reconnaissance, was sent forward to examine the situation and report. When he returned to the company headquarters, the panzer regiment leader, Colonel Forster, was impatiently pacing up and down inside the tent of the command post.

"The Poles are well placed behind the stone walls of their village. It is located on a hill that overlooks our approach," Horst informed the colonel. "We need tanks."

"We have outrun our tanks," Forster replied. "They will not come until tomorrow. We have traveled so far in such a short time that the tank treads have worn out by the roads and they must halt for repairs."

"With all due respect, sir," Horst resumed, "then we should withdraw. The Poles are using their temporary advantage to bring up artillery. We saw it being moved into place."

"Withdraw!" snorted Forster. "Unthinkable! The only field pieces the Poles can muster were surplus twenty years ago. We will continue the attack."

"Perhaps we should at least call for air support," offered Horst's company commander.

"Agreed," replied the colonel, and the three men started for the radio set up in the colonel's armored half-track. Without any warning, Horst found himself flung backward across the tent, which partially collapsed on top of him. Fighting clear of the folds of heavy canvas, Horst hugged the ground as a rain of Polish artillery shells burst around the site.

Crawling free of the tent, Horst came upon his company commander, dead. Next to him, propped against a tree trunk, was Colonel Forster. The man's left arm was shattered, and he was unconscious. Behind Horst was a thick line of trees and a tempting depression in the earth like a ready-made trench. Ahead, across an open space of some twenty yards, was the command vehicle and the radio equipment.

The ground continued to quake as incoming shells straddled the targeted camp, but Horst moved steadily toward the half-track. The radio operators had bailed out of the open-topped vehicle and were huddled underneath it. "You!" Horst shouted to a shuddering communications lieutenant. "Get up there and call in the Stukas!"

The man, wide-eyed with fear, shook his head. "Are you crazy?"

"Do it," ordered Horst, "before they pound us to pieces here!" He drew his Luger from its holster and waved it in the man's face. "Now!"

High-explosive rounds proceeded to drop, each one threatening to be the direct hit that would end the matter altogether. Horst forced the man at gunpoint to get out from under the half-track and climb up into it. Spent pieces of shrapnel clattered all around from another near miss, and the frightened lieutenant appeared ready to dive back underneath.

Horst was just behind the radioman when he felt a sharp pain. Protruding from the back of his leather glove was a steel splinter about two inches long. Horst waved his pistol, gesturing toward the dials of the radio set and the wheels and keys of an Enigma encoding machine. As the man reluctantly put on the headphones and sat down in front of his equipment, Horst laid aside the Luger and yanked the jagged blade of shrapnel out of his hand.

"Get on with it," he ordered through gritted teeth. "Here are the coordinates."

Moments later, both Horst and the radio operator were back under the half-track. Five minutes of further explosions passed, some so near as to make the two tons of armored Kommando-Panzerwagen bounce off the ground. Finally, unseen by the figures huddled under the vehicle, a trio of tiny black dots appeared high overhead. Diving earthward, the banshee scream of their sirens penetrating even the blasts of exploding shells, the Stukas swept toward their objective.

Following the release of their five-hundred-pound bombs, the dive-bombers veered back toward their base. From a distance, the deep-pitched *crumps* did not sound like much in comparison to the artillery rounds, but their efficacy was total. Two of the Polish guns were knocked out, completely destroyed. The crew of the remaining cannon abandoned their position and fled.

Dearest Lori:

I didn't write yesterday . . . or has it been two days? Can't write much now either . . . too tired. No sleep for close to 40 hours.

We came north much faster with the current. Crystal clear fall morning in the south and then saw the cloud of smoke hanging over Warsaw, lit from underneath by all the fires. It looked like the mouth of hell.

Once inside the city the riverbanks were so packed with fumes we could hardly breathe, much less see. So many shattered bridges and sunken ships that it took forever to go two miles. Rails and girders from bombed rail lines stuck up here and there out of the river like reeds in a pond. Had to pole our way around them.

Swollen dead bodies float everywhere, like abandoned, overstuffed scarecrows. Smoke that burns our eyes and makes everyone cough also keeps us from smelling anything else.

We're crammed on board like sardines, but nobody complains now. If the boat was any bigger, we'd never make it through.

The bombing raids continue. The Nazis drop death blindly into the smoke, not caring what they hit.

Shouted news from people on the banks is that Radom—twenty miles south of here—is already surrounded by Nazis. We might be the last boat to make it this far.

They also say General Guderian's XIX Panzerkorps has nearly cut Poland in two. Someone said the Polish government fled the city yesterday. Maybe just a rumor. Where could they go?

We're all stunned. No word yet from Captain Orde about his new plan.

Not even the most optimistic of the Zionist boys wants to stay in Warsaw now, and Herr Frankenmuth is frantic to get home and check on his family.

We're going. Not sure what we'll find north of the city.

I'll write when I can.

All my love always,

Jacob

Kevin Miller nursed his second pint of Guinness and surveyed the bus stop outside the Coal Hole pub. Situated in the corner of the Savoy

Hotel building, the Coal Hole had become Kevin's local hangout. Perched at a high table near the window, Kevin occupied the ideal place to observe Lori and Elisa and their bodyguards as they caught the bus. With a pint of beer in his hand, the newspaper open before him, and a cigarette in the ashtray, no one suspected he was working.

It was 5:27. The number six bus that usually carried Lori Kalner back from work to the Savoy Hotel pulled away from the curb. Lori had not disembarked. Kevin scanned the flocks of pedestrians moving past the window. There was no sign of her. Earlier Elisa Murphy's bus had come and gone, and she also had failed to disembark.

Had the women changed their daily routine?

Kevin stared sullenly at the back of the departing number six.

Suppose they had been warned to vary their routine? Had they gotten off the bus a block earlier? ridden two blocks farther?

Kevin sighed and took a sip of beer. He would hate to give up this place and return to following them everywhere. The window of the Coal Hole was the ideal reconnaissance point. Comfortable. Warm. And as long as he still had an inch of beer in the bottom of his glass, no one would ask him to leave.

Someday, Kevin knew, either Elisa or Lori would arrive at the bus stop unaccompanied by the watchdogs, and then Kevin would give them a ride all the way to the end of the line.

But not today.

Where were they?

The proprietor wiped down his table and emptied the ashtray. "Kevin? Another Guinness? It's 'alf five. We'll be closin' at six on account of the curfew. You've just got time for one more."

"The curfew," Kevin muttered in disdain. "Blackout! As if the Germans will ever bomb London, eh? Keep us working stiffs from enjoying our pint or two in the evening."

There was a hint of amusement in the barkeep's eye. Perhaps it occurred to him that he had never seen Kevin work. "Too right. Bad for business. Me missus took the kiddies down to her mother in Kent. When the Jerries have done with Poland it'll all get back to normal, make no mistake. It's a Guinness, right? And a jacket potato?" The barkeep grinned a gap-toothed smile.

"You know me well."

"Think we should put a brass plaque on this table for you. *Reserved for Kevin*. Three pints of Guinness and a jacket potato. You've got a routine, you see."

"Well, then—" Kevin cleared his throat—"tonight I'll have a bowl of soup and a Black and Tan."

"Do you mean it? Changin' the pattern, are you? You'll ruin my day, Kevin. Yes, you will."

"I know what you mean."

∽

Primrose Hill
London, England

Dearest Jacob,

Today we moved into our lovely white terrace house on Prince Albert Road. We are almost directly across from Regent's Park and the Zoological Gardens on one side and Primrose Hill Park on the other. The authorities at the zoo are also evacuating some of the animals. I heard lions roaring as we moved our few meager boxes of belongings into the house. I daresay that I am not sorry they are taking the lions away to the zoo in Edinburgh if they make such a racket! Every day more and more houses and flats are vacated as people evacuate for the country and men join the army. I read that one in eight houses in London is now empty.

When the danger of bombing is past, Elisa and Murphy say we will bring our mothers and the children home from Wales to this nicely furnished house that costs us only one pound ten shillings a week. Over three floors there are five bedrooms, two baths, a kitchen, and a dining room, as well as a library with shelves and shelves of books all written in English that will help me learn the language better. There are also two reception rooms furnished in very dark old Victorian furniture, but Elisa says if we strip off the terrible flocked wallpaper and paint everything in creams and pale blues, it will brighten the place up. Perhaps we can reupholster the chairs and the sofa with a light fabric as well. In the ground-floor reception room is a very old and out-of-tune grand piano. Elisa says she knows a fellow who will tune it very inexpensively. I will not play it until he comes, however, for fear of making the wolves at the zoo howl.

At the recommendation of Mr. Churchill, Murphy has replaced the London policemen and hired a retired Scotland Yard detective to watch over us. His name is Inspector Stone. He is a widower in his sixties who is as silent as his name implies. We are only aware of his presence because of the unending aroma of pipe smoke. He brought his clothes and a radio when he moved in. He will sleep in the bedroom off the kitchen.

When I step out onto the sidewalk, I can see the spire of a

church five minutes from here. Elisa says that many members of the
BBC orchestra attend services there and that it has a wonderful
pipe organ in the loft. I think we will go there this Sunday morning.

The bus stop is across the street, and it is only about a 30-minute
walk for Elisa across Regent's Park to the BBC headquarters,
where she performs with the orchestra. Very lovely old plane trees
and now, of course, the antiaircraft batteries in place give one a sense
of protection.

Out the back door there is a private terraced garden that we
shall soon plant thick with vegetables. There is a wonderful big tree
in the center that will give us shade in the summer months. The
leaves are starting to turn.

I do wish you were here, Jacob! I pray every day for your
health and safety. And I beg God that you will soon come to
England to me!

Your loving wife,

Lori

೨೦

My dearest, dearest Lori:

I'm so glad you're safe in England! Oh, Lori, you can't believe the
horrors here!

Herr Frankenmuth's wife and daughter-in-law (Hans' wife)
and Hans' baby girl are all dead . . . killed by a direct hit on their
house. They died on the first day of the war, before we ever went
south.

Herr Frankenmuth just sits and stares, saying nothing. Alfie
sits next to him, patting his shoulder.

Hans ran up and down the streets, begging to be given a rifle to
kill Germans with, then disappeared.

We're in Wyszkow, trying to sort out what to do next.

The villagers who fled into the woods to escape the bombing are
returning. In fact, people from outlying villages are here, too,
pushing carts, carrying babies, dragging the sick and wounded on
cots. They are all heading into Warsaw. Despite what we tell them
they'll find there, they say the Polish army will never let Warsaw be
captured and that they'll be safer there than out here alone.

Some who came from the farthest west have already met Nazi
soldiers who laughed and spit on them but let them pass.

We only have a small radio. Only German stations are still on the

air, and they claim to have captured 60,000 Polish troops and that
IV Panzer is already in the suburbs of Warsaw.

I feel sick... my heart hurts, you know?

God keep you safe.

All my love always,

Jacob

P.S. Just heard... Captain Orde says we're going east, up the River
Bug as far as we can get, even to the Soviet border. He says the
Russians have declared their neutrality and that our British
passports will protect us. What will happen to Lucy and the Zionist
Pioneer boys, who have no passports, no one talks about. I trust
Captain Orde... and Alfie says, "Trust God."

10

A Solemn Promise

The American convoy pressed on over rutted highways lined with endless miles of refugees traveling through ruined villages.

Often Mac McGrath wound the key of the cinecamera, leaned out the window, and recorded small beginnings of what would surely grow to be great misery.

He held Eva's hand, gazed earnestly into her face, and made her a solemn promise, like a man who might be falling in love: "The film will be played in American movie theatres so people see for themselves what's happening."

Richard Lewinski, the strange, red-haired Jew who shared the automobile with them, replied to Mac's pledge in French. "*Il faut en finir . . . This time we must put an end to it.*" Lewinski had uttered no words but those since they had fled from Warsaw. Nor did he speak again until, at last, the convoy entered France.

Poland was doomed. The armies of Great Britain were still on English soil. France had only begun to mobilize.

A French army staff car met the convoy at the checkpoint. Bits and snatches of conversation informed Eva that they had come personally to collect Richard Lewinski and that he was the most important treasure to escape from Poland.

Mac trotted off to film the French poilus checking the papers of the American ambassador.

Lewinski gathered his gas mask and scanty belongings from the backseat of the car. Eva remained in the vehicle, praying no one would question the validity of her British passport.

Almost as an afterthought, Lewinski paused, kissed Eva's hand, and whispered in Polish, "Dear young lady, it is plain to anyone with ears that you are not who you say you are. I can tell by your accent you are entirely someone else. I recognize you." He held up a long bony finger to silence her objection. "Your secret is safe with me. Now, one more thing . . . it is also clear the American buffoon has fallen in love with you. He is like a boy who balances on fences and stands on his head to impress a girl. When you sleep he stares at you with painful longing. And why not? You are very beautiful. An unforgettable face, I would say. A face I would not forget."

She blushed and thanked him.

Lewinski shrugged. "It is true. And when you are awake and he is asleep, you stare at him the same way. When you are both awake you try not to look at each other at all. Love. It is evident. So, will you accept some insight from a fellow who is your countryman?"

"You are from . . ."

"I spent my boyhood summers in Czechoslovakia with my grandparents in your village. Your father is Franz Weitzman, is he not?"

"Yes. Yes! But how long have you—"

"And you are Eva."

"Yes."

"I remember you from Brendizi's."

"The ice-cream shop."

"Indeed. I was afraid if I spoke to you at all I could . . . possibly compromise your safety. But here we are. Safe. And since your father is not here to speak to you, I will say to you what he would say, Eva. You have heard that Americans are all overdressed, noisy, irritating tourists with no knowledge of geography, who have cameras dangling from their necks. This American Mac McGrath with his camera bears out part of the equation. However, he has a heart. I heard him say he would like to accompany you to London. To deliver you safely to your employer there. Yes? Very good. I would say this McGrath is a very good fellow. A goodhearted fellow, though none too bright if he believes you are in any way English. However, you could do worse. Go with him to London. Perhaps you will survive. Perhaps you will have a happy life. I do hope so. Farewell."

He kissed her hand again and then hurried away to the waiting French staff car.

◯◯

Kevin Miller craned his neck to see around a beefy English businessman whose florid face obstructed the bus stop outside the Coal Hole. Two days had elapsed since Kevin had last spotted his quarry, but he had not been overwhelmed by anxiety until now.

Cold jacket potato sat in a congealing pool of butter.

Warm Guinness was flat and sour in his mouth.

What if Elisa and Lori had escaped his surveillance and moved elsewhere? Worse yet, what if they had been evacuated from London to some remote part of Wales?

Jostling the table in his urgency for answers, Kevin spattered his coat with grease in his haste to leave the table and return to the Savoy's lobby. He barged in ahead of a wealthy couple arriving by chauffeur-driven limousine, then banged his fist in frustration on the revolving door when he got halfway around, only to find further motion blocked by someone exiting too slowly to suit him.

Beyond an oval of dark red, thick woolen carpet that framed barrel-backed, overstuffed chairs and mahogany bookshelves was the reception desk. When a horse-faced clerk frowned disapproval at Kevin's lack of decorum, Kevin forced himself to slow his pace and compose his thoughts.

"I have an urgent message for Elisa Murphy. Is she still stopping here?" Holding his breath, Kevin waited for the clerk's reply.

"She is not," the attendant replied haughtily. "The party has checked out."

Kevin's heart sank. "Left a forwarding address? The matter is urgent, as I say."

The hotel employee consulted a box of file cards. "Messages may be delivered to Mr. John Murphy, in care of Trump European News Services."

Kevin waited.

"That's all the information I have, sir." The clerk sniffed. "Will there be anything else?"

Kevin shook his head and headed for the exit. He had to think, had to have a plan before he said anything about this to Erich.

What to do next?

～

The din of children's voices in the basement of the Cathedral of St. John was deafening. Rows of long tables crowded under the low stone vaults were packed with hungry young refugees guzzling soup and tearing off chunks of dense black bread.

It was forbidden to speak about who, if any among them, was a Jew.

The Sisters of Mercy had given a three-day course teaching these two hundred Jewish refugees from Muranow Square how to properly make the sign of the cross before prayers were said, when to kneel, and how to genuflect when Mass was being read. After this careful instruction, meant to save their lives and protect their protectors, the girls were admitted to the congregation of Gentile children. One by one they had been assigned a younger Gentile child to care for. This duty kept them busy and prevented any unnecessary questions from being asked about Polish accents heavily tinged with Yiddish.

Mikka Najinski had been placed in charge of a very bright four-year-old boy who had lost both parents when their home had been flattened by a bomb. He had bright blue eyes and hair so red it might be called orange. His name was Rex. He spoke only Polish, and that with a lisp. This gave Mikka great opportunity to practice the language. Rex did not notice her Yiddish accent. He loved stories and playing with toy automobiles that Mikka made out of blocks of wood. At night he slept with Mikka's stuffed toy dog beneath his arm. She called him "my cherub" and was comforted in the thought that he was much worse off than she could ever be.

A week had passed. The end of Warsaw was near, and yet Mikka had not written in her journal. Tonight, as Rex slept deeply on his pallet, Mikka remembered her diary and took it out. Tucked in the pages was the letter Rachel Lubetkin had given her to take to the priest.

So! A whole week and Mikka had failed in the last promise she had made to her best friend in the world! Truth to tell, Mikka had hardly given Rachel a thought.

This night the German guns boomed louder, Mikka thought. The Polish artillery was becoming less and less frequent until finally there was none at all.

Across the stone floor lay a sea of sleeping children. Near the arch of the entrance, the little priest stood locked in serious conversation with Sister Angeline and the American newswoman, Josephine Marlow, who had been stuck in Warsaw since the Nazi invasion. Were they discussing what must be done with so many mouths to feed and the Nazi lion crouching at the gates of the city?

Mikka fingered Rachel's letter for a moment, then began to pick her path over the prone bodies of her comrades.

Sister Angeline, sweet-faced beneath the garb of her order, glanced at Mikka's approach.

Father Kopecky, haggard, the stubble of a beard growing thicker by the day, blinked thoughtfully at the girl and finished what he was saying. "At all costs! It is not only a danger to a few; it is a danger to the many. The countryside if we can. Then over the border."

Mikka stood patiently at a distance while they discussed what to do with so many, many children.

Then Sister Angeline summoned Mikka with a crook of one finger. "Mikka?"

Mikka did not know if she must make the Christian sign of the cross when approaching the priest. She did so, just to be safe.

Rachel's envelope extended before her like a sword, Mikka took three large steps forward, averting her gaze from the large wood crucifix that hung around the priest's neck.

"What is it, child?" Father Kopecky took Rachel's letter. "What?"

"Sir, it is a letter from my best friend. From the daughter of the rabbi of Muranow. She begged me to give this to you. Begged that you see this, sir. That you read her prayer and offer this prayer on the altar of this church. For the Jews of Muranow."

He did not chide her though she had said the word *Jew.* He held the white paper carefully and studied the intricate flourish of Rachel's handwriting with interest.

Mikka knew what it said:

> *To the priest of the Cathedral of St. John*
> *A prayer for my people . . .*

"Thank you, child. What is your name?"

Mikka looked nervously at Sister Angeline for permission to speak her Jewish name. Sister nodded.

"At my home I am Mikka Najinski. Here my name has become Gruen. 'Green.' "

"Your father?" the priest inquired. "Is he the dentist? Dr. Najinski?"

"Yes, sir."

"Then you are his darling Mikka. The poet. He spoke of you to me when I was last in to see him."

At these words, meant kindly, meant to comfort her, Mikka began to sob uncontrollably.

Sister Angeline rushed to embrace her. "Mikka! What is it? You've been so brave. A tower!"

Through her tears Mikka explained, "I forgot to give him the letter. Oh! I should have given him the letter! I promised Rachel I would give it to him, and I forgot!" Mikka's heart felt as though it would break within her. Papa had spoken about her to this priest. He had talked about her gently as he pulled a tooth or fitted a partial plate.

"Oh, Papa. My papa. Papa told him I was a poet, but I haven't written anything new at all. How will I remember it all? How?"

"You will remember enough, child." Sister stroked her hair and let her weep. "Yes. There will be enough to remember."

～

Dearest Lori:

We're tied up to the bank of the Bug River, somewhere east of Wyszkow. It's about one hour till day, but we're all too tired to go farther, so we cut tree branches to hang all over us and will sleep here for now.

Herr Frankenmuth gave us the fishing boat and stayed behind. He said he had no heart to try to escape, that he should have died with his wife.

Hans never came back.

Captain Orde can operate the machinery. Some of the other Pioneers and I take turns steering. It's not like we can get lost or anything, but in the dark we spend a lot of time straining our eyes and jerking the wheel away from imaginary obstacles. About once an hour, all night long, we run on a very real sandbar. Since we're going so slowly we can usually back off them, but sometimes we stick there until a bunch of us climb out and wade alongside to make the boat lighter.

Captain Orde says in one more night we'll be out of fuel anyway.

For the last ten minutes as I write this I've been watching something drifting down toward us. It looks like a very small boat with one or two people in it . . . a rowboat, maybe?

It's not a boat. Just a bit of planking with a dead . . .

Lucy says she prays for you every morning and night.

All my love always,

Jacob

～

"Of course this is Richard Lewinski. He may well be the most important person to have escaped from Poland. He is certainly the most important man in Paris! Including you, Bertrand." Colonel Andre Chardon viewed the peculiar, red-haired figure of Lewinski through the two-way mirror in the Paris headquarters of French Military Intelligence at 2 bis Avenue de Tourville in the seventh arrondisement of Paris.

Colonel Gustave Bertrand scratched his head in amazement at Chardon's words. "I did not say otherwise, Andre. I only asked if this odd duck was indeed our Richard Lewinski. *The* Richard Lewinski."

Andre nodded. "Indeed."

"It is difficult to imagine, Andre, that the fate of France, as you put it so clearly, could rest in the hands of one so . . . unusual."

The two men silently considered the wild red hair, the blank stare on the pale, thin face, the flannel shirt that was buttoned crookedly, the untied shoelaces, and the gas mask clutched in the right hand.

"He is in deep thought," Andre remarked.

"I would have said he was catatonic. Or worse. One of the living dead perhaps. When we bring him his food, he eyes it as if it is poisoned, nibbles a bit, and then consumes it with the enthusiasm of a hog at the trough. But the rest of the time he is as you see him before you now—a great lethargic zero. He has said nothing to anyone since he crossed the Polish border and left the care of the American ambassador Biddle in Bucharest. He wept silent tears behind his gas mask when I brought him here to Paris. He has scribbled this note." Bertrand handed Andre a slip of paper.

Andre read the childish scrawl aloud:

> "Attention!
> Nazi pigs, you have not deceived me!
> I will converse with no man but Colonel Andre Chardon."

Andre laughed at the sentiment.

"Flattering, Andre?"

"A brave soldier, our Richard. Here is proof of the cause he believes in."

"Your old friend believes with all his heart that we are Nazi agents, instruments of Reinhard Heydrich in the employ of the German Secret Police. And so . . . there you have it." Bertrand shrugged. "I think he is quite insane, Andre. But I leave it to you."

"It is understandable that he should be suspicious, Gustave—that he should be cautious. First he lost his parents in Germany. Then his wife and child were killed in Poland by a German bomb. He is fighting the only way he knows how to fight: by refusing to acknowledge anyone at all. Suppose he was right about you and yet proceeded in his work?"

"If Richard Lewinski was correct in this hypothesis, he would be dead."

"True."

"So—" Bertrand spread his hands in a gesture of helplessness—"the fate of military intelligence may be in the hands of a lunatic, and the fate of the lunatic must be entirely in your hands. Shall I cover him in gift wrap before you take him home, Monsieur? Or is he colorful enough?"

11

A New Identity

The prow of the ferry cut through the placid waters of the English Channel.

"She's crossing the Channel like a hot knife through butter." Mac tapped his pipe against the rail, dislodging charred tobacco.

Eva stared down at the dark waters. "This is my first time on the sea."

A gleam in his eye, Mac corrected her. "What? Never been to England? And you with a shiny new British passport? Shiny new name . . . Julia. Better not let the British customs officials hear you talk like that."

"Oh. Yes. I mean, no! I mean . . . I . . . wasn't thinking."

"I'll say. They'll bundle you right off to jail as an alien threat to national security."

"Mac? When did you know I wasn't . . . what I said I was?"

"That you weren't English? Easy. From the first time you opened your mouth. No—" he smirked— "before that. The instant I saw you walk across the foyer of the British Embassy. I said to myself, 'Mac, old buddy, she's no English girl. Too pretty.'"

Eva frowned and looked away. "How very unkind."

He raised an eyebrow. "I meant it as a compliment."

"Unkind to the English women."

"Stout, sturdy types, most of them. Legs like balustrades. The rest of 'em angular. All jaws and elbows."

Her blue eyes flashed annoyance. "You shouldn't say such things."

Packing his pipe, he grinned. "Why not? It's true."

"You shouldn't say such things about good English women and because . . . because you have called me by another woman's name."

Mac looked puzzled. "Yes? Julia? Isn't that what your passport says?"

"No. Not that. I mean, you've called me Josie. On the quay before we boarded the ship. Several times on the journey. In the car. Yes. Josie, you said . . . "

"Did I now?" Mac's fingers scratched his stubbled cheek.

"You know you did. Josie. Who . . . is she? This Josie whose name crowds out all other names from your thoughts?"

"I've been worried about her. She can take care of herself, but I haven't heard she got out of Warsaw. She's a reporter. She's not English either. She's American. A widow. The widow of an old friend of mine. And when he died—was killed in a bombing raid in Spain—well, I set myself to help Josie get through it."

"And you . . . you fell in love with her in the bargain?"

Mac inhaled deeply. "I . . . I've thought that might be the case. Yes. I did think I might marry her if she'd have me. And then . . ." His eyes searched Eva's face for some sign of encouragement.

She put a hand to her cheek as she warmed beneath his gaze. "Don't, please. I am not used to having a man look at me like that."

"Like what, Eva?"

"You know."

His lips turned up in a weak smile. "I do. I mean . . . very confusing." He took her hand. "You've shaken my resolve. See?"

She pulled away. "Don't. We're from different worlds, you and I."

"Right. You're nothing but a kid. Don't know what got into me. Sorry."

"You are a brute to look at me like that. To smile at me as if . . . as if . . . and all the while you are in love with another woman."

"So it would seem. You're right. Sorry. I just . . . must be all this fresh air. The White Cliffs of Dover looming ahead. Yes. Didn't mean to imply . . . anything between you and me."

"Good."

"I won't say any more about it if you don't. Ever. Deal?"

"Yes. Of course. Deal."

Mac stuck out his hand, and they shook on the bargain. They would not allow themselves to even mention the possibility of love. Not ever again.

"So. There. Those are the famous White Cliffs of Dover?" she asked.

"Right. We'll catch a train from there to London. Murphy will meet us. Elisa, too, if she can. You two will get along nicely, I think. But remember, don't mention to anyone that you're glad to be in England for the first time ever. I'd hate to see you spend the war in jail for forging documents."

The Fleet Street coffeehouse where Kevin Miller kept up his surveillance of Trump European News was crowded with journalists of competing wire services and rival newspaper chains. To see the way ears pricked up when nearby conversations dropped to whispered levels put Miller in mind of the exotic locales portrayed in spy films: Casablanca, Algiers, Lisbon, Hong Kong. . . .

Except that the Sunnyside Bun Shoppe was decorated with overly cheerful yellow curtains inside its blackout shades, and in place of slinky femme fatales, the waitresses were all bustling, middle-aged types, wearing starched white pinafore aprons.

"'Ave another sticky bun, dearie?" Kevin's waitress inquired.

The thought made him nauseous. A dozen cups of coffee and five cloyingly sweet pastries combined into a roiling stomach weight well over Kevin's limit. He calculated he would be allowed at least one delay without reordering. "Waiting for someone," he mumbled.

The waitress frowned, obviously eager to clear his place and fill the space with more than a single customer. She slashed her pencil across her pad, ripped off the top sheet, then dropped the plate containing his bill onto the table with a clatter. She moved off without saying anything.

Abruptly the waiting came to an end.

From the glass-and-bronze front door of the TENS office, John and Elisa Murphy emerged, and right behind them, Lori Kalner.

Kevin's heart beat faster. Now to follow them to their new home.

He fumbled in his pocket, dropping a handful of coins into the plate with his tab. He glanced out the front window up Fleet Street, scanning for the black cab he might need to maintain the contact. Would they travel by cab? private car? walk to the tube station?

When his gaze eastward produced no results, Kevin turned his eyes west and found himself staring at a purposeful John Murphy striding across the street directly toward him. There was no time to flee, no time to plan. Kevin shrank back in the corner as Murphy entered the shop.

The reporter's eyes scanned the room, passing Kevin's face without stopping. Murphy greeted a trio of other newsmen, then remarked to the counter attendant, "A half-dozen lemon tarts for takeaway, please, Gertie."

Kevin took another bitter swallow of coffee and pretended to fumble with the coins on the plate as if uncertain how much to tip. He looked awkward, amateurish, and he knew it, but he had learned something interesting: Beneath the left arm of Murphy's suit coat was an angular bulge that could only be the butt of a revolver.

Kevin's own fingers twitched toward the pistol he carried in the pocket of his raincoat, but he refrained from touching it, managing to regain that measure of control.

In the end, following the Murphys home was not difficult at all.

Miller did not even have to instruct someone to "Follow that cab." Instead he and his quarry rode the same double-decker bus, with Murphy, Elisa, and Lori Kalner seated comfortably inside while Kevin boarded at the last moment and sat at the back. When he saw them stand up just before the stop for Regent's Park Zoo, Kevin inwardly exulted that he had succeeded.

John Murphy helped Elisa and Lori down from the bus at the corner of Prince Albert Road and Albert Terrace. They crossed Prince Albert toward a crescent of Georgian houses that climbed the east side of Primrose Hill. Beyond the row of homes loomed a church spire and the autumn-tinged leaves of a massive plane tree.

An altogether pleasant and safe neighborhood.

Kevin exited the double-decker after them and remained at the bus stop as if awaiting a transfer to another line. From the zoo the piping of birds in the aviary, monkey chattering, and the woeful howls of something unknown pursued the trio toward the redbrick home on the corner.

Murphy already had a key in his hand.

Their own place then, and not a visit to a sick friend.

Kevin struck a match with his thumbnail and lit a cigarette while he watched them ascend the flight of steps to the entry. When they entered the building, he smiled broadly.

The setup would be much the same as at the Savoy: wait for a target to join a crowded queue at the bus stop, step up behind her, a quick shove, and . . .

The only problem was that this area was much less populated than the Strand, and there were no nearby businesses into which Kevin could quickly disappear.

No matter. The operation was back on track.

⟨��⟩

The iron girders that formed the arch of London's Waterloo Station were lost in the smoke of trains arriving from the seacoast. Anxious family groups hung about in knots, awaiting the arrival of friends and family who, by the thousands, streamed home to England after narrowly escaping the Nazi slaughter.

Every citizen in England knew someone working on the Continent who had been forced to flee the instant Poland was attacked.

Murphy waited on the platform as the Southeast Line train from Dover rattled beneath the great dome of the station. He reread Mac's telegram:

MURPHY STOP ARRIVING WITH JULIA SMITH FROM WARSAW TENS OFFICE STOP 1 PM WATERLOO SEP 16 ON DOVER TRAIN STOP BRING ELISA STOP MAC MCGRATH

But Murphy had not brought Elisa. From the sound of Mac's telegram, only he and the girl were arriving in London, not Jacob Kalner and Alfie Halder. Until Murphy knew if the two young men were alive or dead, he decided not to involve Elisa or Lori.

But this was good news, wasn't it? The falsified British passport, along with a TENS press identity card made out to Julia Smith, and fifty pounds emergency cash tucked into the document had at least reached Rachel Lubetkin.

But what about Jacob Kalner? And Alfie Halder?

Mac's wire was excruciatingly short on useful information.

Murphy studied the rumpled slip of paper. As the days and hours passed there was less and less hope that the two young men had survived. If Jacob Kalner was still alive, if he had escaped from Warsaw, would he not have let Lori know?

Mac's request for Elisa to be present on the platform was ominous. What shape was the refugee girl in? Leaving her family behind? her life? Yes, Murphy thought, Elisa would know best how to handle the trauma of separation. He would phone her from the office and let her know once Julia Smith was safely in London.

Rachel Lubetkin was only thirteen years old, though her British passport had been created from the identity of an English child named Julia Smith, who had been born and died at the age of three months twenty long years ago. The birth certificate of the dead infant, taken from the Hall of Records in Essex, had provided the basis for Rachel's new identity.

The Zionist Underground had obtained several hundred British passports for Jewish children trapped behind the borders of the Reich through this device. Many had traveled on to the British Mandate of Palestine. Taken into kibbutzim, they were creating a new life for themselves and laying the foundation for the new nation of Israel. The birth certificates of dead English children added another layer of meaning to the word *resurrection*, Murphy thought. Yet for Murphy and Elisa, there remained a great sadness. However many Jewish children they and the Underground had managed to save, millions more were left behind within the stranglehold of Nazi anti-Semitism.

In Warsaw over three hundred identification photos of Jewish children had been delivered to the Underground immigration committee in London for processing.

Too little. Too late.

In the end Murphy had only managed to deliver three out of the three hundred as shells fell on Warsaw.

Over the bobbing heads of disembarking passengers, Murphy spotted Mac as he stepped from the train. In the only gentlemanly behavior Murphy had ever witnessed from Mac, he then turned to assist a young woman descending onto the platform.

She was older than Murphy expected. Rachel Lubetkin was supposed to be thirteen. But this was no adolescent. Wearing a broad-brimmed, white straw hat with a blue ribbon around the brim, her features were lost beneath the shadow. She had the figure of a full-grown woman. It was plain enough to Murphy even at a distance that she was extremely fragile. Her short-sleeved, blue-checked cotton dress hung loosely on her. She grasped Mac's arm to steady herself. Clearly the ordeal of her exile had taken its toll on her health.

Murphy was relieved he had not brought Lori.

Mac and the young woman were alone.

No Jacob.

No Alfie.

Mac—rumpled, hair askew as if he had slept on his head—waved broadly as he saw Murphy. Towering over his charge, the broad-shouldered newsman stooped and looked directly into her face as though trying to make her understand something. The straw hat bobbed in acknowledgment. Mac's face split in a broad grin. He cupped hands around his mouth and shouted joyfully, "Hey, Murphy. Murphy! We made it!"

12

The Straight Story

Six reporters were crammed into the cluttered London headquarters of Trump European News Service. Murphy led Mac and Eva through the maze of desks and filing cabinets to his office. The room was an eight-by-eight cubicle enclosed by a half wall topped by windows. Murphy's name was stenciled in silver on the door:

John Murphy
Editor in Chief

Most of his office was taken up by a graffiti-scarred oak table that served as Murphy's desk. The table and four ancient Windsor chairs had been salvaged from a three-hundred-year-old pub demolished in St. Albans, just north of London.

Mac glanced around approvingly. "You've come up in the world."

"Ain't much, but it's home." Murphy removed a stack of books from a chair and offered Mac and Eva seats. Poking his head out the door, he asked his secretary to brew tea and scrounge up a few cookies or something.

"Where's Elisa?" Mac stretched his long legs as far as he could.

"Setting up house. We rented a place in Primrose Hill. Vacated by an American cloth merchant. A Georgian across from Primrose Park and the zoo."

"Nice digs."

"Cheap enough. The guy was in a real hurry to get back to America when war broke out. Elisa can walk across Regent's Park to the BBC. The orchestra, you know. The government has shut down all the theatres and music halls. The *Times* editorials are more about that than the fact that Britain hasn't sent one plane against the Nazis. Anyway, there's nothing left but the BBC orchestra. Elisa's working every day but Saturday."

"I told Eva about her. Hoped she could be here to meet her."

"I didn't tell her or her niece, Lori, that you were coming in. Sorry, Mac. Not yet. I've got to have the straight story before I tell her anything. See, I left three British passports in Warsaw. So far this one is the only pigeon that's come home to roost. Two young men were supposed to be with you, Eva. One is Jacob Kalner. He's married to Lori. The other is Alfie Halder. The Nazis consider him too useless to live. And the rabbi's daughter, Rachel Lubetkin, was to be the third. Not even Rachel made it. I couldn't tell Elisa you were coming until I got the whole story."

Eva placed the passport on Murphy's desk and poured out everything she knew about Rachel Lubetkin. She translated and read aloud the letter Etta Lubetkin had written to her father in Jerusalem. Showing them the photo of the Lubetkin children, Eva recounted how Rachel had appeared out of nowhere and insisted that Eva take the passport.

Hot tea and scones with apricot preserves remained uneaten on the tray as Eva continued the tale. "But there was no one with her. Not Jacob Kalner. No one else. She was alone as far as I could see. It all happened so quickly. She told me only that she could not leave her parents or her brothers. And that she was glad I am also a Jew. She told me we could be sisters. But there were no companions with her."

Murphy steepled his fingers. "At least we can be sure the passport made it to Rachel. And yet she gave it away."

Eva's sad gaze remained fixed on the photograph. "I have thought about it so much. Every day. About how she didn't want to leave her family. I . . . thought about myself . . . I mean, my own family. Czechoslovakia. I would not have left them if I had known what was coming. But I did not know. And so when Czechoslovakia fell, I stayed in Warsaw. Rachel's brothers. Look at them. The baby. This letter Etta Lubetkin wrote to her father in Jerusalem. So full of hope. I think love kept Rachel from going. And a different kind of love made her give me this. Please, you are Americans. Your American president Roosevelt must try to do something for the children. To get them out of Warsaw. To their grandfather in Jerusalem. Surely when England and France come to their aid . . ."

Murphy and Mac exchanged knowing glances. Whatever could be done now to intervene would likely be too little and too late. News from the German front lines was bleak. Only Warsaw held out, and it was being pounded into submission.

Mac did not look at her when he replied, "Eva, England isn't going to send soldiers to Poland."

"But how can that be? England declared war! Can they let Poland be defeated?"

Mac replied, "A declaration of war is only words at the moment. Hitler knew the British government could not lift a finger to fulfill its promise to Poland in time to save Poland. If Hitler had seen even a glimmer of strength in Prime Minister Chamberlain, he wouldn't have attacked."

Eva's face had the look of someone who has just heard that a family member has been beaten and left to die in the street. "So that is the way it is? No hope for Rachel Lubetkin. Or Etta? Or for Etta's children? That's how it is?" Eva bowed her head, clutched her stomach, and began to rock, as if in deep mourning.

The men did not speak as the reality of the situation sank in. If the free nations could not help a country under attack, what hope did a single individual have of being saved?

Murphy directed the next question to Eva. "You'll be staying on in London? looking for work?"

Eva managed to regain her voice. "I thought . . . perhaps as a translator."

Mac snapped his fingers. "Sure, Murphy. That's it. You need a translator. TENS can do a series on the refugees. Stories firsthand. She'll be great."

Murphy agreed. "Right. You can start tomorrow. You'll need a place to stay. I'll ring Elisa. Tell her you and Mac have just come in from the Continent. That you need a nice meal. A roof over your head and a bed. A good night's sleep. Things will look better in the morning."

Mac and Eva smiled gratefully as they rose from their seats.

"So, Murphy," Mac added, turning back at the office door after Eva had already passed through, "how's Josie Marlow? She bring back great stuff?"

Murphy frowned. "Mac . . . Josie hasn't been around. I mean, nobody's seen her since Warsaw."

꩜

Primrose Hill
London, England

Dearest Jacob,

This evening Murphy brought home two visitors to stay at the house. Both have come from Warsaw. Mac McGrath is a news photographer whom I believe will be working for Murphy and Trump European News. The other is a young Czech woman named Eva

Weitzman. She is a Catholic of Jewish heritage who was cut off from her home and family when Hitler invaded Czechoslovakia. She says that the fact that she and her family were Catholic did not save them from the Nazis. I knew at once what she was saying. We had a lot to talk about. She is only a little older than I am. She told us the story of how she came to hold the passport that saved her life. She showed us photographs of the family whose daughter gave her the passport and a very sad letter from the mother of the children in the photograph. She is desperate to find some way to help them. But none of us has any hope that there will be any more rescues.

Her appearance with Mac gave us all hope that you also must have received your passport. She had no information about that, of course, only that Warsaw was in such chaos all along the route of their escape.

It is plain to Elisa and me that Eva Weitzman and Mac McGrath have fallen in love. Mac is a funny duck. He only looks at her when she is not aware of it—as if he is afraid for her to know how he feels. One wonders if his heart was terribly broken some time in the past.

Elisa and I like them both very much. Eva will start work at the TENS office as a translator and will be staying with us for a while. She is my size, and I am loaning her some of my clothes until she can go shopping. Mac will stay in a boardinghouse near the TENS office.

I will be glad to have the company of Eva when Elisa and Murphy need their time alone. Eva enjoys playing chess, and I shall challenge her soon.

I miss you very much, Jacob. I will sign off now and say my prayers for you and Alfie and Papa and the world. May we all rest in the safe hands of Jesus during this very dark night.

I love you,
Lori

P.S. Eva Weitzman is very kind. She just rapped on my door, and we spoke for a few minutes. She told me that she knows how it feels to worry about family. She has not heard from any of her family since Prague fell. We prayed together for our beloved.

❦

Dearest Lori:
We have had a bit of good luck.
Last night, when I was steering, Alfie told me to turn the wheel to the right. I argued with him that the bend curved the other way.

We almost crashed into a wrecked ship lying half sunk against the bank. There were two dead men on board . . . the others must have run away.

Anyway, now we have barrels and barrels of fuel. Enough to make it to Brest, Captain Orde says.

Also food.

But best of all, we found a portable radio. The ship's captain must have been a rich man because the radio is almost brand-new . . . a British-made Phillips All Wave receiver.

We heard a Polish-language broadcast from Moscow. Captain Orde translated for the rest of us who don't speak it. The news is all bad for Poland. The Poles asked Russia for assistance. Stalin says he would have helped, but since Britain and France have declared war on Germany, the USSR must now remain neutral.

No one will help Poland before it's too late, it seems.

The Polish government has fled to Brest, where we are also going.

Hearing all this will likely cut the heart out of the Poles who are still resisting.

But perhaps you know all this already.

We have finished loading all that can be salvaged from the wrecked ship; we also buried the two men.

Tonight we'll go farther east.

I still don't know what Captain Orde is thinking. If we reach the Russian frontier, what will we do then?

All my love always,

Jacob

"Do you read Polish?" Father Kopecky, the priest of the Cathedral of St. John, passed the letter to Josie Marlow.

She scanned the beautiful script and noted the signature at the bottom: *Rachel Lubetkin.* "Sorry. No," Josie replied in French.

"This is from the thirteen-year-old daughter of the rabbi of Muranow. Rabbi Lubetkin. A good man. A wise man. Just the sort the Nazis will kill first if the Polish army is not victorious."

"She didn't come with the other Jewish girls?"

"No. She wouldn't come. She is made of the same stock as her father. No. Poor child. She has written me, asking that I will find room for her baby brother, Yacov. He is the youngest of the Lubetkin children."

"A baby."

"A few months old. But I can't. Can't put the other children at risk by taking in a circumcised child. I . . . can't."

"Father, what will happen to them?"

"Everywhere the Nazis have gone the slaughter of the innocents has been replayed as though the Christ child had come again to Bethlehem. And Rachel mourns for her children."

Josie studied the incomprehensible plea. "What can be done?"

"You are American. America must hold the key to this! America has remained neutral. You must carry this news—not only of one child, but the peril of millions—back to your own countrymen."

"I will. You know I will."

"Perhaps then your President Roosevelt will take in some of our children. Not just the girls . . . but . . . we must pray . . . we must . . . pray. How can I take in even one circumcised boy when so many children would be put at risk?"

Josie returned the girl's letter to him. Father Kopecky smoothed the paper gently and laid Rachel's request on his desk blotter. He was still pondering it sadly when Josie left him.

⊙

Primrose Hill
London, England

Dearest Jacob,

Today as I walked to the market in the village, I saw schoolboys marching through the park with broomsticks on their shoulders. Cardboard gas-mask containers hung around their necks with twine. Several wore tin pots on their heads for helmets.

At first I wondered why these rosy-cheeked English children had not yet been evacuated to the country. Then the memory came to me of the Hitler Youth marching in step through the streets of Berlin. I remembered when they stopped to throw stones through the windows of your uncle's shop and the day your nose was broken when fifteen Hitler Youth beat you and your brother outside the schoolyard because you were Jewish. Surely those cruel Nazi boys have grown up to become the SS soldiers who swarm across the borders of Poland.

And one day soon these innocent English schoolboys who march across Primrose Hill Park with their mother's pots upon their heads will grow big enough to die in a foreign country fighting against the evil that threatens to swallow the world. These sweet boys will die because in the beginning so few protested what the Hitler Youth did to German Jewish children. My father saw what was coming; when he raised his voice, it cost him his freedom. Now they have silenced all opposition. It is too late to stop the slaughter that must surely come upon all the world.

Oh, my dearest Jacob, where are you now? May the God of love and mercy keep you safe from those little Nazi boys who grew into monsters, nourished by the bread of hatred.

I love you,

Lori

Dear Lori:

If you ever come to read this, I hope you can make it out. I lost my pen, you see, and have only this stub of a pencil to use.

We very nearly lost everything yesterday, and today we are on foot.

It was nearly sunset. The engine was warming up. A German plane—a Dornier, I think—must have spotted us by the smoke the old tub puffed from her stack, because he came diving out of nowhere, shooting up everything.

Most of us dove over the side.

He made two passes and set the boat on fire.

When he left we got back aboard and put out the fires, but the motor is wrecked. Can't go upstream with no motor.

Two of the Zionist boys were burned on their hands and faces. Lucy hurt her arm, but Captain Orde tied it up in a sling.

Alfie said tall, golden men stood guard over us and didn't let anyone get hurt worse. Captain Orde says it's a miracle none of us were killed.

We saved what we could, but now we're walking to Brest.

I thought all of Poland was flat and ugly. Well, it mostly is. But they have also the deepest, darkest forest here I've ever seen. We heard some strange buglings that Captain Orde says are elk. He says near this forest is a herd of buffalo. Wolves live here, too, he says.

Funny, I wasn't frightened when we got strafed. No time, I guess. But this forest scares me.

Maybe it's because it's so thick, or maybe it's because I have no idea where we're going or how, or maybe it's because all the time I'm going directly away from you, farther away all the time.

All my love always,

Jacob

P.S. Saved the radio. Sometimes we can almost make out BBC—London. Makes me think of you.

P.P.S. Werner-kitten is afraid of the forest, too, and stays on Alfie's shoulder all the time.

13

Consumed by Fire

Smoke rose from the inferno of Warsaw, blotting out the sun for one hundred miles. The ring of German fire and steel had encircled the city for weeks.

Although most of Poland had fallen, Warsaw refused to surrender. The boom of one hundred heavy guns resounded with the Nazi reply to this final defiance. Unending waves of Luftwaffe bombers dropped their cargos of incendiary bombs on churches and hospitals filled with wounded. The streets were littered now with thousands of dead and dying. The heat of the fires cracked the windows. Not one building in the city remained undamaged by the ceaseless barrage.

At 8:30 AM a frantic radio message was received in Budapest:

> "At this moment German heavy artillery . . . shelling Warsaw . . . German planes bombed Little Jesus Hospital only a few minutes ago. The left wing of the hospital . . . grave for hundreds of wounded soldiers, women, and children . . . Opera House, the National Theatre, and the Polytechnic School are on fire. . . . German artillery now is concentrating its fire on the center of the city. . . . All these days of siege . . . difficult to keep order in a city of a million and a half people when death and destruction . . . Those still able bring what aid they can to the hungry . . . wounded . . . dying in the streets."

The broadcast ended with a desperate plea.

"We hold to hope . . . awaiting quick aid from our British and French allies!"

In that same hour France and England, who had declared war against Germany, still debated what help to send.

There would be no military aid from the West. Still, the Polish army fought on in Warsaw. The weapons of fallen soldiers were given to civilians—women, old men, and boys—who held the barricades. Pounded by the distant German artillery and the Stuka bombers, the defenders did not see the face of the enemy who slaughtered them. They simply died, still believing that their allies would come. One hero at a time, Poland and Warsaw perished while France and England clucked their tongues and offered nothing more substantial than sympathy.

Josephine Marlow, the last remaining member of the Associated Press in Warsaw, covered her head as yet another explosion rocked the great edifice of the Cathedral of St. John above her. Ancient dust and flecks of mortar rained down on the carpet of wounded who lined the floor of the vaulted crypt.

The groans of four hundred sounded like one continuous moan. There was no more morphine for pain. The last of the disinfectant had been used the day before. Now bottles of vodka served as both antiseptic and anesthetic. The most severely wounded had been taken to the main hall of the cathedral, where the priest moved from one to the other, administering last rites. Here in the crypt were the women and children who might survive . . . if medicine could be brought for them in time.

Josie followed Sister Angeline as she offered hope, cleaned the wounds, and changed the bandages of her patients. Carrying a precious bucket of boiled water, Josie ladled its contents into parched mouths.

Josie knelt to offer a drink to a young Jewish woman of about eighteen who had lost the lower part of her right leg in an artillery blast. She clutched Josie's grime-covered sleeve. Her dark eyes were frantic. She cried out to Josie in Yiddish and would not release her grip.

"Sister Angeline." Josie called for help in French, which was the common meeting place between English and Polish for the two women. "What is she saying? What does she want from me?"

The young woman pleaded with the nun, who translated for Josie. "She thinks you are French," explained the sister. "She wants to know when your French soldiers will come to save us from the Nazis."

Josie sat back on her heels and put her hand on the young woman's hand in despair. She looked into the face of Sister Angeline. "What do I tell her, Sister? What? That I don't think the French or the English will come? Do I tell her that I am American? That we're not even at war with the men who blew her leg off? That, as a member of the press, if I survive the shelling I can probably walk away from here to freedom with the blessings of the German High Command while all the rest of you are . . ." Her voice faltered. Eyes brimmed with helplessness and anger. She had sent two dozen wires throughout the siege, each more desperate than the one before. She did not even know if her stories had gotten through to the AP in Paris.

She had stayed too long in Warsaw and now was trapped like everyone else. Only her entrapment was not an automatic sentence of death as it must surely be for this young Jewess with half a leg. The SS had shot wounded numbering in the tens of thousands. What hope for mercy could there be for those in the crypt who reached up to Josie for an answer she could not give them?

Josie covered her face with her hands. She was filled with anger and shame. With every bomb that fell, she found herself inwardly raging against the senselessness of this slaughter. Angry at the brutality of the Nazis, she was also angry at the useless courage of the Poles. Could the Polish High Command still believe that Chamberlain and Daladier, the French prime minister, would ride in to break the siege of Warsaw like the cavalry in a bad movie? Only one word—*Surrender*—would stop the destruction! Why did the Polish High Command continue to hold out in the face of inevitable defeat?

Sister Angeline put a hand on her shoulder. "Josephine? *Ma chèrie*," she said gently. "Soon it must come to an end for us in Warsaw. We will stay and face what we must with God's help. We will each fight on in our own way. You must live. You must go from here and tell them what you saw. Tell them . . . yes . . . we were afraid. But even so, we held out until it was no longer possible. Perhaps it will help them to fight if they remember that Poland died alone, yet with courage."

"Oh, Sister!" Josie cried as the terrible roar of an artillery shell howled overhead, bursting somewhere beyond the church. Thunder succeeded thunder, drowning out screams as a dozen explosions followed the first blast. The ground shook. Sister Angeline threw herself across a patient as a section of wall collapsed on them both. The air of the crypt clouded with choking dust. Josie crouched down and shielded her head as bricks tumbled from the pillars, and the ceiling at the far end fell in on fifty wounded.

Then there was silence. Josie sat up slowly. She was uninjured. The place where Sister Angeline had been was covered by debris. Josephine crawled toward the heap, crying out the name of the sister. Her voice echoed in the shattered crypt. Outside, the distant rumble of artillery suddenly stopped, and there was only the voice of Josie.

The church sustained a direct hit. For hours Josephine worked numbly beside a priest and a few ragged soldiers to dig out the victims from beneath the rubble. Josephine's hands were torn and blistered from the rough edges of the bricks. Her clothing was shredded and soaked with sweat and blood.

And then, for the first time in over a week, Josephine walked out into the night. She looked up and thought of words to describe what she had seen in this place. There were none adequate to the task. She tried to simply observe—to detach herself from the scene and mentally record the images of war. *Useless. Senseless. Waste.* These were the words that came to mind.

Two soldiers carried Sister Angeline out onto the pavement. Her wimple had come off in the blast, revealing short, graying hair. Covered with dust, her face was serene, almost joyful in death.

Josephine stood over Sister Angeline for a moment, realizing she had told the sister everything about herself in the last two weeks. But what did Josephine know about Sister Angeline? Only that she fought a different kind of battle than the soldiers at the barricades.

The sky above Warsaw glowed orange with flames that engulfed the main buildings of the city. Josie shielded her eyes against the brightness as the town hall and the Gothic edifice of the ancient castle were consumed. Acrid smoke billowed as if the earth had opened and hell had risen to engulf Warsaw.

The dead were laid out on the shattered stone pavement outside the church. Row upon row. So many. So still. The fires of the fallen city were reflected in the lifeless eyes of the brave.

No one spoke. Silence was punctuated only by the disintegration of collapsing buildings. The German artillery had stopped. Was it finished then? Was the siege over? Had the last Polish child died defending the last barricade?

Josephine sank to the ground as the fires crackled behind her. She was thirsty. Somewhere she had lost the bucket of cool water with which she had comforted the condemned.

೧೨

Dearest Lori:

We made it! We're in Brest! I didn't know we were so close.

When we finally got out of that forest, just around one more bend of the river we saw it. There's a big fort on an island in the river.

The Polish government really is here. There are four Polish army divisions here, too. They have ammunition and are talking about counterattacking the Nazis. They still expect Russian help.

When we show our British passports, people grab our hands and pump them till I think something may break. They call us "allies" and "friends."

They are especially cordial to Captain Orde. They seem to think he's a British officer preparing for a drop of British paratroopers and supplies.

That's the rumor anyway.

They are not so welcoming of the other Jewish boys, but Captain Orde says we all work for Trump European News, and so far that seems accepted.

We're staying in the dormitory of a boys' boarding school. The students have all been sent home.

I saved the news that will interest you most till last.

Captain Orde and Lucy are married!

She protested, but he insisted. He said if they were married his British passport would apply to her, too.

I don't think Captain Orde is Catholic, but after he explained everything to a priest, they got married in St. Christopher's Polish Catholic church.

I was his best man. Alfie stood by Lucy's side. Our clothes were pretty ratty, but Alfie had his hair combed, and somewhere he found a sky blue ribbon to tie around Werner's neck.

Captain Orde almost lost his voice. The old priest had to twice ask him to speak up.

Lucy looked beautiful and blushed.

Not so beautiful as you, of course!

They still have a working telegraph here. Maybe I can send you a telegram.

Finally things are getting better.

All my love always,

Jacob

꙳

The road leading from Lodz to Warsaw was packed with Polish prisoners of war shuffling against the flow of Wehrmacht tanks, mobile artillery, and troop lorries. Disheveled, bloody, and filthy, the captured Poles made a striking contrast to the victorious German troops.

Captain Horst von Bockman, now company commander in the 8th Armored Reconnaissance Regiment of General Stumme's 2nd Light

Division, watched the tide of conquered men divide and move into the roadside ditches as the heavy machinery passed. The picture was, he thought, a perfect summation of the war. The Poles had fought with the tactics of the last century. The antiquated Polish divisions had dug in along a border stretching for fifteen hundred miles. While the German Luftwaffe served as artillery, bombing airfields as well as civilian centers behind the lines, the highly mobile Panzerkorps of tanks and motorized infantry had broken through and cut the Polish units to pieces. Within ten days, General Guderian's tanks had covered two hundred miles. In Zabinka they finally met a rare Polish mechanized unit. Polish tanks were being unloaded at a railway siding. They were destroyed before returning a single shot.

Horst von Bockman was proud of the performance of the men in his unit. He had led them through the Polish lines, often meeting enemy resistance before the main body of German troops reached the front. Unlike the Luftwaffe, which had been blooded in the Spanish civil war, this had been his first taste of real combat. Four years of hard work and sacrifice had finally paid off. He had found the first victory exhilarating, and yet today, as he observed the Polish prisoners being herded away by the SS, he felt ill at ease.

For a week he had been anxious to leave Poland for the Siegfried Line. At first he explained away his misgivings. He told himself that he was simply impatient to get to the western front, ready to face the French and finish what had been left undone in 1918. But the rumors of mass graves and the results of SS execution squads were every hour being confirmed as fact.

A motorcycle reconnaissance team of two men had come upon an open grave filled with Polish officers. Reported to von Bockman and then up the chain of command, the grizzly discovery had been dismissed as a burial place for Polish soldiers killed honorably in action. On the face of it, this answer seemed to satisfy all but the two who had seen the site. It could not be, they explained. Every Polish officer in the ditch had been executed by a single bullet in the back of his head!

As their commander, von Bockman warned them to keep their mouths shut about it. Talking could get them into trouble. They had done their duty in reporting the incident; now they had better forget it. The matter had been passed on to higher authority than his own, and it could not be his concern any longer.

Now, as the distant rattle of machine-gun fire echoed from the otherwise calm woods, von Bockman could not forget it. For him and others in the German Wehrmacht, the glory of their patriotic war was rapidly dissolving into meaningless slaughter by Hitler's Waffen SS.

"We'll be here until Christmas," von Bockman muttered to the fresh-faced young driver of his armored car.

"By Christmas we will be in Paris," corrected Sergeant Fiske, the tank commander who had been sent with the dispatch ordering von Bockman forward to general headquarters outside Warsaw.

The line of withdrawing Wehrmacht troops seemed endless, disappearing into the smoky eastern horizon, which marked the site of the continuing bombardment of the besieged city.

"With all the Wehrmacht marching to the western front, I suppose Poland will belong to the SS," von Bockman remarked bitterly as a group of six soldiers with the death's-head emblem on their caps emerged from the edge of the woods. Von Bockman did not go on to express his sense that the SS supermen aimed to be the only two-legged creatures left alive in the occupied territory.

Sergeant Fiske inclined his head, acknowledging the harsh reality that now faced the conquered nation. He shifted uneasily in his seat, evidently visualizing the same unexpressed image of slaughter. Then he changed the subject. "Well, Captain, you may be right. We won the war in a few days. It will take us till Christmas to pull the army back to fight the French. You are the reconnaissance expert. Is there another road to Warsaw?"

Von Bockman nodded. They made their way two kilometers back down the highway to where a narrow dirt track branched off and twisted through a string of deserted and ruined villages, eventually leading toward Warsaw. Burned-out shells of buildings and collapsed roofs identified the arbitrary targets of Hermann Göring's pilots. Six milk cows lay bloated in a field where they had been machine-gunned, no doubt for sport. The road was littered with debris left behind by fleeing civilians.

Von Bockman looked away and covered his nose and mouth against the sickly aroma that permeated the air. This was what he would remember most about Poland, he decided. In practice maneuvers he had never thought about what a battlefield would smell like after only one day in the hot sun. He imagined that Poland would stink for a thousand years, for as long as the Thousand-Year Reich.

They passed the charred remains of what had been a steeply gabled farmhouse. The fine stone barn across the yard was still intact. A dead plow horse, still hitched to the plow, lay in the furrowed field where it had fallen. There was no sign of life. Von Bockman wondered what had happened to the family that lived here. Bits of furniture and clothing were strewn everywhere around the gutted residence. A kitchen chair lay beside an overturned cradle; on the step, a woman's yellow calico dress; across a rail fence, the trousers of a small boy; trampled in the dust, a doll with a broken porcelain head. They had not warned him about such sights when he was a cadet longing to see action.

Now all he wanted was to walk with Katrina in the sweet pine forest that bordered his family estate in Prussia. He closed his eyes and called up his wife's image. At twenty-five, she was not what would be considered fashionably beautiful. Dark-haired and hazel-eyed, she was the opposite of the perfect Aryan vision of womanhood. She was only five feet, two inches—a full foot shorter than he. Fine-boned and fair-skinned, she was a delicate contrast to his sunburned complexion, hawklike nose, deep-set blue eyes, broad forehead, and jutting chin.

Katrina preferred riding breeches to dresses and Wellington boots to high heels. Her stride could match his in a hike through the forest. An excellent horsewoman, she could match him jump for jump on a cross-country ride. Her father owned one of the finest Arabian stud farms in the world. Katrina preferred working with horses above everything in life, she said, with the exception of making love. This she did with the same enthusiasm as a cross-country ride.

In the beginning Katrina had been dangerously opinionated about Hitler and the National Socialist movement. She had openly displayed her contempt when Hermann Göring purchased a large boar-hunting preserve in the Schönheide, north of Berlin and bordering the estate of Katrina's father. At a Christmas party she had expressed the opinion that she would love to see Fat Hermann's head stuffed and hung on the wall of his trophy room with the rest of the Nazi swine. The comment was repeated, and neighbor Göring was not amused.

Horst had been privately warned about it. The suggestion was strongly made that, for the sake of his career, he keep company with a woman who had the correct political opinions. *Dangerous* was a word that was emphasized. About that time the arrests of dissidents, Democrats, Communists, and church leaders became commonplace. After that, Katrina kept her sense of outrage and her sense of humor to herself.

Horst had married her in the summer of 1937, in spite of the official warning that she was a political handicap. His career had not been harmed by the union. Horst believed that this was quite possibly because half the generals in the Wehrmacht secretly shared her opinion about Fat Hermann and the Nazi barnyard. What would she say, he wondered, if she could see Poland?

Katrina kept his mind occupied for another dusty hour until they turned onto a main road. Traffic headed toward Warsaw was light. Joining a procession of a half-dozen military vehicles, they were stopped at an SS roadblock on the outskirts of a still-smoldering village.

"Orders from General Guderian," said Sergeant Fiske, presenting the papers to the arrogant SS soldier blocking the way.

"You will have to go back." The man barely glanced at the official documents, passing them back through the window of the vehicle as the staccato popping of machine guns resounded beyond the blockade.

"We are ordered to Warsaw." Agitated, Fiske looked past the SS officer even as he argued. "You can see. The general himself—"

The SS officer cocked an eyebrow impatiently. "We receive our orders from SS-Obergruppenführer Heydrich. And our orders are that no one passes through the restricted area until mop-up is finished."

Von Bockman leaned forward. "Mop-up? Guderian's Panzerkorps took this area last week. Fifty thousand Polish prisoners were captured. I was here. What is left to mop up?"

"We receive our orders from Heydrich alone."

"Then you should let SS-Obergruppenführer Heydrich and the general discuss their differences. In the meantime, I outrank you. The siege of Warsaw continues, and you are blocking the way of officers ordered to battle at the front." A slight smile. "Sergeant Fiske, check the identity papers of this SS whelp. Perhaps he is not German at all. He is willfully obstructing our progress."

Fiske drew his pistol and opened the door of the vehicle as the SS soldier stepped back. His eyes narrowed at the insult. He raised his hand, conceding that he had lost the argument. "Heil Hitler!"

They returned the obligatory salute and passed through the blockade and into the village.

On every corner there were black-shirted SS with submachine guns guarding groups of terrified civilians—sobbing women, children, old men. A few blocks beyond, thick, black smoke poured from a gaping hole in the onion dome that topped the village synagogue, drawing the gaze of von Bockman.

He peered out the window slits of the vehicle. What was going on? This village had surrendered to Guderian without a shot being fired.

"Pull up there," he ordered the driver as they neared a group of laughing SS who congregated near the fountain in front of the synagogue.

Smoke billowed out. Flames licked the frames of the broken stained-glass windows. The wind caught the smoke, clearing a view to the open front doors.

Fiske gasped. "Horst! Look!"

Von Bockman followed Fiske's gaze to a sight that made him reel.

Three men were crucified on the heavy wooden doors of the burning building. First hidden by the smoke and then revealed for an instant by a breath of wind, they had been stripped to the waist. It was evident that they had been savagely tortured. They were, thankfully, dead as the tongues of flame shot out to touch them. The word *JUDE,* "Jew," was scrawled in blood on the stone wall. It was a picture of hell.

Von Bockman and Fiske leaped from the armored car, interrupting the conversation of the dozen SS guards who stood as if there were nothing unusual about the scene.

"You!" Von Bockman rushed toward a sergeant whose smile faded at his furious approach. "What is this?"

The sergeant saluted as did the others. "Jews, sir. Caught hiding Polish soldiers."

Von Bockman grasped the man by his shirtfront, pulling him up on his toes. Bile choked off his voice. "Who . . . has done . . . this . . . ?"

"We act on orders. From the top. Such offenses against the Reich are punishable by death. And the death must be an example to others among the population who might benefit from such an example." The explanation was made in a tone that expressed the SS sergeant's agreement with the reasonable nature of crucifixion as punishment for such a crime.

"Whose orders?" von Bockman demanded, shaking the SS soldier.

An amused voice behind him replied, "Mine alone. Obergruppenführer Reinhard Heydrich. And you are?"

Von Bockman threw the sergeant back, then whirled to face the tall, slender, broad-shouldered figure of Reinhard Heydrich, general of the SS. Heydrich's sharp blue eyes narrowed with contempt for the outrage of von Bockman. Thin lips twisted into a smile as the color drained from von Bockman's face. Horst realized that he was meeting the man known as "The Butcher."

"Heil Hitler?" Heydrich intoned.

"Heil Hitler," came the submissive reply of Fiske and von Bockman in unison.

Heydrich nodded and considered the two with new interest. "That's more like it." He walked slowly around the two men as a butcher might inspect a side of beef. "What are you doing here?"

Fiske fumbled for the papers. There was a rumble as a portion of the synagogue roof caved in. Fires crackled. Smoke swept across the square and touched them, making their eyes sting. "Trying to get to Warsaw, Obergruppenführer. We are under orders. You see?"

"This is a restricted area. You were allowed to pass at the barricade?"

"Yes, sir."

Heydrich glanced sharply toward the blockade, then with a jerk of his head and a snap of his fingers sent two of his minions to arrest the guard. "Sloppy. Careless. Not acceptable behavior in the Einsatz-truppen," he said coldly. "So. You have lost your way." Rocking up on his toes, Heydrich peered down his long nose at them. "An easy mistake to make, I suppose." He laughed and slapped von Bockman on the back. "It would be best if you get back into your car now and find another route to General Guderian, gentlemen. I will overlook your error. This time." He glanced at the papers. "Company Commander von Bockman, is it? And Sergeant Fiske? Be assured I will remember."

As the armored car sped away, Horst von Bockman did not look back at the synagogue as the doors were finally consumed by the fire.

Lori:

The Nazis are here, in Brest.

Overnight panzers rolled out of the west and north. I heard it was Guderian's column, but I don't know.

We barely made it here ahead of them. There are already artillery shells falling in the center of town.

The Polish troops are firing back from the old fortress on the island, but I don't think their guns are as big as the ones the Nazis have.

Radio reports from Moscow worry Captain Orde. He told me the Soviet news agency Tass quoted Stalin as saying ethnic Ukrainians are being mistreated by the Poles.

I said, "So?"

He said, "The last Ukrainians we met shot at us, remember?"

Also, that's the exact sort of thing Hitler said about protecting the Volksdeutsche . . . right before he invaded the Sudetenland.

Got to go. Captain Orde says he has a plan, and he wants to discuss it with me before he tries to explain it to the whole group.

Love,

Jacob

P.S. Here's the plan: We're going to Moscow. If Russia's neutral, then the TENS bureau in Moscow can help us. Maybe we can catch a Russian ship to England!

14

A Blanket of Silence

Yom Kippur. The Day of Atonement. The last letter from Etta remained unopened on the table of Rabbi Shlomo Lebowitz. The old rabbi was fasting. He would not allow himself the nourishment of reading what might well be the final correspondence from his daughter.

Ten days before, as the new moon rose over Jerusalem, the shofar had announced Rosh Hashanah. The Jewish Quarter of the Old City had celebrated the New Year holiday with the hope that the Polish army could hold back the flood of German invaders.

But throughout the Days of Awe that followed, the news trickling into Jerusalem from Poland had gone from grim to hopeless.

Now, on the anniversary of the siege and desolation of the Temple in ancient Jerusalem, Warsaw was in flames. On this most holy Day of Atonement, two thousand years of Jewish culture in Europe were being irrevocably blasted to oblivion.

And what of Etta and Aaron and the children? Compared to their lives, even the destruction of a great city seemed of small importance to Rabbi Shlomo Lebowitz. Did they still live?

The old man left his home and made his way through the narrow streets of the Old City toward the Western Wall of Solomon's Temple. The story was told that this part of the wall had been built by the beggars of Solomon's Jerusalem. On the day of the Temple's destruction, angels had linked their wings around the wall and given the command: *"This, the work of the poor, shall never be destroyed!"*

The Shekinah glory of God remained in this place, and at certain times the very stones wept for the destruction of the Temple. Would they weep today for the new desolation? the old man wondered.

A space of only twelve feet separated the Wailing Wall from the shabby houses of the Muslims of the Moroccan neighborhood. Today that space was packed with worshippers who covered their heads with prayer shawls and lifted hands and eyes to the sheer face of hand-hewn rock.

At a respectful distance, armed British soldiers stood guard over the assembly. In years past, more than one pious Jew had turned his face to the wall and found himself face-to-face with the Eternal, thanks to a well-aimed stone hurled from a Muslim rooftop onto a Jewish head.

Rabbi Lebowitz welcomed the presence of the English, even though he never worried about the rocks of his petulant Arab neighbors. He had decided early in his life that there was no better spot for a Jew to die than in the posture of fervent prayer before the Holy Wall.

He turned his face up to the slit of blue above him as he covered his head with his prayer shawl. He knew the prayers by heart, but still he turned the pages of his siddur to the prayers of the High Holy Days. His voice joined the others in a dissonant song that somehow blended into the harmony of one voice and one prayer to heaven.

The Amidah was recited:

> *"Blessed art Thou, our God and God of our fathers . . . who will bring a Redeemer with love to their children's children for His name's sake."*

The shofar sounded, reminding rabbi and congregation that in spite of their grief, the Eternal was sovereign in the world, that He remembered the deeds of all men and the Covenant of Abraham, and that someday He would send the Redeemer.

Was this not the time? the rabbi silently prayed. Would it not be best if Messiah would appear at this moment and bring home the children of the Covenant to Jerusalem? And the children and grandchildren of Rabbi Lebowitz, too?

Where was Etta in the desolation? Where were her husband, Aaron, and the children?

"They are in the hands of the Eternal," the old man reminded himself. "And He sees them just as He sees me."

Was there a better place for Rabbi Lebowitz to remind the Eternal not to forget them? In all the earth, this was the one place where a chink remained open to the throne room of the Almighty. The old man had come with his petition written on a slip of paper. He reached up and urged his request between the blocks of stone.

As always, he was sure he heard the fluttering of angels' wings above him. Perhaps the stirring of their wings carried the prayer of the rabbi near to the ear of the Almighty. Did they wait each day to hear the same prayer recited by an old man? He felt the breath of angels on the breeze.

> *"With Your mighty hand carry Your children home to this place, this small piece of earth that is so near to Your throne. For the sake of Your Name. For the sake of Your Covenant, call to the north and bring them home, that the kingdom of Messiah may be established, and His throne endure forever in Jerusalem! Omaine."*

The gathering of Yom Kippur was more solemn than usual this year. There were none present who did not have some link with the community trapped in Warsaw. The wealth of Poland had founded and supported many of the Yeshiva schools and synagogues here in Jerusalem. Now what help could they send back?

As the holy day passed, Jews flocked to the headquarters of the British Mandatory Government, each volunteering to be allowed to fight in the British forces against the Nazis on Polish soil. They were politely turned away; no one told them that no British forces were being sent to Poland.

Rachel cradled baby Yacov and sat beside her mother in the women's section of the worship.

Silence covered Warsaw like a blanket beyond the Jewish district. Some said it was the silence of peace. Had the Russians arrived ahead of the Germans? Among the secular Jews that was the hope.

Others said it was the peace of the grave. Soon would come the crash of Nazi jackboots upon the cobblestones of their beloved city.

Then what?

In the basement shelter of the Jewish Community Center the congregation of Rabbi Lubetkin prayed and sang blessings for the end of the day:

> *"Blessed are You, O Adonai! Blessed are You who knows our going out and our coming in! Blessed are You O Eternal, who knows . . . "*

The hammering of fists on the doors disrupted the service.

Papa did not look up from beneath the prayer shawl that covered his head.

Morris, a surly young Communist, crippled by polio as a child, moved to the door and threw back the bolt, flinging the doors wide.

Rachel turned her face and cocked her head to hear the news, though she knew she should have been listening to Papa's prayers.

Three filthy Polish fighters, ragged and agitated, stumbled into the basement. One was Tov, the younger brother of Morris. The voices of the congregation fell away until Papa prayed alone.

Tov declared, "The Polish government has fled. All of them! All!"

"Who won?" Morris grasped the arms of his brother.

"The armies of Poland are . . . no more!"

Morris cried, "Is it the Russians? Is it?"

A rapid shake of the head gave the dreaded answer. "The Nazis. There are mass graves in every Jewish village they passed through. The Gestapo and the Waffen SS come together. Executions. They will be in the city before nightfall!"

Mama went ashen at the news. Baby Yacov slept on. David and Samuel clung to their mother. Rachel's heart began to beat rapidly. Why had Papa's prayers not been heard?

Morris covered his face with his hands and wept. "We should fight them here! Here in the streets. Someone give me a rifle! I am not afraid!"

Tov tried to calm him. "Morris. Brother! Comrade! There are no bullets left to fire."

Morris slammed his fist into his palm. "Then stones! We must resist, or they will kill us all!"

Tov replied, "They have dropped leaflets." He passed one to Morris. "If we resist, they will kill first our families. The innocent among us. Morris, they say if we surrender peacefully . . . if we lay down our arms, we will live."

Morris turned to face the gaping congregation. "You believe them?"

Silence. What else could they do but believe such a promise? hope it was true?

Papa's prayers came to an end. *"Blessed are You, O Adonai, who knows . . . Omaine."*

Tov stepped forward and addressed the crowd. "Look! All of you! Get back to your homes. When they come, don't make it easy for them to round you all up. They must not find all the Jews of Warsaw in one place. Go home! Go quickly!"

All eyes turned to Papa. He closed the prayer book and removed the tallis from his head. He did not raise his eyes from the book in his hands.

The congregation erupted.

"Rebbe, what shall we do!"

"Where should we go?"

"They will kill every Jew. Like in Munich!"

"Rebbe! I saw what they did in Berlin on Kristal Nacht!"

"And I was in Vienna. Concentration camps! Public executions!"

"I fled from Prague! They rounded up so many at random. Pulled my brother from the bus. Firing squads! Executions! Young men strung up from streetlamps on the boulevard!"

"Rebbe! What can we do?"

At last, when every fear had been shouted again and again, Papa raised his hand for silence. "Tov is right. We do not want to make it easy for them. Split up. Each family to your own home. The bombing is finished. Go home. Each apartment block elect a representative. We will meet here tonight and discuss what must be done."

There was a mad scramble to exit the shelter.

Rachel, her mother, father, and brothers stood back and waited until they were alone in the midst of the rubble of left belongings.

Sunlight streamed through the open portal. The smell of decaying flesh was on the wind.

Mama hugged Papa. "Aaron! Oh, I had such hope it would be the Russians."

Papa stroked Rachel's cheek, mussed the hair of David and Samuel, and said with conviction, "Like the three faithful Jews in the days of Daniel, we stand before the blazing furnace. Remember the story? Children, do not fear the Nazis! Are they worse than the enemy who took our people captive in those days? It is in the fire we will meet Messiah face-to-face. He will walk with us even there, if it is written that we must also be thrown into the flames."

15

Opera Houses and Small Poets

It was after dark when Rabbi Aaron Lubetkin led his family out of the shelter through the rubble-strewn streets toward home.

Had their home survived? The neighborhood looked as though a giant had carelessly walked through, crushing this house and that shop underfoot.

Rachel covered her nose and mouth against the stench. In the distance the glow of still-raging fires illuminated the skyline in the direction of the National Opera House.

The family walked several blocks without speaking until they were once again inside their own flat.

Nothing had changed. Nothing. The electricity was off, so Papa lit an oil lamp and held it up to chase the shadows away. In the library were Papa's leather-bound volumes. Gilt lettering reflected the light.

In the dining room Mama's blue-and-white china remained on the shelves. Shabbat candlesticks needed polishing, but they had not been stolen. It was as though the house of Rabbi Lubetkin had been watched over by angels, Rachel thought. The Lord of all the angel armies had cupped His hand over the house of the rabbi and kept it there as the bombs fell. Would the protection remain with them?

"So," Papa said in room after room as they climbed the stairs, "very good. *Nu?* Etta, look! Fine, fine."

David stood at the window of Rachel's bedroom and stared out over the rooftops. "Papa? The fire. Look, Papa? Why would they bomb the Opera House?"

Papa had no reply.

A hard, desperate knocking sounded at the front door. Mama started to go alone to answer it. Papa stopped her. "No, Etta!" His voice was sharp, as though he were warning her not to step in front of a bus. "All of you. Stay here."

He took the lamp and left them in the dark. They remained back from the banister as Papa cautiously approached the foyer. "Who is there?"

A man's voice, half choked with grief, replied, "Rebbe! Rebbe Lubetkin! It is I, Doktor Najinski!"

Rachel involuntarily took a step forward. This was Mikka's father! What was wrong? Had something happened?

Mama grasped Rachel's arm and held her back.

Papa opened the door. "My dear Doktor Najinski!"

The dentist entered the house and stood wringing his hands. In the glow of the oil lamp he was as gray as concrete. Dark circles were under his eyes. "Rebbe, it is my wife. We have had bad news. Our little Mikka. Mikka was crushed and burned when the bombs fell on the Cathedral of St. John."

A cry of horror escaped Rachel's lips. Not Mikka! Oh, how could it be? Mikka the poet. The scribe who would remember everything. Write it all down so the world would never forget. Mikka had not even lived one month into the war!

Papa set down the lamp and took Dr. Najinski's hands in his own. "I am so very sorry."

The dentist babbled on. "Our little Mikka is dead, you see! My wife . . . oh, Rebbe! She blames herself. She says that God has punished us because we sent Mikka away. Oh, Rebbe! I fear my wife will take her own life if you do not come immediately!"

Papa called up the stairs, "Etta? Do you hear?"

"Yes. Yes." Mama's tone was dull, stunned. "You must go, Aaron. The children and I will be fine here alone. Go now. You must."

Rachel collapsed into her mother's arms.

It was not supposed to be like this. Opera Houses and small poets burned up. No.

Rachel looked heavenward for a brief moment. But no, there was no answer.

⟨♋⟩

Josie Marlow slept with her back against the sandbags that surrounded the shattered Cathedral of St. John. The still-raging fires illuminated Warsaw in a hellish light. She was awakened just after midnight on September 27, 1939, by the priest's gentle voice.

"Josephine? Child?"

She opened her eyes reluctantly. For a moment she could not remember where she was or how she had come to be here. Was this a dream?

Father Kopecky's face was pale and drawn. He smiled sadly. "The major has come to take you away from here."

She blinked in confusion and rubbed her burning eyes with the back of a blistered hand. Silhouetted against the backdrop of fire was a horse and a Polish officer. The horse was tall and sunken in the flanks. Flecks of lathered sweat dotted his dark hide. He snorted, his eyes wide with resentment against the smoke and fire and the smell of death. The Polish officer patted the animal's neck and spoke calmly to him.

The priest extended his hand, helping Josie to her feet. "The Germans will be at the gates of Modlin Fortress at sunrise. The major has come from Polish High Command to take you there. The streets are impassable to motorcars. You will have to ride."

Josie nodded slowly in comprehension and wordlessly staggered to the officer and his mount.

The officer bowed slightly and clicked his heels. He greeted her in perfect French. His features were half hidden beneath the shadow of his cloth cap. By his tarnished saber, tall boots, and mud-caked spurs, Josie knew he was a member of the aristocratic Polish cavalry that had ridden out against the tanks of the German Panzer division in the first hours of the war.

"Your horse," she questioned. "I thought they had all been killed." She had heard that the animals that had survived the brutal cavalry charges had been butchered to provide food for the starving city in the last days of the siege.

"Not all, Mam'zelle." He bowed again. "We have a long way to go, if you please. It is dangerous."

She embraced the priest, who blessed her.

"Remember us," Father Kopecky rasped. "Tell them."

Mounting, the major extended his hand and helped her up behind him. The horse danced nervously, iron-shod hooves sparking against the cobblestones. Somehow it seemed appropriate to Josie that her last journey through the ancient city would be on horseback. Warsaw had always been a dream from another age. Trams and automobiles had seemed foreign to the grace and chivalry of the city. It was that grace and chivalry that had met the mechanized brutality of the National Socialist armies, only to fall forever.

"Hold tightly to me, Mam'zelle," the officer warned. "Press your face against my back and close your eyes. You must not look!"

She thanked him and leaned against him, closing her eyes. The rough wool of his tunic smelled of sweat and cordite and smoke. Then she remembered the admonition of the priest: *"Tell them!"* Her eyes snapped open to memorize the ruins of the city she had loved second only to Paris.

Now it was almost unrecognizable. Great heaps of bricks spilled out across the streets, making passage difficult for the horse. Once-stately rows of buildings resembled a comb with its teeth broken out in irregular intervals. Shards of glass were embedded in the trunks of blasted, leafless trees in city parks, and uncollected bodies of the dead lay everywhere.

The enormous stone citadel that guarded the Vistula River was pocked with shell holes. A torn Polish flag still waved where it had been run up on a shattered staff.

When Josie had arrived in Warsaw only one month earlier, the boulevards had been brightly lit with neon signs. Sidewalk cafés had been packed with people. Queues for theatres had wound around the blocks. Now everything was still except for a skinny dog that sniffed through the debris. Along the route to Modlin Fortress there were no voices. No light on the broken marquees of the theatres. Only the fires and the smoke that swirled upward to cover the full moon in a veil of red.

Men and women slumped over barricades of furniture and sandbags. Were they only sleeping?

Turning off the main thoroughfare, Josie and the soldier picked their way carefully through a neighborhood of flats that seemed less damaged than the city center. The fire was behind them now. Above the roar of the inferno came a sound so startling that the major reined the horse to a halt.

From the dark hulk of a stone synagogue came the soft, sad voices of men singing. The melody drifted out through the empty window frames of the domed building.

Josie spoke to the soldier for the first time. "What are they singing?"

"It is an old song," he replied and then translated the words for her.

> "Let the priests, the ministers of the Lord,
> weep between the porch and the altar,
> and let them say . . .
> Spare Thy people, O Lord, spare them."

It seemed to Josie that they waited in the center of the deserted road for a long time, although it was only a few seconds. The soldier spoke softly. "God is too high up to hear and France too far away. . . . This is the end for them. We Poles may somehow survive for a better day, but when morning comes, it means the beginning of the end for the Jews." He bowed his head, and Josie felt him shudder. Then he nudged the horse onward past the shadow of the synagogue.

The first light of approaching dawn was straining through the smoke when they arrived at Modlin Fortress on the outskirts of Warsaw. After being challenged by a young soldier, they passed beneath the arched gates where the remnant of the Polish army waited to surrender.

Josie imagined a cup of hot tea. Maybe just a slice of bread. How long had it been since she had eaten? She figured three days at least. And it had been fourteen hours since she had even a drop of water to drink. She licked her parched lips and asked for water. A cup of cloudy liquid was handed to her. She thought better of it and handed it back.

"We have nothing left, Mam'zelle," the Polish major apologized. Then he explained that they had run out of food and ammunition at the same time. The last assault against the enemy had been made with bayonets fixed. They had no choice now but to surrender or die. Maybe the Germans would give her breakfast when she was on their side of the line with all the other foreign correspondents who had no doubt been brought forward for the occasion.

"For your safety, it is best if your American press compatriots witness that you are alive and well when you leave us. The Nazis will treat you with courtesy and release you unharassed to your countrymen if there are witnesses. No doubt they will even have hot tea for you, Mam'zelle."

He had not meant the statement to be an accusation, but Josie was stung by a sense of guilt. What witnesses would there be to the Nazi treatment of the captured Polish prisoners after the international press was ushered back to Berlin? What of the Polish intelligentsia—the professors, doctors, lawyers, and politicians who now were superfluous to a state that no longer existed? And what record of the Jews of Poland who sang their hopeless prayer in the night?

In the morning light, Josie could see that her escort was in his early twenties. His eyes were gray. He had a shy, boyish smile, fair hair and complexion.

"I did not even ask your name."

"I am Count Alexander Riznow, Mam'zelle." He kissed her hand. "My family fled to London. If you could find them . . . my mother. My sisters. Tell them that you saw me and that I send my love."

"I will," she promised, accepting the torn scrap of paper with names and a London address hastily scrawled on it. In this way perhaps she, too, could be a witness that when she saw him, he was alive and well.

The German demand for surrender was to be answered at 6:00 AM by a white flag run up over the Modlin Fortress. The German front lines were two hundred and fifty yards from the gates. At six o'clock exactly, two Poles stood ready with the white flag. They were seconds too late for the impatient Germans, who sent one last barrage into the walls, sending everyone in the fort to their bellies and killing one last Polish defender.

Shouts and angry cries arose. When the dust cleared and Josie raised her head at last, the flag was up.

The siege of Warsaw was over.

Josie walked unsteadily toward the line of German officers. The world was spinning as she heard her name spoken by the officer who escorted her.

The German general, von Blaskowitz, looking very clean and untouched by the conflict, turned his gaze on her. "Fräulein Marlow."

"Associated Press," she managed to say as the scene before her became yellow, and a border of darkness closed on her consciousness. "Consider yourself liberated. Along with all of Poland." She saw his mouth twitch in a near smile just before she blacked out.

Dear Lori:

We're under arrest.

But it's not the Nazis. It's the Russians.

Two days ago we heard the Polish government flew out of Brest headed—we heard—for Rumania.

Captain Orde said if they were clearing out, so should we. So we went east, following the Dnieper-Bug canal, caught a ride on a truck carrying other refugees, made it to a town called Pinsk . . . and ran right into the whole Russian army.

Radio Moscow said that on September 17th, 40 Russian divisions went into battle on a line from the Ukraine all the way to Lithuania. Russian planes dropped leaflets saying they were coming to help the Poles. Their lead tanks had white flags, and they were greeted in the streets with cheers.

The smiles turned crooked when the Russians rounded up all the local police and the mayor and the aldermen. It seems Stalin says that since the Polish government has "ceased to exist," the Russians must step in and "restore order."

Lucy said, "Poor Poland."

Captain Orde just nodded.

And since we're not Poles or Nazis, or Belorussians or

Ukrainians, the Russians have locked us up until they figure out what to do with us.

They took the radio, but let me keep the notebook.

The potato soup is thin, but the black bread is good. The army colonel in charge of us seems friendly enough. Every time he sees Captain Orde he smiles and says, "Jolly old England!" Must be all the English he knows.

Their political officer, the commissar, is another fish altogether. Thin body, thin face, thin nose, and disapproving stare . . . I think he thinks we're all spies. They took away our passports.

Captain Orde says I should stop writing letters to you for now, because Comrade Commissar might believe I'm making notes of troop strength or something and have us shot. (As if we can see anything from this farmhouse where we're being kept!) We're allowed to walk between the house and the barn, but that's all.

All my love always,

Jacob

The German military victory review took place in one of the few neighborhoods of Warsaw that remained relatively undamaged. The Führer watched the goose-stepping parade of fifteen thousand troops from a hastily erected grandstand on Ujazdowski-Allee, where the foreign embassies and legations were located. On this street, colorful leaves still remained on the trees that graced the lawns of large Georgian mansions. Windows that had rattled from bomb blasts were dark with the grime of smoke but unbroken.

Horst von Bockman stood at attention beside his troops in the cool autumn afternoon as Hitler addressed them.

"On September first, at my order, you lined up to defend our Reich against the Polish attack. Today I greet the troops sent against fortified Warsaw. This day ends a battle that has given evidence of the best that is in German soldiery. We stand closer together than ever and we have cinched our helmets tighter. I know you, faithful to your belief in Germany, are prepared for any sacrifice!"

His words were greeted by a thunderous roar from the thousands of handpicked troops who had come to meet him. Would they be required to fight again? The German chancellor had been sending the West persistent hints that perhaps some settlement might be reached now that Poland was in the pocket of the Reich. There was some feeling that once again the British Prime Minister Chamberlain would look the other way and that France would simply suggest the whole matter be forgotten and the war called off. Already the theatres and nightclubs of Paris had reopened, and the wartime restrictions eased. The citizens of those allied nations worked to keep their daily routines as they had been in peacetime.

In Germany every man, woman, and child lived with the reality of war. The allies in the West lacked the determination to force a war over the dismemberment of a feudalistic nation like Poland, it was said. Having seen the gruesome face of war, Horst hoped now that Poland would be the last battle. He wondered what the citizens of Warsaw were thinking as they heard the cheers of their conquerors.

It was probable that even during the parade, not one Pole was aware of the presence of the German Führer in their conquered city. Cordons of German troops with fixed bayonets had closed off Polish access to all the buildings on the route from the airfield to Embassy Row. The houses and buildings had been cleaned out to rid them of any "suspicious elements."

After the Führer's speech, the route that took Hitler and Himmler back to the airfield passed the devastated National Museum, the Polish Foreign Office, and the Hotel Europjeski. The downtown shopping area had been demolished, with huge craters in the middle of the main streets and tram rails twisted like pretzels. In both the suburbs and the center of the city, deep trenches and tank blockades remained, made from overturned trolleys, automobiles, paving stones, and sandbags.

Horst von Bockman was among the honor companies that accompanied Hitler and Heinrich Himmler to the plane that would carry them back to Berlin. Hitler now turned to the international press corps and passed along a warning. His words were clearly meant for publication:

"Gentlemen, you have seen for yourselves what criminal folly it was to try to defend this city. I only wish that certain statesmen in other countries who seem to want to turn the whole of Europe into such a shambles as Warsaw could have an opportunity, as you have, to see the true meaning of war."

Hitler then turned his attention to a pretty, chestnut-haired woman who stood near the front of the crowd, among the cadre of American reporters.

Sergeant Fiske leaned closer to Horst and whispered, "The American woman trapped in Warsaw during the siege . . . a Fräulein like her alone with eighty-five thousand Polish soldiers. Not bad, eh?"

The weariness in her clear blue eyes reminded Horst of what he had seen in the faces of the conquered Poles. She met the gaze of the Führer fearlessly and without any trace of admiration for the leader of the German people.

Hitler admonished her, as though she somehow represented all those who had resisted his will in Warsaw. "So, now you see how unwise it was to oppose German might. They were fools. And you were foolish to remain with them."

She did not reply but continued to stare at him in silent defiance. Her expression caused the ranks of troops and the journalists around her to stir uneasily. Horst imagined that after this encounter, the American would be put on the next plane out of the Reich. Hitler prided himself on the adoration of women and his ability to charm them. This female journalist was clearly unmoved by his attention and unrepentant. Perhaps she had seen too much on the Warsaw side of the lines.

The Führer continued, raising his voice to the others in the crowd as he turned his back on the young woman. "These ruins stand as a lesson to all those who seek war with the German Reich. Those Polish leaders who incited their people to violence have brought this destruction upon themselves. To defy the will of Germany is suicide."

The statement was a literal truth for those who had led the futile Polish opposition in hopes that France and England would deliver them. The mayor of Warsaw, Stefan Starzynski, was now reported to have committed suicide after the fall of his city. It had been his shaky voice that had broadcast messages of hope and courage and finally desperate pleas for rescue. Known as "Stefan the Stubborn" after he declined to accept the German ultimatum, he had organized the civilian brigades and inspired the populace to stand its ground. The claim of suicide was the official version of his disappearance. But Starzynski had been a devout Catholic, which made suicide improbable. Horst had heard that the mayor met a different end at the hands of the SS.

As the silver trimotor lifted off, carrying the Führer and his henchman back to Berlin, Horst caught a ride back to Pilsudski Square. The Centrale Hotel, where junior officers were billeted, was only slightly damaged by bomb blasts. The windows in his room were cracked, and the brick facade was pocked by shrapnel. It was as if the artillery gunners had deliberately picked out this hotel as a kind of safe zone with the thought in mind that the German officers would need a place to sleep after Warsaw fell. Better to blow up a cathedral than a hotel.

Before the war, Horst had visited Warsaw a dozen times for the pleasure of it. Proud, joyful people had populated broad, brightly lit boulevards and stately homes. What he saw now sickened him.

Horst sent a wire to Katrina, telling her that he would be in Prussia for a short leave within a matter of days. He imagined her face when she got the news: ecstatic. But he felt no emotion even in the thought of home. He ate a tasteless meal in the company of officers who laughed too loudly and drank too much; then he walked past the armed guards in the lobby and out into the Warsaw twilight toward the Vistula River.

It was nearing curfew, so there were few Poles out on the streets. Here and there, beneath the watchful eyes of German soldiers on the street corners, small groups of people picked through the rubble, trying to salvage personal belongings. Without exception the black armband of mourning was on every Polish sleeve. Horst did not stop to ask if they were mourning the loss of family members or the loss of their nation. Their sad, weary faces displayed the privation they had endured during this descent into hell. When they looked up at him, their eyes were full of hate and bitterness. He was no longer a man; he was The Enemy.

Horst walked quickly toward the bank of the river and sat down on a heap of broken bricks. At home a view of the river had always comforted him . . . something about the slow current passing by. But there was no comfort here. Bits of debris bobbed on the flow. A fishing boat drifted past, belly-up, like a dead fish. The warehouses on the opposite bank were charred ruins.

He decided he would not tell Katrina about Warsaw. It had been one of her favorite cities. She shared with the Poles a love of the finest Arabian horses in the world. How many times had she struck up a conversation in a Warsaw café and ended up talking bloodlines until morning? If Katrina could see this, no doubt she would also wear a black armband.

His head ached. It had throbbed for days until he became accustomed to it. This was the first moment he had relaxed enough to identify the pain. He thought about the strong, gentle fingers of Katrina stroking his forehead. She would soothe away the ache he felt and make him forget what he had seen. The hands of Katrina would heal his inner wounds, and he would be whole again, proud again, a soldier for the Fatherland, ready to fight again without remorse.

He pushed his hat back and looked up at the sky. It was the only thing in Warsaw that was still beautiful, untouched. The western horizon was streaked with pastel banners that faded into star-flecked purple in the east.

He silently watched as the last light deepened into night. The approach of footsteps went unnoticed until a woman spoke from behind him.

"Get up!" she ordered in broken German. "Slowly, please, Herr Nazi. Herr butcher. I have a gun."

He stood, unsnapping the holster of his sidearm.

She heard the click and warned him, "Try it and I will shoot! I have nothing to lose. Drop your weapon. Now."

He obeyed.

"There's a good little Nazi." She moved nearer. "Kick it over to me."

He nudged the weapon just beyond her reach with the toe of his boot. Her voice was young. Horst could hear the fear as she spoke, although he could not see her face. Her shadowed form swayed a bit as she debated how best to retrieve the Luger.

"What do you want?" he ventured.

"Shut up!" she snapped.

"Surely there can be no benefit in murdering me. You will only get yourself shot in doing it."

"Being out after curfew is enough to get me killed, Herr Nazi. What more can they do to me for shooting you?"

"Good point." He laughed aloud at the insane logic of her predicament. "So. Are you prowling around in the dark to ambush Germans? What is your name?"

"Sophia," she answered without thinking, disarmed by the innocuous question. She seemed to consider von Bockman. "I have a child three miles from here near Muranow. I heard they were distributing bread near the Cathedral of St. John. I came for the bread. Night fell before I could get back."

"Did you get your bread?"

"Yes." She held up half a loaf as proof.

"Then perhaps we can be of some mutual service. I will see you safely to your home, if you will not shoot me."

Again the long silence of consideration. "Why would you . . . ?"

A powerful beam of light ruptured the darkness. The young woman cried out and shielded her eyes from the blinding glare. She had no weapon. Her precious bread fell to the ground. She dropped to her knees and scrambled to recover it.

"Halt or we shoot," commanded a voice out of the spotlight's glare.

Crouching like a cornered animal, she covered her head with her arms. Horst heard her whisper, "Poor Jules! Oh, Jules," and then her words were choked by a muffled sob.

"Are you all right, Captain?"

"Of course. This was nothing. Nothing," Horst replied indignantly. "She came for bread for her child and was caught out after curfew. She is not . . ."

Two patrolling SS stepped up, holding machine pistols at the ready, covering the Polish woman as if she were a rabid dog. "Thank you, Captain," one of them said smoothly. "We will take it from here."

"I . . . wait a moment," Horst said. "Surely she can be detained until daylight and then allowed to go home?"

"Of course, of course, Captain. If you will step aside, please."

Horst still stood, unmoving, between the SS patrolmen and the woman. The faces of the men seemed unconcerned; there was no anger or threat evident in their eyes.

"Come now, Captain, what do you take us for? Just stand aside, please. We will see that she is taken care of."

Horst nodded curtly, then looked down at her upturned face.

Her expression showed a glimmer of hope.

"You hear them? They will not hurt you," he said.

"Thank you, Herr Captain." Sophia rose to her knees as Horst reluctantly moved to the edge of the flashlight's glow.

In the same instant a blast of machine-gun fire tore through the Polish woman, throwing her back down the embankment into the Vistula.

Silence.

Horst stood wide-eyed and panting from the sudden violence of it. The black waters closed around the body. The loaf of bread, saturated with her blood, lay beside his Luger.

The two black-uniformed SS strode forward. One, a boy of eighteen, kicked the bread aside and retrieved Horst's weapon. "It seems we were just in time, Captain," commented the young man. Smoke from the barrel of his pistol curled up, encircling his grinning face. "It is dangerous to be out after dark. Two of our fellows were murdered last night by prostitutes. The Polish women are as dangerous as the men, you know. Just as fanatic. By the way, thank you for your quick wits. You disarmed her suspicions completely. It is so much easier if they do not think of trying to run—"

"That will be all." Horst cut him off and retrieved his cap from the heap of broken bricks. "She only wanted something to feed her child." He pointed to the proof of her intentions, then pushed past the SS guards.

"She should have gotten it in daylight."

"I will find my own way back," Horst said angrily, declining their offer of safe escort to the hotel.

⟡

The red-and-black Nazi flag hung from the window of Herr Flugelman's linen shop across from the house of Rabbi Lubetkin. A large sign in the window declared *Jews and Dogs Not Welcome*.

Rachel finished setting the table, then closed the curtains against the offending view.

"Mama." She glanced in the mirror at the yellow Star of David stitched on her dress. The Nazi bombs had ceased to fall on Warsaw, and yet lives continued to be blown apart. "Why has Herr Flugelman done this? He has lived in Poland. Sold Shabbat linens to us Jews as long as I can remember. Why, then?"

Mama's face was tight, her eyes downcast. "He is afraid."

"Afraid?"

"Of what they will do to his shop because he is here in the Jewish district. Afraid they will think he is also a Jew and that they will destroy his business."

"But who will buy from him now anyway? Gentiles don't come onto our street anymore."

Mama straightened the silverware. A lot of fuss for cabbage soup and bread, but it was Shabbat and so the tradition of linens and silver and fine china at the evening meal would be honored.

Mama remarked absently, "Herr Flugelman will have to move soon. Never mind. Never mind. So far we are still free."

Rachel gripped the back of a chair and inhaled deeply. "Mama, I have something to tell you." It sounded like a confession.

Mama looked up sharply. "What is it?"

"I sent a letter with Mikka when she went away to the church."

"A letter?"

"To the priest."

"And?"

"I asked him please to help us. Our family. Told him it wasn't fair that only Jewish girls got to go away and be safe. Told him about my brothers. About the baby and how afraid I was that the Hitlerites would kill him like the Egyptians killed the babies in the days of Moses."

"And?"

"I asked him to please pray for us. . . ."

"A good request made to a kind and good man."

"And I asked . . . please . . . that somehow if things got very bad for us here . . . if he would find some way to . . . to . . . save the baby." Rachel's voice cracked.

Mama said nothing. Her face was very sad as she stared at the silver Shabbat candlestick. She winced as though some deep pain coursed through her, then met Rachel's gaze. "Let's hope he got the letter before Mikka died, eh? Let's pray he read it and . . . and . . . we will pray he is not like Herr Flugelman, eh?"

◌

Lori:

I'm scared.

Captain and Frau Orde, and Alfie and I have been moved to a prison camp near a town called Mayzr.

I don't know where the Jewish boys are. We were separated on account of our British passports.

All day long today trains of cattle cars passed here. They are full of Polish soldiers . . . being taken to Siberia. One train pulled onto a siding. The prisoners were allowed out to have one cup of water each.

We talked through a barbed-wire fence to a Polish lieutenant of artillery. His eyes were sunken, his face a mask of hopelessness. He said his division got surrounded and cut off. They took a vote, and the whole division decided to surrender to the Russians instead of the Nazis.

Siberia is the result.

He had other news, too—maybe rumor, maybe true.

The Russians and Nazis have divided Poland between them. They even had a joint "victory" parade in Brest.

And there's still worse news. Captain Orde asked the lieutenant if he'd heard the names of any of the Nazi commanders.

The man said the Nazi frontline troops were being replaced by SS-Einsatztruppen, led by a General Heydrich.

Captain Orde said, "Oh, dear God," and bowed his head.

Lori, Heydrich is the one who said his unit does housecleaning—rounding up Jews, pastors, university professors, and other . . . undesirables.

You and I both know what that means.

I pray for your father every night.

We've heard stories about Polish Jews who fled east, only to be rounded up by the Russians and handed over to the Nazis!

We don't know where Peter Wallich and the others are.

And that's still not the worst.

That ugly commissar called Alfie "mentally deficient." So far they've left him with us because of his British passport . . . but they know Alfie and I aren't really English.

I'm scared. I'm writing this in secret, when Comrade Commissar and his Russians aren't around.

Alfie says he sees angels . . . but the only angel I can picture is you.

Pray hard.

All my love always,

Jacob

16

Death at the Burgerbraukeller

Georg Elser peered up and down the alleyway behind Munich's Burgerbraukeller, exactly as he had each night for the past month. Seeing no one, he placed the carefully filed and oiled key into the lock on the delivery entrance door and slipped through into the dark interior. Elser had made the journey through the storerooms to the stairs so many times that he needed no help from the flashlight to find the way.

At the sound of a low growl, Elser stopped and fumbled in his coat pocket. "Here, Ajax. Good boy," he called softly. The noise of the watch-dog's warning rumble changed to the thump of a friendly wag as the German shepherd recognized Elser's voice. A moment later Ajax was happily munching a sausage and Elser was taking the steps to the gallery two at a time.

The faint glow coming through the high windows in the beer hall's assembly room lighted the row of turned posts along the low railing of the balcony. Just ahead, in the center of the balustrade, loomed the brick pillar that supported both the gallery and the roof.

Now Elser switched on his flashlight, its lens covered with a blue handkerchief. The faint glow seemed no more than an errant beam of moonlight in the echoing hall. Using his pocketknife, Elser levered free a strip of molding and then snapped open a cleverly disguised panel in the back of the column.

The pale shine of the flashlight probed into the hollow of the sup-posedly solid pillar as Elser bent forward to examine his handiwork. The onetime watchmaker traced the wires leading from the batteries to the alarm clocks and from the clocks to the dull gleam of the brass artillery shell into which Elser had stuffed fifty pounds of high explosive.

He read the numerals on the faces of both the primary and the backup clocks and compared the position of the hands to his wrist-watch. "Running a touch fast," he murmured. He did a brief mental calculation, then breathed a sigh of relief. "It is all right," he whispered. "By nine tomorrow night it will only be fifteen minutes ahead . . . perhaps that is even better."

Satisfied that all was in order, Elser carefully closed the secret panel and replaced the molding. On a sudden impulse he bent forward again and placed his ear next to the pillar. The faint ticking that reached his hearing was softer than his own excited pulse.

՚Ⱳ

The sixteenth reunion of the Old Fighters of Hitler's Brownshirts promised to be a raucous affair. In the company of his comrades from the beer-hall putsch of 1923, the mighty Führer could relax, swap stories, and reminisce about the good old days. No foreign dignitaries to impress, no disapproving generals glowering around—nothing but pure adoration from the cadre of Hitler's earliest supporters.

Of course, in the fall of 1939, nothing was without political overtones, and no occasion for a public appearance was without its propaganda value. This night Hitler's address to his old cronies would also be broadcast to the Reich and the rest of the world.

The beer hall was crammed to capacity and saturated with a thick blue haze of cigar smoke and puddles of beer. The Old Fighters knew how to celebrate, and several foaming steins of lager had already sluiced down the throats of the party faithful before Chancellor Hitler made his appearance.

When at eight o'clock Hitler's booted step entered the room, all the chairs scraped hurriedly back, and a disorderly forest of tan sleeves popped up in ragged salute. His entry, twenty minutes earlier than expected, caught the audience by surprise. The band on the stage hastily blared out the "Horst Wessel" song while everyone remained standing at attention. The Führer crossed the hall to the lectern just below the balcony, which was also packed with eager spectators.

Taking his place directly in front of the Nazi banner that hung from a massive brick pillar, Hitler approached the bank of microphones and began to speak. He recalled for the crowd those memorable days before the Nazi Party had come to power, and he extolled the patience and faithfulness of the Old Fighters. Soon tears rolled down many cheeks.

He had their full attention when he started to speak of the list of German grievances against the Western democracies: "The German people have been injured, shamefully wronged. No redress has been offered to our suffering, no correction made of injustice. The British and the French attack our unity of pride and purpose in the name of freedom. What hypocrisy! Where is the fairness in that odious document called the Versailles Treaty? Where is the freedom for the German people to fulfill our destiny?"

He paused to let the magnitude of the injustice sink in. "England and France bear a heavy burden for provoking Poland into attacking us . . . let them pay close attention to the consequences!"

A roar of approval went up from the crowd, and five minutes of *Sieg Heils* laden with smoke and beery breath rocked the chandeliers. Even the Führer seemed overcome by the response, for he began to wrap up his talk after only fifty-five minutes instead of the customary hour and a half.

His cherished comrades in arms begged him to stay and drink with them, reliving more of the old days, but he would not be persuaded. By ten minutes after nine, the last salute had been offered and the last hail to victory shouted to the rafters. Chancellor Hitler, much to the disappointment of the Old Fighters, got in his armor-plated Mercedes and returned to the Munich train station.

Elaine Snow entered the lobby of the Insel Hotel on the German side of Lake Constance at 8:30 PM. Her assignment was a simple one. Glued beneath the binding of a volume of Goethe was a Swiss passport for the man Georg Elser. She had been forewarned that Elser was a strange little man. The photograph on his forged passport showed a dark-haired, glowering face. He was missing his little finger on his left hand if she needed another way to identify him. He would recognize her by the red cape and matching beret she wore.

They were to meet here as if they were old friends. She would do most of the talking, as usual. The fugitives were nearly always too nervous to eat or converse with her, so she kept up a running monologue about her daughter, Juliette, and their home in Luxembourg. It was as though she was continuing one long conversation that had stretched on for three years. If all of her clients were somehow miraculously gathered together in the same room, they could each recite some small part of the history of Elaine's daughter from the age of two.

After enjoying dinner and her own monologue in the converted cloister of the old Dominican monastery, Elaine would give Georg Elser the book with his passport sealed inside. She would bid him good night and then cross back over the frontier to Switzerland. From there the fellow was on his own. It was likely she would never see him again.

A train ride back to Luxembourg City, and Elaine would be home by tomorrow night and back in her role as an entertainer, a singer. It was that simple. She had done the same thing a hundred times in the last three years, each time allowing German and Austrian Jews to escape to the neutrality of Switzerland with new identities.

Tall and fair, she had the look of purest Aryan breeding. The guards on both sides of the border liked to see her coming. Long ago she had offered the explanation for her frequent visits to Lake Constance. "I have family there." No one guessed that her "family" included anyone on the run from the Nazis. Nor could they imagine that Elaine Snow was a Jewess born in the French province of Alsace just before Kaiser Wilhelm started the last war with France. Her two uncles had been killed in that struggle. When Hitler came to power, Elaine declared that any enemy of the Nazis was a friend of hers. Her present secret occupation of courier paid quite well, but she liked to think that her motives were based more on conscience than money.

The work had become more difficult since the invasion of Poland and the declaration of war. This afternoon, Friedrich, the elderly German border guard who regularly stamped her passport at the crossing, warned her that soon the Gestapo would send a man to look over his shoulder. He was not happy with the intrusion. Life had been pleasant for him so far. He might ask to be transferred to the regular army if the secret police became regular fixtures at the little outpost he had manned for twenty-two years.

Perhaps the border guard did not know that the entire shoreline of Lake Constance was already crawling with General Reinhard Heydrich's brutal watchmen. The neutral Swiss side was just as contaminated as the German side.

Now in the Cloister Restaurant, Elaine sipped her wine and smiled toward the table near hers where two men in dark suits ate their sauerbraten without speaking to one another. Gestapo. Clearly. She could tell by the way they cast sideways glances at her. She knew her looks—what others called "strikingly blond and beautiful"—garnered attention, but she had learned how to use that to her advantage. After all, these men were only sour-faced swine who had learned their beer swilling and table manners in a beer hall in Munich.

The radio was playing in the lobby. The growling voice of Herr Hitler penetrated the pleasant atmosphere of the Cloister Restaurant as the Führer vomited his hatred for the West at the annual gathering of the Old Fighters. Hitler's broadcasts were required fare these days on the

German side of the border. Everyone had to listen or at least pretend to be interested. Elaine raised her head as though every word was dear to her. When he reached the end, she nodded in approval at the resounding heils that followed.

The Führer had finished his anniversary tirade early this year, the announcer said. He was leaving the Munich beer hall well before schedule. Elaine was certain that this was a grave disappointment to the party faithful, but she was relieved to have the music of Bach replace the sounds of the reunion. She would enjoy her poached salmon in peace as soon as the absent Georg Elser appeared.

Twenty minutes later the waiter poured her another glass of wine and asked if she would still like to wait before ordering.

"He will be here," she replied pleasantly. "He is always late. I will order for both of us. I have a train to catch at ten." She ordered trout for Elser and salmon for herself, then sipped her wine as the radio concert was abruptly interrupted by the trembling voice of an announcer.

> *"Just moments ago, as our beloved Führer drove away from the Burgerbraukeller in Munich, a terrible explosion rocked the hall where hundreds were gathered to honor him. The toll of dead and wounded is unknown. Guarded by fate, the Führer is totally unharmed by the blast, which was obviously designed to take his life! More news will be forthcoming. Heil Hitler!"*

The Gestapo agents sat up in alarm. They whispered frantically to one another across the table. The shorter, more Neanderthal-looking of the duo stood, dug in his pocket for change, and scurried off to find a telephone.

Elaine crooked her finger at the waiter. "My friend is obviously delayed. I will eat without him. I have a train to catch," she explained again.

At her words, the ears of the remaining Gestapo agent perked up.

Elaine sighed heavily. It was plain that this abortive attempt to kill the German leader was going to make her work as courier more difficult. Tonight the Bahnhof would be overrun with official slime, tearing out the lining of every coat and slitting open tubes of toothpaste to check for diamonds and secret messages. No one would escape the scrutiny. Perhaps if Hitler had died in the blast, she might consider the outcome worth the inconvenience. But at best, a few dozen Nazi drunks lay smashed in the rubble, and Hitler was free to pursue his vengeance. Now Elaine would have to endure a strip search by some hairy-lipped Nazi matron. Most unpleasant.

She ate her salmon. The béarnaise sauce, which had been excellent before everything wonderful had been rationed in Germany, was mediocre.

The apelike Gestapo agent came back to the table but did not sit down. He leaned over his companion and spoke in hushed, urgent tones. Then he turned toward Elaine and swaggered to her table.

"May I join you, Fräulein Snow?"

The salmon made a knot in her stomach. So here it was. So soon? She was not even trying to cross the frontier into Switzerland.

"It seems that you know my name, but I do not know yours."

"Allow me." He smiled. His teeth were stained with tobacco. "Herr Gustaf."

"I am expecting a friend, Herr Gustaf."

"Yes?" He sat down, not heeding her polite protest.

"He has been delayed."

"We have heard." He was toying with her now. Had he learned the information from the Cloister waiter, or was there something else? He placed a hand on the red leather cover of Goethe. "You enjoy fine literature, I see."

"Herr Gustaf, really." She blotted her mouth with the linen napkin and placed it beside the plate of unfinished salmon. "If my friend should see me here with another man . . ."

"Ah, but he will not, Fräulein Snow." He held the book up and flipped through the pages.

Her heart pounded faster. She tried to swallow but could not. Where was Elser? What had happened to him?

"I have a train to catch."

"I do not think so, Fräulein. Not a train out of Germany, at any rate." Picking up a butter knife, the Gestapo agent pried the corner of the endpaper.

The room swam around Elaine. She feigned indignation. "What are you doing? A friend asked me to give the book to Herr Elser. What are you—?"

"To Herr Georg Elser, Fräulein Snow?"

"Georg. Yes. The book is a gift from . . ."

The battered Swiss passport fell onto the table. "Well, well. Just where Herr Elser said it would be, Fräulein Snow." Herr Gustaf narrowed his eyes and considered her with amusement. "We picked him up a few minutes ago at the Bahnhof. Frightened little fellow. He had a few clock gears in his pocket and a postcard of the beer hall in Munich that has just blown up. Naturally we were alerted to be on the lookout for anyone attempting to cross the frontier tonight."

"I do not know what you're talking about." She stood and tossed a few bills on the table to cover the cost of her meal. Now every head in the dining room pivoted toward her. The second agent approached and, with crossed arms, blocked any retreat.

"We have been watching you for some time. Hoping you would lead us to a trail of traitors. How long have you been at your work? A Jew, are you not?"

"I am a citizen of Luxembourg. I protest this arrogant—"

"You are in the Reich now, Fräulein. It is best you come quietly," Herr Gustaf whispered. "You are under arrest, I fear. There is a train waiting . . . to take us all back to Munich."

❧

The rain that had fallen on Paris for a week finally stopped. A thin glaze of ice coated the bare branches of the trees that lined the River Seine. Mist floated up from the water, shrouding the two islands in the river that formed the oldest part of the city of Paris.

Ile de la Cité, crowned with Notre Dame Cathedral and the crenulated towers of government buildings, resembled a great ship moored by bridges between the Left and Right Banks of the Seine. Ile St. Louis, a quiet, residential island populated by wealthy Parisians, seemed like a smaller ship tethered behind Notre Dame. The two islands were linked together by the bridge known as Pont St. Louis. And together, the islands, known simply as the Cité and l'Ile, linked the distant past to the present.

At No. 19 Quai d'Anjou was a large four-story stone house on Ile St. Louis facing the Right Bank of Paris. Built in 1658 for the mistress of a bishop, it had in later years housed a succession of generals, poets, and the American statesman Benjamin Franklin. In 1849 the house became the Paris residence of a prosperous wine merchant named Chardon.

This afternoon, ninety years later, his great-great-grandson, Colonel Andre Chardon, looked out from the window of the study. A carload of policemen were just driving away, having returned Andre's houseguest. Andre turned to regard the thin figure of Richard Lewinski, perched on a settee near the fire.

The pale man with the explosion of red hair was hunched over, playing with a loop of string. He resembled a woodpecker plucking at a stolen bit of twine. The gas mask, which he had been wearing while walking along Boulevard St. Michel, was beside him on the couch.

At least Lewinski had been able to remember Andre's name when the gendarme stopped him for questioning. The police had returned Lewinski to the house on Quai d'Anjou, where Andre convinced them that the eccentric mathematician really did suffer from allergies and wore the mask against the fumes of Paris automobiles, not for some sinister purpose.

"Richard, you must wait for me if you want to leave the house," Andre requested, "or I will have my driver take you. You must think of your own safety."

Lewinski glanced up from the complicated eight-sided figure he had just constructed from the string. "Safety, Andre? You have always made me feel safe here in Paris. You know that. Why, back in our days at the Sorbonne you—"

Andre interrupted the reminiscence. "That is what I am trying to say, Richard. I will see that you are protected, if you will not wander off."

From the halfhearted nod that was Lewinski's only reply, Andre knew that his message had not gotten through. He sighed heavily as Lewinski headed back down the stairs to what had become his apartment. What a responsibility, and all because Lewinski had specifically asked for Andre when he approached the French Embassy in Poland to request asylum.

Andre was still musing about his friendship with the gifted engineer when the housekeeper announced that Colonel Gustave Bertrand had arrived. Minutes later Andre and the colonel joined Lewinski in the basement apartment.

A large wooden cabinet, open at the top and front, perched on a worktable. Trailing colored wires and black electrical cords and exhibiting shiny metal disks and a hand crank, the device looked like someone had set off a bomb in an organ grinder's instrument.

"The work goes well?" Bertrand inquired. "It progresses?"

Lewinski gave no sign that he had heard the question. An uncomfortable silence stretched into several minutes, finally punctuated by a piercing cackle from the scientist. "It is five! I knew they would not stop with three or four! Two more wheels gives them almost 12 million combinations instead of only eighteen thousand! Can you imagine?"

"Does this mean that your work is progressing?" Bertrand demanded. "Yes or no?"

"What? Oh, yes, yes, definitely advancing." Lewinski dismissed the inquiry with a flutter of his hand and was instantly engrossed again in his study of a fistful of wires.

"How does this thing work, anyway?" asked Bertrand, stretching out his hand toward the cabinet.

Lewinski glanced up from weaving his tangled filaments. "I would not touch that if I were you. Curiosity killed the cat."

"Is he kidding?" Bertrand asked.

Andre could only shrug in reply. "We do not want to upset him."

The two men retreated up the stairs, leaving Lewinski to continue manipulating a project that seemed no more than a colossally overgrown version of his loop of string.

"Are you certain that he is a gifted scientist, or just a crazy one?" Bertrand asked Andre.

"Bear in mind that SS General Heydrich wants Richard dead. Hopes he is dead. Richard was employed at the highest level of the factory that built the Enigma code machines for Wehrmacht. That should tell us something about the value he had in Germany. If Heydrich knew Richard was here . . ."

"Wandering around Paris . . . lost . . ."

"No matter how it appears, Richard Lewinski is the best mind in the world at what he does," Andre soothed. "Remember, he worked at Princeton with Einstein."

"Why do I not feel reassured?" commented Bertrand dryly. "Have you ever tried to make sense of Professor Einstein's writings? But enough of this, Andre. I have another reason for coming to see you today. It is necessary for you to go to England."

"England? But how, Gustave? I can't leave Lewinski alone for more than an hour without him wandering off. Why just today—"

"I know all about it. I will supply some men to watch the house around the clock. If he gets out, they will follow and return him safely."

"Richard cannot work under scrutiny. He is like a child. He says his best ideas come when he's riding the Ferris wheel at the Tuilleries. You cannot put a guard around a mind like that. Richard will not have it. You will have to call my brother, Paul."

"Will not have it?"

"He cannot be made to feel like a prisoner. We were children together. His father and mine taught at the Sorbonne."

"Right." Bertrand wiped perspiration from his brow.

"What is so important in England?" Andre changed the subject as they entered the study.

"You know that British Intelligence is also working on Enigma. Colonel Menzies of MI6 wishes to hear about our friend's progress and will share what they have. If your mad scientist produces the miracle we are hoping for, we will be able to read all the German transmittals . . . every battle plan transmitted from their High Command, every Luftwaffe deployment, every U-boat directive . . . but we must know how the machine has been modified."

"And the British?"

"They have two machines and are trying to reason out the modifications by taking those devices apart. They want to confer about it."

"They always do."

Bertrand cleared his throat nervously. "And there is something else, Andre. . . . Sit down."

Andre obeyed, settling into a padded leather chair opposite Bertrand. "What is it, Bertrand? Am I being demoted?" He tried to joke, but something was terribly wrong.

"No." Bertrand patted his pockets, looking for a smoke. "I know it has been a long time since you and Elaine—"

"Elaine Snow?"

Bertrand nodded, then bit his lip as if searching for the right words. "She has been arrested."

"Elaine?"

"Gestapo. In Constance. German side of the frontier. It was nothing really. She was acting as courier. Taking a passport to a German. Well, the Gestapo caught up with her. Accused her of being part of the Munich beer-hall plot."

"Ridiculous. She would not harm a fly."

"Hitler is no fly."

"What happened? What was she sent in to do?"

"It was a passport. Just like a thousand others, more or less."

"We've got to approach them. Pay a ransom."

"And if we do so?"

"Maybe there is some chance."

"But, Andre . . . she confessed."

"Confessed!" Andre bellowed. "What did they do to her?"

"If we approach the Nazis in this instance, all of France will be implicated. Herr Hitler has a keen interest in the case. He wants her shot. His ego needs to believe that there was a conspiracy. She has a perfect background he is looking to blame: a French Jewess. You see how it is."

Andre could hardly breathe. "You are telling me she is going to be executed? Just like that? She has . . . a child."

"Yes. We are aware. I am sorry. But there is nothing to be done. I wanted to tell you myself."

Andre covered his face with his hands. "Now you have done your duty. Leave me to mine. Go away, Bertrand. Just go away."

17

Not All Is As It Seems

For a while after her return to England, Josie Marlow wore the borrowed clothes of a fellow newswoman. But she was hopelessly out of style in wartime London.

A cartoon appeared on the London news kiosks, courtesy of *Punch* magazine, to sum up the autumn British fashion craze: A tall, bony-kneed Highlander, dressed in his kilt, observed an Englishwoman who was clothed in her new khaki uniform. The caption read, with thick Scottish burr: *"M'gawd, womin, ye look turrrrible!"*

War had a curious leveling effect on ladies' dresses in London. Khaki on women suddenly became fashionable. Josie had lost everything but the clothes on her back in Poland. Circumstances had elevated her title from foreign correspondent to war correspondent. And war correspondents, even from neutral countries, were all having military-style uniforms made up by the tailors on Saville Row.

Unlike her male journalistic counterparts, Josie did not have the funds for such extravagance. Gold braid and tasseled epaulets were beyond her means. The Mussolini-look just did not suit her. So she went to Moss Bros. & Co. Ltd., 20 King Street in London, where advantageous terms for uniforms had been arranged by the Associated Press. There she was sensibly clothed on the AP expense account.

For a total of thirty-nine pounds, seven shillings, and threepence, she was fitted with two tunics, two skirts, a uniform cap, a greatcoat, four blouses, four pairs of stockings, regulation shoes, tie, and gloves. Undergarments were extra. Not willing to have some AP accountant know how many bras and panties she owned, she paid for those items out of her own pocket.

It saved the problem of picking out an entirely new daytime wardrobe, Josie told herself. It would simplify packing, would it not? And when news of this European fashion disaster got back to the States, surely every woman would rise up with one voice and declare that America must enter the war! The military might of the U.S. must make the world safe again for the fashions of Schiaparelli! It was indeed possible that men would be more inspired to go to fight for a woman dressed in Schiaparelli than for a woman clothed by Moss Brothers!

Ah, well. The whole world was topsy-turvy. She gazed into the mirror of the tailor shop and muttered the words of the Scot in his kilt. "Josephine, ye look terrible!" She now appeared identical—almost—to every other young service-age female in London. Large or small, buxom or flat-chested, pretty or just pretty homely, in a dim room they were hard to tell apart.

Josie stitched the press badges onto the shoulders of tunics, blouses, and her greatcoat. She was official, at last. She returned her borrowed clothes to Canadian newswoman Rhonda Grafton, who was now also decked out in Moss Brothers fashion. Rhonda, who had gained weight since she came to England, let Josie keep the cobalt blue evening dress. Rhonda informed her she must wear it in Paris if ever there was an occasion and if the French had not turned sensible like the English.

So this comprised Josie's entire wardrobe: the uniforms, the underwear, the cobalt blue evening dress. Pitiful indeed.

It would take a man with imagination to look through the khaki exterior that sashayed up Fleet Street and down Oxford Circus and through the revolving doors of Harrods.

Rich girls bought their uniforms from Harrods. They paid much more, but the extra expense was wasted. The effect was still khaki. Even the word seemed appropriate to the drabness of the color. *Khaki. Khaki. Khaki.* Say it fast, and it sounded like someone retching.

෨

"So." Murphy settled into the booth across from Mac at The Green Man pub. "Elisa wants you to come to supper tonight."

"Can't."

"Is it Eva?"

"Is it that obvious?"

"Hard to miss. You'd have to be blind not to notice. She's a looker all right."

"And I'm trying not to look. She's a kid. Just twenty-two. I'm almost ten years older than her, Murphy."

"War has packed a few years of wisdom into callow youth." Murphy sipped his warm Coke as Mac nursed a pint of stout.

"It's not just that. There's someone else. . . . You know Josephine Marlow."

Murphy's eyes raised in surprise. "Danny Marlow's widow?"

"Look, Danny and I were great friends. He was some kind of heel when it came to the way he treated her, but me and Danny were pals all the same. He kept Josie's picture in his wallet. I saw it every time he opened it to pay some Spanish barmaid for her favors." Mac winced. "So, after Danny was killed . . . I wrote Josie. Wrote her a lot. When she came to Europe, I got to know her. Sort of fell for her in a way." Mac shrugged. "Once I started down that road and as much as told her I cared about her—put myself in line after Danny you might say—how can I meet somebody in a convoy escaping from Warsaw and fall head over heels?" He slugged the last of his stout and shook his head in disgust. "I'm as bad as Danny Marlow if that's the case."

Murphy scratched his chin. "How does she feel about you?"

"Which one?"

"Josie, to start."

"I dunno. She made it back, thank God. I'm meeting her today at the Langham. I'm going to ask her. It's the right thing to do."

"You love her?"

"I dunno. Maybe. I worry about her. I always have. When she was Danny's wife and that's all I knew about her, I worried. I mean, married to a guy like Danny."

"Okay. How does Eva feel about you?"

"Dunno. I'm trying not to ask. Trying not to let her tell me. She's so young. Innocent, like. And I'm so . . . you know what I mean, Murphy. My hide has been nailed to the barn door a long while. I'm set in my ways. I mean, how did you know? With Elisa?"

"Couldn't get her out of my mind."

"Yeah? Well, how can I spend months thinking about Josie Marlow, thinking about taking the plunge and then—now—Eva comes along?" Mac glanced at his wristwatch. "There. Typical. See? I'm late." He tossed a few coins on the table. "Listen. Thanks for the care, Murphy. Just wish I had it in me to settle down like you and Elisa. But . . . you know?"

"Good luck. See you at the office."

Spurs clicked against the floor of the Berlin Gestapo Headquarters as SS General Reinhard Heydrich sauntered toward the film-screening room.

Mousy and innocuous in appearance, Gestapo Chief Heinrich Himmler sat in his wooden rocking chair and cleaned his glasses.

"Heil Hitler, Heydrich." Himmler did not bother to look up as Heydrich entered the Spartan room. "Mein Gott, Heydrich, take your spurs off. Do you think you are a cowboy?"

Heydrich sat down hard and raised his legs to imbed the spurs in the arm of Himmler's chair. "What is it you want, Herr Reichsführer?" Heydrich asked in a bored tone. "And this had better be worthwhile! I have plans tonight with a pretty Mädchen destined for great achievements in your breeding program." He tossed his gloves at Himmler. "So you see? This had better be important. I was about to make a significant contribution to Lebensborn tonight. Maybe create another little Reinhard; who knows?"

Himmler stared at him with amusement. Muscular, athletic, and brutish, Reinhard Heydrich was the exact opposite of the soft-looking former schoolmaster who now ran the German Secret Police. But Heydrich was also the German ideal of manhood.

"It is good to see that you are eager to populate the Fatherland, Heydrich. But here is one thing you may find almost as interesting as copulation."

"Impossible."

At that, Himmler raised his hand and snapped his fingers. Instantly the room was darkened. The ticking of the projector from the projection booth sounded like a time bomb. The silent images of an American newsreel appeared on the screen.

"It is the American ambassador to Poland. Herr Biddle. He left Warsaw with a caravan of automobiles all stuffed with frightened people. . . . " Himmler lightheartedly narrated the scene displaying a coatless Biddle helping to paint *USA* on the top of a vehicle. The next picture cut to the low approach of a Messerschmidt as it sprayed the road and scattered refuges in every direction.

"Yes?" Heydrich crossed his arms and sighed. "So the Luftwaffe chased the American ambassador. Amusing, but my Fräulein is waiting, Himmler. Will you get to it?"

Himmler held up his finger as if in readiness to make the point. The camera panned over the dust from the road and lingered on the broken bodies of slaughtered refugees. It caught the stunned and terrified expressions on the faces of the survivors, finally moving in on a bizarre figure wearing a gas mask. For just an instant the mask was raised, revealing the taut features of a man.

At this moment, Himmler shouted to the unseen projectionist. "Halt!"

The eyes of the frozen image stared in horror directly at Himmler and Heydrich.

"Where did you get this?" Heydrich sat up with a start, his spurs clattering on the floor.

"Can your Fräulein wait now, Heydrich?"

"Richard Lewinski!"

"Quite." Himmler sat back with satisfaction. "Escaped from Poland under the protection of the Americans."

"But . . . his colleagues from the University in Warsaw informed my staff . . ."

"It is well-known that men under extreme torture will say anything, make up any lie they think their captors wish to hear. His colleagues in Warsaw knew you wanted Lewinski dead, so they said he was killed. It made their deaths quicker. You will have to teach your men more delicate methods of extracting information. It is the hope of life that makes a prisoner tell the truth when pain is inflicted."

"So Lewinski is alive," Heydrich said in amazement.

"Last seen in Budapest."

"How did you come by this film? Astounding!"

"The newsreel was shown in every theatre in America, my dear Reinhard. Uncensored. Taken by an American cameraman. A member of our Bund in New York runs a moving-picture theatre there. He had the bright idea that the film might be some use to us. It seemed worthwhile to know who was important enough to catch a ride out of Poland with the American ambassador. Your Lewinski was the only member of Biddle's entourage who remained an enigma, if you will pardon my double entendre. I recognized him instantly, the first moment I viewed the film."

"He is still in Budapest?"

"We have a number of agents working on it. My guess is that he is back in America by now with his old friend Albert Einstein. Possibly as you said, he is no threat to our project. But who can say? I suppose his potential is enough . . . considering his outspoken opposition to the Reich."

Heydrich's mouth was a hard line of determination. "He must be liquidated."

"If he is in America, the matter is easily taken care of with such a brilliant idiot as Lewinski. He will step off a curb and under the wheels of a bus perhaps. Drown in his bathtub. Or perhaps slit his wrists?"

"That is best. Suicide. His wife and daughter died in Warsaw. That much has been verified. He had no other life except for his mathematics.

Reason enough to kill himself. We have agents in America capable of carrying out this action?"

"If Lewinski arrives on the doorstep of his American colleagues from Princeton . . . if he wires them or telephones giving his whereabouts, he is a dead man. There are three men—American Jews—whom Lewinski worked with closely during his student days at Princeton. Each one is being carefully watched. Telephone conversations monitored. Everything that can be done is being done. Lewinski will one day make contact with one of his old American friends and then . . . " Himmler touched his hand to the hilt of his dagger.

"Keep me informed."

"That was my intention." Himmler gave a tight-lipped smile. "So! Enjoy your evening, Heydrich. My compliments to the Fräulein. Heil Hitler."

Beyond the khaki, the sandbags in Piccadilly, and the air-raid shelters, except for blackouts and handbags containing gas masks, London seemed quite unaffected by the war.

The salon of London's Langham Hotel across from the BBC was crowded with radio-broadcast staff taking afternoon tea. Josephine Marlow shoved her trembling hands deeper into the pockets of her greatcoat as the maitre d' greeted her.

"Your reservation, madame?"

"Thank you. I'm meeting someone. Mac McGrath." She looked past him, scanning the opulent room that hummed with conversation punctuated by the clink of teacups.

At the mention of Mac's name the expression on the face of the maitre d' turned sour. "Yes." He sniffed. "Mr. McGrath. Indeed." Without further conversation, he regally led Josie through a mass of tables peopled by older men in pin-striped business suits and older, nonmilitary-type women with fox stoles draped from their shoulders.

In the far corner of the oval room, Mac was seated at a small table behind a potted palm. The teapot and cups were already in place. He was out of sight of the elegant crowd but clearly not out of the thoughts of the Langham staff.

Dressed in brown corduroy trousers, a blue tweed jacket, and a turtleneck sweater with a comical bow tie, Mac looked decidedly out of place. Josie guessed that he had come without the tie and had been fitted with a spare from the Langham cloakroom.

Battling the potted palm, he stood awkwardly at her approach. With the build and features of a prizefighter, his usually cocky expression was filled with remorse as he held out her chair.

"Good to see you, Jo. I mean . . . I'm glad . . . really glad you're . . ."

"It's all right, Mac." She tried to console him with a smile, but she kept her coat on and her hands in her pockets. It would not help his tender conscience if he saw that her hands were trembling.

"Look—" he lowered his voice and leaned toward her—"I didn't know you hadn't left, or you know I never would've—"

"Please, Mac. Nobody's blaming you. And see . . . I'm okay." She took her napkin and shook it out, then laid it on her lap. But she clasped her hands together under the table.

He had to say it. "You told me you were leaving. I telephoned Mike at Warsaw AP. He thought you had gone on the night train. You know? I mean, I thought you were out of there before the first bombs dropped. I showed up at the embassy, and a bunch of us all made it out together. Except you. What happened? Where'd you go?"

"It doesn't matter. I just stayed behind." Should she tell him that she had decided to stay over in Warsaw one more day? that she had intended to call him that morning and tell him she didn't mean any of the things she'd said?

"Well, look." He poured the steaming tea and then picked up the dainty cup in his large square hand. "I want you to know . . . I don't have any hard feelings. I know what I said that night. I was hurt . . . angry . . . I didn't have a right to be, but that's the way it goes. Anyway, I thought about it all the way to the Rumanian border. Nazi planes spitting bullets at us like mad hornets . . . anyway, you're right. This is no kind of life for me to inflict on somebody like you."

"Mac, please don't—"

He held up his hand. "No. Lemme finish. You're a wonderful dame—girl, I mean—beautiful and classy. You deserve something better than what you had. Danny used to say that. In Barcelona, the night before he was . . . well, that night we got plastered. That was the night he pulled out your picture . . . and told me about you. He said if anything ever happened to him, I should tell you to get hooked up with a banker or an insurance salesman. Anything but another journalist. He was right. But when I met you face-to-face, I couldn't help wishing that I was a banker instead of what I am." He tugged on the bow tie. "But I'm not . . . and I fell in love with you." His face was pained. "Then when I heard you were still in Warsaw, I just about went crazy. If I hadn't asked you to come . . ."

"I would have been there anyway. I had my own story to write; didn't I?" Josie did not dare pick up the cup. She was trembling so badly that the contents would have spilled. She looked away, trying to think about something besides Danny and Spain and Mac and Warsaw.

"I think you should go home."

"I will. Back to Paris. But I've got an assignment here. The evacuee children. And then I can go home to Paris."

"Not Paris. I mean *home*. Back to the States. Back to teaching English lit and a quiet, normal life again. Out of that getup." He gestured at her uniform.

"I see you're not impressed by the latest style." She laughed. Of course Mac would hate seeing women in uniform. And from the look of his clothes, he would also be the last journalist in Europe to visit a tailor.

He ignored her attempt to change the subject. "A girl like you . . . needs to meet some nice guy and have kids."

Josie smiled, hoping he would not see what a knife his words were in her heart. "I've grown accustomed to this getup, as you call it. And Paris is home. And I . . . I'm not interested in meeting a nice ordinary guy and having kids."

"Why not?"

"I was happy with Danny. No one can ever replace that."

Mac inhaled deeply. Now she had slipped in a knife. "No, I guess not. I hoped maybe . . . for a while I thought maybe I could make you happy like he did."

She wanted to put her hand on his arm, to comfort him somehow, to let him know that maybe with time something might come of what she felt for him. But she would not answer him with hope that she could not find in herself.

"Maybe someday, but it's just too soon, Mac. I told you that."

"Well, we've come full circle, haven't we? I'm talking like a first-class chump. Sitting here pretending to like tea, when it would have suited me better to meet you at The Green Man pub with a pint of Guinness in my fist."

She laughed. "This does seem out of character."

"For me maybe, but not you. This suits you. You know that. And I didn't mean to bring me into your life again. You were right and honest with me from day one. I know all that now, and I won't bother you about it anymore. I guess that's what I wanted to tell you. That and . . . that I'm glad you made it outta there."

"Me too."

He checked his watch and tugged the bow tie loose. "Well, that's that. I gotta run. An appointment across the street at the BBC. The censor is looking at my film. They always cut the best stuff. Maybe I can slip the guy a bribe. So. Maybe I'll see you sometime. Who knows, huh?"

He was on his feet, pushing his way out from the potted palm. Kissing her lightly on the cheek, he strode out of the room and tossed the tie at the maitre d' without looking back.

18

A Surprise Move in the Game

From his window on the second floor, Andre Chardon's younger brother, Captain Paul Chardon, looked out across the athletic fields and the stables behind the Ecole de Cavalerie. It was not a very distinguished view, such as Colonel Larousse's office provided of the formal cobblestone square at the front. Paul's panorama was less of the tradition and ceremony of the school and more of the boyishness of the students.

Just now, for instance, there was a wholehearted game of capture the flag in progress. A mound of horse manure, covered with a purifying blanket of early snow, represented the besieged fort. The object of the struggle was an improvised flag made of toweling on which had been painted a blue cross of Lorraine. One team, marked by scraps of someone's blue shirt in their back pockets, defended the hillock against the red contingent.

The leader of the blue squad, seventeen-year-old Gaston, with his wrestler's build and personality, had sensibly deployed his troops in concentric rings around the base of the hill. Each of the three guarding circles had four piles of snowballs so that a supply of ammunition was within easy reach.

Opposing him as chief of the reds was a fellow cadet captain who was growing a scruffy beard to make himself look older: Gaston's best friend, Sepp. The forces belonging to Sepp launched their assault en masse across the open field against the south face of the embankment, ignoring the other sides of the hill.

From Paul's vantage point, it seemed that Gaston's defenders had a two-to-one numerical advantage. Why was Sepp's red team so small? He opened the window in order to hear as well as see.

There were yells of bravado and shouts of disappointment. Three of the reds went down, pelted by a quantity of snowballs from the higher elevation, but then Sepp's advance broke through the lowest line of Gaston's defense and killed three blues by ripping off their cloth pieces.

Commander Gaston, seeing his front threatened, called for the unoccupied defenders to shift around to the south side of the heap to help drive off the enemy. Paul noticed that Sepp did not press home his attack, content to stay at the extreme edge of the range and keep the blue team busy.

In another minute, Paul saw the full development of Sepp's strategy. From behind a tangled thicket of wagons and farm equipment farthest from the mound came a rush of the remaining reds. Led by good-natured Raymond, speediest and, at sixteen, youngest of the cadet captains, the wave of new attackers was halfway up the hill before Gaston had seen the danger.

A furious battle ensued. The blues, caught between the two foes, had to fight on twin fronts at once. Gaston bellowed for courage, for not giving ground, but his troops were forced backward. Tangled with each other and unable to retrieve their supply of snowballs lower on the hill, they fell to well-placed shots and the speed of the assault.

Raymond sprinted past the last ring of defenders, seized the flag, and scampered back down the hill and out of reach of the angry Gaston. The game broke into a free-for-all, in which everyone threw snow missiles at everyone else. Gaston wore himself out chasing a grinning Raymond, who taunted him with the flag, always staying just a few yards ahead.

⁂

The mess hall was oak paneled and had high ceilings; mounted racks of antlers made it resemble an ancient hunting lodge. Paul Chardon gathered the cadet captains around him at the dinner table. "What did you learn from the game this afternoon?"

The three boys glanced at each other.

"Were we supposed to learn something?" Gaston blurted. "We thought it was just for fun."

"True." Paul nodded. "But it may be that even play contains valuable lessons. Sepp?"

"I suppose I learned that strategy is as important as force. Gaston expected my attack across the most level ground where the approach was the easiest. He saw what he expected to see, which is why the surprise worked."

"Raymond?"

The smiling young cadet captain chose his words carefully so as not to offend his older and easily angered friend. "Even though we had to dodge around obstacles and started from farther away, our speed made up for the advantages of the hill's defenses."

"Gaston?"

The young man with the pale green eyes and the fighter's crooked nose replied grudgingly, "I learned that a good defense is not enough if the enemy catches you off guard."

Paul motioned for the boys to stack their dinner plates. When a space had been cleared on the table, he unrolled a map of northern France that showed the location of the school on the River Lys, the Belgian border, and part of the frontier with Germany. "Let us look for a little broader application of today's struggle. Here is the Maginot Line." He pointed to the well-known ramparts that lined France's eastern boundary. "Here are the flatlands of Belgium. All right, Gaston, you are the German commander. Where do you attack?"

Gaston studied the chart. "I cannot risk a frontal assault on the Maginot, so I launch west against Belgium—ignoring their neutrality, of course—then swing south toward France."

"And what will be France's response to that thrust?"

"Move all forces into Belgium from this side."

"Does everyone agree with both statements?" Paul asked.

Sepp frowned and leaned forward over the center of the diagram. "What about this area here? Between where the Maginot fortifications stop and the plains of Brussels?"

"The Ardennes Forest?" Gaston argued. "Any force moving through there could not be significant. Everyone knows it is impassable to heavy equipment."

The discussion was interrupted by the arrival of a messenger with a telegram for Paul. "Excuse me, gentlemen," he said, opening the envelope.

The argument continued over whether an attack through the Ardennes could be similar to the surprise movement in the game.

"I must excuse myself," Paul apologized. "I am called to Paris on military business and must leave at once."

The cadet captains rose when he did and stood at attention as Paul exited the room.

◑

The three cadets continued to stand after their captain left the room. "I bet he is being promoted and placed on active duty with a cavalry division," Raymond said.

Gaston looked unhappy. "They cannot do that to us. We will end up with some old geezer again like that retired colonel we had before Captain Chardon."

Sepp clapped his friend on the back. "You may have to put up with it, Gaston. Can it be that you are the only one who has not noticed: Captain Chardon wants active duty more than anything else in the world."

⌘

It was raining, clearing the smoky London haze. The pavement was shiny wet. Men and women hurried down the street beneath an unbroken canopy of black umbrellas. It was a mournful day. Even the sky was weeping, Eva thought.

She sat quietly beside Mac as the taxi carried them to Waterloo Station. For an instant their hands brushed. She glanced up. His warm eyes met hers, holding her in his gaze.

She wanted to say all the things she had come to feel about him, but now that he was leaving, her courage failed. And if he was not still in love with that other woman and loved her, as his looks sometimes seemed to indicate, why did he not say so?

"How long will you be in France?" she asked him.

"As long as it takes, I guess." He patted her hand as if to comfort her.

She was not consoled. "Will you come back to London soon?"

"Sure, kid. I'll try. If there's no news in France, well . . . I'll try to get back occasionally."

"The woman. The one who broke your heart? Josephine? She will be in France?"

"I . . . don't know, Eva. Even if she was . . . well, it doesn't do any good to talk about it, does it, kid?"

"I'm sorry, Mac. . . . I didn't mean to pry."

The great dome of Waterloo Station loomed ahead of them.

"Pry away. Pry the door wide open. There's nothing inside to talk about."

"You know this will be the first time since we fled from Warsaw that I will not see you every day."

"Are you saying you'll miss me?"

"Should I? Should I say it, Mac?"

"Eva . . . I've sort of gotten used to you, you know. I mean . . . I mean . . . Eva."

"You will be safe? careful? You promise you won't stand on the bonnets of any moving cars while the Nazi planes are strafing?" She felt suddenly desperate. She longed to hold on to him, to keep him from leaving. What if he never came back? What if he was killed?

"I promise. I'll hold the camera up and keep my head down. Okay?" The taxi pulled into the rank. "Okay?" Mac lifted her face as if he might kiss her. "Okay, Eva?" But he did not kiss her.

"Sure, Mac. Be safe. Come back soon."

He chucked her chin as if she were his kid sister. "Soon. You bet." Mac paid the cabbie extra and gave him the address of the Primrose Hill house. Then he leaped out of the taxi and dashed through the rain into the station.

Eva watched him until he vanished, noting that Mac was the only one in the crowd without an umbrella.

The moment Captain Paul Chardon reached Paris, he went to headquarters. He was told that Commander in Chief Gamelin wished for him to attend a dinner being given at the Hotel Edouard VII on the Right Bank.

Paul was excited. The only reason he would be summoned to attend a soiree for the High Command was if he was about to be promoted and given an active-duty assignment. Finally, it seemed, all those letters he had written about strategic concerns had come to the attention of someone important.

The chiefs of the Grand Armee had taken over the finest restaurant in Paris for their gathering. The Delmonico, located in the hotel at No. 39 Avenue de l'Opera, was world-famous for its oysters, caviar, and *canard à l'orange*.

When Paul arrived, the group had already collected for aperitifs. The first person he recognized was Colonel Charles de Gaulle, easily spotted because he was the tallest figure in the room. Paul joined the group surrounding de Gaulle and discovered that it included General Gamelin and Gamelin's aide, Colonel Pucelle.

De Gaulle was expounding his theory of modern armored warfare. "It is absolutely essential that armored forces operate as independent units capable of getting the most out of their firepower."

"But surely, Colonel de Gaulle," Pucelle argued, "you realize that tanks and other armored vehicles are most effective when they screen the advance of the infantry. If they were to be concentrated into separate sections, they could not be used for scouting and for forward protection of the poilus."

De Gaulle snorted. "Just because we call tanks the cavalry does not mean they can be used like horses. The Germans—"

Pucelle drew himself up to look de Gaulle square in the chest. In a haughty voice he demanded, "You would quote the Boche in opposition to the views of your own commander in chief?"

De Gaulle bent his head and stared down his great beak of a nose at Pucelle. "I meant no disrespect to General Gamelin," he said, bowing to

the general. "My sole motive is to ensure that the Grand Armee remains
the most modern and respected fighting force in the world."

"And following the guidance of the leaders who won the Great War
will not accomplish this?"

Paul could see that de Gaulle was without support among the officers who were listening. Gamelin's protégé, Pucelle, was doing all the
talking, but the aging commander in chief nodded his agreement.

De Gaulle had overstepped the bounds of protocol by writing a book
criticizing all French army training and organization. But for all the big
man's arrogance, Paul believed that he was correct. "Excuse me," he said.
"I concur with Colonel de Gaulle. The role for tanks in modern warfare
has changed since they were used as mobile fortresses in 1918."

Pucelle gave him an icy stare. "And who are you?"

"Captain Paul Chardon, chief instructor at the Ecole de Cavalerie in Lys.
I was advised to come here to receive orders from the commander in chief."

"Yes, Captain. I am familiar with those orders." Pucelle drew Paul
aside and away from the higher-ranking officers. "Your brother, Colonel
Andre Chardon, is called away from Paris. You are needed to . . . I do not
know exactly, but Colonel Bertrand of Military Intelligence asked for
you to stay at your family home for the time your brother will be gone.
You may go now, Captain."

Paul felt stricken. "That is all? Nothing further?"

"There was not time to put it in writing before this dinner, which is
why I sent for you to come here. Good evening, Captain."

Paul saluted smartly, biting his lower lip. He bowed to General
Gamelin and Colonel de Gaulle and left the restaurant feeling bitter.

⚬᷄᷅

General Gamelin watched Paul's exit, then called Pucelle for a private
word. "Make certain that young Chardon never receives an active-duty
assignment. We do not want to give radical ideas like de Gaulle's any further support. Keep that captain back with the horses where he belongs."

"Exactly my thinking, General," Pucelle agreed.

⚬᷄᷅

Primrose Hill
London, England

Dearest Jacob,
*The weather grows colder in England and, sadly, so does the fever
against the Nazis. The corpse of Poland is barely bled out, and*

already there are rumors that once again Chamberlain's government may be secretly negotiating peace terms with Hitler.

Can this be? I fear the rumor may be true, and I ask myself when it will stop.

Eva Weitzman has proved to be a great help to the TENS news staff. She interviews refugees and translates the stories of their horrors very well in English. These stories are wired to America in the hopes that there will be some indignation among the people of that great land. But Murphy says they are lulled to sleep, as if Hitler's atrocities are fiction rather than fact. He believes it will take some catastrophic attack on American soil to awaken America. I do hope everyone remains vigilant, or I believe the swastika flag may one day be flying over the Houses of Parliament.

There still remains an entrenched anti-Jewish sentiment here in this nation, as if the Jews of eastern Europe somehow have caused their own trouble. We have learned that many British remain very pro-Arab in part because of the romantic notion of Lawrence of Arabia and the Bedouins fighting the Huns during the Great War. And yet, even now Hitler courts the Muslim Arabs in the Middle East. He has taken the Grand Mufti of Jerusalem, Haj Amin el Husseini, under his dark wing and plans to fight against England in the British Mandate of Palestine.

The English government fears an alliance between the Nazis and the Muslims, which is why they have not allowed persecuted Jews to immigrate to the Mandate. You must know all of this, of course, but the facts are new to me and only recently understood when they were discussed over the dinner table with Murphy and a Christian official who is in the Foreign Office.

It's terrible that so many lives could be saved if Jews could only return to the ancient land of Israel, and yet this is prevented by Chamberlain as another form of appeasement!

Eva Weitzman is so grieved over the Lubetkin family. It is as though they have become her own family. We pray for them daily together. I cannot think what else we can do now that the Nazis are so firmly in control of Poland.

Where are you in all this, my darling? I pray for your safety every hour of every day. I wake in the night, and your name is on my lips. Surely God sees you and will keep you safe to return to me.

I love you,

Lori

19

On a Mission

Twilight dissolved rapidly into complete darkness as the battered Renault rolled down the long hill into the capital of the province of Lorraine. Mac McGrath squinted unhappily through the murky windscreen at the vague shapes in the blackness. His headlamps had been painted over until they were mere slits of feeble light.

One hundred and seventy-five miles east of Mac's permanent lodging at the Ritz Hotel in Paris, the medieval town of Nancy was a maze of crooked houses, twisted lanes, and narrow alleyways that climbed in almost vertical switchbacks. Charming in daylight, the town had become a treacherous place at night since the beginning of the war. As headquarters for the operational group consisting of the French Third, Fourth, and Fifth Armies, Nancy took the blackout seriously.

Mac cursed the night, cursed the cold, and cursed the Paris bureaucracy that had delayed his departure just long enough for him to arrive after sunset.

After he had been assigned by Movietone News to cover the French army after his return from Poland, it had taken him forever to maneuver his way through the paper minefield of forms and interviews to obtain his permit to enter the forward areas.

He dropped the Renault into first gear and crept along the lane. The scent of diesel exhaust and the rumble of a truck vibrated from somewhere on the road in front of him. Head and shoulders protruding out the side window, he scanned the blackness and spotted the dim taillights of an army lorry. Provided the lorry was not lost, not German, and headed into Nancy, Mac was in luck.

The truck led him to a shadowed mass, which turned out to be the train station. From there he easily remembered his way to the Hotel Thiers. It was just across the square, but it still took ten minutes to find the entrance to the hotel garage.

Behind the blackout curtains, the lobby of Hotel Thiers was surprisingly well lit and felt comfortably warm after his six frigid hours on the road from Paris. A parade of French and British uniforms tramped across the green marble floor while an old Frenchman with mop and bucket mumbled about paw prints and swept away their tracks in an unending effort.

The old man paused midstroke and cast a dubious glance at the American Press Corps patch sewn on the shoulder of Mac's well-worn Burberry topcoat. With sharp suspicion, the janitor glared at Mac's brown corduroy trousers, the blue turtleneck, the lapel of a gray tweed jacket, and finally the mud on the newcomer's shoes. He waited until Mac stepped to the registration desk before he resumed his task.

Behind Mac, through an arched doorway, male laughter and the aroma of garlic and hot bread drifted out of the brasserie. Mac's stomach rumbled. He was as hungry as he was tired.

There was no clerk behind the registration counter. A woman's angry voice, engaged in a telephone conversation about the price of butter, shrilled from the back office. Mac rang the bell once and then again impatiently.

A dark-eyed, heavy, middle-aged woman wearing a black sweater and skirt stepped into the doorframe. Her weary face betrayed disdain for his American Press Corps emblem.

"You are American," she said in the same tone she had used to declare that the price of butter was immoral and the dairyman was a thief. Putting her hands on her broad hips in a defiant gesture, she stated flatly, "Americans stay across the street at the Hotel d'Angleterre, Monsieur."

"That may be. But I've been driving several hours in the blackout. I myself ran over three cows and a German saboteur on the road. It's too dangerous for me to walk across the street in the dark, madame, even to get better hotel accommodations. I would like a room with a private bath. If you please?"

"We have private baths for our French patriots on leave from the front, Monsieur."

Mac arched his scarred eyebrow. "Do you have such a room available? empty? tonight?"

"*Oui*, but—"

"I'll take it. Since it is available."

She sighed. "Since it is unoccupied tonight . . . it will be ten francs additional."

He knew full well that across the road, the Hotel d'Angleterre had only shared baths and toilets. American and British newsmen would be lined up in the gloomy hallways to use the facilities at all hours. Some would resort to bathing at 3 AM to avoid the rush. Others would stop bathing and simply rub themselves with Scotch once a day to kill the germs.

Mac smiled patiently and passed her the ten-franc note.

"And when will you be checking out, Monsieur?"

"Noon . . . in a month or two." Mac knew he would be back and forth to Paris a dozen times between now and then. He did not want to suffer through registration more than once. He would keep the room on a long-term basis.

Pursing her lips, the woman eyed the old man with the mop who had paused to listen to the interesting exchange. With a disgusted shrug, she shoved a registration form and a police questionnaire across the walnut counter and retrieved a room key from a row of pigeonholes. This she tossed onto the register. One last scornful look at the American patch; then in a regal gesture she rang for the hall porter and disappeared into the back office without additional comment.

The upper corridors of Hotel Thiers were as black as the darkest street in Nancy. Whether this was a plan devised by the thrifty proprietor to save on utility bills or to keep German planes from spotting the hotel and blowing it to smithereens, Mac could not tell. Groping toward his room, he imagined that more hotel guests perished by falling over banisters or tumbling down the stairs than would ever be killed by the Luftwaffe. Heart attacks brought on by the terror of bumping into fellow guests in the pitch-black corridor might also be on some casualty list. Overall, the upper-story atmosphere of the Thiers was something like the perfect setting for a murder in a Charlie Chan movie.

The black curtain in his chamber was drawn and the light switched on. His room, on the second floor and facing the square, was indeed equipped with toilet, tub, and sink in a tiny alcove that must have been a closet at one time. At least he would not find himself climbing into a bath with a perfect stranger from down the hall during a blackout. True, he would have to step over the toilet to get to the sink, and the tub was designed for one of the Seven Dwarfs, but it was his very own.

Painted pale blue, the sleeping area was small. Very small. Not made for entertaining. Beneath the window was a writing desk with a reading lamp and a straight-backed chair. Hotel stationery was neatly fanned out on the blotter beside a pen. Against the right wall was a narrow bed with

a dark blue coverlet and no pillow. Above the bed hung a poorly executed oil painting of the Alps. On the opposite wall towered a monstrous Victorian bird's-eye maple armoire. Along with a veneer of a
thousand little maple eyeballs, it had carved ball-and-claw feet, which
made the thing look like it might walk out of the room in search of human flesh to devour. Mac would recommend it dine on the desk clerk as
first course.

"Just what I like," Mac muttered, tossing his canvas duffel into the
belly of the armoire. "A room with personality." He ran a hand wearily
over the coarse stubble on his cheek. "It ain't much, but it's home."

It was not home, certainly. No place was. Sleeping in the back of
army lorries or under bridges in the middle of a rainstorm was no kind
of life, but it was his living.

Nancy would soon be filled with journalists from New York and
Fleet Street and a dozen other newsreel services. Most members of the
press corps were old friends. Even the newcomers were aware that Mac
had been here from the beginning.

Mac had recorded the landslide toward war with the dedication of a
man who believed he had a mission: "Just show 'em the facts on film.
They'll rise up with one voice and put a stop to this!"

The foolish idealism with which he had first pursued his goal embarrassed him now.

Yes. Through his lens they had seen the German Luftwaffe in action
during the Spanish civil war. Hadn't Mac filmed the dead civilians in the
streets of Barcelona after the bombings? That long, still row of slaughtered Spanish children laid out awkwardly on the sidewalk. Hadn't he
captured the face of the mother holding her dead son in her arms? Did
the audience think her tears weren't real? Did they imagine that the dead
child would open his eyes and live again?

The list of political blunders that had blazed across the screen in
thousands of American theatres seemed endless. Terrifying!

America and the free world were plenty informed, yet knowledge
that others suffered had not eased the suffering. Perhaps seeing it right
there in black and white, squeezed in between the cartoon and the pre-
views of coming attractions, had only made people numb. Maybe they
observed death and tyranny with a detached interest, as though it could
never reach out and touch their lives with a personal horror.

Just another preview . . .

Spain had been a preview of what happened in Poland. Poland was a
preview for the show about to open in France. Now nothing could stop
the blitzkrieg from engulfing millions. It was too late.

Death waited patiently just on the other side of the French Maginot Line. And so Mac had come here to wait as well.

He had survived the fall of Poland . . . a sort of personal miracle it had been. Yet tonight he had the sense that everything he saw there was child's play compared to what would inevitably arrive here on the doorstep of Hotel Thiers.

In the meantime, this would be home for a while. At least until the German offensive began in earnest.

Mac would make himself comfortable in this little room with the private bath until some Stuka dive-bomber unloaded its cargo on the roof. Just like a Stuka had done to the Bristol Hotel in Warsaw. Then Mac McGrath would pack up his camera and check out.

◌◌

It had taken weeks for Josie Marlow to track down the London residence the Polish count, Alexander Riznow, had given her the night he'd spirited her away from the Warsaw siege.

She had made the young officer a promise to seek out his family—his mother and sisters—but it seemed to Josie that perhaps the countess did not want to be found. Josie had made several inquiries at Whitehall about the whereabouts of Countess Riznow and had been questioned and gaped at as though she were a spy.

At last Josie put an ad in the *Times*:

> *Seeking Countess Riznow. Son sends love.*
> *Please reply. Confidential. The Times. Box 240.*

After two days the reply arrived on monogrammed, watermarked, heavy bond stationery. The countess and her two teenaged daughters had taken up residence in a small flat not far from Sloane Square, at No. 3, Flat G, Beaufort Gardens. The note gave no telephone number but offered an invitation for tea on Thursday afternoon.

It was raining when Josie stepped out of the Sloane Square tube station. She was twenty minutes early, so she wandered past the windows of Peter Jones Department Store before entering the tangled streets in search of the flat.

Beaufort Gardens was a lovely Victorian neighborhood. Stately redbrick houses were topped with steep slate roofs and a forest of chimney pots.

No. 3, near the corner, overlooked the leafless trees of the communal gardens. The Riznow residence was on the third floor of the building, and the lift was no longer running because of some war regulation.

Josie shook the rain from her umbrella in the lobby and pushed the buzzer to Flat G, indicating that she had arrived.

Moments later, even as she raised her hand to knock on the door, it swung open. A young woman of about eighteen, with red, puffy eyes, greeted her in halting English.

"I speak French," Josie replied, knowing that most of the Polish aristocracy used French as their primary language. Then she introduced herself as the woman who had placed the ad in the *Times*.

The girl seemed relieved. She stepped aside and escorted Josie into a pale, cream-colored sitting room warmed by a tiny coal fire. Three banks of rain-streaked windows overlooked neighboring rooftops. Draperies were pulled back to let in the light, and yet the atmosphere was gloomy.

"Mother," said the girl cautiously, "this is Madame Marlow. She placed the ad. About Alexander."

A silver-haired woman wearing a long black dress of bygone elegance, Countess Riznow sat beside the window. She pivoted her head slightly, as though she was only vaguely aware of Josie's presence and infinitely weary. She extended her hand in a regal gesture. "How do you do."

Her English was much better than that of her daughter, Josie thought.

"Won't you please sit down, Madame Marlow? We have no servants these days, but Danielle will serve us tea."

Josie took a seat, feeling awkward and not entirely welcome. "I have been trying to reach you, Countess. I have been back in London for several weeks."

The woman nodded one slow signal of acknowledgment, as if this meeting was a perfunctory duty.

Josie continued. "Your son, Alexander, gave me your London address, but the Nazis took it from me when I left Warsaw."

"Of course." The countess waved her hand, and her daughter retreated into the kitchen.

"He was quite well when I saw him last." Josie tried to sound cheerful and enthusiastic. Could she penetrate the spell of despondency that permeated the little room?

"He was well." This was not a question but a flat, unemotional comment, as if the memory was her own. "Alexander . . . *was well*. . . ."

"Yes. I was at the Cathedral of St. John during the siege. He came to take me out on the last night before the surrender. He asked that I bring a message to you in London. He wanted me to tell you that he loves you all and that he is well."

"Is that all?"

"There was no time for anything else, Countess. Except . . ." Josie bit her lip and examined the toes of her black military pumps. "Your son is a wonderfully brave young man. He . . . and the others who held Warsaw . . . well, I cannot say enough. I was there, and they were extraordinary. They held the city to the last bullet, madame. I know that God will not desert such men as your son. He will survive. I just know it."

For the first time Countess Riznow turned her face toward Josie. Her eyes were full of sorrow and some embarrassment. "Madame, it is kind of you to come. But . . . I cannot let you continue. My son—my courageous Alexander—is dead."

Josie blinked dumbly at her. In the kitchen the teakettle came to a hissing boil. She heard the muffled sobs of the woman's daughter. "I . . . I don't know what to say. I am sorry."

"You meant well to come. But have you not heard? They killed them all. All the professors. Doctors. They cleaned out every hospital of the sick and wounded. Then all the officers. All the aristocracy. Entirely, madame."

"How can you be sure?" Josie asked in a horrified whisper.

"A friend, Jan Franciszkanska, escaped death with a bullet through his arm. My son stood beside him in a ditch as they faced execution. It happened quickly. The men waited. The SS fired machine guns. Alexander's body fell on Jan. He lay there beneath the corpses until the SS left. All night he waited. Then . . . he crawled out. He escaped from Poland." She shrugged. "I can be sure, Madame. My son is dead. My homeland is dead. But I thank you for coming all the same."

20

A Life in Exchange

St. Mary's Catholic Church
Hampstead Heath
London, England

Dearest Jacob,

I am writing this letter from the pew of a tiny Catholic church in the suburb of Hampstead Heath. I have come here with Eva, who woke up this morning in need of spiritual solace. Over breakfast she broke into tears. I thought it was because Mac McGrath has gone to France and she is clearly in love with him, though he does not know it. But when Elisa and I pressed her, she confessed that she dreamed all night about Rachel Lubetkin and the little boys in the Lubetkin family in Warsaw. "What can I do?" she cried.

Elisa said she must go to church and pray until the answer came to her or until she found peace. So we all bundled up and left this morning with Inspector Stone to drop Elisa at the BBC, and then we transferred to another bus and rode up the hill to this lovely little village of Hampstead and St. Mary's Church. This is the oldest Catholic church in London. It was a secret church where persecuted Catholics used to worship. It looks on the outside like a little white row house on the lane. I would never have known it was there. When you walk inside it is a lovely jewel box of a place. Very quiet, and the presence of the Lord is here.

Inspector Stone, who is an anti-Catholic Scottish Presbyterian, *is outside right now, puffing away on his pipe. Not having a pipe to keep me warm, I remained inside writing while Eva knelt at the altar and prayed most of the morning. There was a short Mass at noon, the first Catholic service I ever attended, and the priest gave a fine sermon on the Scripture that warns that anyone who harms one of these little children would be better off with a millstone around his neck and thrown into the deepest sea. The priest said that with what is happening to Jewish children all over Europe perhaps there are not enough millstones in the whole world to deal with those who have allowed injury to innocent children by simply doing nothing.*

As I listened I thought, Well spoken! Closing my eyes, I could not hear any difference between the faith of this godly cleric and my dear papa.

Eva took this sermon as a sign from God that she was meant to come here. She believes that perhaps there is some answer, some way to help the rabbi's children. Even now as I write this, she is in the office of the priest, speaking to him.

I do hope he can help her. If there is nothing more to be done, perhaps he will help her be at peace. She is an interesting person. A Catholic Christian with a deep faith in Christ, and yet she has not forgotten that she is by heritage Jewish—like you, Jacob—and she wants to help her people. I like her very much, and I am glad she came to stay with us.

We pray together for your safety. For the safety of the children of Israel. How many millstones will be required for the pacifists who let this horror come upon God's beloved children?

I love you,

Lori

⟨∞⟩

Eva Weitzman's attention remained fixed on the crucifix that hung on the wall above Father Brocky's desk. The swelling of grief threatened to choke her. How could she explain that her own life seemed somehow intertwined with the lives of the Lubetkin children? And since the fall of Warsaw, who could say if they were even still alive?

The kind old priest held the edges of the photograph gently. He placed it on the blotter and reread Etta Lubetkin's letter to her father in Jerusalem. At last he commented, "The girl here, Rachel? She looks enough like you to be your sister."

"That is what she said to me. Something like that, when she gave me the passport. I told her my name, and she said she was glad I was a Jew. Glad that she could give it to a Jew and save my life. I did not tell her I am a Christian, Father. I was afraid, really, deep down, that she would take it back."

"And now?"

"Now I am ashamed that I was afraid. And . . . and isn't my Jesus also her Messiah? I thought about it when I heard the homily today. How can we let them just be slaughtered? The Nazis appeal to anti-Semitism by calling Jews Christ-killers."

"And yet our Lord came as a Jew to take the sins of all men upon Himself that we might be clean and whole before the Father in heaven."

"Yes. I couldn't say it so well as you, but I believe it. I believe He came to take my place and buy my life by offering His own. Oh, Father Brocky," Eva cried, "isn't that what Rachel Lubetkin did for me, too?"

"Yes. Like Christ Himself it seems the girl has offered her life in exchange for yours. Quite a gift you've been given. A close-up object lesson on how salvation works." He appraised her solemnly. "You're alive and free. She may not be alive. If she is, she is not free. What will you do with the gift she gave you, Eva?"

"What can I do? What? How can I help her? These little boys. Her brothers. How can I help this family?" Tears brimmed in her eyes.

"I do not doubt you were led here. What men and governments will not accomplish without love and mercy as their creed, the merciful Savior through His church may be capable of." He picked up the photo. "We are all a part of the one body of Christ. From the rising of the sun to its setting we are called to be united in His love."

"I was so in hopes I would find a solution."

"Put it in the hands of the Lord now." The interview was at an end. "Mind if I borrow these? The photo? The letter to the rabbi in Jerusalem? The Lord has laid the burden of these children on your heart for a reason. You must continue to pray for a miracle, Daughter. For Rachel. For her brothers. I'll be seeing you at Mass now, will I?"

"Yes, Father."

"Good. That's good then. I'll inquire about the family. Now you must keep this under your hat, girl."

☙❧

Primrose Hill
London, England

Dearest Jacob,
Something truly did change in Eva after our visit to St. Mary's
Church in Hampstead. She seems very much at peace. She left the

*photograph of the Lubetkin children with Father Brocky and goes to
worship there often.*

*She will not speak to me of details but says that perhaps there is a
way to help the Jewish children of Poland. She says we must
continue to pray that God will go before them and open a door
through the sea for them to return to their homeland.*

*I thought of you when she said that. Where are you tonight, my
darling? I pray that God will open a path through the sea and lead
you home to safety.*

I love you,

Lori

The central London landmark known as Admiralty Arch was almost buried under a twelve-foot-high thicket of concertina wire. The barbs were
as wide as a man's hand and looked more like lance heads than thorns.
Andre Chardon's identity papers and the orders directing him to consult
with the First Lord of the British Admiralty were examined three times
before he was allowed to go upstairs. On September 3, when Chamberlain had broadcast that Britain was at war with Germany, he had also announced that Churchill was to join the War Cabinet. Now Churchill
faced his second major war with Germany as First Lord of the Admiralty.

Andre was escorted to Winston Churchill's war room by a secretary,
but he was asked to wait outside while Churchill finished his regular
6:00 AM consultation with his briefing officer, Captain Richard Pim.
When Pim came out, he was carrying a stack of manila folders, each of
which had a red label bearing the words *Action This Day.*

Pim shrugged when he saw Andre staring at the heap of projects. "Go
right in," he said with a cheerful grin. "I think he's cleared the decks for
you now."

The rotund, dressing-gown-clad figure of Winston Churchill was
studying a wall map of the North Atlantic. In it were pins representing
the whereabouts of British warships, merchant ships, and the last reported sightings of German U-boats. "Andre, son of my old friend," he
said, drawing a black drape across the wall, "how good to see you again."

Andre looked around the room. All the walls were covered in dark
curtains that presumably hid more maps and charts. It gave the office a
very somber look. "A pleasure to see you also, First Lord."

"No ceremony," Churchill insisted, then with sympathy added, "I
am aware of the situation with Elaine. I'm sorry."

But Elaine Snow was not the subject that had sent Andre to Churchill's office, and Andre said nothing except a muted thank-you. "I am directed to tell you, without being able to give you details, that the work on the German code is progressing, but slowly. We are hopeful of a breakthrough but do not expect it to come soon."

Churchill stuck out his lower lip in thought, then walked over to the room's lone window and stood gazing down on Horse Guard's Parade. "It is of the utmost urgency," he said at last. "This delusion your people call the *drole de guerre* and ours call the Bore War is really a sinister trance! The fate of Holland and Belgium, like that of Czechoslovakia and Poland, will be decided by the next move. We must come upon concrete evidence of what follows in Hitler's infamous plan."

Andre wished that he had more positive information to offer. He wished he could reinforce the confidence of this man who was the backbone of British resolve.

Churchill continued speaking, now almost musing aloud. "The Nazis try to frighten us with their propaganda. But we are not frightened. Hitler tries to reassure the neutrals with solemn promises and guarantees . . . which is why they are frightened! They remember how he kept his other promises! I tell you, Andre, either Hitler and his minions will be destroyed, or all that Britain and France stand for will go down. And if that happens, the United States will be left to single-handedly guard the rights of man."

"You do not believe that it will come to that?"

The great head moved ponderously from side to side. "Only bullies and cowards support Hitler. The rest of the entire world hates the monstrous Nazi apparition. Once the Allies are awake to the danger, we shall not draw back until this business is finished, once and for all."

"Then," said Andre, "we must hope that the slumber will soon be over!"

"You and I, and others like us, are awake already. If we do not fail in our duty, others will soon arise to share the burden," Churchill concluded. "But come along now; Clemmie would never forgive me if I did not take you upstairs for a visit. We recall with great fondness the times we spent at your family's villa in the South of France."

"How is your wife, sir? I heard about her automobile accident. Is she all right?"

"Bruised and shaken, but quite strong and willing to be on the road again. A bit like the national honor of our two countries, eh, Andre?"

❧

Clementine Churchill sat at her desk in the pale yellow morning room, answering correspondence. Wearing a navy blue dress trimmed in white, she looked the female counterpart of the First Lord of the Admiralty. Her straight Grecian nose and classic features were still beautiful in spite of her fifty-odd years.

Her face erupted in a pleased smile as Andre entered the room with Winston. Only as she rose stiffly did the aftereffects of her accident show.

"Andre! I was hoping you wouldn't get away from here without dropping in."

He embraced her gently and kissed her on both cheeks. "I was concerned for you, Clemmie. I read that you and your automobile have been tilting with brick buildings!"

"The driver swore he saw that nasty Hitler standing on the corner in Surrey." She laughed. "He tried to smash him like a bug, and I found myself sitting in a shopwindow like something on display."

"Sit down, Clemmie," Winston growled.

She ignored her husband and led Andre to a settee beside the bow window. Still holding his hands like a delighted auntie with a nephew, she scrutinized him just as she used to do when he was a child. He half expected her to proclaim that he had grown.

"Every time I see you, you've grown to look more like your handsome father at this age. He would have been proud of you, Andre. And your mother as well." She patted his cheek. "It's been too long since we saw you last. Summer seems like a century ago now. When Winston told me you were coming, I had the cook make up profiteroles just for you."

"A treat we cannot easily get in the patisseries of Paris, Clemmie. *Merci.*"

Churchill cleared his throat and scooped up a prowling gray kitten that rubbed itself across his legs. "Well, you two don't need me for your tea party. I'll get back to work."

The cat under his arm, Churchill retreated down the stairs. Perhaps, Andre thought, Clemmie had warned him that she wanted to have a personal word with her godson.

Tea and profiteroles were served. Andre felt more like a child in the presence of Clementine Churchill than in any other woman's.

"Do you notice anything since last you were in London?" she began.

"Apart from gun emplacements on the roof of Harrods, barrage balloons, gas masks, and sandbags everywhere?" He smiled. "It is the same in Paris, *ma chèrie.*"

"Listen." She raised her chin regally. "Do you hear it?"

He strained to hear whatever noise she was contemplating, but there were only silence and the ticking of a mantel clock.

"What is it?"

"Silence." She smiled. "London is as still as Chartwell. No church bells. No taxi horns or train whistles. No sirens. No unnecessary noise. Winston says it was his idea. They let it out that the ordinance for silence was to enable the air-raid wardens to hear aircraft. But I think it was so Winston could tolerate living full-time in London after years of peace at Chartwell."

"I would believe such a motive," Andre replied with a laugh.

They spent the next thirty minutes discussing the Churchill children as well as Andre's brother, Paul.

Finally Clementine came to the purpose of the tea and pastries. Her expression turned suddenly serious. "We were shocked to hear the news about Elaine."

"Luxembourg has appealed for her release," Andre stammered. "The offer was made to deposit a large ransom in a Swiss account if she might be released. Hitler will not hear of it. He is convinced that the plot against his life was either of British or French origin. And that Elaine— poor Elaine—had something to do with it."

Clemmie nodded slowly. She took Andre's hand. "What about the child, Andre? Have you thought of her?"

"I think of little else. The war . . . yes. It is almost a diversion to my troubled thoughts these days." He grimaced and shook his head. "She is with Elaine's father. An old and bitter man . . . I cannot think what to do."

"You will do the right thing; I am certain," she replied kindly. "How old were you when you lost your parents, Andre?"

"I was nine. Paul was five."

"Yes, I remember. A tender age, darling. A lonely time for you. But then you had your brother and your grandfather." She let the memory of that time convict him.

"Grandfather. But for him it might have turned out differently for Elaine and me. For the child."

Clemmie rose and held up a finger commanding Andre to wait. She retreated through a door and returned a minute later carrying a delicate, porcelain-faced doll and a thin, green leather volume.

"These were your mother's. The doll she gave me when she left for France to marry your father. She told me that one day I might like to pass it along in case she had a little girl. Until now I thought I should never be able to fulfill my promise to her. Of course she had sons, and so we held out for the possibility of grandchildren someday. This—" she placed the book into his hands—"Milton. *Paradise Lost*. We struggled through literature class together, she and I. All the notes in the margin are hers. Some lovely thoughts. I thought you might like these things. Perhaps you may wish to pass the doll along. Her name is Clementine."

Unable to reply, Andre nodded and held the doll in his hands. At last he spoke. "Well, she has your eyes, Clemmie. They look into a heart, do they not?"

"Perhaps, Andre, dear boy. But your heart is on your sleeve in this matter. Easy to see. It always has been."

21

The Lion Crouched on the Doorstep

Throughout the days that followed the return of Horst von Bockman from Warsaw, the face of Sophia, the murdered Polish woman, haunted his thoughts.

Quartered at Berlin's esteemed Adlon Hotel, with two dozen other junior officers who had distinguished themselves in battle, Horst had kept mostly to himself. This morning after breakfast, he pulled fellow officer Putzi Dietrich aside. Putzi had been a childhood friend. They had gone through cadet school together and now shared the same rank, commanding different companies. If any man would understand the disillusionment Horst felt, his old friend would.

The two men walked slowly beneath the leafless canopy of trees in the Tiergarten. Horst began to tell Putzi about the three crucified Jews in the village and then about the young Polish woman at the river.

"Enough." Putzi held up his hand to silence Horst. "I do not want to hear this, and you don't want to talk about it. Not to anyone, Horst. You understand? The war is over in Poland for us. We fought honorably and won. What happens beyond that is none of our business. We have careers to think about. Families."

He leveled a chilling gaze at Horst, as if the very mention of doubts was somehow treasonable, before he continued. "You heard it. General Stumme has sent in commendations for us. That is why we are called to the Chancellery. Does that mean nothing to you? Do you want to risk all that because some overzealous SS shot a woman? It is not our business, Horst. Compassion has always been your weakness. You are too soft. This time compassion is misplaced, even dangerous. Hatred is a soldier's medicine. It makes us live; it inspires vengeance! Pity the enemy, and you betray Germany."

This was the sensible response, Horst knew. He thanked Putzi, as if this counsel had somehow relieved his conscience. But the words of his friend were no comfort.

That same afternoon Horst stood ill at ease among the twenty-four newly promoted majors in the Entrance Hall of the Reich's Chancellery. The dark marble floor was adorned with expensive carpets and the walls hung with fourteenth-century tapestries showing hunting scenes.

The Entrance Hall, the only room in the Chancellery in which smoking was permitted, was the most popular room in the building for diplomats and government officials to congregate. But since Horst did not smoke, it was small comfort to him. At any rate, he was doing at least as good a job controlling his nerves as the other Panzergruppen commanders; they were smoking furiously.

The newly promoted officers being sent to join General von Rundstedt's Army Group A had been summoned here to Berlin to meet the Führer personally before being given leave and then dispatched to their respective assignments.

The commander in chief of the western front, General von Rundstedt, strode into the Entrance Hall from the curtained doorway to the diplomatic reception salon. The flashbulbs of a half-dozen cameras popped as the young men snapped to attention and then followed von Rundstedt through the salon into the chancellor's private living room.

The dark leather sofa was occupied by Joseph Goebbels, minster of propaganda, and high-ranking Nazi leader Martin Bormann. A score of other exalted officials of the Reich were grouped around the room. Among them was SS General Reinhard Heydrich, who spoke in low tones to fat Hermann Göring about the art of fencing. Horst looked quickly away from the SS general, in hopes that Heydrich would not remember their encounter on the road to Warsaw. Heydrich and Göring ignored the arrival of the majors, who waited in uncomfortable silence marked by the deep-voiced ticking of the clock over the renaissance coat of arms on the fireplace.

Horst was perspiring as the door leading to the private rooms of Adolf Hitler opened. The Führer entered. All conversation stopped. Goebbels and Bormann stood to acknowledge Hitler's arrival. General von Rundstedt and the others saluted crisply. Accompanied by the probing lens of the photographer, the general presented each of the majors in turn.

Beads of sweat formed on Horst's forehead as Hitler walked slowly down the line toward him. Like a proud father, the Führer spoke to each man as his deeds of valor were recited. But Horst heard neither the accolades nor the response of the German leader. Voices became inaudible beneath the pounding of Horst's heartbeat in his ears. The collar of his uniform felt as though it would strangle him. He stared ahead, catching the form of Hitler approaching down the line.

Then Reinhard Heydrich stepped directly into Horst's vision. Heydrich cocked an eyebrow and gave a tight-lipped, secretive smile. He silently mouthed the words, *Congratulations, Major von Bockman*. Horst swallowed hard and blinked back the sweat that trickled into his eyes. So Heydrich remembered their meeting—remembered Horst's protests.

"Allow me to present Major Horst von Bockman, Führer," offered von Rundstedt. "Distinguished himself several times in the early days of the battle . . ."

Hitler scrutinized Horst. He nodded and smiled at the recital of the young major's accomplishments. Yet when Hitler smiled, cold eyes seemed to peer deep into the doubts and dread of Horst's most secret thoughts. Hitler patted him on the shoulder. "Relax, Major. Surely you did not tremble like this when you faced the enemy." He laughed, and everyone in the room laughed with him.

Horst managed a feeble smile. "No, Führer."

"Well, then. We can trust that you will continue to do your duty for the Fatherland."

"Yes . . . Führer."

And so the personal attention ended. Now the gathering was strictly a matter of putting the final touches on an event that would be published in the propaganda sheets.

Hitler stepped back by the fireplace to address them all. The flames behind him, he began to speak. "I have summoned you here to impress upon you the importance of the mission with which you are charged. You are soon going west to redress the unspeakable injustices inflicted upon the German people by the Versailles Treaty. Each of you has demonstrated in the recent Polish campaign that you have grasped the requirements of modern warfare: speed and unrelenting attack! We must not get bogged down in a war of attrition. When we strike, strike hard! You tank commanders and others of Panzerkorps Hoth, with Reinhard and Guderian, will be in the forefront of the Lightning War. We will not only even out an old score, we will teach the world a lesson about battle that it has never seen before."

Von Rundstedt thanked Hitler on behalf of the group for receiving them and for the benefit of his insight. "Perhaps, Führer, you would like to command a Panzer division yourself."

"If only it could be," Hitler agreed without a trace of doubt about his ability to act in such a capacity. "Unfortunately I must remain where I can command a view of the larger picture of the war. But know this—" he addressed the panzer officers—"I will be following your progress with great interest. You are the future generals of our Thousand-Year Reich. One day you will tell your protégés of this meeting. And since you are soon to face the French, may I recommend that you study the best work on the use of motorized units in modern warfare."

"That would be the word of General Guderian?" inquired von Rundstedt.

"No." Hitler corrected the general with an impatient wave of his hand. "It is written by a French colonel . . . his name is de Gaulle. Know your enemy well, and you will defeat him." He turned back to the young majors. "Have any of you studied this book?"

Horst timidly raised his hand, as did Putzi Dietrich and two others who had been students under Erwin Rommel. The work of the Frenchman evidenced his genius, but Horst was also aware that it had been largely ignored in France. Less than five hundred copies had been sold. Fifty of these had gone to cadets trained by Rommel in Germany.

"Then you shall continue to lead the pack," Hitler finished. "Now, I have a speech to prepare. If you will excuse me." Chased by resounding heils, he stepped from the room. Only then did Horst draw his handkerchief and mop his brow.

"Well, you survived meeting God face-to-face," Putzi Dietrich said softly.

Reinhard Heydrich stood just behind Putzi. "Major von Bockman is a survivor, I think. Aren't you, Major?"

"O-obergruppenführer Heydrich," Horst stammered. "It is good to meet you again."

"A little pleasanter surroundings than last time, eh, von Bockman?" Heydrich smirked. "Although it is always pleasant to do one's duty for one's country, is it not? One can sleep soundly at night knowing that duty is first. It is everything."

Putzi went pale. No doubt he was wishing he had not heard Horst's story about the SS action in the Polish village.

"Yes, Herr General," Horst agreed, although the nearness of Heydrich made him feel ill.

"I kept my promise to you." Heydrich smiled coldly. "I did not forget. You interest me, Herr Major von Bockman. A man of such tender conscience and yet such courage. An odd mix for a soldier. Better suited for a priest perhaps." He laughed. "But then you are not interested in living the priestly life of celibacy. You are married, I understand. Yes. A lovely woman. Tell me, does she share your enthusiasm for duty? Or only your tender conscience?"

Horst felt beads of sweat gather on his forehead again and an unseen hand close around his throat. Question followed question without a break for Horst to reply, and when Heydrich had asked enough about Katrina, he left Horst with the certainty that every answer would be found. And that every answer had better agree with Reinhard Heydrich's concept of duty to the Fatherland.

At that moment Horst made up his mind: No action of his, no word—not even a thought—would vary from absolute attention to duty. Anything else would not only endanger his life, but Katrina's as well.

⚭

Dearest Lori:

Haven't written more because of Captain Orde's warning, but now it doesn't seem to matter.

I think we're going to be shot tomorrow.

All day long today Russian firing squads executed people. Captain Orde says it's the NKVD . . . the Russian version of the Gestapo.

They shot wounded Polish soldiers.

They shot the aldermen of some villages who were accused of hiding Polish soldiers.

They shot villagers accused of being traitors or spies or intellectuals or Jews.

It seems anybody with an old score to settle can bribe the commissar and . . . that's it.

Alfie and I were forced to dig long trenches for . . . well, you can guess what for.

Saw Peter Wallich and the others . . . they had to dig, too. Peter said they're being kept in a wire pen with no shelter and given two pieces of bread a day . . . but so far all are still alive.

Captain Orde heard the commissar haranguing the colonel about us. Says we should all be shot, and that waiting longer to hear back from Moscow is a waste of time.

Captain Orde has apologized a hundred times for getting us into this mess. He frets about Lucy most of all.

I love you. Why can't I write more? There are a hundred thousand things I want to say to you, but when I begin to scribble, the words just won't come.

You may never know what happened to me, but maybe in your dreams you'll remember me, just as I see you every night in mine.

All my love always,

Jacob

P.S. Alfie is just as cheerful as ever . . . says we'll meet in the Promised Land. I guess he's right.

❦

"Lori? Lori? Are you upstairs?" Murphy slammed the door of the Primrose Hill house and tossed his briefcase onto the foyer table. "I need a word with you."

"Down in a minute," Lori called.

Murphy glanced at a note in Eva's handwriting. She had gone to the market. Murphy frowned. He had been hoping for support from Eva or Elisa when he gave Lori the bad news.

There was no easy way to tell Lori the truth. Murphy stretched his hands out to the coal fire in the grate of the reception-room fireplace.

Elisa was late getting home from the BBC. Inspector Stone had gone to fetch her. Murphy wished someone were here to help him. Lori would see the news on his face the minute she laid eyes on him.

Lori's footsteps sounded on the landing and then the stairs. "Murphy? What is it? Everything all right?"

He turned, inhaled deeply, and sighed. "Lori . . . I . . . today I got a call. . . ." Dread clouded her face. She knew. Did he have to say it?

She blanched. "Who? Who is it?"

"I . . . I've . . . I'm sorry, Lori. . . ."

"Is it Jacob? Is it?"

"Your father."

She closed her eyes as the weight of it pressed down on her. "Papa," she whispered. "Oh, Papa."

"Sorry. So sorry, Lori. There's no easy way to tell you."

Her head bobbed once in acceptance. "How?"

"The report from the Reich Chancellery to the American Embassy simply said Pastor Ibsen died of . . . suicide . . . while in prison."

Her fists clenched, Lori nodded once again. "Impossible! But they would say that."

"Yes."

"When?"

"Didn't have a date."

"I'll need to go to Mama. To Wales. Tell her myself, Murphy. All this time she's been praying. Hoping. Hoping the Americans could do something. Get him out of Germany."

"I'm sorry." Murphy felt helpless. "Lori, I know how you must feel."

"No. No, you can't know, Murphy. No one in America seems to know or . . . or they would surely stand up to Hitler. No one cares that my father has been murdered because he was a Christian trying to help Jews. No one cares what the Nazis did to him because he was one of the few in Germany to speak the truth. No one in America cares. Not the ordinary people. Especially not politicians. They're all too oblivious to believe what is happening to us over here. Easier to believe lies of evil men than to stand up and confront evil with the truth."

"You're right. Yes. As long as it hasn't been on our own front step we've let the world outside our borders go to the devil."

"And so the devil will come knocking on America's door, Murphy. And then the devil will break the shiny American lock and kick in your lovely American door. It is only a matter of time before apathy will devour you from inside your own borders."

Murphy knew she was speaking the truth. It did not take a prophet to see a clear vision of what was coming. No doubt the Nazis had murdered Pastor Ibsen. Probably tortured him to death, then called it suicide. "We'll need to arrange for a bodyguard to go with you to Wales. Inspector Stone has bronchitis. Like half the population of London. Barely able to stay on his feet, let alone travel far."

"I'll leave tomorrow. Alone. I need some time alone. Some time with Mama. Please. We'll want some time together to sort this out."

ᑯᑭ

Eva's frequent dreams of her mother and father and brothers in Czechoslovakia dissolved into nightmares of their torture and deaths at the hands of the Gestapo.

The news that Lori's father was dead struck Eva to the heart. She lay awake and tried not to listen to Lori's quiet sobbing, which penetrated the walls of the old house, but it was no use. In Lori's grief, Eva's longing for her lost family was renewed. She buried her face in her pillow and wept silently for her loved ones.

It was after midnight when Elisa knocked softly on Eva's door.

Eva wiped her tears away with the back of her hand. "Come in."

The door opened a crack. Light streamed through.

"Eva?" Elisa asked tentatively. "May I come in?"

"Please. Yes. Leave the light off." Eva sat up in bed.

Elisa, dressed in a white nightgown, sat in the chair beside the wardrobe. The light was behind her. "We've kept you awake. I'm sorry."

"I have my own memories to keep me awake."

"Yes. Your family. I'm sorry. How long has it been?"

"Just over a year. They were in Czechoslovakia. Just across the Polish border."

"I'm sorry," Elisa said again, as though there was nothing left to say. "Now Lori's father. When will it end?"

"Only when someone stands up and fights," Eva said angrily.

"Yes. How upside down it has seemed to me these years as Hitler marched over one free nation after another. The only way to stop him from murdering people like Lori's father and your family is to fight. Make him stop. And yet even now I don't think America will do anything until the lion is crouched on its doorstep."

"Lofty words of peace from the pacifists will not save one life. Only destroy the innocent," Eva declared. "How is it a man of peace like Lori's father dies because he protected the innocent and his life is considered somehow of less importance than staying on good terms with the butchers who murdered him?"

"Lori has been asking the same questions all night. I have no answers. You know she hasn't heard from her husband since before the day the Germans invaded. It's hard."

"There is still hope for her. Lori's husband may still be alive. She's lucky, you know. Yesterday was my mother's birthday," Eva said softly. "No one left to remember but me. My mother would . . . you know . . . want me to go on. Make a life. Fall in love. Marry. Have children someday. I am the only one who made it out. She would not want me to give in to despair, but there are times . . . times I am so . . ."

"Is it Mac?"

"Yes. A fine man. Good and brave."

Elisa sighed. "He's a coward about love, Murphy tells me. A fellow needs to be brave to fall in love in such a time."

"Yes. Well, perhaps he has not found that sort of courage yet. He's in love with another woman. I'm sure of it."

"His eyes tell another story. I saw the way he looked at you."

"He left nothing behind for me when he left for France. Not his heart. I do not hold his heart." Eva's thoughts turned to Mac again. For the thousandth time. Her longing for him came unbidden, like an uninvited guest. "I should like to see him again when all this is over."

Elisa did not reply for a moment. Then, "Listen. Lori and I are going to Wales. To the farm. Our mothers are there with the children. Lori needs to be with her mother now. And I am desperate to see my baby girl. We thought—Lori and I—that maybe you would like to come with us. You've not been outside of London. Such a gloomy place lately. That part of Wales is lovely. Would you like to come along?"

"My work. At the office."

"I've asked Murphy. He said you could write a few stories about how the evacuees are doing in Wales. We're leaving early tomorrow. I couldn't wait until morning to ask you."

Eva brightened. The countryside! What a change that would be from the cold gloom of London. "Well, then. Yes. Yes, of course. I can help with the children. I am—I was—a schoolteacher, you know."

"Then it's all settled. The three of us. You'll need to pack."

∾

Primrose Hill
London, England

Dearest Jacob,

The news about Papa we have been fearing has come. Papa is dead. The Nazis claim he committed suicide in prison. It is a lie, of course. Papa would never have taken his own life. Anyone who ever knew him or heard him preach about suffering for Christ and remembered how he risked everything to defend the helpless would know what a foul lie the Nazis have told about him.

Mr. Crawford, an assistant to the American ambassador in London, rang Murphy at the news office to tell him there was information at last about the fate of Karl Ibsen. Murphy went with me to the embassy. There we were taken to a cramped office to meet with Mr. Crawford. He told me I should sit down. He brought me tea and gave me a letter that had the official seal of the German Chancellery on it. It had first been relayed to the American Embassy in Berlin, then passed on to London. It was written in German and translated into English. It said very tersely that the prisoner, Reverend Karl Ibsen, had committed suicide in prison on September 1, 1939. This was the day Germany invaded Poland.

Mr. Crawford told me how very sorry he was. He said my father's resistance to Nazi inhumanity and the resistance of his church was well-known and admired in America. I asked him, why then did America not speak up to help my father and men like him when he was arrested and tortured? Why didn't Roosevelt come to the aid of the church when Papa and other Christians protested against the Nazi policy of euthanasia and persecution of Jews?

The poor fellow could not explain. I suppose it was unfair of me to say such a thing to him. After all, he is not the one who makes such policies. It is not his fault America has done nothing, nothing, nothing to help good Germans oppose Hitler.

I am angry. My heart is broken. For Papa. For the tragedy of what Germany has become. For the fate of Christians and Jews together who fall into the hands of such evil men.

I prefer anger over the waves of grief that pound me and threaten to drown me. How I wish you were with me!

I cannot let Mother hear this news in a telegram. Not in such an unfeeling and heartless way. Elisa, Eva, and I will go to her side in Wales and tell her face-to-face that Papa, our beloved, has gone to be with the Lord. He is a martyr for the righteous cause of Christ's Kingdom. The lies of the Nazi murderers I will not tell her. And then we will weep together.

I love you,

Lori

22

A Ticket to Shrewsbury

It was cold. The wind of late autumn swept through the plane trees of Regent's Park, stripping away the last foliage. Antiaircraft emplacements, sandbags, and slit trenches were littered with fallen leaves.

Kevin Miller turned up the collar of his raincoat and glared at the threatening sky. The bench at the bus stop across from the white Georgian house of John Murphy was damp. Kevin's ears hurt. Where were Elisa Murphy, Lori Kalner, and the third young woman who lived at the house? Where was the stone-faced private bodyguard who had been escorting the women everywhere in London since they had moved from the Savoy?

Kevin blew his nose. He should have been in bed, not chasing after two enemies of the Reich in such damp weather.

So where were they? Perhaps they had caught the flu like Kevin. Cheerful thought. Maybe some unfriendly microbe would finish them off and save Kevin the trouble! Then he would clip out their obituaries and submit them to Erich Bain with the claim that he had gotten close enough to sneeze on them and kill them.

The wind picked up. Kevin shuddered and broke into a cold sweat.

A London taxi pulled to the front of Murphy's house. The driver, sensibly swathed in layers of coats, muffs, and mittens, bounded to the door. It opened as the man raised his hand to knock. Lori Kalner, leather traveling valise in hand, stepped out, followed by Elisa Murphy and the third resident. Elisa turned and embraced John Murphy. Both Lori and Elisa wept quietly.

What was happening? They were going somewhere in a taxi. Lori

Kalner and Elisa Murphy without a bodyguard for the first time in weeks. Somewhere with a valise. Traveling . . . where? Not a short journey. No. Not with baggage. They were leaving London. Perhaps by train. Was this the opportunity Kevin had been waiting for?

The cabbie loaded the luggage and held the door as the women entered the taxi.

Kevin leaped to his feet and scanned the traffic of Prince Albert Road for a cab to pursue his quarry. He waved his kerchief as a taxi rounded the curve and slid to a halt at the curb.

"Available?"

"Aye. Where you headed?"

Kevin jerked his thumb toward the cab across the road as Elisa waved to Murphy from the backseat. "Ten pounds to you if you keep up with that cab."

The driver shrugged. "Get in then."

⟶⟵

From the Murphy house to Paddington Railway Station was just a ten-minute ride even in heavy traffic.

The grinning driver presented his palm to Kevin as they stopped directly behind the cab carrying the three women. "Ten pounds, you said. Well, I'm taking a holiday after this. Is she your fiancée or something? Running off without you?"

Kevin felt the cold sweat of fever trickle into his eyes. He fumbled for the cash. No time to regret the cost of the ride. There were Lori, Elisa, and the other one. Unaccompanied for the first time in weeks. How was Kevin to know they had only been going to Paddington?

Wordlessly he slapped the cash down and bolted, leaving the bemused cabbie to contemplate his great fortune.

Kevin followed on their heels. Elisa and the other woman left to find the lavatory. Kevin was close enough to touch Lori. Close enough . . .

Pretty thing, Lori Kalner was. Eyes red-rimmed with tears, she blinked up at the departure board, then walked slowly toward the ticket queue. She did not notice Kevin standing just behind her. Close enough to overhear her destination—Wales by way of Shrewsbury.

She would never make it that far.

A woman waiting in front of Lori struck up a conversation with her. "Travel these days! Almost impossible to get anywhere!"

"Yes. I'm going to Wales."

Lori's slight foreign accent was greeted with suspicion. "A long way."

"Family."

"Bad news?"

"Yes. My father. I'm going now to be with my mother."

"But you're not English."

"No. No. My father was a pastor in Germany. Arrested by the Nazis. My mother and brother and I escaped, you see."

The traveler's eyes brimmed with sympathy. "Terrible. Terrible. Who would have imagined it would come to this? I was in Austria just before the Anschluss. Hitler's Gestapo arresting Jews right and left. And now a Christian pastor, you say! Who would have thought!"

Lori thanked her for her sympathy but said little else. Her eyes remained fixed on the floor. She did not seem to notice Kevin's frank stare.

Kevin's head throbbed. He coughed into his hand, then fumbled in his pocket for a fresh handkerchief. Wales was indeed a long way. He formulated a plan. He would also purchase a ticket to Shrewsbury and would follow Lori to the crowded platform. Give her a shove beneath the iron wheels of the train as it pulled in. Then he would simply board the train, ride out a few stops, turn around, and come back to London. A few days in bed, and he would be back on the job.

The line inched forward. Lori reached the window and counted out twenty-six shillings each for three tickets.

"Here you are then. Track 11. Pleasant journey."

Lori turned and was gone.

No worries.

A fit of coughing seized Kevin. He braced himself on the counter as the world spun around him.

The pleasant, bespectacled clerk peered at him with concern. "You all right, then?"

Kevin nodded. "Shrewsbury . . . return, please."

"Shrewsbury. With a cold like that? You should be in bed."

"You're a doctor? Just give me my ticket."

"Twenty-six shillings."

Kevin doubled over with a renewed spasm of coughing. He grasped the ticket and shoved it into his pocket without bothering to wait for change.

The great hall of Paddington echoed with the din of thousands of voices. Still thirty minutes before boarding time. Where were Lori Kalner and her companions?

Kevin staggered into the throng in search of her. Where had she gone?

◎

Lori, Elisa, and Eva sat at a table in the corner of the Paddington tea shop and sipped tea in silence.

Warming her hands on the cup, Lori thought of her mother. *Poor Mama.* What would she do now that Papa was dead? How would Helen Ibsen manage to face life without him?

Twenty-five years they had been married, and Lori had never heard either of her parents utter even one cross word to the other. They had been childhood friends. Just as Lori and Jacob had always been friends before they had fallen in love.

Lori bit her lip and tried not to imagine what she would do if news came that Jacob was dead. How would she manage to go on without him?

Elisa asked quietly, "Lori? Are you all right?"

Lori nodded. Opening her valise, she pulled out the notebook that contained her letters to Jacob. She had intended to write him on the train, tell him how she felt about the news from Germany. But here was a thought that could not wait to be written down. Lori did not open the notebook but replied quietly to Elisa's question, "Here's something, Elisa. For the first time, you know? For the first time—ever—it occurred to me how much like Mama I am. And I am not going to Wales as a daughter to comfort my mother, but as a woman to comfort a woman who has lost her beloved. As I wait to hear news from Jacob—or about Jacob—I think I may know my own mother better at this moment than I have ever known her in my life. Perhaps in seeing how she gets through this terrible news I will also get through whatever faces me on the road ahead."

"Yes—" Elisa patted her hand—"I know. I do. I felt the same with my mother after Murphy and I were married. She's become my best friend. No one else I would trust to watch over Katie and the boys."

Eva did not speak but gazed intently over Lori's shoulder. It seemed as though she had not heard a word Lori and Elisa had said. From behind her raised teacup she whispered, "Don't look now, but . . . there is a man over there staring at you, Elisa. First at Lori and then you. By turns . . . no! Don't look now. Not until I say. He got out of a taxi just behind ours. He was standing near Lori in the ticket queue. I think . . . I think I've seen him near Primrose Hill. Riding the bus. Staring. I thought it was because, you know, the way some men stare at women. But I don't think so." She sipped her tea and whispered again, "Look at him now."

Lori turned and glanced at the stranger in the brown raincoat. Familiar? Could he be following them? She shook her head. "I don't know."

Elisa was likewise unhelpful. "So many faces every day."

The PA system announced that their train would soon be arriving on Track 11. Lori gulped her tea and rose from the table. Involuntarily she looked toward the man.

He was indeed glaring angrily in their direction. He appeared to be near Murphy's age—thirtyish, thin, and fevered looking. Drunk? His hat was shoved back on his head. Eyes were red. Perspiration poured from his face and soaked his collar. And yes, he was staring openly at her. Blocking the exit.

Two gentlemen pushed past him. He remained rooted like a tree, swaying in the doorway. Waiting. Waiting for her. Waiting for them. Lori was almost sure of it.

But to what end? Yes, she was the daughter of an avowed enemy of the Reich. But now that Papa was dead, why would anyone care about her?

A chill coursed through her. She prayed silently, *Lord, help me. I am afraid. Silly. Oh, help me not to give in to this.*

She dismissed her fears. She told herself she had simply become paranoid.

The fellow began to cough. He staggered back and leaned against the wall of the tea shop as Eva started toward the exit.

"He's quite ill, then," said a plump, balding man to his wife as they sat down at the table next to Lori and Elisa, who were gathering their belongings to follow Eva.

"Yes, Horace. Look there. Somebody ring a doctor!"

The pursuer slumped forward and crumpled to the floor.

A crowd gathered. "Who is he?"

"No luggage."

"A ticket to Shrewsbury."

"All the way to Shrewsbury and no luggage?"

"He's burning up. It'll be a quick trip to hospital. He's not going to Shrewsbury today."

Lori clasped Elisa's hand and followed Eva. Lori was the only one of the three women who looked closely at the unconscious man before they hurried to catch the train.

23

From Lamb to Lioness

It was generally agreed by the Fleet Street crowd that Josephine Marlow, widow of good ol' Danny, had left for Warsaw an unopinionated lamb and had returned a lioness. She had been, in the political sense of the words, "born again." To the seasoned journalists in London, this change was infinitely irritating. Little Josie spouted off like Winston Churchill at the very moment when American isolationism was at a fever pitch. Even the English were wondering if going to war over Poland was such a good idea after all.

The great debate between the young widow and Konrad Lock of the Hearst syndicate was sparked by a discussion of the failed assassination of the Führer in Munich. The bombing aroused as much interest as *Gone With the Wind*. It was discussed by everyone in Europe. The arrest of French entertainer Elaine Snow as a conspirator had made international headlines.

This afternoon the whole thing was being rehashed by a troop of correspondents gathered for a very long lunch in the Savoy Grill. There was nothing else newsworthy happening, so why not eat and talk?

Josephine was starry-eyed with hope. "They'll get Hitler sooner or later. Even the German people secretly despise him."

Konrad puffed up in disagreement. "They adore him. He's another Caesar to the Deutchlanders."

"Then why try to kill him?" Josie insisted. "They know what he stands for. They're basically decent people."

Konrad considered her with a cynical twinkle in his eyes. "You've forgotten Kristal Nacht already, my dear?"

There was nothing to say to that. She passed the baton to Ernest Ward of *The New Yorker*. He accepted but also ran the opposite direction from Josie's opinion. "They love the beast all right. He's built a bankrupt, starving, pitiful democracy into a thriving nationalistic dictatorship. The trains run on time. They've scraped the bums off the streets, wiped out the loonies, euthanized the sick, and turned the asylums into maternity wards for pregnant SS bimbos reproducing little master-race replicas. What are a few Jews compared to that? What is principle compared to that?"

Josie sat forward and raised her chin in indignation. "But this Elser man . . . the bomb."

Konrad shrugged. "One little psychopath who likes to blow things up. That's all. The Germans love their Führer. They are as convinced that they are the master race as we Americans are convinced that we are one nation under God. In God we trust."

"Well, isn't it true?" Josie shot back. "We fought the last war for democracy, for freedom, for an ideal."

There were a number of looks exchanged around the table. The responses were polite chuckles and a few groans.

Konrad, who was clearly pope and chief apostle of the Doctrine of Cynicism, corrected her. "We fought the last war because the Germans sank our ships and because we insisted on freedom of the seas. We fought the last war to protect our investments. This gag about making the world safe for democracy is propaganda that American politicians use to draw in the hillbillies who could care less about freedom of the seas or investment. Like the Crusaders, those guys dying in the trenches needed some moral reason to leave home and die. And their mothers needed some noble cause to help ease the pain when the telegram came from the War Department."

"That is the ugliest thing I have ever heard," Josie proclaimed rather self-righteously. "Young men are not sent to die for other people's money! Everything we believe in, everything that is true and decent and honorable—that's why we were in the last war and why we must come into this one as well!"

But Konrad was sure of himself. He continued as if she had not uttered a word. "The democracy thing is a terrible ruse, full of holes. You really think America can deliver God and democracy to the rest of the world? The rest of the world doesn't really want either unless there is some economic benefit. They want their Hitler and their Mussolini and their Stalin and their Franco. As long as the trains run on time and there's a chicken in every pot, then people can take ideals, moral righteousness, and God—or leave them."

This had clearly disintegrated from friendly discussion to outrage for Josie Marlow. She glared back at Konrad. "You're dead wrong. I was there, you know. I saw the faces of the Polish people. Watched them at the barricades. Heard their prayers. Prayed with them for deliverance."

"And were their prayers answered?" Konrad smiled smugly.

"Not yet. But it isn't over, is it? God will answer for the right. The Allies have gone to war over Poland."

"Leave God out of this for a minute. Poor God gets tangled up in the middle of all sorts of quarrels, blamed for everything. Now ask yourself. Do you think anyone cares about Poland, Josephine? This is not about Poland. It's about those idiots, Chamberlain and Daladier, finally drawing a line in the sand so that the entire economic wealth of Europe does not end up in the hands of Hitler."

"And the people? What about them?"

"The Jews, you mean." Konrad laughed. "As if anybody cared about the Jews of Europe. I mean cared enough to do more than just talk, talk, talk about them. Poor Jews. Not even the Poles like their Jews. England shut down immigration into Palestine. The Brits are still tossing illegal Jewish immigrants into concentration camps, both in the Middle East and here in England. Go down to Kent and have a look for yourself, if you don't believe me. They're behind wire down there—refugees from Nazi Europe. And good old America has closed the floodgates, *slam-bang!* All Roosevelt cares about is getting elected to a third term. America will get into this thing as soon as our economic interest is seriously threatened, not until. And certainly not for the sake of the downtrodden. There is no God but Mammon in America. That is what the slogan means on our bills: *In Money We Trust; For Money We Fight; For Money We Bury Our Sons.* If God is interested at all, I don't believe human motives fit anywhere into His agenda."

So there it was. Konrad won the bout with a knockout. Josephine, who thought she had all the answers, backed into her corner. She listened politely to the rest of the conversation, which covered everything from the rifling of American mail by the British authorities to the lousy media censors.

Was Konrad right?

She was shaken by the logic of his arguments. She felt the whispers at her back as she left the Savoy. She saw the nudges and the winks and was embarrassed by her idealism. Was she foolish to hope that somewhere in the horror of war God still existed, still reached out, still changed the course of human events for the sake of righteousness and the value of human life?

She walked out into the gray afternoon and thought about Alexander

Riznow, the young Polish count. She flushed again at the trite optimism she had expressed to his grieving mother: *"Your son is a wonderfully brave young man. I know that God will not desert such men. . . . He will survive. I just know it."*

Obviously God had not. Alexander Riznow had died—horribly—for what? And the others? All the young Germans on the Siegfried Line and the Frenchmen on the Maginot? Both sides declaring that God was with them.

Gott mit uns! Perhaps it was, as Konrad claimed, just a jolt of propaganda to ease the pain of dying.

⸻

Josie sat across the desk from Charlie Morris, London AP chief.

Heavyset and white-haired, he had a drooping mustache that reminded Josie of Mark Twain. A true Southern gentleman, Charlie had been born in Valdosta, Georgia, in 1880 to the granddaughter of Confederate general Stonewall Jackson. He had covered the Spanish-American War in '98 and had come to London just in time to write the feature story on the funeral of Queen Victoria. Staying on nearly forty years, he was the principal European correspondent through the last war.

Charlie was a father figure to the younger members of the press. He had seen them come and go by the shipload. His Chelsea home was always open in the high standard of Southern hospitality.

This afternoon he kicked the door of his office shut and leaned back in his cracked-leather chair. He steepled his fingertips and waited, as if hoping Josie would speak first.

She did not. After all, it was Charlie who had called her into the office. Was she in trouble?

He cleared his throat. "Heard you had a little problem with the boys at the Savoy."

She felt the color climb from the collar of her uniform blouse to her hairline. "Not much. I mean . . . a little."

"I heard Konrad cut you up, chewed, and spit you right out like a chaw of tobacco."

"He's a cynic."

"That may be so. It *is* so. But he's right."

Josie put her head in her hand. "I give up, Charlie. I can't go over this again."

"Can't say I blame you, honey," he said gently. He drew a deep breath and continued. "You want to talk about what happened to you back there? Poland?"

"Something important." How could she explain? "I woke up, sort of."

He nodded and smiled. "I figgered. Lemme tell you, honey, I've seen folks wake up. I remember when I was a boy in Valdosta, and a young man died of typhoid. Back then you had to get the body in the ground right away. Well, it was after dark when we all tramped down to the cemetery for the committal service. There we stood by lantern light around the headstones. Prayin' and preachin' and singin' and such. Just then, up the road, came the town's worst drunk. An orn'rier drunk you never knew! He spotted us down there in the cemetery and thought the Lord had come and the dead had risen from their graves!" He laughed and slapped his knee.

Josie laughed with him.

Charlie continued. "It scared him so bad that man was sober ever after. He was a changed man. And you know? He began to preach to everybody who would listen. Then he preached to everybody who didn't want to listen. He became a general nuisance, arguin' with anybody about just about everythin'." He shrugged. "Folks in Valdosta liked him better as a drunk."

"Thank you, Charlie." Josie shot him a hard look. "The moral is loud and clear. Can I go now?"

"Now, now, honey, I don't believe you do hear me. I'm not sayin' you're like that fella. But here it is. Konrad was right in every cynical, nasty thing he said."

"I was talking about ideals, moral obligation."

"You mention such things to newsmen and you'll be flayed alive. You think it's bad here, wait till you get back to that white slaver Frank Blake in the Paris office."

"I have to go back, Charlie. Thanks for the care."

He studied his hands, as if considering his words carefully. "Danny won't be there."

"I know that."

"He would have been spoutin' off the same stuff as Konrad, you know. Your husband was a first-class cynic. He didn't die for a cause. He died because he was doin' his job and got under a bomb."

"I have few illusions about Danny's nobility. But I loved him."

"Paris could be rough for you just now," Charlie warned.

"I'll keep my mouth shut."

He mopped his brow and took a sip of tea. "God ought to smite a person dumb the instant the light comes on inside. That way there'd be no temptation to explain it. No argument about moral right or wrong or the existence of God. No way to let slogans substitute for actions. If only Christians couldn't preach on and on like that Valdosta drunk! Only way we'd have to tell other people about the love of God would be to show it, to live it. Give a cup of cool water to someone who is thirsty. Comfort some kid. It's not a church or a religion; it's a way of life. It's a different kind of war. It never ends."

Josie nodded, grateful that he seemed to understand. "That's what I want to do, Charlie."

"There are goin' to be a lot of kids in need of comfort before this is over, Josephine. There's no stoppin' it now. For all the reasons Konrad gave, this is likely to be a long, mean, ugly war. Whoever is left standin' at the end will win. And if you get in the middle of it and live out the light as you see it, maybe nobody is ever going to say thank you. Maybe only God will ever know what good you do. Are you willin' to face that?"

"I want to make a difference, Charlie. I don't want to just die without making things better by having lived. Isn't this the time . . . such a time . . . when the world needs people who measure convictions against God's love and then act on the best impulse they have? In Warsaw, up to the end, I saw people who lived and died just that way. And suddenly I saw how small and blind my own soul had been. What difference have I made? It seems to me I must be alive for some reason I don't know yet."

Charlie grinned. "That's what I thought you'd say. But trouble comes when you live out your convictions. You're young and full of hope, and you ought to be warned. I've seen souls wake up before, Josephine. You could get hurt." The old gentleman put his hand out to her. "If you need to come back to London, I'll have a place for you."

᠆ᡋᢙ

It was growing cold and threatened rain. Horst drove along the low ridge that led to the gravel drive of Arabian Nights Stud Farm. The pastures were empty; the rail fences that in warmer months separated yearlings from weanlings and weanlings from broodmares stood stiffly in piles of autumn leaves.

On such a day, Horst knew, Katrina would be exercising the horses in the shelter of the small indoor arena and lunging them in the round pen.

Like the horses she bred and trained, she hated the gloomy, damp months in northern Germany. Her father was purest Prussian, as hard and unyielding as a block of ice. But her mother was Italian, and the hot temperament and love of the Mediterranean climate had been passed along to Katrina. Often Katrina blamed her excessive love of Arabian horses on the Italian side of her heritage. Horst had come to agree with Katrina that she did indeed match most of the characteristics that marked the best of that breed: fine-boned, delicate features, intelligent eyes, a passionate disposition, seemingly inexhaustible energy, and a love of warm climate.

Smoke rose from the chimneys at either end of the stone stables that joined the domed riding arena. Horst followed the recent tracks of a large double-axeled truck that was backed up to the arena doors.

No use driving past the barns and stables to the enormous Georgian-style redbrick mansion that crowned a low hill overlooking the farm. Katrina would, no doubt, be where the horses were.

He parked beside the canvas-covered truck. It bore the insignia of a Wehrmacht troop lorry, except that the benches had been removed and the empty floor was covered with horse manure. A scarred wooden ramp leading from the truck into the dark interior of the stable evidenced that horses were either going or coming today.

Horst almost regretted that he had not warned Katrina that he was coming. She was in the middle of something. Now here he was, hoping she would be ecstatic about his surprise arrival.

The sound of unhappy neighing emanated from the far end of the building. He strode in, grateful for the sudden warmth and the sweet, familiar scent of hay and horses. Rows of alert Arabians peered out at him from behind heavy wood stall doors. Pert ears twitched expectantly, and every equine face turned toward him. Placards bearing the names of Greek gods, ancient heroes, and constellations hung above each stall, but Horst knew their names without the aids. Othello, black as a crow's wing, gave a familiar nicker as he passed. Venus, dapple-gray and elegant, pawed the floor and wagged her head impatiently as he walked on without stopping. Prometheus, muscled and impatient, stretched out his long neck to be touched.

There was the familiar, and yet there was much that had changed since August.

He walked past what had been the tack room. Where were the saddles and bridles? A bed and a small chest of drawers filled the space. A heavy blue wool coat hung from a hook that had previously held lunge lines.

From the upstairs quarters that had been the residence of two stable-boys the laughter of children penetrated the planks. Children? The stablehands were unmarried adolescents. Perhaps the sounds were from the cook's grandchildren, he speculated as delighted squeals followed him through the tall double doors into the arena.

Within the oval enclosure, twenty mud-caked, unkempt Arabian horses milled around in restless apprehension. Katrina, at the opposite end of the arena, studied the animals over the fence. Horst remained in the shadowed doorframe, watching her as she pulled herself up to sit on the rail. She was dressed in a black jacket over tan riding breeches and tall black boots. Her expression showed some displeasure at the condition of the horses. Behind her, in the shadows, stood a white-haired old man; a tall, thin young man; and a mousy young woman about Katrina's age. All three appeared to be exhausted. The strangers were silent and grim as an officer in the black uniform of an SS lieutenant gestured toward the animals and spoke in low, insistent tones to Katrina. One quarter of the way around the arena were Hans and Adam, the two stableboys.

"Excellent broodmares," said the officer. "General Göring is most anxious . . ."

Katrina did not reply for a long moment. Then she blurted out, "When I saw these mares in Poland last summer they were . . ." She turned her head and her words were lost to Horst, but he could tell she was angry. "Now . . . just . . . prisoners of war . . . tell Herr General he shall have my bank draft, and that I will need to keep Herr Brezinski and his son and daughter-in-law in my employment to help get the animals back into condition."

At this, the stooped old man looked down at the ground. Only in that instant did Horst recognize Walther Brezinski, the head trainer of Poland's finest Arabians. He was also a Jew. Brezinski had aged almost beyond recognition since Horst had last seen him.

"The general . . . not authorized . . . this Jew . . . Brezinski was only to assist with the mares until delivery."

"I cannot purchase the animals unless Herr Brezinski and his family members remain part of the agreement. You can see my stables are full. There are three mares in foal. The Reich has drafted my best help, including my veterinarian. I have all the stock I can manage now. The deal I struck with General Göring was Brezinski *and* the horses . . . or nothing. The armaments industry of the Fatherland has six hundred thousand Polish war prisoners now at work in factories on German soil. Surely the Fatherland can spare me three in the interest of maintaining the most elite breeding program in the world. Either that or risk the production of Arabian horses inferior to those bred in prewar Poland."

Horst crossed his arms and leaned against the doorframe to wait until the scene was played out. *Bravo, Katrina.* If there was anything these SS imbeciles were obsessed with, it was breeding programs.

"Frau von Bockman . . . I have not the authority. . . ."

"Then you had better telephone the general. I understand he is ten miles away at Karin Hall. He will not be pleased if you, by your own authority, violate his word of honor . . . the word given to me in this transaction. The telephone is in the office." She snapped her fingers and called a stableboy to guide the officer to the telephone. "Adam!"

The boy sprinted to the side of the lieutenant and led him into the office as Katrina remained perched on the railing. There was silence except for the snorting of horses and the scuff of hooves against the turf. Brezinski did not speak or move.

Horst dared not disrupt Katrina's resolve by suddenly appearing on the scene. She was doing well without him. She was strong and savvy. Hiding her long friendship with Walther Brezinski; his son, Jan; and daughter-in-law, Nadia, she pretended that her only interest was in the welfare of the horses. Prove to a Nazi that a Jew was essential to the well-being of the mares, and then perhaps the Jew had some value. Nazis prided themselves in their love of animals, after all.

A few minutes passed. The officer emerged from the office. "Reichsführer Göring concurs that Herr Brezinski and his assistants remain in your service. He makes you personally responsible for their custody, however. He wishes to receive the bank draft at once."

"What else?" Katrina replied in a steely voice. Then to Brezinski she snapped an order. "All right. Get the mares groomed and fed while I attend to business. You will be quartered in the barn."

This seemed to please the SS lieutenant.

Walther Brezinski, who had often sipped tea with Katrina and Horst on the veranda of his fine estate in Poland, nodded silently without looking his savior in the eye.

Horst retreated back into the stables. He was scratching the soft muzzle of Othello when the SS lieutenant strolled past him alone. The man cast a startled look at Horst, who greeted him with an enthusiastic "Heil!" The SS lieutenant left without further conversation. Horst walked back toward the arena and this time stood beneath the floodlight.

Brezinski wept as he led a sorrel mare from the herd. Speaking to the animal in French, he called her *"Ma chèrie"* and promised her she would not have to endure any further abuse since coming to the estate of his dear friends.

Katrina spoke quietly to Jan and Nadia, gesturing toward the horses and smiling with great relief. Nadia glanced up, spotting Horst at the far end of the arena. At first sight of the uniform, her smile faded and she went pale.

"Don't be afraid, Nadia. It's only me," Horst called as he took off his peaked cap and tossed it into the air.

Katrina whirled around at the sound of his voice. With a little cry, she ran to him, calling his name. "Oh, my darling!" She threw herself into his arms. "You're here! Oh, Horst! You wouldn't believe . . . can't imagine . . . what it has been like here since you have been gone!"

⌾

The quiet elegance of Arabian Nights Stud Farm was disturbed by the shouts of children playing outside. When Horst asked about the presence of so many strangers at his home, Katrina explained that they were children evacuated from Berlin. But Horst had not been aware that the panic about possible air raids had touched Germany as it had England and France. He watched them playing tag and then, at the call of a chaperone, run to their supper, which was served each night in the stables.

He was glad when darkness fell and Katrina called up to announce that his dinner guests had arrived.

The white linen cloth that covered the long table was trimmed in Battenburg lace. The oval dining room was large enough to comfortably seat fifty guests, but tonight the table was set for four. Century-old Meissen china gleamed on sterling silver chargers, flanked by the Sheffield tableware Katrina had purchased on their honeymoon in England. Finger bowls, wine and water goblets glistened in the candlelight.

For all this refinement, the dinner to celebrate Horst's safe return was simple German home cooking, just as Horst requested. Included on the menu were roast pork with potatoes, spaetzle noodles, applesauce made with apples from their own orchard, and imported French burgundy wine.

Instead of a big celebration with little-known acquaintances and party functionaries, Horst had insisted that they invite only Katrina's sister and brother-in-law.

"Kurt and Gretchen Hulse are company enough. Let us just be glad to be together, without having to perform," he had said wearily.

The war, and the fact that both men would soon be leaving again to rejoin their units, lurked on the fringes of conversation. And so while the atmosphere was pleasant, it was also restrained.

Horst stood and raised his glass in a toast to Kurt, who served with aerial reconnaissance. "To my friend Kurt, the eyes of the Wehrmacht. And to the greater glory of Germany. May you continue to fight with honor and courage, and return from your service to our Fatherland in safety."

Suddenly the atmosphere in the formal dining room of the Arabian Nights Stud Farm had more in common with the naked tree branches pointing like bayonets outside the picture window than with fairy tales and happy endings. Standing beside his chair with his upraised glass, Horst felt as if he had accidentally spoken in some unknown language. Katrina, Gretchen, and Kurt remained seated, staring at him.

Katrina spoke up, trying to deflect what she saw coming. "Let us

drink to your safe return, Horst—yours and Kurt's—and to your continued protection."

But no one raised a glass.

"What is it?" Horst sat down slowly. "Has something happened?"

"That's right, Horst," Kurt said. "You need to be sitting down for
this." He glanced at Katrina. "It is no good, Katrina. We had better get
this out in the open. The only three people I completely trust in the
whole world are in this room, and I need to talk."

Kurt was dressed in civilian clothes, even though he was a military
observation pilot. In contrast, Horst was wearing his full uniform with
his newly attached major's insignia. Horst had believed that being
home, returning to a hero's welcome and the congratulations for his
promotion, would revitalize his eagerness for the fight. Now he wasn't
so sure.

"I only saw combat from the altitude of my Henschel recon plane,
but I saw enough! It wasn't what I expected—not the heroic defense of
the Fatherland that I enlisted for," Kurt continued.

Visions of what he himself had seen in Poland flooded over Horst,
but he could not let such a remark go unchallenged. *Duty,* he reminded
himself. *Only duty gives safety.*

"Come now, Kurt!" Horst improvised. "I know what you are saying,
my friend. I have also been troubled in my thoughts. But to talk openly
about it before the women will only make us sound like weaklings—or
worse, cowards. Look at it this way: The overwhelming power of our
forces meant that the war got over sooner rather than lasting longer.
Probably lives were saved by the speedy conclusion."

Kurt's voice fell almost to a whisper. "It seems you have been reading
Joseph Goebbels' propaganda, Horst. The king of lies. But the truth is that
war in Poland was quick but not painless. The agony continues and grows
each day for the conquered. Even propaganda cannot excuse murder."

Horst tried to shrug off Kurt's serious mood. "War is no pleasure
cruise on the Rhine."

"I am not speaking of war. I am speaking of murder."

"Then perhaps you should not speak at all." Horst became suddenly
dismayed. He again saw in his mind the Polish Jewess being gunned
down.

"Since when have we been afraid of the truth?" Kurt gave a bitter
laugh. "I can answer that myself. Since Hitler became chancellor."

"This is not the place," Horst flared.

"Where are you?" Kurt leaned forward and searched the face of his
friend. "Horst von Bockman is—was—a man of honor. Do you want to
be associated with murdering innocent women and children?"

Gretchen laid her hand on her husband's arm. She was an older reflection of Katrina, but quieter and more reserved. "Please, Kurt," she begged. "We cannot say such things to the ones we care about."

"This is important," Kurt argued.

"I agree," Horst replied. He spouted Wehrmacht textbook doctrine. "To know the true feelings of those who are next to you in battle is essential. How could anyone trust you to come through for them, knowing that your sense of duty is halfhearted, to say the least? Duty has nothing to do with politics."

"Oh yes, hide behind your precious belief in duty," Kurt said scornfully. "Hitler knows exactly what he's doing with his blood oaths and his voodoo ceremonies. You talk just like one of them!"

"One of whom?" Horst said coldly.

"You know what I mean . . . the SS! Ignorant, savage, murdering brutes who hide behind their oaths of duty and loyalty when they commit acts of terror like a pack of wild dogs!"

Horst and Kurt rose from their chairs. They glared at one another across the table. Horst clenched and unclenched his fists, as if ready to jump at Kurt's throat.

"Please, please," Katrina pleaded. "Sit down, both of you. Kurt, I am sure you didn't mean to compare Horst to those horrible monsters, did you?"

Kurt ran his hands through his dark, slicked-back hair and fell heavily into his chair. "No . . . I . . . no. I am sorry, Horst. It's just that . . . I flew over too many Polish villages where the SS had been."

"And?" prompted Horst, though he already knew the answer. It was as if everything he had kept bottled up inside was now spilling from Kurt.

"You are right," Kurt said. "Enough of this. I've ruined a perfectly fine evening. A man cannot weep for the entire world. Even Poland is too big. In days like these he must chose carefully who and what he may shed tears for. It is too dangerous to do otherwise."

Horst unbuttoned his tunic's top button in order to breathe better. He felt choked, so he reached for his wineglass, knocking it over. Red fluid splashed across the white tablecloth, and drops of it spattered on Katrina's white blouse.

The discussion could not end yet. "It should not have happened," Horst managed to get out. "But it will be different in the West. It will be a real war, man to man, against an enemy that is ready for us. What is a man if he does not honor his oath, Kurt? Think of that."

Kurt raised his gaze from the slowly congealing gravy on his plate. "And what is a country that does not keep its promises, Horst? Do you think that all the pledges and guarantees and assurances coming out of the Chancellery will keep our tanks from rolling over Belgium and Holland? Neutrals, Horst. Neutrals! Innocent people who believe that not taking sides will keep them safe! Do you really believe Hitler will keep his sacred word of honor? Does anyone believe it anymore?"

"What will you do then?" Horst demanded. "Refuse to serve? Leave Gretchen at the mercy of the Gestapo while you rot in prison?"

"No," Kurt said quietly. "I am sending her out of the country, to Switzerland first." Kurt glanced sharply at Katrina. "You have not told him your mother and father are not coming back from Switzerland?"

Horst sat back, stunned. To Katrina he stammered, "N-not coming back?"

She nodded but did not look at him. "It is better. Father has friends . . . people who know. The Gestapo has a thick file on Father. It was a matter of time."

Horst blinked at her in amazement and then turned his inquiry back to Kurt. "And what about you?"

"I mean to join them in Switzerland, if I can. But there is something I have to do first . . . a friend and I . . . we mean to convince Belgium that they are not at all neutral in the Führer's future plans."

"But how could you?"

"I fly over Belgium every day, Horst."

"That is not what I mean. I mean—" Horst tapped his finger to his heart—"this! To betray your country, your honor."

"I lost my country long ago. I seek to preserve my honor now," Kurt replied simply. "Even if my dearest friend should report me. I had to tell you, Horst. We will not likely meet again soon. I had hoped you would understand."

There was nothing more to say. Horst could not betray Kurt for his disloyalty because to do so would also condemn Gretchen. But by remaining silent after hearing such treason, he was himself condemned, and Katrina along with him. As these thoughts spun around in his head, he stared at the drop of wine on Katrina's blouse. It was so like a bullet wound, just over her heart.

24

Friends in High Places

Bettws-y-Coed, Wales

My dearest Jacob,

Long hours on many trains brought me at last to this lovely world. The nearest village is Bettws-y-Coed, which is pronounced in lyrical Welsh "Bettoosycoed" and means "Chapel in the Wood."

The farmhouse where Mother and Aunt Anna and the children live is in a quiet glen surrounded by pastureland. It is no more than a thatched stone cottage of three rooms. Two tiny bedchambers above one main room. The boys sleep together in a feather bed in one room. Mother, Aunt Anna, and the babies occupy the other. Eva and I have the best of all accommodations, for we sleep on the floor near a cast-iron stove that serves for both cooking and heating. Elisa is overjoyed to be reunited with baby Katie. I think she may stay on here.

The boys have learned to fish, thanks to an old fellow who keeps a small herd of sheep across a stone fence. He has taken a liking to Mark and Jamie, and Murphy and Elisa's adopted boys, Charles and Louis, and every afternoon after school he takes them on excursions to fish in the Conway. Mother says almost every night there is good fresh fish to eat. Milk for the babies comes from healthy goats. Mother and Anna attend church at a Protestant chapel in Bettws. Aunt Anna plays an old organ there. The pastor and his wife remember very well when Papa came to London to

preach at Buckingham Chapel in the church of Martin Lloyd-
Jones about the Christian struggle in Germany and coming
persecution.

Mother was at peace when I brought her the news about Papa.
She said she had known it somehow. Her dreams had been of Papa.
His words. His faith. His kindness to all. He was truly the hands
and voice of Christ alive and vibrant in a terrible hour.

In this little village we are surrounded by peace everywhere we
look. In the love of the people. Their souls are as filled with music as
their language. They sing always—as they walk and when they sup.
At worship and in work you hear their voices raised in song to their
Creator.

Papa is gone. His murderers are still alive, still continuing to
plunge the world into darkness. But I am at peace in this place.
Regaining my strength through prayer and remembering my
father's teachings in the Scriptures.

Mother says that what is happening now must somehow signal to
every believer that this is a spiritual battle. She reminded me that
whenever God is going to do something mighty, Satan attacks
Christians and Jews in the most horrific way. And yet Darkness is,
in in the end, always defeated by the light of only one candle.

Before I came to Wales, I did not know that David Lloyd
George—a friend of Winston Churchill—was the prime minister of
England in the first war. He started his career as a Welsh
Protestant preacher. They say that he is now and always was a great
believer that someday the nation of Israel would be reborn. He is a
Member of Parliament, though he is now very old, and supports a
Jewish homeland with Jerusalem as its capital.

I only wish there was an Israel for all the Jews of Hitler's
Europe to flee to. It seems there is nowhere in all the world that Jews
can call home but that place.

I pray daily that you have reached those blessed shores. The
Promised Land. Are you there now, my dearest husband? Or are
you with Papa? The Promised Land. It is not only a name for
heaven, Papa said. It was eternally promised by God as a homeland
here on earth for all Jews. One day the promise of God will be
fulfilled.

I take many long walks through the woods. I sit and pray long
hours beside the waterfalls. Every day more children evacuated from
London swell the population of the village. They are welcomed with
joy and affection and soon are singing the lovely Welsh songs and

*trekking to places called Fairie Glen! It seems very far away from
what is happening in Poland.*

*My courage is renewed by my mother's courage and a belief that
somehow the enemy of all mankind will be defeated.*

*I will return to London with Eva in a few weeks so that I might
be there when you come home to me. There is much work to do, and I
will take back with me the strength to do it.*

*One day, perhaps, you and I will come back to Bettws-y-Coed
together. It is, to me, like heaven.*

I love you,

Lori

∾

"Pneumonia. He died just after midnight, Mr. Murphy. Kevin Miller is
the name used on his identification papers." Inspector Dunston of Scotland Yard pulled back the sheet, revealing the face of the corpse on the
slab in the morgue. "Do you know him?"

Murphy blinked down at the body. "Never seen him before. American?"

"German-born. Naturalized British citizen."

"Sorry. Nobody I recognize. What is this about?"

Dunston's eyes narrowed briefly as he gestured for the corpse to be
returned to storage. "Come along." He escorted Murphy to a poorly lit,
windowless office with a gray metal desk, one steel chair, and a black file
cabinet.

Opening a file drawer, the inspector withdrew a tan folder and
placed it on the ink-marred blotter. "Where is your wife?"

"My wife?"

"Elisa, isn't it?"

"She's in Wales. In Wales with Lori Kalner and . . . a friend. Our children are there. Elisa's mother and Lori's mother evacuated with the first
wave. Lori's father died, and the three of them traveled north to—"

"Wales. Left out of Paddington, did they?" Dunston slumped in the
chair and steepled his fingers.

Murphy sat on the desk. "Yes. Paddington."

"Thursday. Thursday. So. You're saying your wife and Lori Kalner
and another woman left London on Thursday out of Paddington."

"Yes. But what has this got to do—"

"Kevin Miller collapsed in Paddington Station on Thursday."
Dunston opened the folder. "He was carrying this." Holding up a ticket
to Shrewsbury, he pressed it into Murphy's hand. "And he had these

photographs of your wife and Lori Kalner on him." Dunston spread two dozen photos of Elisa and Lori like a deck of cards.

Murphy felt his stomach turn. "So he was . . ."

Dunston nodded and pushed a notebook across the desk. "He's kept records of their coming and going. See there. Times. Dates. Bus routes. Good job you hired Inspector Stone as a bodyguard. You see here. From the time you were staying at the Savoy until . . . well, until Thursday. You yourself know how significant your wife and Lori Kalner are to the Gestapo. Several near misses. Miller had plans to throw one or both beneath the wheels of a train. I would suggest that you send Inspector Stone to Wales immediately until you can get them to America."

"Sure. I mean, you'll verify all this? The danger? Verify it with the American Embassy for us? They've been dragging their feet on the visas."

"It's already been seen to. Within a month or two your wife and children will be on their way. You have friends, it seems, in high places, Mr. Murphy."

"Yes. Friends in high places." Murphy smiled grimly as he silently breathed a prayer of thanks.

"As for Lori Kalner, that will be more difficult. Perhaps she will be safe in Wales. At any rate, I would ring Inspector Stone. Nazis are something like cockroaches. See one skitter across the kitchen floor, and you can be certain there are a hundred more lurking beneath the icebox."

⤸

Conscious that she was an outsider among a family in mourning, Eva threw herself into taking up household chores and looking after the seven-year-old-twins, Charles and Louis.

She remained in the background while Lori and her mother, Helen, took long walks or reminisced by the fire and prayed together. Jamie, the eleven-year-old son of Karl Ibsen, expressed his grief at the loss of his father solely through angry outbursts and hikes into the hills. Mark, Lori's eleven-year-old brother-in-law, watched Jamie with sympathetic eyes. Mark still didn't know the fate of his parents, Leona and Richard Kalner. Elisa said more than once that she wished Murphy was there so both Jamie and Mark would have a man to talk to.

Elisa and her mother, Anna, both remarkably alike in appearance, demeanor, and even the sound of their voices, likewise busied themselves on behalf of the grieving mother and daughter. They were relatives, so their nearness did not seem like an intrusion.

Eva wondered if Lori knew how lucky she was to be surrounded by love in such a difficult time. Eva had been utterly alone in Warsaw when news had come in October 1938 that her entire family had been rounded up with over two hundred other Jewish residents of the village and taken into the woods by an SS platoon. They had never returned.

What Eva would have given to have been with them. A few minutes of terror, and then it had all been over for them. They had left life together. *Together.*

Only Eva remained. Living outside the unassailable border of Lori Kalner's grief, Eva did not speak of her own loneliness or regret. Neither Lori nor her mother, or anyone else in the household, was fully aware of what Eva had lost or what the miracle gift of Rachel Lubetkin's passport had meant to her.

Possibly a new life. With Mac McGrath. Possibly.

Not an hour passed that she did not pray for Rachel Lubetkin. Rachel, who had made the choice to stay and perhaps die with her family. It was a choice Eva understood and envied. Eva, who had no one left to live for, continued living nonetheless.

Each weekday after lunch Eva volunteered to walk three miles into the village to pick up the mail and any groceries that were needed. The trek through luxuriantly wooded hills to Bettws-y-Coed kept her out of the house until almost suppertime. The days were growing short. The sun rose late and set early. Eva timed her going and coming so she returned to the lane that led to the house and waited beside an ancient oak until she saw the lamp was lit and placed in the window.

The occupants of the house did not know it was her signal to reenter their world. They did not realize she lingered in order to give them time when they might weep together or speak of Pastor Ibsen tenderly without an outsider overhearing.

There were stars in the sky tonight when Eva reached the farmhouse. Her fingers were stiff from the autumn cold. She had carried salt and a five-pound sack of flour home from the village.

A car was pulled to the side of the road.

A tall, dark-haired man in his late twenties stooped to peel away the blackout paper from his headlamps. Perhaps there was no blackout in Wales. Turning at her footstep he seemed startled by her curious gaze. "Can't drive these roads with no headlamps."

"I don't imagine the Germans will bomb Wales."

He stood, crossed his arms, and leaned against the automobile. "No. Nothing here but evacuees, farmers, and fishermen."

She smiled. "You are clearly not in either of the first two categories."

"Right. Angler. Out to catch the big one before my regiment is called up to fight the Hun."

"So. This is the way you English prepare for war. You go fishing."

"Have I been insulted?"

"Not at all."

"I'm relieved. I came here to fish and play a bit of solitaire. And you? Are you a farmer or an evacuee?" His eyes hardened.

"Neither." Eva, suddenly uneasy, took a step back into the lane that led to the house. "On holiday. Staying with friends."

Was he probing her for information?

"You're not English. The accent. Not German. Czech? I would say Czechoslovakia. Clearly."

"There is no Czechoslovakia."

"Point taken. Well. Anyway. I had hoped to be checked into my lodgings by now. An early day tomorrow. Plenty of big fish hiding in the rocks and rills of the Conway, I hear. Pardon me. My name is Erich. And you?"

"Julia." Eva clutched the basket of groceries close and offered the false name on her passport.

"Do you have a last name?"

"Julia will do."

"Well, Julia, may I trouble you for directions? Which way to the village of Bettws-y-Coed?"

"Three miles along the road. Straight on the direction you're headed."

"Thank you. I'm sure we'll meet again. I'll be staying at the Swan. Wish me luck. Fishing." Somehow his smile was unnerving.

"Good luck then. And good evening."

☙

It was half past eight in the evening. Eva enjoyed this hour on the farm more than any other. Supper done. Dishes washed and stacked. Schoolwork completed. A game of chess left unfinished on the table.

The older boys were all in bed, sleeping beneath the down quilt like a pile of puppies. Elisa rocked Katie beside the fire. Baby Alfie slept in Lori's arms. Helen Ibsen sat near her as she mended a tear in Jamie's shirt. Anna Lindheim played Brahms on the ancient upright piano in the corner.

Eva attempted to better her command of English by reading aloud from a voluminous volume of *The Old Curiosity Shop* by Charles Dickens.

> "The messenger soon returned at the head of a long row of urchins, great and small, who, being confronted by the bachelor at the house door, fell into various convulsions of politeness; clutching their hats and caps, squeezing them into the smallest dimensions, and making all manner of bows and scrapes, which

> the little old gentleman contemplated with excessive
> satisfaction, and expressed his approval of by a great many nods
> and smiles. . . ."

Elisa remarked wryly, "All that in one sentence! A person would die of suffocation if she tried to read it all in one breath."

Lori added, "This explains what is meant about the English being so long-winded."

Helen bit off the thread and knotted it. "Yes. These English fight the war against the Nazis much like Dickens writes. With a great deal of verbiage and very little being accomplished in the end."

Eva laughed and closed the book. "Tea, anyone?"

At that a loud rapping sounded on the door.

Anna's music fell silent. Each task and pleasant thought came to an abrupt halt.

"It's half-eight." Anna swiveled around on the piano stool.

Helen placed her sewing in the basket. "Who would be out this far from the village at such an hour?"

The knocking sounded again, more insistent.

Eva tossed her head and squared her shoulders. "Probably someone broken down on the road. I'll see." She crept cautiously forward and laid her cheek against the door. "Who is there, please?"

The voice resounded, "It's Murphy! And Inspector Stone! Open up!"

It was a joyful reunion in spite of the ominous news Murphy brought and the fact that Eva especially remembered the man at the train station. It was decided that perhaps the women and children should stay in Wales until passage could be arranged to take them all to America.

Inspector Stone, silent through the entire recitation of facts and probabilities, eyed the fishing rod that hung in the rafters over the dining table. Though his stony expression did not change, Eva noted his glance continually returned to the fishing gear.

"So—" Murphy swilled the last of his second mug of tea—"Inspector Stone will stay here on the farm with you. Not that we think anything could happen way up here . . . but the fact remains: You were being followed."

Elisa sighed. "I was thinking that we should all just pack up and go home to London. Take the children back home. It seems so foolish to stay so far away from you when there are clearly no bombs falling. Both sides staring at one another across the Maginot Line in France. The British army trickling across the Channel. There is no war, Murphy. As lovely as this is . . ."

Anna Lindheim narrowed her eyes imperiously. "What my daughter is saying, Murphy, is that the outdoor plumbing is a difficult arrangement with so many women and children in the same dwelling. Even if the war begins in earnest . . ."

"It's not a matter of *if*. It's a matter of *when*," Murphy said. "Twenty thousand British Nazis are known to be in England. Elisa, you're staying in Wales until I can find a way to get you and the kids to America. All of you. Inspector Stone will stay on."

The hitherto silent bodyguard cleared his throat and glanced at the rod again. "Aye. Raised on a farm, I was. I'll play the part of a hired hand. The village folk'll naught think a thing of it."

"And who'll take care of you, Murphy, with all of us here?" Lori cocked an eyebrow.

"I'm leaving for France. I'll join up with Mac McGrath there."

25

Greetings from the Phony War

There were few American war correspondents awake and moving in the lobby of Hotel Thiers this morning. Enough champagne and brandy had been consumed in the brasserie press meeting the night before that Mac did not doubt many of his fellow journalists had gone to bed still fully dressed in their splendid uniforms. Of course the owners of those garments would not wake up until sometime after lunch. Blackout curtains had a way of making a man with a hangover believe it was still the middle of the night when it was really high noon.

Mac predicted this would cause no end of grief for the hotel valet, who would be expected to press myriad pairs of wrinkled trousers instantly and restore slept-in jackets to their original crispness. No doubt there would be a lot of rumpled newsmen wandering around Nancy before the day was finished.

Only Ted Munroe, radio broadcaster for Mutual, had thought to have more than one outfit made for himself. Normally his duds would have made Mussolini's tailor jealous. But last night, Lou Frankovitch had spilled—or perhaps thrown—a plate of spaghetti on Munroe's tunic, and Munroe had been too far gone to notice. It had been an interesting gathering for the eagles of newsdom.

There were about twenty survivors at 7 AM when the croissants and fresh butter and steaming coffee were put out on the long table in the lobby for the French army press officers and the international journalists.

Midbite, Mac was relieved to spot, among the other nationalities, one American he knew who was completely alive, showered, shaved, and dressed in plain tweed hunting clothes.

John Murphy looked up from lively conversation with a French officer. He waved at Mac, tugged his tweed lapel, nodded in approval of Mac's civilian clothes, and raised his coffee cup in salute.

Mac sauntered over to Murphy. "What are you doing here, Murphy? I thought you big-cheese bureau chiefs only sent the little Indians out to the trenches."

At that Murphy pulled out his wallet and showed snapshots of his wife, Elisa, holding their baby, the two Kronenberger boys, a pretty niece named Lori with an infant, a mother-in-law, and assorted others dear to his heart. "They're all up in Wales. On a farm. Until I can get them to the States," he explained. "I couldn't stand London anymore. It's a lousy, dark, lonely place when a guy's got a desk job. I got . . . irritable." He shrugged. "Fog. Coal smoke. Thought a little fresh air at the front might do me good."

"You forgot your uniform."

"Yeah. You, too." Murphy grinned.

"Ted Munroe brought two."

A long pause. Murphy cocked his head. "We could borrow one."

"The one without meatballs," Mac suggested. "We could divide it up. Epaulets, gold braid, and brass buttons. There's plenty to go around."

"I don't know. On second thought . . . if the Heinies spot us at the front with that stuff on, they'll shoot us down like generals."

A French press officer, who looked remarkably like the large half of Laurel and Hardy, announced pleasantly that the correspondents must be divided into teams of two men, with each team to be escorted to a different area of the western front. It had all the makings of a Boy Scout field trip.

Being the only two Americans who had underdressed for the occasion, it seemed natural that Mac and Murphy join forces. Assigned to a French cavalry liaison officer for the day, they shared the amiable understanding that there was no competition between them for whatever story they might discover. If there was a story . . .

Murphy studied the young, serious French captain who spoke in solemn tones to his superior officer. "Our guard dog," Murphy remarked.

"This whole trip is canned ham. A tour of the factory."

The Frenchman scratched his head and read over a slip of paper that contained the destination of the day.

"We're a bunch of old ladies on a guided tour of Atlantic City. That's all."

"Where else do you want to go?"

"Elsewhere."

"We could get arrested . . . shot at." Murphy smiled slightly, as though that was a pleasant thought.

"That would be a story, anyway. Stick with our elegant friend here, and we might as well be climbing the Eiffel Tower. What about it?"

Moments later, pockets stuffed with croissants and cheese, Mac and Murphy walked nonchalantly down a corridor to the kitchen and then out the back door of the hotel. They arrived at the garage in a roundabout way as a caravan of official government Citroëns, loaded with official government guests, clattered off en masse toward the great concrete block houses of the Maginot Line. Mac's battered Renault followed the tedious progress at some distance and then peeled off down a side road toward a village nestled in the valley sloping down to the Saar River.

The lane passed through a series of hops fields, rimmed with sheaves of tall stakes stacked together like tepees. Sunlight broke through the clouds and shone on the high peaks of the Alps that protected the eastern border of France. At first glance the countryside seemed like something lifted off a postcard, pastoral and undisturbed by the nearness of war.

But it was too quiet. No smoke drifted from the chimneys of St. Wendel. No dogs barked as Mac and Murphy entered the town. There were no people in the streets. The rubbish of unswept autumn leaves blocked the steps and doorways of homes and businesses.

"Nobody home," Mac whispered as the reflection of the passing Renault was caught in shopwindows that still displayed merchandise. "Evacuated."

Mac pulled up in front of the Hotel St. Wendel and stepped out. There was no sign of shell damage. No indication that this tiny fragment of France had been injured in any way. But a terrible dread permeated every brick and cobblestone of the dead village. A glance through the window of the hotel restaurant showed cups and plates of half-eaten food rotting on the red-checked cloth that covered the tables.

Then they heard the thunder of artillery and the thin, high scream of a shell somewhere up ahead.

"Guess we're headed in the right direction," Murphy said wryly as he peered through the window at dusty bottles of wine and withered salamis hanging like stalactites above the bar. "Good thing we brought our own lunch." Then he offered some explanation for the eerie discovery. "It's the German planes they're scared of. Not German artillery. Not tanks or infantry. Little St. Wendel is all tucked away safely behind the Maginot Line."

"No. They'll go around. And they'll fly over," Mac added with the certainty of one who had seen it all before. "Too bad the French generals haven't figured that out."

Murphy looked up. Clouds scudded across the sky in close formation. Farther to the west the tiny dots of a fighter squadron passed somewhere near the Maginot. "But the people . . . they heard about the Stukas over Poland, and so they've run away. Poor dopes. They can't run far enough away, can they, Mac?"

Mac gave a quick shake of his head. "No. Not far enough. Or fast enough. Might as well have stayed home and finished supper."

"France has the Maginot, and England has the English Channel."

They climbed back into the Renault.

"They'd better hold the Nazis here, because England's got no place to run to," Murphy continued. "And it's twenty minutes by air across the Channel. . . . Sandbags and slit trenches all around London. You know we've got barrage balloons up over the Thames, just waiting for the Luftwaffe. Paint faces on the balloons and the Thames would look like Fifth Avenue and the floats in Macy's Thanksgiving Day parade. What I wouldn't give to have my kids there to see it. The parade, I mean." He sighed.

Mac felt a wave of pity for Murphy. "I'm glad I'm not . . . " Mac thought through his meaning, choosing his words carefully. "This whole deal is tougher to handle when a guy's got a family to worry about, I guess."

John Murphy lapsed into a troubled silence. Doubtless he was thinking about his wife and kids all tucked away in Wales, which was not far enough or safe enough after all. He was wishing he had them on the other side of the Atlantic Ocean. Maybe that was the only safe place left to run to.

⨌

When Mac and Murphy arrived at the front, German artillery batteries on the opposite shore of the murky River Saar were hard at work. Above the trenches, 155-millimeter shells passed over with an ear-splitting crack.

Mac ducked lower and considered the information he had been given by the French artillery captain at the blockade an hour before. The captain had smiled with some secret amusement as he examined the pink press passes that allowed Murphy, Mac, and Mac's camera a front row view in the zone des armées. Had the captain noticed the surprise on Mac's face as a shell exploded on a hillside a half mile away?

"It is not really war up here, Monsieurs. Only afternoon target practice. We send the Boche a gift, and they return the gesture in kind. It is nothing, really. This is not Poland."

Then the captain had rapped his knuckles against the old-style American army helmet perched awkwardly on Mac's civilian head. Here was a truly serious matter. "Your tin hat, Monsieur. It looks British. Keep your head down, or the Boche will blow it off." He smiled apologetically. "If they think there are English soldiers in the trenches, they are likely to get nervous and really start something." With that advice, he sent the journalists off like rats in a maze to capture the reality of life in the trenches.

The reality in 1939 was no different than it had been in the war of 1914–1918. Cold, filthy, and miserable, the trench system had been cut into the yellow clay of the bank that sloped a few feet above the level of the Saar River. The walls were lined with woven willow. The upcoming winter was going to be hard and lousy. The lining was bellied out, and the mud had broken through in places.

Mac and Murphy made their way through an unoccupied communications trench that zigzagged toward the main lines. At any point, Mac could have filmed the entire terrain, both German and French sides, by standing on a firing step and peering over the parapet. Murphy discouraged him from this by improvising the posthumous narration of Mac's newsreel in thousands of American theatres: "You are now seeing the last footage of the so-called Phony War along the French front, filmed by the daring Movietone cameraman, the late Mac McGrath. . . . "

Mac smiled appreciatively, then paused a second longer to listen to the hacking of a machine gun and the continuous popping of rifles on the other side. Then, remembering the German dislike of British-styled helmets, he resisted the temptation to stick his neck out and trudged on.

The duckboards on the floor of the trench were muddied and scarred from months of heavy boots and rifle butts. There were no visible bloodstains. A shell screamed past close overhead. Mac and Murphy plastered themselves against the sandbags until a loud *crump* sounded not far behind the lines.

"Too close," Mac muttered as the acrid smell of cordite filled the air.

Around one more corner, the support trench emptied into the front line. Mac unsheathed his DeVry cinecamera and gave the key wind a crank.

There were ten French soldiers in this section firing rifles and submachine guns. They stood on the firing step and took aim through gaps in the sandbagged parapet. Their trench coats were caked with mud. The amount of firing along the line indicated that the trench was fully manned.

As Mac raised his camera, a machine gun let off a clip almost in his ear. His knee-jerk reaction ruined the filming. He braced himself against the sandbags and began again.

Through the viewfinder he saw a lieutenant detach himself from the jumble of filthy uniforms and look at the camera and the two journalists in puzzlement. Lowering his rifle, he hurried toward them.

"Bonjour, Monsieurs?" There was a definite question in the tone, as if a couple of tourists had lost their way to the Eiffel Tower and had somehow blundered onto the western front. This was a battle zone, after all.

"Good day," Murphy returned cheerfully as a deafening barrage roared over, drowning out his voice.

Mac gestured upward with the camera and then added in his best French, "The Heinies are really pouring it on!"

As if to confirm his statement, the shell exploded a few hundred feet behind their position, and the lieutenant forgot to ask either man for his papers. After all, what fool would be there if he was not required to be?

"What is going on?" Murphy shouted. Tides of sound surged around them as the *crump* of French guns answered their German counterparts.

During a momentary lull, the lieutenant explained, "The Nazis have been at it for several days now. Last Thursday down the line a German captain went down to the river to smoke a cigar and hurl insults at the French army across the way, as was his custom every morning. To try our patience and show off to his men, I suppose. Our captain grew weary of this hairy Boche. He got on the loudspeaker and told this fellow to cease his obscenities and go back to his Nazi pillbox at once. More insults were exchanged. The Nazi cocked a snook at our fellows! He went too far, this Nazi. What can one expect? Our captain shot the Boche, who fell over, a very surprised dead man."

The lieutenant glanced up at the sky with a pained look as yet another barrage whined over and then, after a series of rapid explosions, died away. "We were none of us happy that our captain shot the Nazi captain. It was like killing the lucky mascot, if Monsieur understands my meaning. Every morning the Boche pig insulted us but nothing happened. Now he is dead, and so now here we are, and the insults are more deadly. The Boche have advanced some on our territory. There—" he pointed—"you see, they have taken Spichern Hill. Captured French soil. Although it is in no-man's-land, it is listed in all the guidebooks as French soil. *Baedeker's Red Guide Books. Michelin Blue Guide.* It is most distressing. We have a monument to all the old battles up there."

Mac reloaded his camera and did not mention the names of all the empty frontline ghost towns in the guidebooks that were also listed as French, although not one citizen remained in residence. The face of Lorraine had changed since September and would likely alter more as time passed.

The officer indicated that Mac and Murphy should stand on the fire step, look through the opening in the parapet, and see the disaster for themselves. The Frenchman handed Mac a pair of field glasses.

The black waters of the Saar River twisted through the middle of a flat meadowland that rose gently to a sparsely wooded hill crowned with a pillbox and ringed with barbed wire. The concrete had been painted bright red and garnished with a number of black swastikas.

The French captain clucked unhappily. "That hill has been like a soccer ball over the centuries, Monsieurs. French. And now, as you can see . . . "

Spichern Hill was definitely German again. Well forward of the heavy concrete defenses and tank traps of the French Maginot Line, the loss of Spichern Hill did not matter much as a strategic position for the defense of French soil. For the Germans, it was more like winning a game of king of the mountain.

The French generals believed with fervor that the great forts of the Maginot Line would keep the German Wehrmacht on their own side forever. The Nazis could sit on Spichern Hill and shout obscenities all they wanted, but they would not get past the Maginot. They could send artillery barrages until the end of time, but they would not pass the Maginot! This motto was emblazoned on the black berets of the Maginot defenders, was it not? *Ils ne passeront pas!*

For the French riflemen in the forward trenches of no-man's-land, however, the loss of Spichern Hill was one of personal insult. Their fathers and grandfathers and great-grandfathers had died fighting the dreaded Huns over that mound.

The huge black-on-red swastikas emblazoned on what had been French concrete were somehow like the ghost of the dead German captain rising up to cock a snook at every patriot on the line and their ancestors as well! For this reason, although there was nothing much to see and no one close enough to shoot, the Frenchmen were firing their rifles every time an artillery shell roared overhead.

"Why are your men shooting?" Mac focused the field glasses on the Spichern Hill pillbox.

"We keep the heads of the Boche down. We know—but of course—they are not going to attack! We know we shall go on sitting here and dying of boredom. We shall go on shooting our machine guns at soldiers who might as well be stuffed with straw for all the harm they'll ever do to us! This is not Poland. We are not soldiers anymore; we are night watchmen. On duty till we die of old age, the way this war is going. We are the sort of guards they put outside bank vaults." He jerked a thumb in the direction of the Maginot. "Behind us is the great Maginot vault. *Ils ne passeront pas!*"

"They shall not pass." Murphy blanched and repeated the famed words of Field Marshal Petain in English as well, as a succession of stretcher bearers approached. The two Americans stepped on the fire step and flattened themselves against the revetment as they passed by.

Mac turned off his camera and watched the procession from the safe distance of his viewfinder. There were nine young men on the stretchers. Two were alive. Their skin was a waxy yellow color. They licked their blue lips with grayish tongues. The color would not show in the black-and-white-and-gray footage of the newsreel. Some of the others may have been alive. It was hard to tell. Blood dripped from the ends of the litters onto the boots of the stretcher bearers and down to the muddy duckboards of the trench. Two bodies had been gathered up and loaded piecemeal onto the stretchers.

Mac gave the grim parade twenty-five seconds of film. As he did so, the words of the lieutenant ran through his mind: *"Not soldiers anymore . . . night watchmen. On duty till we die of old age."*

Mac kept the camera rolling. He had seen this all before. For each of those nine broken French boys, this might as well have been the front lines of Poland.

How old were they? Eighteen? Nineteen? The prime age of all cannon fodder. They might just as well have faced the Panzer divisions bare-handed and shouted *"Vive la France"* as they fell like heroes! Or galloped out across the field on warhorses like knights of old to fight single combat against a German tank!

They were just as dead even though they had waited here patiently beside the Maginot with their rifles. They had believed that this war was not war, not Poland. They had wished they were home. They had talked about things young men talk about—the future!

The Maginot Line had not saved their lives. Confidence and boredom and dreams of glory had all come to an end. Now who would tell their families that this war was supposed to be the Phony War, the Twilight War, the *Sitzkrieg*, the *Drole du Guerre*, a joke?

Reports of light casualties were no comfort to the guy who got a shell bounced on his head. For that man, this was as much a war as any war had ever been. One man could die only one time, and after that, he would not care who occupied Spichern Hill. And those he left behind would not care about the loss of the hill but would mourn all their lives for the loss of the man.

Mac tried very hard not to think of such things. Or else how could he stand in this bloody trench and go on shooting footage to enlighten the civilians back home? He had given these dead and the dying twenty-five seconds of his life, and he would not give them more. He switched off the cinecamera and switched off his mind.

"I've got my lead paragraph," Murphy muttered grimly. "Greetings from the Phony War. Your son is dead."

Mac and Murphy stayed long enough to eat lunch with the soldiers, who valued news from Paris. For three hours they talked about theatre and women and philosophy and good food. They did not talk again about the war. No one ever asked them for their press passes. Mac and Murphy could have been German spies sent by the Führer to mow them all down, and they would never have known.

⸎

It had been five days since Mac and Murphy had paid a visit to the front lines. Five uneventful days. Since Hotel Thiers was crowded, Mac and Murphy had agreed to share a room. Tonight they also shared a plate of sausage and eggs for dinner in the seedy café across from the hotel. *So much for the glorified reputation of French cooking,* Mac thought as he held up his fork and allowed grease to drip from the morsel.

It was raining. Not the wild, stormy kind of rain that cleared the air and sent people dashing for cover, but a damp drizzle that oozed from the sky and seeped into joints and made old dogs moan when they got up.

"So," Murphy remarked through a mouthful of sausage, "I heard Josie Marlow is coming back to France."

Mac frowned. "Is this supposed to cheer me up?"

"Thought you might be interested."

"That cloud has no silver lining. No light at the end of the tunnel. Whatever happy cliché you can think of relating to springtime and roses and love does not apply to me and Josie Marlow."

Murphy shrugged. "Just testing the water."

"Neither hot nor cold when it comes to Josie."

"Good." Murphy wiped grease from his chin.

"Yeah? Good? Why's that?"

"Got a letter from Elisa in Wales." Murphy patted his jacket pocket.

"What's that got to do with Josie coming back to France?"

"You talk in your sleep, that's what."

"So?"

"Eva."

"I never remember my dreams." Mac fumbled for unbuttered toast and pretended not to care. So Murphy knew Mac had been dreaming about Eva. "Lousy cooks, these French. Guys are starving in the trenches because the food's so bad."

Murphy would not be deterred. "Five nights in a row you've been talking to Eva at three in the morning."

"Is that supposed to mean something? She's . . . attractive. And she's also almost ten years younger than me."

"My mother is ten years younger than my father. He was thirty-two. She was twenty-two. They've got five kids."

"But Eva . . . Eva'd never be interested in a bum like me."

"That's what you told her last night. You were snoring like a hog in the sunshine, and all at once you were talking to Eva, telling her she could do better than falling in love with someone like you. I tend to agree. But love is blind. Sometimes deaf. She'll have to be deaf to sleep in the same room with you. But that's one of those little secrets she'll discover after the wedding." Murphy shoveled in the eggs and let Mac chew on that detail awhile.

"Wedding."

"You asked her to marry you."

"Did I? And what did she say?"

Murphy patted the letter in his pocket again. "She told Lori's mom she's in love with you. Old and decrepit though you may be, Mac old buddy. At thirty-one . . . is that right? Mac! You're that old and never been kissed?"

Mac blinked dumbly at Murphy. "Can I read the letter?"

"Get your own letter." Murphy tore the return address from Elisa's letter and tossed it to Mac. "Write Eva. Tell her she's the woman of your dreams. That'll settle it. She's in love with you, and you're an idiot if you don't do something about it before someone else nabs her."

Mac held the address gingerly by the corner and stared at it. *Bettws-y-Coed, Wales. What kind of place has a name like Bettws-y-Coed?* "She . . . loves . . . me?"

"Only God knows why, but there it is."

"You think so?"

Murphy piled on another helping of food as if he liked it. "Don't tell her you snore. Trust me."

26

The Crossing

⌾

The Channel crossing from Dover to France was like a homecoming for Josephine Marlow. Now the world looked somewhat level again. The nightmare of Warsaw had receded into a distant dream. Josie's personal pain had begun to heal. No German bombs had been dropped in London, and the evacuated children were trickling back to their city with the hope that perhaps no bombs were ever going to fall on Great Britain.

The attention of the press had returned to France once again. American women wanted to know what effect the war would have on fashion, art, music, and culture, the Associated Press insisted. Throw in a few human-interest pieces on the work of the Red Cross, and it was the kind of assignment that required almost no emotional commitment. Josie wanted nothing more demanding than that. Traveling with her old friend, Alma Dodge, who had just been transferred from Fleet Street to the Paris copy desk of the AP, Josie was eager to be back in Paris.

Dark waters blended with the low, slate-colored sky of the late afternoon. The windswept coast of England seemed peaceful; the white-chalk Cliffs of Dover looked like bedsheets hung out to dry.

Less than thirty miles across the English Channel was a different picture. Hundreds of seagulls circled above the French harbor at Boulogne-sur-Mer to scream insults down at the human intruders on the docks. Gone were the herring boats and the ferry loads of tourists with their bags of bread crumbs to feed the birds of Boulogne. Of the thousands of khaki-clad men moving down the gangways of the big ships, not one even looked up at the gulls or seemed to hear them.

The din of officers' shouts and curses mingled with the roar of engines. Quayside, shiploads of military lorries, tanks, and troops were being unloaded to join the swelling ranks of the British Expeditionary Force in France.

Boulogne had been invaded by the English before. Henry VIII had taken the port in 1544. His son had given it back to France in 1550. In the eighteenth century it had become a convenient rendezvous for English duelists intent on killing one another in single combat. Then came the tourists, debtors on the run, and disenchanted British literati. The uniformed hordes appeared again in 1914 when the British arrived to help their French allies fight the war to end all wars against the Kaiser and his Huns.

Twenty-five years later, the BEF was back in Boulogne for much the same purpose. To hear Winston Churchill tell it, the issue might have been settled without disturbing the gulls of Boulogne if Herr Hitler would meet him in single combat:

"Every bully is a coward beneath the skin. And der Führer is a bully in the first degree. Tweak the little paperhanger's nose, and then we'll see!"

The problem of Hitler had, unfortunately, grown beyond the ability of one man to settle it. Now it would take millions of men and the armies of nations.

As Admiral Nelson had told the troops at Trafalgar, England expected every man to do his duty. Tweaking the paperhanger's nose was number one on the list of priorities for every soldier who arrived through the Port of Boulogne. Second on the list was to get back to England alive. In the meantime, there were the pleasant prospects of meeting beautiful French women and seeing Paris.

The little Frenchman behind the bars of the ticket booth at the train station knew all these things about the soldiers who packed the trains out of Boulogne-sur-Mer on their way to Paris. This is exactly what he was trying to explain to the two young American women at the head of the line. "Mademoiselles! You must not ride on the third-class car. It is filled with the soldiers of the British Armees!"

"*Merci.* But we have obtained our ticket vouchers from the Thomas Cook Agency in London, as you see." Josie fumbled with the leather ticket wallet. At a salary of twenty dollars a week, she could not afford to upgrade her ticket to second class. She pulled out the itinerary. "You see, Monsieur . . . " She put her finger on the line that read *Night train. Boulogne to Paris. Third class. Arrival Gare du Nord. 5:15 AM.*

"Mademoiselle." He ran his hand over his withered face in frustration. "So many soldiers, Mademoiselle! Common soldiers. On their way to Paris for a . . . for a good time. . . . "

Behind Josie, Alma Dodge spoke up. "Tell him we don't care. Tell

him we don't mind. Tell him we just want to get to Paris by morning!"
Alma had been with AP for three years in England and had never been to
Paris. The marriage of a valued copywriter on the Paris staff had left the
vacancy Alma had been waiting for. She did not want to wait a moment
longer than necessary.

Josie drew a deep breath and thought through her response in her
most refined French. "Monsieur, we do not have the funds to upgrade
our travel to a first-class sleeping compartment. I have made this trip two
dozen times. I do not mind third-class seats. We do not have funds . . . "

"What are you thinking of? This is a war, not high tourist season. I do
not care how many times you have traveled on this train. It is not like it
was before the war. Have you traveled to Paris since the war began?"

"I have been gone for some time, Monsieur."

He grimaced and tried again. "I myself am the father of eight girls,
Mademoiselle. I tell you now that third-class travel these days is like riding in a cattle car. You are two lovely heifers. The rest are bulls. The journey takes twice as long these days. Nine hours to Paris with the young
bulls. Understand?"

Josie pretended to study the itinerary. "Oh."

"*Oui,*" he said with relief. "You have come in the middle of a war. I
cannot understand how two young American ladies are here at this time.
You should have come last summer before this Hitler fellow got into Poland and started all this fuss."

"I am a member of the press, you see. Here to cover the effects of the
war," Josie said distractedly.

"An American woman a journalist? In France?"

"For the Associated Press. Well, what does it matter? It does not solve
the problem. I am slightly impoverished, at any rate. We have no funds
to purchase space in a private compartment and—"

The man raised his eyes to heaven. "I would not be able to go home
with a clear conscience." His face puckered angrily. He closed his eyes
and raised his hand for silence.

An English voice shouted up from the end of the queue, "What's that
old froggie about, then? Makin' time wif them birds 'isself? I been
practisin' me French for jus' such a chance meetin'!" The comment was
cheered by fifty soldiers in the ticket queue. A string of French phrases
about love was butchered in cockney enthusiasm.

The clerk shuddered. It was a nightmare unequalled since Henry VIII
landed in Boulogne! Two women nine hours with this . . . he took the
third-class vouchers, inked his stamp, and clamped it down with a resounding *VOID*. After that he retrieved two new cards from the second-
class drawer and filled them out carefully.

"It is senile old generals and brainless politicians who ride first class in France. That would be the safest place for young ladies. Second-class compartments are mostly reserved by officers of lesser rank. You will have to sleep sitting up, but at least you will be safe from the mob. I assign you to the compartment of a French colonel. I only just issued his ticket," he said in a paternal tone. "He is older than the foot soldiers, but you must still be on your guard. You are a woman—two women . . . I must think of my daughters. If they were here . . . but the colonel, he is French, Mademoiselle. And in matters of love, one old French bull is, I am certain, the equal of a carload of these young English bulls. Only you will not be trampled in the rush." He sniffed.

Josie smiled. "*Merci*, Monsieur. One Frenchman will be easier for us to keep an eye on."

He slid the tickets across to her. "No charge. *Vive la France!* Next please."

A sea of British khaki parted as Josie and Alma lugged their baggage toward the train on platform number 3. Offers of assistance came from several dozen of the young British bulls. Josie, mindful of the ticket clerk's warning, pretended not to understand a word of English and pushed on without stopping. She spoke to Alma in French, warning her not to look, speak, or smile at the soldiers. In spite of Josie's instructions, Alma looked and smiled.

The French colonel already occupied Compartment F. He was asleep, sprawled out to take up an entire bench seat. A copy of the Paris newspaper, *Le Journal*, covered his face. The headlines of the thin issue announced the execution of a former French singer who had been implicated in the attempt on Hitler's life in Munich. The photograph showed a strikingly beautiful blond woman in a black dress with a plunging neckline, perched beside Maurice Chevalier on top of a grand piano. It was an old photograph. Josie glanced at the story. How odd it seemed that one woman would be given almost an entire page of rationed newsprint when so many had perished in obscurity. The French had a flare for the dramatic. Thankfully, however, as the two women settled into the coach, the reality of war was little more than a dramatic headline covering the face of a snoozing Frenchman.

Josie noticed the expensive riding boots, overcoat, and cap of the French officer stashed above him in the luggage rack. His clothing showed no sign of the hardships of life in the trenches. Perched on the back of his seat, a porcelain doll dressed in white lace gazed across at Josie and Alma with serene blue eyes.

Alma shrugged and gestured toward the doll as if to dismiss the concern of the ticket taker about the lone French bull.

Josie nodded in amused agreement, then opened the window to look out as the din in the train shed increased. The old man had been right about the matter of the third-class travelers.

It was still twelve minutes until departure, but the long, forest-green train to Paris chuffed impatiently. The red signal light glowered down on the scene in the station like a disapproving eye. On the tail end of the platform, swarms of soldiers cursed and pushed impatiently to board the third-class cars. The tin roof reverberated with angry shouts. Those first men on board began to pull their friends into the cars through open windows. A conductor fought his way out from the mob and hurried toward the front of the train. He had lost his hat. His coat was torn at the sleeve.

"We must depart immediately!" he shouted. "There is no more room in third class!"

"Stampede," Alma whispered.

Behind her a strong, resonant male voice replied from under the paper. "Riot, Mademoiselle. The window, if you please. Close it. Pull the shades. And lock the door." But the colonel did not change his position.

Josie obeyed, closing the window with clumsy fingers as the first group of soldiers broke off from the mob and ran toward the uncrowded second-class cars.

"'Ey, mates! There's room up there!"

Suddenly three hundred men turned to the front of the train and swarmed toward them, leaping into second-class compartments as the whistle shrieked and the train lurched forward.

Josie locked the door but did not pull the shade as five men sprinted alongside them, gesturing and shouting to be let in. She and Alma watched the mad dash with horror as two of the men fell to the pavement. The other three kept coming as if they could race the train and somehow beat it.

"Come on! Give us a lift, girlie!"

"Poor things." Alma put her hand on the glass.

They looked so hopeful and childlike. Josie's fingers were on the latch. For a moment she considered opening the door. Could it hurt? Three homesick boys who wanted only to get to Paris?

"Enough!" the colonel shouted. He sprang to his feet, throwing the paper to the floor. With a wave to their pursuers, he reached around Josie and pulled down the shade. He remained standing in the center of the cramped space until the voices died away.

Josie looked up at him, embarrassed somehow that she had not obeyed his command, yet angry that he had not opened the door for the young men.

The colonel was not such an old bull after all. In his early thirties perhaps and darkly handsome, he was over six feet tall even without his boots. A small green-leather volume of Milton's *Paradise Lost* protruded from the right pocket of his unbuttoned tunic.

He grinned at Josie and bowed awkwardly, with a gesture as if he had doffed his hat. He did not seem to notice that Alma was beside her. He swayed slightly. Was he drunk? The doll smiled placidly from behind him.

"Poor fellows missed the train. Well, war is hell, they say." He sat down hard on the padded bench and closed his eyes. "That is what they say." Using a leather portfolio as a pillow, he stretched out on the seat and reached up to touch the leg of the doll as if to make certain it was still there. Then he groped for his newspaper.

With an unconcealed expression of amusement, Alma retrieved the rumpled sheets of *Le Journal* and spread it over the face of the colonel as the night train to Paris rocked and gained a steady rhythm.

⁂

The note was slipped under the door of the Lubetkin family flat in Nazi-occupied Warsaw in the afternoon. It was addressed to Rabbi Aaron Lubetkin and written in German by a trembling hand.

> *Verstecken Sie sich heute abend!*
> *Hide yourselves tonight!*

An early snow had fallen all day, dusting the soot-blackened streets of Warsaw with a fine white powder. The grime of multiplied millions of coal fires was covered by early evening, and still it continued to snow without letup. Steep slate rooftops, chimney pots, and wrought-iron balcony railings took on the appearance of miniature alps. Patches of white grew to heaps on the gables, then slid away in small avalanches onto the cobbled streets. Charred rubble from September's bombs and the freshly turned earth of mass graves were lost beneath the soft contours of newly fallen snow. The all-pervasive stink of death that had hung over the city suddenly vanished. Warsaw, once called the Paris of eastern Europe, was beautiful again.

The heaviest snowfall in half a century covered the scars on the landscape and made the German soldiers playful.

It was no surprise to Rabbi Aaron Lubetkin that there would be a need to protect his wife, Etta, and their four children from some planned Nazi action against the Jewish community.

From the window of their flat across from the Jewish cemetery Aaron could see hundreds of new graves filled with old friends. The synagogue was burned. His congregation was scattered, decimated. The shop across the street had long ago been boarded up.

For weeks Aaron and Etta had kept small bundles packed at the door for themselves and each of their four children. They had slept fully dressed and ready for whatever might come in the night. They had prayed and waited to hear from the priest who had promised them forged passports.

But the sender of today's warning remained a mystery. *Hide yourselves tonight!*

Etta cradled baby Yacov and stared glumly at the note in her husband's hand. "It could be a trick. You know the decree. If we try to leave without permits . . . if we are out after curfew . . . and if our new identity papers are not ready? The priest might know. Telephone him, Aaron. He might know."

Aaron let the telephone of Father Kopecky ring twelve times before he hung up. The priest was not there, but somehow Aaron found comfort that the telephone still worked. An odd bit of normalcy in a world turned upside down. They were not cut off entirely. Not yet.

In October, forty-two-year-old Aaron, along with all Jewish men between the ages of fourteen and sixty, had been compelled to register for forced labor. When asked his occupation, Aaron had answered truthfully, "Mosaic craftsman." The beady-eyed official at the desk made no mental connection to the laws of Moses or Mosaic studies in this declaration. He simply listed Aaron as a tile worker and waved him on.

Already the German general government had established twenty-eight labor camps in the Lublin district, twenty-one at Kielce, twelve in the Krakow region, and fourteen in the area around Warsaw. Men were conscripted off the streets daily to work in conditions worse than those of slaves. They disappeared without a trace, leaving families to grieve and wonder at their fate.

Aaron studied the note, then glanced in the mirror at his Semitic features. Dark eyes. High cheekbones above a black beard.

Verstecken Sie . . . Hide yourselves tonight!

There was no place in the world for Aaron to hide and not be recognized for who he was. *"Good Shabbes, Rebbe!"*

But Etta? Who would challenge such a beauty? Aquiline nose, cobalt blue eyes, shining black hair. Father Kopecky had told him as long as Etta did not speak, she could pass for a Gentile and a Catholic. Forged passports were being made for her and the children. There were still ways to get out. Even now. Bribes could be paid. There were officials who, for enough money, would look the other way as a woman and four children traveled south through Hungary and Yugoslavia, then by ship, perhaps, all the way to her father's home in Jerusalem.

Hide yourselves tonight!

Aaron had never told Etta of the priest's concerns. There were no forged documents that could transform Aaron's features. No bribe spread far enough down the line to stop some petty Nazi official in some obscure outpost from rightly suspecting Aaron's face and accusing his eyes of Jewishness. Then they would all be condemned, would they not?

He glanced out at the snow-covered cemetery. So peaceful . . .

"You and the children must go tonight to Father Kopecky."

"Not without you, Aaron." Etta was trembling.

He flared. She must not question. "Yes! Without me, Etta! Remember, tonight you are a Polish widow on your way to Mass with your children. *Nu!* Just like we talked about. I will come after. Following. Always following. Never together! You understand, Etta. We must think of the children now!"

The children.

Beautiful Rachel, just like her mother. It had been months since she had worn a dress. Tonight she was outfitted in a boy's knickers, stiff-collared shirt, tie and jacket, woolen socks and scuffed boots. Her long black hair was braided and pinned beneath a woolen cap. Etta wanted to cut it for the sake of safety. What if the cap blew off? But Rachel had wept, and Aaron had relented. A few streaks of soot from the stove concealed the clarity of her complexion. Still, she made a very pretty boy indeed. Too pretty. She had learned never to look anyone in the face lest they notice her blue eyes and long lashes and suspect the truth. There had been too many young girls raped on the streets of Warsaw lately. It was a long road between here and the safety of Jerusalem.

"Keep your fists in your pockets," Aaron warned his daughter. Her gloves had been stolen last week. Disaster. Her delicate fingers lacked the squareness of masculinity. Surely even a detail so small could be noticed. "And keep your eyes only on the toes of your boots. You understand, Daughter?"

"Yes, Papa." Fists were thrust deep into pockets and eyes looked instantly downward.

It pained Aaron that she understood the reason for this charade so completely. She was only thirteen, and yet she had seen so much.

David, at ten, also understood. He raised his chin and mocked his sister. "I told you how to stand. Not with your feet so close together." He demonstrated a masculine stance. Head cocked to one side, feet apart, toes slightly out, toothpick dangling from his lip.

Six-year-old Samuel joined the instruction. "Walk like this!" He strode past her, arms swinging like a miniature soldier marching to war. "See? You walk that sissy walk of yours, and it will be our own boys in the neighborhood who beat you."

"Papa said keep my hands in my pockets," Rachel protested. "How can I swing my arms and . . . ?"

Aaron passed her his gray wool gloves. "Wear these." They dwarfed her hands. The thumb was missing, but Samuel was right. The masculine effect was better when she swung her arms, lengthened her stride, and marched a bit.

Through this last-minute rehearsal, baby Yacov slept peacefully in Etta's arms. Etta sat in silence, sometimes looking at the sleeping child and other times staring at the snow gathering on the windowsill. Aaron knew the scene behind her was reflected in the glass pane, but she did not watch it. She did not want these images burned into her mind. Her eyes were full of other memories, as though she was hearing other voices and seeing faraway moments of their life together. Did she suspect that Aaron would not—could not—follow her and the children?

He tried not to look at her. He came close and touched the tiny hand of Yacov. He kissed Etta on the cheek and then bent to brush his lips across the soft brow of the baby. But he did not look into the eyes of Etta.

"He is too young to remember all this." Etta sighed.

"I am glad for that at least." Aaron knew the child would not remember him either, and he was not glad about that part of it.

"Are you?"

"Yes," he lied. "He will wake up in your father's house one day and think that there has never been any place but Jerusalem. Only peace and joy. Safety." He faltered. "I never should have brought you here. Or I should have sent you home last year. Found a way."

"I am glad the other children will remember what it was like in Warsaw for us . . . I mean before." She searched the face of Aaron. "You will come, Aaron?"

"Yes," he lied again. He could not let her see his eyes. She knew him too well.

"Aaron, look at me!" Her voice quavered. Behind them, Rachel marched back and forth across the stuffy little room as her brothers coached her. "Aaron, I need . . . I need . . . you to look at me!" Etta whispered hoarsely.

He glanced at the windowpane, and his eyes met hers in that shadowed reflection. In an instant he saw she had read his intention. How long had she known he would not come? Such grief in the knowing! How much better it might have been . . . so much easier . . . if they had gone on pretending.

She rose and turned to him, stroking his cheek. He caressed her face as the baby slept cradled in her left arm between them.

"They will all remember . . . I promise . . . that it was good here for us. They will! And someday when this is over . . ." Etta bowed her head against his chest as words became small and died away in the face of truth.

There would never be a someday for them.

ᘒ

Eva lay awake in the darkness. Soft footsteps in the bedroom above the kitchen told her Helen Ibsen was also up.

Moments later the glow of Helen's candle illuminated the kitchen. Helen rummaged in the primitive icebox, withdrawing a glass bottle of milk.

She glanced down at the makeshift beds where Lori and Eva slept. "Oh. Eva, dear," Helen whispered. "Did I wake you?"

"No. I was awake."

"A glass of milk?"

"Sure." Eva sat up and hugged her knees.

"My mother used to swear by hot milk and butter to help a person sleep. I think it's an old wives' tale. More likely by the time you're up and get the milk and find the saucepan and heat the milk and drink it down you're just tired out and ready to go back to bed, eh?"

"My mother . . ." Eva faltered. No good talking about her mother. Not tonight. Not when dreams of a mass grave had awakened her in a cold sweat. "I dreamed of Rachel Lubetkin. The girl who saved my life. My mother was with her. My mother . . ."

Helen seemed to sense Eva's grief. Her tone was laced with sympathy. "My dear. Your mother."

"Yes. Yes."

"Well then. The reason you're awake?"

Eva nodded and buried her face against her knees as Helen poured milk into the pan and added a pat of butter and a pinch of salt. "You have said so little, my dear. But you're in England alone?"

"Yes." Eva resisted the emotion that constricted her throat. "Alone."

Silence. Helen stepped over her and stirred the embers inside the old cookstove. "It'll just take a moment. Then we'll sit up and drink our milk together, eh? Talk about old times if you like. Pray for those you're worried about. You know it's no good at all to carry such a load alone."

"You have grief of your own. I didn't want to trouble you."

Helen sighed. "No trouble. No, no. We carry one another's burdens.

Every day now I've watched you do for us and never ask anything in return."

"My mother loved the Scripture *Bear ye one another's burdens.*"

"The fruit does not fall far from the tree, as they say. So you must be very much like your mother."

"I hope to be. That would be my prayer. She is . . . Mother . . . was . . ."

Helen sank down beside her and put an arm around her. Eva leaned against her and began to weep softly as she had not wept from the first day she had learned the fate of her family. "Please, Helen, will you say to me all the things my mother would say? If she were here? Speak to me . . . all the things I think I knew once but have forgotten. Please, Helen. For my mother's sake . . ."

Helen soothed, "There, there. Yes. It's all right. Go ahead. Oh, Eva! There will come a great day when Jesus will wipe every tear. Yes, every tear! But that day is not now. Not yet. And so . . . we must weep together. For those whom we loved. For the lost world we once knew. For the dark road we must walk until at last we reach the light. And then the True Light will embrace us. And you will see your mother and father and . . . all the others. And Jesus will wipe away even the tears we shed tonight. This is what your mother, watching you from heaven, wants you to know tonight."

27

The Twilight of Courage

The night train to Paris had been quiet since the dining car closed some hours before. Blackout restrictions required that the passage be made in darkness in the unlikely event that a German Heinkel might wish to bomb the rail lines. The shade was up, so the light in Compartment F was off.

The moon broke through the clouds, illuminating the snow-covered farmlands in a pale blue light. Josephine, her forehead pressed against the cool glass windowpane, watched the countryside slide by as Alma and the French officer dozed.

The world beyond the train seemed peaceful. Tiny villages dotted the valley. Steep-roofed houses with unlit windows clustered around tall, Gothic church spires. Rows of leafless poplar trees divided fields and defined the boundaries of roads and farms and lives.

In the moonlight, beneath the blanket of snow, the world seemed perfect, almost holy.

The calloused hands of the old man reached out for his wife in the darkness, and she lay against him as she had each night for fifty years.

In those little houses, men and women raised their children together, ate their meals together, laughed and cried together.

The weary farmer sighed with contentment as his wife slid her hands along his back and said his name.

Unseen by those on the speeding train, couples whispered secret things and made love in warm feather beds.

The clock on the nightstand hammered out the seconds as the impatient young husband pulled his bride to him, and she yielded eagerly.

Each day and night, beneath those steep roofs, the sacrament of ordinary life was performed while the train to Paris passed by, changing nothing.

How Josie envied the people she imagined behind those darkened windows! Once again the ache of loneliness welled up in her, constricting her throat until she could barely breathe. Beyond the neat rows of poplar trees was everything that she had ever dreamed her life with Daniel would be. She had wanted nothing but Daniel. To share his bed and bear his children, to be young together and then grow old, one ordinary day at a time.

He had not shared her dreams, however. In the first six years of marriage, they had spent a total of sixteen months together. While he had traveled the world on assignment with the AP, she had stayed behind to teach school. She had built her own ordinary life without him. In the summer of 1936 she had joined him in Paris, and they had fallen in love all over again.

Less than a year later he had died while covering the Spanish civil war. And something within her had died with him.

A widow at twenty-seven, she had no job, no place to go. She longed only to remain in Paris, where she and Danny had had the best of one another.

They were good to her at AP. She got a job as a reporter. Some said she was a better writer than Danny had been. More heart and soul, they said, not knowing that whatever passion Josephine had put into her writing was borne of her own personal grief. And so she had built a life without Danny after all.

The shadow of a cloud drifted across the face of the lopsided moon, blocking its light. The world was dark again, yet the image of Danny's face was clear and bright in her mind. The memory of the dead had crowded out all thought of living. She wanted to love again. There were moments when she thought she had found what she was looking for in Mac, but somehow she had let that die, too.

"Beautiful, is it not, Mademoiselle?"

The quiet voice of the colonel startled her, but she did not acknowledge him. Instead she snapped her eyes shut and pretended to be asleep. She wanted to think only about what she had lost. She resented this intrusion on her grief.

"Forgive me, Mademoiselle. I am afraid I gave you a bad impression this afternoon." He tried again. "I did not intend to be rude."

With a sigh, Josie raised her head and shifted in her seat, inching away from his outstretched legs. She was glad he could not see her face.

"We thought perhaps you were . . . ill." She did not tell him that she really thought he had been drunk.

"In need of sleep."

"You missed the evening meal."

"You are . . . American. There are no tourists since September."

"My friend and I are with the Associated Press office in Paris."

"Yes? I know of it. P.J. Phillip is a friend of mine."

"P.J. Phillip is *New York Times*, but that's close enough. We eat at the same café and attend the same press conferences."

He frowned in consternation, trying to rectify his error. "Let me see. Associated Press . . . there was a fellow I knew some time ago. Daniel Marlow."

"My husband."

He blanched. "I am sorry, madame. Clumsy of me."

"Quite all right. Danny had a million friends. Everyone knew him."

"You are working in Paris for a while?"

"For a while."

"You are not afraid of Nazis, Mademoiselle? That they will bomb Paris?"

She did not tell him that she had been in Warsaw. That her dreams were full of Stuka dive-bombers and the thunder of artillery and the screams of the dying. "I hope that will not happen, Monsieur. I hope that France will not let that happen."

"Every able-bodied man is called up, Mademoiselle. The sandbags are heaped up everywhere. Notre Dame. The Opera House. The Louvre. Everywhere. A precaution they say. But we have all seen the news films. What they did to Warsaw. Paris is crowded with the refugees from Poland. The Jews from Germany. Austria. Czechoslovakia. They would say there is reason to be frightened."

"You have family in Paris? A little girl?" Josie could just make out the silhouette of the doll behind the colonel.

He did not reply. He had closed his eyes again? drifted off to sleep? Or had she somehow intruded on his privacy just as he had done, unwittingly, to her?

"Duty calls me back to Paris," he replied after a long moment. Then silence settled between them. She did not ask what duty he had to face. She did not ask about the doll or Christmas plans or his family. Somehow she sensed that she had come too near a painful place in the French colonel's thoughts.

Nor did he question her further. The only safe topic, it seemed, had been the war, the Nazis. Would they try to do to Paris what they had done to Warsaw? Who could say? For strangers on a train, nothing remained to be discussed.

Alma stirred and sat up. "How much longer till Paris?" she moaned.

"Four hours, Mademoiselle," the colonel replied in a voice so heavy that Josie was certain he wished he had more time before the train arrived at Gare du Nord.

"*Merci*," Alma slurred. "My neck will be bent like the hunchback of Notre Dame by then." Then she promptly went back to sleep.

For a time, the colonel sat silently across from Josie. Was his face turned toward her? She knew he was awake. She wondered if he would speak to her again. He did not.

A half hour passed before he slipped on his boots, stood, and wordlessly left the compartment. For a brief moment the moon broke through the clouds. Light shone on the pretty face of the porcelain doll in the white lace dress.

At last Josie was lulled to drowsiness by the gentle motion of the train. Using her sweater as a pillow, she settled into the corner and drifted into a dreamless sleep.

⸙

Katrina lay sleeping beside Horst in the enormous four-poster bed. She was turned away from him, lying half in a shaft of silver light that fell across the curve of her back. Her skin glowed with a sheen so beautiful that the sight made him ache inside. He wanted to start over again, to pull her against him, awaken her with passion that could help him forget everything but her.

And that was his problem, he mused. In trying to make himself forget, he had somehow forgotten how to make her happy.

Tonight their lovemaking had lacked the joyful abandon they had always felt when giving themselves to one another. He had been demanding and impatient. He could see from the confusion in her eyes that she was troubled by the change in him. He had lain awake beside her, unable to sleep, until her breathing had deepened.

Now, lost in hopeless thoughts, he got up, wrapped himself in a down quilt, and moved into the sitting room to brood beside the window.

Perhaps his trip home had done more harm than good. Perhaps it was better for a soldier to steel himself for the horrors of battle, to build resolution on a foundation of hatred for the enemy, and not to allow himself the softer emotions. He should bottle up love and compassion, stick it on the shelf until everything was over and he could come home for good.

But that was not the answer either. He did not hate the Poles, much less the French against whom he would next be engaged. Horst sighed heavily and parted the sheer curtain to stare out at the night. He shook his head at the realization that the only hatred he felt was directed at the murdering SS swine.

And he loathed himself. He detested the fact that he was connected to the death of the Polish woman by the river. What weighed most heavily on his mind was the fact that he had known the SS would not really let her go. It had been a convenient fiction, designed to save face and protect his tender conscience. But deep down he reckoned that he was a coward after all, since by standing aside he had let them kill her.

Katrina had more courage than he did, and his knowledge of this separated him from her. There were moments when he thought he saw contempt in her eyes when he talked of duty. Often he wondered if she would have gladly gone to prison except for the fact that she thought she could oppose the Nazis more effectively by remaining free. Her courage frightened him.

Thin wisps of smoke rose in the moonlight from the chimneys of the stables. Horst felt a flash of irritation at Katrina. Twenty-two little girls, supervised by two middle-aged women, now lived on the upper floor of the stable.

"Evacuees from Berlin," Katrina had explained.

Horst had not pushed her for details, but he had his suspicions.

Embers on the grate of the sitting-room fireplace glowed deep orange. Horst tossed another spadeful of coal onto the fire and stirred them into flame.

"Horst?" Katrina called as she entered the sitting room. She had pulled on a silk robe that clung to the contours of her body. "Why aren't you sleeping?"

"I couldn't." He stabbed at the coals and then let the poker fall with a clatter.

She took a chair beside the window. Drawing her knees up under her chin, she appeared childlike in the moonlight as she gazed down on her domain.

"Do you want to talk?" she asked.

"About what?" His irritation was evident.

"About whatever happened out there?"

He stood to his full height and stretched his hands out to the warmth of the fire. "I would rather you tell me the truth about those children down there."

"What about them?" she replied with unconcern.

"Are they Jews?"

"How should I know?"

"You should know!" His anger flared. "You're playing with fire, Katrina! Old Brezinski is one thing. You played that hand cleverly. Yes, he is essential to the welfare of the horses. When you have permission from Göring himself . . . Göring can change his mind and send the Gestapo out here to collect the old Jew whenever he likes. You will have to let them take him, too! But those children and the women. Nuns, are they not? They cross themselves at every turn. They look like nuns even without their habits. Pious-faced crones. Turned out of their convent? Threatened with arrest? How can you expect to protect them? Do you know the penalty if you are caught?"

She jumped to her feet and matched his anger with outrage. "I told you! I do not know anything except that Father Johann asked if I had room for children from the city."

"This was just before they hauled the good priest off to Dachau, was it?"

"I do not know any more than what I have told you, Horst. I do not want to know more. I do not ask questions."

"You understand the penalty for keeping a collection of Jews beneath your roof? Little Jews though they may be. Even in your stable? Your punishment will be the same as theirs! Dachau. Sachenhausen. How long until one of your stableboys reports you?"

"You are no better than every coward in Germany!"

"I do not want to see you hurt."

"Only *you* have the power to hurt me," she retorted. "And you use it very effectively."

"I do my duty."

"You do your duty?" She laughed bitterly. "Then do it. Serve whatever twisted evil god you must and call it duty. But I also have a duty!"

"They will kill you."

"My life is the only weapon I have. If I am afraid to lose it, then I have lost the battle already. You . . . *Major!* . . . surely you know this." The words rang with scorn.

"I have faced death with courage!" he shouted.

"You face death in battles against men who never were your enemies, yes? Then what is it you fear more than dying, Horst? You fear the disapproval of these Nazi monsters who call you brave and brother and comrade! You value their good opinion of you more than you value your own opinion of what is true and good! You fear their accusations of cowardice even more than death. And that marks the twilight of your courage. You have sold your soul to them, Horst, for a profane lie they call sacred honor. They own you."

"I have lost you," he said miserably.

She stood silently before him. "No. It is you who are lost. What happened to you in Poland, Horst?"

"I . . . Katrina . . . I am . . . forgive me." He sank to his knees.

"You should divorce me before I bring dishonor to your career. I want you to leave me, Horst." Her voice was without compassion. "You are not a cadet playing war games anymore. Poland was not military maneuvers."

"You think I do not know . . ."

"Then what are you doing?"

"What I must do! I have no choice. Where is the way out?"

She could not answer the deeper side of his question, but she raised her arm and pointed toward the snow-covered drive that led to the road. "There." Then she retreated to the bedroom and closed the door, locking him out.

⚭

Aaron Lubetkin stood at the darkened window and surveyed the cemetery across the road. Behind the high brick wall were ancient, leaning headstones and broken monuments. Marble and granite markers once bore chiseled inscriptions: *Beloved Father . . . Faithful Wife . . . Our Baby.* Now scars from bullets marred those precious words. The stones had been machine-gunned during the recent Nazi desecrations of Jewish graves. Tonight those eerie sentinels marked the path to freedom for Etta and the children. There was no other way out of the Jewish Ghetto. Since November first, the area had been ringed with barbed concertina wire. Only the field of tombs remained open on both sides.

The population of the district had doubled to over three hundred thousand as Jews from other parts of the city had been rounded up and herded into the already overcrowded neighborhood. The tribe of black-coated Orthodox was joined by thousands who had never read a word of Hebrew. Bank clerks, shopgirls, nightclub singers, and taxi drivers suddenly were thrown out of their apartments and trucked across town. Now they scrambled for a few square feet of space in which to live. For years they had blended in, purchasing clothing in the same department stores where the Gentile Poles bought their garments off the rack.

The Ghetto district was a muddle now. Confused Nazis first singled out for persecution those who dressed in the fashion of religious Jews. Those who dressed in modern style were passed by. Then the invaders were reminded of the Aryan maxim: "Everything that looks human is not human." Yellow armbands marked with the Star of David were now required. In that way the "subhumans" were easily identified, no matter how they dressed or what their former station had been in pre-Nazi Poland. Those Jews who did not wear the obligatory armbands and were caught suffered the severest consequences.

At a nod from Aaron, Etta slipped her armband off and then removed them from the children's clothing. Her hands were like ice. The cloth of the yellow bands trembled in her fingers. Did the children notice?

"A short walk. Just through the cemetery. On the other side we will be Catholics going to Mass. You remember . . . like we talked about." Etta tried to steady her voice.

Curt nods from all. Their eyes were wide, faces pale, as they contemplated the penalty for walking out without their yellow bands and trying to leave without papers. They had heard the stories and seen with their own eyes the punishment meted out by the enemy.

"Are you afraid?" young Samuel whispered to his bigger brother.

David replied with a single affirmative nod.

"Are you afraid of the graveyard?" Samuel probed. "Of ghosts?"

David leveled his gaze at Samuel. "No. Not ghosts."

It was not the fear of disembodied evil that shook them all, but the knowledge that all around, the darkest, cruelest Evil had somehow possessed the flesh of living men.

The SS. Those human husks were empowered with inhuman brutality and were omnipotent over those who wore the condemning armbands. Hell had come to Warsaw to search out all Jews and destroy them as quickly as possible. Even little boys like David and Samuel. Even babies like Yacov.

David did not fear a walk through the dark graveyard. He feared those living dead: the soulless Aryan horde who dressed in handsome uniforms with lightning bolts on their collars. He feared the slap of their marching jackboots on the cobblestones and their proud voices raised together in song:

> "Crush the skulls of the Jewish pack
> And the future it is ours and won;
> Proud waves the flag in the wind
> When swords with Jewish blood will run."

Even now those soldiers watched and waited on the other side. Yes. The boy was afraid. So were they all . . . except for the baby.

Aaron raised his hand and muttered, "Quickly now. Go." He turned back to the window as if to promise that he would watch them safely on their way.

A final glance of farewell. Then down the hall and onto the landing, quickly down two flights of stairs, and out past the closed door of the concierge. The sudden coldness of the fall air was like a slap in the face, awakening Etta from the unreality of parting. She gasped, held the baby closer to her, and then stepped away from the shadowed alcove of the entrance.

The street seemed deserted at first, and yet Etta heard the faint voices of terror rustling in the shadows. How many, like themselves, had received the warning?

Hide yourselves tonight!

Fat, lazy snowflakes drifted down and landed on her dark shawl and flecked the coats of the children.

Three steps and Samuel spoke. "Mama, I forgot—"

He was instantly silenced by a rough shove from David. What did it matter if Samuel had forgotten something? What difference could it make now? They had left their whole world behind. What was left of any value that Samuel could have forgotten?

Samuel persisted, his voice choked with sorrow. "I . . . forgot to kiss Papa . . . good night."

Yes. Papa. Left behind.

"You can kiss him when we are back together," Rachel soothed.

We will never be together again! No kissing Papa good night or good-bye, Etta wanted to scream. She fought the urge to run back to Aaron, to ask him if it was such a terrible thing for them to all die together. Could they not face the end together? To beg him . . . how could she go on living without him?

The sleeping baby sighed a ragged breath and turned his face toward her breast. She shook her head, as if to clear her mind for what lay ahead. For these, she must live!

Pulling herself erect, she stepped from the curb and resisted one last look back at the window. The children followed. Crossing the street, Etta felt Aaron's gaze on her back. He was watching their retreat—willing them to go, yet longing for them to stay.

Little Samuel moaned at having forgotten the kiss. Rachel put her hand on his shoulder. "He is still there at the window. Blow him a kiss then, Samuel. Like this . . ." She turned and demonstrated. "You see? He is there. At the window. Good night, Papa."

Samuel imitated his sister even though he could not see Papa. Satisfied at last, they hurried beneath the rusted iron archway above the gate of the Jewish cemetery.

Then David balked a moment and ran back to the gate. He, too, gave a final, tentative wave in hopes his father would see him. After searching the dark eye of the window frame, he reluctantly ran after the others.

They wound quickly down a narrow pathway rimmed by snowcapped headstones. The gnarled branches of an ancient tree towered above them. Only now in the shadow, when she was certain Aaron could not see them, did Etta let herself look back at the dark brick facade of the apartment building.

Every flat and house in Warsaw had been fitted with blackout curtains before the outbreak of war. A precaution against German bombs. What a forlorn and foolish hope the black cloth represented! There had been no hiding from the Stukas.

Tonight, everywhere in Warsaw, blackout curtains remained in place like the black crepe of a household in mourning for its dead. No light shone from the window. There was no sign of life. But Aaron was there in the unlit room, she knew, still straining for one final glimpse of his family.

Just another window, she told herself, again fighting the desire to return to him. *No one there. He is not really there. Nothing to turn back for. She steeled herself. Think of the children! Of life!*

Etta tucked her head against the sharp wind that howled down from the highest hill of the burial grounds. At the bottom of the slope they descended, snow had piled up dangerously deep. The paths had not been cleared since the first snowfall. Heavy drifts tugged at Etta's hem, holding her back like the dread-filled, grasping clutch in some terrible nightmare.

Behind her, little Samuel struggled on. He stumbled, fell, rose slowly, and stumbled again. Not bound by skirts or petticoats, Rachel moved more easily than her mother through the tomb-studded drifts. She grabbed the hand of Samuel, yanked him upright, and then, in marching stride, plunged on after Etta. David trudged along behind.

Rachel, panting, pointed to the crest of the hill they must now climb. She called above the wind, "That way, Mama. Up there. Over the ridge. Past the Levy tomb and then out the gate to the Aryan side!"

Etta nodded, not sparing breath to answer. A dozen times in the last month Rachel had carried messages out to the priest using this route. It had spared her the questioning and the document checks at the barricades that guarded every entrance into the Jewish Ghetto. It still seemed a peculiar oversight that only rarely were Nazi guards posted at the cemetery gates. Tonight she and the children would step from the Jewish side of this valley of death into streets where trams still clattered by and taxis blew their horns.

The church of Father Kopecky was only a few blocks from the portals of the Jewish cemetery. The bells announcing evening Mass echoed across the landscape. But they seemed frantic tonight, clanging wildly without their usual steady cadence.

Etta's stomach churned at the sound.

Were the bells a beacon to prayer? Or a warning?

The pealing died away. For a moment there was only the scream of the wind and the crunch of their footsteps as they began their ascent of the slope. Then another sound, more ominous, penetrated the swirling snow.

Fifty yards from the top, Etta paused beside a headless stone angel. She leaned against the monument and put her hand out, stopping Rachel, Samuel, and David.

"What is it, Mama?" David asked, cocking his head toward the murmuring that undulated with the rise and fall of the wind.

Etta shook her head, demanding silence. She raised her eyes to the brow of the hill, where gray light penetrated the veil of falling snow and silhouetted the tombstones. The glow flickered. Shadows of tombs and pillars lengthened and deepened. The light grew brighter, nearer. It spread out, illuminating the width of the ridge above them. A dog barked and then another. The murmuring became recognizable as the noise of men's voices and expectant laughter.

Terror and realization crossed the faces of the children and their mother in that instant. The soldiers were sweeping through the graveyard! Men with torches and dogs were entering the Ghetto from the other side! They were looking for escaping Jews, blocking the route to freedom!

"Run!" Etta cried. "Don't look back! *Run!*"

No time to lose. Too late to consider the deep tracks they left in the snow. They clawed their way toward the gate that led back into the Ghetto.

Behind them the cry went up: "Footprints! Over here!" Hounds bayed as if in pursuit of a rabbit.

Rachel, dragging Samuel, led the retreat. David followed. Etta and the baby trailed twenty-five yards behind.

"It's Papa!" Samuel shouted and dashed ahead in a burst of joy.

Coatless, Aaron had run from his outpost at the window. Ashen and tight-lipped with fear, he met them at the gate. "Where's your mother!" he demanded, shaking David. At that instant Etta emerged from the shadow. She had no breath to acknowledge his miraculous presence. The thought flitted through her mind that she had gotten her wish. Perhaps they were to die together after all.

Aaron did not wait for her. "The torches! Hurry, Etta!" Gathering the two boys into his arms, he sprinted back toward the apartment. Rachel, bounding ahead of him, took the stairs two at a time. Etta, breathless from the effort and still carrying baby Yacov, reached the flat only seconds before their pursuers stormed the lobby.

The door was locked and bolted as two dozen men, following their wet tracks, swarmed up the stairs.

In the end it had been useless to run. They might as well have waited at the gate of the Jewish cemetery and surrendered there to the soldiers. The warning note, the clanging church bells, the pain of farewell, the dash to freedom, and the frantic terror of the chase made no difference to the final outcome.

After all, the snowfall had made for a festive air, and the German soldiers were playful. It was they who had sent the note. The rumor was their own. They had spread the word in the Ghetto that some action was coming.

> *Verstecken Sie sich heute abend!*
> *Hide yourselves tonight!*

Like hunters flushing game from the brush, they had been ready for the hundreds who panicked and ran. Locks and bolts were broken. The door was splintered by rifle butts and torn from its hinges.

And so in spite of everything, they were taken—this family of six—to await the train in the Umschlagplatz with fifteen hundred others. Together. They all went quietly, with the enemy . . . except for the baby in his mother's arms, who finally awakened to wail in indignation that his sleep had been interrupted.

28

Paradise Lost

The soft nickering from the barn called to Horst as he tossed his valise into the back of the automobile. Two sheets of black canvas tarpaulin formed a three-foot-deep entryway, keeping light from escaping, as Horst entered for one last look at the horses.

Old Brezinski was up in the lantern light, stroking the nose of a mare that was heavy with foal. His face expressed a moment of alarm at first sight of Horst's uniform, and then his shoulders sagged with relief.

"You are up early, Brezinski." Horst stepped to the stall door and stroked the muzzle of the old man's object of concern.

"Up late, Herr von Bockman." The old man did not look at the Wehrmacht uniform. Always before he had called Horst by his first name. Brezinski kept his gaze fixed on the intelligent eyes of the mare.

"I am leaving."

"So soon?"

"Katrina has asked me to."

"Ah. She has forgotten that politics has nothing to do with war. Is that it?"

"Something like that."

Brezinski shrugged as if the mind of a woman was unfathomable. "A pity you must go so soon. You will miss the foal. The mare is due any-time. I could not sleep. Beautiful, is she not?" he said with tender affection. "Her sire was killed in your war. A Polish cavalry charge."

Your war. The words were not an accusation but a simple fact in the mind of the old man. It was Germany's war. Horst's war. As if the whole matter had been something distant, a game played by only one team in which the spectators of Poland had been required to participate in the end.

"I am sorry," Horst said, indeed sorry that such a fine animal had been forced to face the iron hide of a German tank.

"No need to be sorry." Brezinski still did not look at him. "He was bred for battle. Brave horses to carry brave men to their deaths. It is a noble end. We will not see the likes of it again."

Silence. The stirring of hooves in the stalls. The scent of hay and manure and horseflesh. All these familiar things, which had been such an integral part of armies for thousands of years, were not without significance. With those last heroic cavalry charges in Poland, a history as long as warfare had ended. Horst had seen the bloated carcasses in the fields where they had fallen. The horses of Brezinski had simply perished with Poland and had been ground to dust beneath the tracks of tanks.

Horst cleared his throat, breaking the stillness. "As a boy, I loved stories of the cavalry. Alexander's army at Issus. Napoleon at Austerlitz. Waterloo. No matter which battle, it was the cavalry that fascinated me. I would have joined the cavalry of any nation, just to ride and fight."

Now Brezinski turned his head to look Horst square in the eye. "It was a noble profession. The cavalry. It was . . . there was something like love—a passion between the soldier and his mount. You know it. That is why I always liked you, young Horst."

"It was a game played on a level playing field. Man to man. Horse to horse. It was the noblest animal who carried his warrior to the thick of battle."

The old man nodded. "Not always the strongest, but the one with the greatest heart. It was the most courageous man who turned the tide and won the war. I have seen it with my own eyes. There was a horrible beauty in it. Death was not beautiful, but the dying! Now that is all changed. Everything is changed." He looked away down the row of stalls. "I always thought you were like one of these, like my Arabians. Bred for the sport of battle. When we were friends, before this war made us enemies, I said to myself, 'That boy is created to ride Orion into the line of waiting infantry!' It would not matter who you fought against or what you fought for—only that you would lead the charge."

"I was born one hundred years too late."

"You were born beneath the wrong flag." Brezinski chuckled. "Even in this modern age it could have been different for you. To have lived a few hours east of here . . . you would have ridden Orion into the final battle with the Polish cavalry. Just a few miles, an accident of birth, separated you from belonging to Poland. As recently as September you might have fought and fallen with the last men of valor."

Horst did not reply for a time. He smiled at the thought of what might have been. In the last century he would have ridden out with the Prussian cavalry to face Napoleon's army at Waterloo. And there would have been some honor in the terrible victory against the French. "I can still fight nobly against France, old man."

"Can you, Horst?"

"I must. In spite of the flag I am under."

Brezinski nodded. "I suppose it is true. A well-bred warhorse knows nothing of politics. Of who is right or wrong. It knows only the battle. It lives only for the challenge." He extended his hand. "You are a man out of your own time, Horst von Bockman. An anachronism. Hitler hates you, but he will use you. I think you may well die before I do. I wish you . . . what? What can I wish a man who is so unfortunate to fight on the wrong side?"

"Wish me noble men to fight against, Brezinski. Opponents with courage and skill. There is nothing else left for a German soldier to hope for."

⚭

"Next stop: Gare du Nord! All passengers to alight. Paris. Ten minutes. Gare du Nord!"

Josie awoke to the rap of the conductor against the compartment door. The gray predawn light seeped in under the half-drawn shade. It was raining. Drops streaked the glass and drummed against the thin metal roof of the train.

Swathed in blankets, Alma sat in numb silence. The seat that had been occupied by the French officer was empty. Boots, cap, coat, portfolio, and doll were all gone. The newspaper lay scattered on the floor, and the green volume of Milton's verse remained wedged between the cushions.

Josie retrieved the book and thumbed through the dog-eared pages, finding whole underlined passages that might have been written about the conqueror of Warsaw:

> "Farewell happy fields,
> Where joy forever dwells! Hail horrors! Hail,
> Infernal world! And thou, profoundest Hell,
> Receive thy new possessor—one who brings
> A mind not to be changed by place or time.
> The mind is its own place, and in itself
> Can make a Heaven of Hell, and Hell of Heaven."

She read these words of Milton in a new light now. Who but one who lived through those days in Warsaw could understand their meaning?

Josie felt a renewed curiosity about the French colonel. How many Frenchmen read the works of the English poet? A vague sense of disappointment settled on her. He had gone without knowing she shared a passion for Milton's work. He had gone without saying good-bye.

Josie closed the book and tucked it into the pocket of her jacket.

"So when did tall, dark, and horizontal get off the train?" Alma asked, gathering her belongings.

"I didn't notice." Josie feigned unconcern.

"Really?" Alma checked her face in the mirror of her compact and grimaced. "I vaguely recall some conversation between the two of you. Did you tell him the story of your life?"

"You were dreaming."

"It wouldn't hurt, you know. A little male warmth and companionship."

"I'm not ready for that yet." Out of habit, Josie defended her right to remain lonely, to live in her own private hell.

"So you've told every eligible man who gets near."

"Every one of them journalists. One newspaperman is enough in a lifetime, thank you, and a man in uniform is just as dangerous."

"You have now eliminated every male in Europe under the age of sixty."

"I rest my case."

"You've been resting your case for too long, honey. You didn't even get his name? No wedding band, I noticed. But here he is, taking a doll to some kid. Sweet. Sort of a tragic figure, I thought."

Josephine ran a brush through her tangled hair. "Maybe it was his doll. Think of that."

"Huh-uh. Not that guy."

"You meet your first Frenchman on French soil, under a newspaper on a train to Paris, and you turn him into the hero of a Gothic romance novel. *Wuthering Heights* or something. If he had been old and ugly, you wouldn't have looked twice."

"Add rich to the mix and try me." Alma grinned.

Josephine, in her best Snow White imitation, began to hum an off-key rendition of "Someday My Prince Will Come."

"Enough," Alma warned as the train slowed and slid beneath the enormous canopy of the Gare du Nord train shed.

Josie continued. "It doesn't matter how tall they are. Beneath the skin every prince is really just one of the Seven Dwarfs in disguise! If you ask me, our French captain was Grumpy standing on Sleepy's shoulders."

"Cynic."

"I'm just saying . . . all I'm saying, Alma, is that you should keep the dwarfs in mind when meeting men. Especially here. Then you'll never be disappointed."

"Or happy."

"I've tried Happy. Just another dwarf. Not that wonderful." Josie caught her own reflection in the windowpane. She was lying. Happiness had been wonderful. It simply had not lasted. And what remained in the aftermath was worse than if she had never known Danny at all.

"As for me, I'm a realist. I'll settle for any one of the seven as long as he's taller than me and doesn't turn into a frog when I kiss him."

"You're mixing fairy tales again," Josie corrected regally.

"You're the lit major, honey." Alma tapped the cover of Milton's epic. "*Paradise·Lost*, huh?"

Yes. Paradise lost, Josie thought.

The frigid morning air of Warsaw settled in the bones of the Jewish captives as well as the SS soldiers who guarded them in the open air of the Umschlagplatz. It was not mercy that led the guards to move the prisoners beneath the iron roof of the train shed, but their own quest for warmth. Oil drums were packed with scraps of wood and set ablaze around the perimeter. SS soldiers warmed themselves, smoked, laughed, and talked together beside the makeshift stoves. The fifteen hundred Jews inside the ring were forbidden to approach the drums. A boy in his early teens had been shot dead for daring to come too near the blaze and stretch out his hands to steal Aryan warmth. When the boy's father ran to his dying son, he, too, was shot. Now the two lay embracing one another in death as a warning to the others that no violation of SS rules would be permitted.

Midmorning of the day after their arrest, this was the hell in which Aaron and Etta Lubetkin and their children found themselves. They were thankful for one thing: The SS had not yet separated families. Husbands stood beside their wives. Mothers and children still huddled together against the cold.

The train that had been scheduled to take them away had derailed outside the city because of heavy snowdrifts on the tracks. The delay seemed a miracle to Etta. She held the baby, nursed him in the circle of her family, and prayed that someone would come to help them. That the Nazis would tire of their game and send everyone home. Surely the Nazis could not want to spend more cold days guarding Jews in the Umschlagplatz. They must be as tired of this as their victims.

"The priest has heard by now," Etta whispered to Aaron when the guard looked away. "He must know. He will come, Aaron. I know he will."

Beyond the smoking drums, Poles walked cautiously past the group. One guilty glance, and then the pace would quicken. It was no good to look too long or let a guard spot an expression of pity.

A prosperous man in a heavy topcoat stopped beside a guard and asked, "What did they do?"

"Attempted to leave the area after curfew without the proper permits and resisted arrest," came the reply. "Expressly forbidden. Such an act makes them saboteurs against the Reich and the general government."

"But the children?" asked the man.

"Their parents are criminals. Children suffer the same sentence as their parents. You know the penalty. It is the law. Everywhere it is the law. How else are we to keep order? If they think so little of their own children, then they deserve what they get. It would be the same for me in Germany."

This was true, Etta knew. In Germany, Austria, Czechoslovakia, and now in occupied Poland. The National Socialist law dictated that if one family member was guilty of breaking a law of the Reich, then all members of the family suffered equally. Such a cruel edict had slowed acts of resistance against the Nazi state.

Accused saboteurs? Lawbreakers? No matter what the SS officer told the man in the business suit, the only real crime was that Etta and Aaron were Jews. Rachel, David, Samuel, and little Yacov were Jews. This crime had received no pardon within the Reich. There was only one hope. . . .

Etta gazed at the child sleeping in her arms. She brushed her lips against his forehead. Did she love him enough to let him go? Could she, like the mother of Moses, cast him adrift, knowing that she would never see him again? that she would die without knowing his fate?

Was there no hope of saving Rachel or David or Samuel? Older Jewish children were seldom taken in by Poles. If the priest did not come soon, if the SS would not accept a payment of ransom . . . then they would cling to one another and die together with thousands of others in some open ditch in the woods.

But Yacov was so tiny. Etta put her cheek against his. She closed her eyes and pictured the daughter of Pharaoh rescuing a Jewish baby from the river, from the edict of certain death that her father had declared against the infant sons of Israel. The child had grown to be a prince among the enemies of his people until God called him back to lead His people to freedom.

The world had not changed in three thousand years. Were such miracles still possible? There was nothing left for Etta but this terrible, ancient hope. This was the miracle she prayed for now. *Oh, God!* That someone— anyone—would take her baby and walk away from her forever!

Hundreds of passengers who had been crammed on board the train to Paris emptied out into the vast, echoing *salle des pas purdus* of Gare du Nord.

The station seemed almost tomblike. Unlike the teeming, noisy atmosphere of prewar train stations, the quiet was tangible. Chilling. Gone were the blue-bloused porters. Now all the station employees were old men in shabby uniforms that reeked of mothballs. Weary women in black dresses pushed brooms around the enormous hall. Josie hoped that the early morning hour was partly to blame for the grimness of the place.

Formerly rowdy British soldiers disembarked like rumpled little Boy Scouts who had been roused too early by reveille. They staggered toward exits in confused bunches, stopped to peer at signs, turned and wandered back the other way before finally finding their way to the taxi queue or out onto the street.

At the far end of the terminal, Josie noticed a French officer part a group of muddled Englishmen with a certain stride. Was it the colonel? Perhaps he had not gotten off the train at an earlier stop after all. Whoever he was, he knew how to get out of Gare du Nord. Josie nudged Alma in the same direction. Perhaps she could just get close enough to return his book. . . .

He was gone by the time they stepped onto Boulevard de Magenta. Rain sluiced onto the cobbled pavement, overrunning the curbs and dripping melodically from the eaves. The air smelled fresh and clean.

The boulevards were almost deserted. Streetlamps burned in the soft predawn light. Paris was still sleeping.

Josephine stepped into the rain and peered up the street for some sign of the tiny orange Citroën of her friend, Delfina Periguex. Had Delfina received Josie's telegram, asking her to reserve two rooms at the American House for their arrival this morning?

"Are you sure she's coming?" Alma asked as the downpour increased, and the minutes ticked into half an hour.

"No," Josephine answered honestly, inwardly suspecting that the wire had not arrived. For the first time she worried about finding a place to live.

The line of cabs dwindled, and the bus came and went across the boulevard. Alma cast reproachful looks at Josie and, in halting French, queried the doorman about fares to the American House.

"The American House, Mam'zelle?" He seemed surprised. "It is a barracks now. All residence halls are requisitioned for the Armees as well."

Josie had sent the telegram to the graduate residence hall of the university where Delfina conducted research for her doctorate in child psychology. "Cité Universitaire?" Josie ventured.

"Requisitioned for the soldiers, Mam'zelle."

Josie hailed a cab, hoping that the AP office could help them find some place to sleep out of the rain.

At that moment Delfina emerged from the entrance to the Paris Metro, the underground. Her normally perfect blond hair was tucked under a scarf. She had no makeup on her freshly scrubbed face, which made her seem younger than her twenty-five years. She looked as though she had just jumped out of bed. Still, she was the brightest spot in an otherwise gloomy morning.

"Here you are!" she gushed, embracing Josephine and then introducing herself to Alma. "I only just got your wire. Several days late. They've booted us all out of our rooms at the Universitaire to make room for the soldiers, and I spent the night in an air-raid shelter. False alarm, of course; they always are. But no time to pull myself together this morning."

"Where's the orange bomb?" Josie asked about the automobile.

"Broken. We'll take the Metro." She hefted Josie's suitcase, leaving Josie with nothing to carry but her portable Olivetti typewriter.

"But where are we going?" Alma asked, lugging her baggage down the steep steps.

Delfina laughed. "Good news. I've found you rooms at the Foyer International. Boulevard St. Michel. I'm there, too. We'll have fun in spite of the war." Then to Alma, who was looking uneasy at having a stranger arrange her life, she said, "You'll love it; I promise. A walk to Notre Dame. A Metro ride to the AP office. Perfection. Almost perfection, anyway, except the elevators don't run anymore to save on electricity."

"We'll manage," Josie replied cheerfully.

"You're on the seventh floor." Delfina grinned. "But Madame Watson promises to put a chair on the landing halfway up so you can rest. Running down to the cellar in an air raid is the easy part. Getting back to bed, more difficult. This morning I just couldn't face it, and I'm only on the fourth floor. There are no bombs. None at all. I wouldn't even bother to go down, except that Madame Watson is a tyrant. She makes us all go every time the siren sounds."

Josie knew Adelle Watson by reputation only. An American who had come to study in Paris before the last war, she had stayed for twenty-five years, running a hotel reserved for American women students. Josie was surprised that Delfina, who was from pre-Bolshevik Russia, was allowed in.

As if reading Josie's mind, Delfina answered. "Almost all the Americans have gone home, you know, so Madame Watson has become international. The Foyer is a regular tower of Babel. Poor Madame Watson. She can hardly understand anyone. Austrian Jews. Czechs. Rumanians. Polish. Bulgarians. French. The rules are posted in eight languages. She will be glad to see you two."

The rest of the journey was spent with Delfina filling in the details of her life. No longer working with children, she was part of a program studying the psychological effects of stress on combat pilots. Delfina finished by stating that she was finding her current patients much more interesting than two-year-olds. The only thing the two groups had in common was that they were unmarried.

⊂♋⊃

The backseat of the gleaming black Citroën that met Andre Chardon at the Gare du Nord was already occupied by Colonel Gustave Bertrand. As they drove away from the train station, Bertrand said softly, "I'm very sorry, Andre. You know that. . . ."

"I do not want to talk about it," replied Andre abruptly.

"As you wish, of course," agreed Bertrand. "What about the project then? Is there progress?"

Andre shook his head, but not in answer to the question. He gestured to the watchful eyes of the driver in the rearview mirror.

The inability to talk about Andre's mission to England and his unwillingness to discuss his personal affairs left an awkward pall hanging over the interior of the Citroën all the way to the Chateau de Vignolles, thirty miles outside Paris.

The large manor house, surrounded by its parklike setting of lawn and trees, was not a castle in the medieval sense. It had been built in the late eighteen hundreds for a wealthy Parisian family and a host of servants. It was now filled with an entirely different sort of family, all of whom were in the service of secrecy.

The operation going on at Vignolles was known to a select few officers in French Military Intelligence as P.C. Bruno. Seventy specialists in code-breaking were gathered in the chateau, including a dozen Polish refugees and a handful of Spaniards who had escaped from Franco's slaughter. The rest were French army officers.

Even though they were working with the same purpose, none of the cryptanalysts at Vignolles were aware of Lewinski's work. Security precautions dictated that each man knew only what was absolutely necessary. Only Bertrand and Andre had actually seen all three attempts to break the German code.

When a representative of each of the three nationalities had gathered in Bertrand's office, Andre filled them in on the progress of the effort in Britain. "MI6 is convinced that the Germans have added two substitute alphabet wheels to the three on the standard Enigma machine. Not only can the setting and the order be changed, but any one or two of the three can be replaced with the extras. We . . . er, that is . . . we have had this conclusion confirmed by an independent source."

A Polish major sat back and groaned. "That is it, then! It is hopeless! How can we devise a way to predict which three wheels will be used on a given day and to what position they will be arranged? Twenty-six letters on each—it is preposterous!"

"The British agree that the magnitude of the task has increased greatly, but they are not ready to give up," said Andre sternly. "They even have a suggestion for your section, Major."

"Yes, and what is that?"

"Realizing that you have radio intercepts going back to September or before, they suggest that you analyze the opening broadcast of each day. We have been informed that the Germans send test messages. It may be that they were foolish enough to use the same phrase more than once. If so, you might be able to discern a pattern in the repetition."

The Polish major brightened noticeably. "It is true!" he exclaimed. "We will get to work on it immediately."

"There is one more thing," Andre added, holding up a cautioning hand. "The need for secrecy has never been greater. The Germans obviously believe their encoding to be unbreakable, because they use it for everything from the highest levels of Wehrmacht communications to orders received at division levels. This means that as you approach a breakthrough, the Nazis must never suspect what we have achieved, or they would change methods entirely, and all your work would be for nothing. Even now, as little as we know might frighten them into a big alteration."

"We understand," replied the Polish officer. "But who could we tell? We are practically prisoners here anyway." Then with a bow toward Colonel Bertrand he added, "It is a most charming confinement."

On the way out to the waiting Citroën, Bertrand drew Andre aside. "I know you are disappointed that you did not have more to give them. But remember that they know nothing as yet about the project going on in your basement. Perhaps our friend Lewinski has come up with something definite. Perhaps there is good news waiting for you at home right now."

Andre gave Bertrand a bleak look. "I doubt it."

∽

Dearest, darling Lori:

There's so much to tell, but I haven't even had time to jot down a word until now!

We've escaped! We're somewhere in the Ukraine, going down the Dnieper River on a coal barge!

Two nights ago, in the very middle of what we thought was our last night on earth, someone pounded on the door of our shed.

We were sure it was the end.

Captain Orde hugged Lucy and kissed her.

Then the door opened, and Peter Wallich called for us to "Hurry up! Hurry up!"

It seems a Jewish organization called Betar—it's named for a Jewish boy who was killed fighting the Arabs to protect a kibbutz in Galilee—heard about the Zionist Pioneers being held here.

Their leader, a man named Menachem, planned and carried out the raid.

Peter said Menachem was not interested in setting Germans or Brits free—meaning us and the Ordes—but Peter and the others said they wouldn't go without us, so Menachem agreed.

Menachem's only 25 or so, but his hawk nose and staring eyes make him look fierce. Peter says Menachem killed the commissar in his sleep.

Anyway, we're free. Betar bribed the guards on the dock to go away for a while and had already bribed the captain of the ship to take us as far as Kiev.

Captain Orde says there's a British consulate there.
Maybe I'll bring all these letters to you myself after all!

All my love always,

Jacob

P.S. I didn't have a clue about where we were or where we are going, but Captain Orde says the Dnieper, which flows into the Black Sea, has been a highway from north to south for centuries. He says the ancient Romans used it to trade for amber with the Gauls, and that later the Vikings sailed down it to plunder all the way to the Mediterranean.

All I know is that it's taking us away from prison and away from the war.

Alfie says the Red Sea will part on the blackest night on the way to the Promised Land.

30

Crossing the Gulf

The penetrating cold of Wales settled in Inspector Stone's lower back, making the walk to the village with Eva impossible this afternoon.

Eva was grateful for the time alone. Without the inspector escorting her, she walked briskly, reaching the tiny medieval town in time to have a cup of tea in the tea shop where the post office occupied a corner.

"They've rationed sugar now, too," clucked Mrs. Evesham, the round, middle-aged expatriate Londoner who served as village post-mistress, pastry chef, and waitress. She poured Eva's tea and placed a dainty scone in front of her. "I'll do what I can do with honey in the past-ries, but the scones will be deficient from now on. No jam, either."

"Never mind. It's lovely. Lovely on such a cold day."

"I have one thing to say about it. One thing only: clotted cream." She patted Eva on the shoulder. "I'll fetch your mail whilst you enjoy your cuppa. There's a letter for you today, Eva."

"For me?"

"From France."

A third voice, a man's voice, interjected, "Eva? I thought your name was Julia." It was Erich, the fellow she had met along the road by the farm. He sat at a corner table in the shadows. A deck of cards was spread on the table before him.

"My friends call me Eva." She looked away from his curious gaze. "How's fishing?"

"Rotten. Too cold. I've been hanging about here in the tea shop. Playing solitaire. Care to join me?"

"No, thanks. I've got to get home."

"Care for a lift?" He was pushing too hard.

Mrs. Evesham returned and stood between Erich and Eva, placing the correspondence beside Eva's pot of clotted cream. "Three from Elisa's husband. A letter from the Home Guard for Lori Kalner. And then this for you. Looks like a man's handwriting to me." Mrs. Evesham cast a back-off glare over her shoulder at the stranger. "Steer clear of that one," she whispered to Eva.

The letter addressed to Eva was on top. A French stamp. *Eva Weitzman*. Hotel Thiers stationery. *M. McG* on the return address.

Mac? Could it be?

Eva felt the frank gaze of Erich as she slipped the knife beneath the seal. She opened the letter only long enough to read the greeting: *Eva dearest . . .*

A flush colored her cheeks. Eva inhaled sharply and slid the paper back into the envelope. *Eva dearest?* To her? From Mac McGrath? She would have to read the letter somewhere else. Privately. Somewhere no one else could see her face.

She plunked her payment onto the table and gathered her things. When Eva looked up, Erich was still staring openly, a curious smile on his thin lips.

"Boyfriend?"

She did not bother to rebuke him. Mrs. Evesham did it for her. "Cheeky. And what business is it of yours?"

He shrugged, sat back, and resumed his methodical placement of the cards.

"Good news, dear?" Mrs. Evesham asked brightly as Eva headed to the door.

"I think so. Yes, I do. Thank you, Mrs. Evesham. I'll tell you tomorrow. Cheers."

Eva heard the door of the tea shop close as she crossed the street. Erich, tucking the deck of cards into his coat pocket, had followed her.

Followed? Was that too strong a word?

He was staring at her, seemingly amused by her unease. Then his eyes narrowed the way a cat narrows its eyes before the kill. He lit a cigarette and checked his watch.

Eva spotted the red phone booth on the opposite corner outside the dry-goods store. It was one of only three telephones in the village. Who would she call? And what would she say? That a young man was eyeing her with too much interest? Surely there was nothing sinister about such a thing. She lowered her head and quickened her pace.

Erich leaned against the wall and flicked ashes from his cigarette.

She told herself that she really had given in to an irrational fear. Mrs.

Evesham had no doubt sent him out of the tea shop with strict instructions that he could not smoke in the presence of the best pastries in
Wales.

Eva crossed the Llugwy River by way of the narrow fifteenth-century
Pont-y-Pair bridge. On the far side, still within earshot of the village if
she needed to call for help, she paused. Was Erich following her? Five
minutes passed. No one came. She chided herself for foolishness and
breathed a sigh of relief. Fingering Mac's letter, she turned her thoughts
toward him.

Eva dearest . . .

She knew the perfect place to pause and read his letter. At the halfway
mark between village and farm, a trout stream rushed past a large boul-
der. It was a perfect place for reading love letters—if, in fact, that was
what Mac had sent her.

Each day on the journey into the village she had pictured Mac here
with her. Today the anticipation of reading Mac's letter was as delicious
as the aroma of Mrs. Evesham's scones.

Yet what if it was nothing at all? Perhaps this was simply the proper
way Americans greeted one another through the post.

Eva dearest . . .

Eva decided she would walk awhile before she succumbed to the
temptation to devour every word.

ℙ

It was clear to everyone that the SS had every intention of carrying out
some sentence against the criminal Jews and their families gathered at
the Umschlagplatz. Rumor passed among the guards and then among
the prisoners that the Warsaw Judenrat, the Jewish Council, had spent
all night and day negotiating with the authorities of the government for
clemency in the matter of women and children. The authorities remained unbending. For the sake of example, the outcome was determined when the first runaway Jew attempted to enter Aryan Warsaw
without permit or identification. Let all the population of Warsaw look
at these lawbreakers and consider their fate.

In the interest of German mercy, however, and in consideration of
the children, the authorities allowed a ration of bread to be provided to
the prisoners by the Jewish community. The Judenrat sent a committee
into the Umschlagplatz to pass out bread from the meager stores of the
Ghetto. There was no milk, but weak tea was provided in tin cups from
the Ghetto soup kitchen. The Judenrat committee was forbidden to
speak to the prisoners. This order was obeyed even when one member of
the committee spotted his son among the condemned. The father gave

his son his allotted quarter loaf of bread, touching his hand in farewell. The two men spoke only with their eyes, embraced with a look, and parted forever after a few seconds.

When the kitchen committee left, they were allowed to cart off the bodies of the two Jews who had been shot earlier in the morning.

New SS guards had come in the afternoon. The train still had not arrived. A battered kettle, shielded from view by a blanket strung between two posts, served as the only toilet. Permission for use was granted at the whim of the soldiers. Permission was not always given. This seemed to be part of the sport.

By evening, young children napped in the arms of their parents. The older children and women slumped to the cobblestones. Men were forbidden to sit. They slept by leaning on one another.

Etta, who had dozed at Aaron's feet, now let him lean heavily against her back. He dozed, his arms draped over her shoulders. Rachel, still dressed like a boy, held the baby. David and Samuel were mercifully asleep with their heads resting on Rachel's lap.

Etta scanned the perimeter for some sign of Father Kopecky. Surely if he came, the guards would listen to him. Were they not all Christians like the priest? Would they not listen to a priest if he explained that there must be some mistake about the Lubetkin family? The Lubetkins were good people, he would tell them. Some mistake. They were Jews but also friends of his. Etta kept this slim hope alive as the hours passed.

It began to snow again. The facades of familiar shops and buildings across the square were dim behind the veil of white. Etta could just make out the sign of the photography shop where the family had once had pictures made to send to her father in Jerusalem. The photographer and his wife had been kind. The man had made the children smile. How long ago that seemed now. Etta was glad her father would have those photographs to remember them by.

The long, sleek staff car of a Nazi officer drove into the Umschlagplatz. Guards came to attention as a black-uniformed SS colonel emerged. Some among the prisoners stiffened to attention as well, almost as if they sensed that here was a man who demanded respect.

Aaron awoke as a harsh German voice crackled over the loudspeaker: "*Achtung!* Prisoners will rise and form two lines, three abreast, for marching to board the trains. There will be no talking. All instructions are to be obeyed at once. Failure to obey will result in . . ."

Etta shook her sons gently. Little Samuel could not wake up. Aaron gathered him in his arms, as though he was going to take him upstairs and put him to bed. The child seemed unaware of what was happening. David stood slowly and glared at a German soldier who brushed past them, shouting for silence. Rachel passed the baby to Etta. She looked at the toes of her boots and shoved her hands into her pockets as she had been instructed. They took their places near the rear of the column.

The officer remained rooted beside his staff car. He observed the scene with disgust. His arms were crossed and his mouth set in a hard line. He raised his chin slightly, so that he literally looked down his nose at the parade. Two civilian Poles, escorted by a guard, approached the officer.

For a moment Etta did not recognize the man and the woman. They were smiling, nodding, talking cheerfully. The man held a large camera, while the woman had a large wicker basket over her arm and carried a tripod over her shoulder like a rifle. It was the photographer and his wife! They were as pleasant to the officer as they had been to the Lubetkin family. Professional smiles. The officer smiled back at them. He waved his hand and nodded in agreement to their request. They had come to record the deportation of the criminal Jews. Perhaps they could sell the photographs to the newspapers?

A flashbulb exploded as the photographer snapped the officer's picture and then turned to face the prisoners beneath the train shed of the Umschlagplatz. The photographer moved quickly from the front of the line to the back, taking photographs, changing film and replacing used flashbulbs from a pocket filled with new ones. Still smiling. How could he still smile?

Etta nudged Aaron, who followed her gaze to the couple. He shook his head, then looked away. The image of vultures came clearly to mind. They came closer.

· Etta heard the voice of the guard who accompanied them. "There are whole cities now in Germany which are *Judenrein*—free of Jews. You will see it here in Warsaw as well."

The photographer smiled and nodded and snapped another picture of two bearded Jews who glared back at him. Then he lowered his camera and looked directly at Etta. The slim smile did not falter. He looked as he did when he had greeted her at his studio: professional, very pleased to see her indeed.

His wife, a thickset woman with rosy cheeks, walked toward Aaron. She put a finger to her lips and winked at David.

Setting the hamper down near Etta's feet, she turned to her husband and the young soldier. "This group?"

"Ideal," chirped the photographer. He took the soldier by the arm. "Would you give me a hand with the tripod?" The soldier cheerfully threw himself into the task of setting up the tripod, while the photographer engaged him in conversation.

Etta looked down. The woman stood planted in front of her, shielding her from view.

"The priest sent word," the woman hissed through clenched teeth. "Frau Lubetkin . . . the baby . . . hurry."

Etta's heart pounded in her ears. She could hear nothing, see nothing but the open basket between her and the broad back and full skirts of the woman. She felt as though she had been kicked hard in the stomach.

The ancient nightmare was real! She stooped and placed her baby into the wicker case. No time to caress him even one last time. She could not display her grief in any way.

Rachel gasped and choked back words of despair. A warning glance from Aaron silenced her.

The hamper was snatched up. The child was covered by a red wool blanket. The woman moved quickly away from them.

"Very good!" The photographer praised the soldier. "You know something about photography; I can tell!"

The soldier was pleased with himself. He spoke of the German-made camera he had carried everywhere with him since the war began. He talked and talked as the photo of Etta and Aaron and the boys was snapped and the smiling, nodding photographer moved down the line.

The baby began to cry. Etta moaned, closed her eyes, and pressed her face hard against Aaron's arm.

Rachel looked back and whispered, "She is speaking to the soldier. She is taking Yacov back to the shop with her."

And so it was done. The SS guard had never asked what was in the basket. Now he assumed the woman had carried a baby out of the shop and would take the same baby back.

Etta suddenly felt the emptiness of her arms. The column moved forward slowly. She did not allow herself to glance back at the shop, lest some SS guard see her face and know the truth. Her eyes were dry. Her face was like stone. A prayer more painful than her own death had been answered. Her baby was gone.

⚭

The cold air was perfectly still. Far away a cow bawled in a pasture. Nearby the water of the steam rushed over the rocks. Eva's breath rose in a steamy vapor. Since she had left the village, the only human sound in the woods was the crunch of leaves beneath her feet.

It was just past the white stone mile marker that Eva heard something behind her. Out of sight around the turning in the lane, beyond her vision, another traveler was close behind her on the road. A man coughed, cleared his throat, and coughed again.

Who would be out walking this direction? Who would be headed away from the village at this time of day?

If Eva paused to read Mac's letter, whoever it was would catch up to her. She pressed on.

Eva gathered her coat close around her. The chill of fear quickened her stride. She was certain now—almost certain—she had been followed.

The late-afternoon sun was low in the sky, tracing an almost horizontal course in this far northern latitude. The road from the village ran up a steep hill before it descended into the gloom of the swale.

Eva panted as she half jogged, half walked to the top. It felt as though there were chains around her ankles. At the brow she turned and looked back. For the first time she saw who was behind her. It was Erich, striding up the slope as though it were level ground.

He glanced up, spotted her, then began to run effortlessly in his pursuit. "Eva!" he called. "Wait! I'll walk with you!"

Whether unreasonably frightened or not, she felt she must not let him overtake her. Her every sense screamed for her to escape. Hide!

The hillside was almost barren of cover. Patchy clumps of brambles were only knee-deep; no boulders loomed large enough to shelter anything larger than a cat.

And he was so rapidly closing the gap!

Eva scanned the road. No cars were in sight; neither were any farmhouses in view.

A trickle of smoke from the already distant village waved a forlorn hope of comfort and security. Could she double back, avoid him somehow, and reach safety?

He was too close! There was no cover.

Trembling all over, she increased her frantic search for some place to hide.

As the road topped the rise, it veered to the left. To the right was a steep plunge that ended at a river gorge.

At the bottom of the descent, Eva spotted a place where a fallen pine log, no more than twelve inches around, spanned the chasm formed by a seventy-five-foot-high waterfall.

Beyond the canyon was a thickly wooded copse of trees and a tangle of underbrush invisible from the road. The entwined limbs and overarching shadows of the forest beckoned her to bury herself in their embrace. If she could only make it that far—hide in the thicket until darkness set in—he would never find her!

But could she make herself cross that gulf?

"Eva!" Erich called again, gaining on her. "What are you running for?"

Taking a deep breath, she plunged down the gorse-covered incline. Halfway down, the weeds gave way to bare shale rock. Eva's feet slipped and she skidded, landing on her back. She slid to within feet of the brink.

From here the seven-story drop to the rocks below appeared even higher, the path to safety even narrower.

Mist from the falls drifted up; the fallen log glistened with it.

Kicking off her shoes, Eva raised her skirt and placed her right foot on the log. The roar of water cascading over the falls drowned out Erich's voice.

Don't look back! Don't look down!

Fixing her eyes on the far bank, she crept out, heedless of the enormous boulders and swift rapids directly beneath her.

Only thirty paces to safety. Just thirty. Twenty-nine, twenty-eight . . .

Suddenly Erich's voice was just behind her, at her back. "I could shoot you now if that's what I had in mind! Stop!"

She forced herself to ignore him, closing her mind to threats, entreaties, and commands.

Twelve, eleven . . .

He stepped onto the log just as she reached the other end and leaped onto firm ground. She whirled to run. A thornbush snagged her skirt, holding her fast.

"This won't do any good, you know." Erich's city shoes were slick-soled. He balanced cautiously.

"What do you want?" she cried, tugging at her skirt. "Leave me alone."

"Not interested in you." His arms were extended like a tightrope walker. A pistol was in his right hand. He was smiling, enjoying a contest he was sure he would win—the hunter enjoying the sport before the certainty of the kill. "If I wanted you dead, I could have shot you on the road."

Three tottering steps carried him well out onto the span.

"Then why? *Why?*" she shrieked as she fought to free her skirt.

"You should choose your friends more carefully." He placed his feet gingerly on the slick surface. Two quick steps. A pause. "Elisa Murphy. Lori Kalner. These traitors from a family of traitors. They think they can hide from the Reich."

The thin log yielded slightly beneath his weight. He glanced downward, grimacing.

"What do they matter now?" Eva pleaded as he neared the halfway point.

"Eva! Surely you know why. They are examples. Proof to the world. You can't win. Can't hide from the Reich. I am merely the extension, an arm of the Reich courts. A bounty hunter sent to bring German criminals—these fugitives—to justice."

Three small steps. He reached the center. The falls roared beneath him.

"You killed Lori's father! Isn't that enough? Now you'll kill her, too?"

He nodded once, concentrating as the trunk narrowed. With each forward step, he spoke one word. "These . . . Jew-lovers . . . were . . . condemned . . . in . . . a . . . German . . . court."

The fabric of Eva's skirt finally tore. She fell backward onto the ground beneath the jagged end of the fallen log.

In an instant she knew what she must do. Leaping to her feet, she braced her shoulder under the dead wood and heaved upward with all her strength.

The trunk yielded, only slightly at first.

"No! Don't!" Erich cursed. He swung the muzzle of the pistol toward her, but when it crossed the center line of his body it threw off his balance and he struggled to regain it.

If she couldn't lift it and his weight, could she at least shake it or tip it sideways?

Erich brought the pistol up in a slow arc. The muzzle gaped toward the water, then the log, then the far rim of the gorge. . . .

Grabbing the tree trunk with both hands, Eva braced her feet in the muddy gravel, then flung herself to the side just as a shot rang out, echoing and reverberating down the ravine.

31

A Vision of Blue

It was late before Andre Chardon completed his reports at Vignolles and returned to Paris. He was in a gloomy mood as he removed his luggage from the car in front of his home. Tucking the doll from Clemmie Churchill beneath his arm, he climbed the steps slowly and looked back toward the Seine. The blue strip of light from the staff car headlamps barely illuminated the pavement of Quai d'Anjou as the vehicle crossed the bridge. Paris seemed a gloomy place tonight.

Only now did he let himself think about Elaine. She was gone, and that was irrevocable. The City of Lights had paid her homage in the newspapers. Her voice and her songs had been played all day on Radio Paris. It had been almost beyond bearing for him when he entered the staff lounge at Vignolles and heard her singing.

Mercifully, Andre knew that by tomorrow the city and the world would move on to other matters. Soon enough Elaine Snow would be forgotten. At best she would be a footnote in history, possibly remembered by a few Jews in Palestine as "the woman who gave me my passport in Constance one night." But there could be nothing more. The human mind absorbed the news of another's death with a kind of surreal acceptance, as though the one who died had never lived at all. The faces of the dead became like that thin blue light, barely illuminating memory.

He entered the foyer of the great house. It was dark and quiet. It suddenly occurred to him that Elaine had been here only one time. That fact made the memory more difficult to deal with. There was no jumble of images to sort out. No past. Only the one, present, immutable vision of her standing there. . . .

She wears the cobalt blue satin evening gown. Her hair shines golden in the light. Her eyes are clear, and more blue than the dress. She turns her face toward the door as I say her name. Her eyes hold me. . . .

Too real! Too near! Until this instant Andre had been able to keep the finality of her death at bay. Now, as the reality settled heavily on him, he wanted company. Anyone.

Peering down the stairs, he saw that the lamp in Lewinski's workshop was out. Climbing the curving staircase he checked on his brother, who was sound asleep and snoring. Andre considered waking his brother, but he did not. Paul would want to talk, to console him, but there could be no consolation tonight.

He closed the blackout curtains in the study, then snapped on the light and tossed his valise in the corner. Placing Clemmie's doll on the bookshelf, he poured himself a snifter of brandy and sat down heavily in the leather chair that faced the enormous walnut desk. He had sat in this very chair and faced his grandfather the day the news about his mother and father had come. He remembered how the old man had glowered down at him and Paul. The drooping white mustache made his appearance even more grim. It was only the mustache Andre could recall now, not tears or eyes or trembling hands. Only the white line curving downward above his lip. How it had quivered as he spoke! All these years Andre had imagined that the old man was furious at him.

"Have courage. Your father and mother were murdered by the Boche yesterday in Louvremont."

Andre stared at the white mustache that floated now before him in a blue haze of memory.

Have courage. Elaine was murdered by the Boche in Munich.

Andre sipped the brandy as the door opened. Paul, blinking at the light, entered the room.

"I thought I heard someone." Paul wrapped his burgundy robe around himself and sat down uninvited.

"Only me." Andre held up the snifter in salute. "Care to join me?"

"I just did." Paul yawned.

The two brothers did not speak for a long moment. The ticking of the mantel clock measured seconds at a ponderous pace.

Paul inhaled deeply. "I suppose you have heard the news. Elaine."

Controlled and cool, Andre replied, "Everyone in Paris has heard. The radio broadcasts."

"Yes." Paul considered Andre with hard eyes. "Is that all you want to say about it?"

"I am sorry. Of course." Emotion was choking him. He wanted to shout his rage, but he remained calm.

"You are a lot like the old man, Andre." A half smile tugged at the corner of Paul's mouth.

"What do you mean?" It was an insult; Andre was certain. He knew Paul had lost respect for him since his affair with Elaine Snow and the child.

"You do not remember the way he sat there and glared at us the day Mother and Father died?"

Andre did not admit that he had just been thinking of it. "Vaguely."

"He was telling us that his son was dead, and his wife with him. The grief of that! What he must have felt! To speak to us of courage at such a time . . . he spoke the words, and saying it made it true for him. Remember? *'Be brave. You must not weep!'*"

Of course Andre remembered. He closed his eyes and thought about Elaine's child. What was to be done with her? What must he do? He rubbed his forehead and glanced toward the placid doll on the bookshelf. As though he were speaking to the child, he thought the words: *"Have courage . . . your mother . . . Elaine is dead."*

Emotion burned in his chest.

Paul grinned and ran a hand through his hair. He shook his head as if he still could not believe it. "He was so cool, that mean old man. I grew up thinking he did not care that Father and Mother died. That we were left alone."

"What are you saying?"

"He was not really angry at us, you know. That day? I did not need to be brave. I wanted to be held." Paul shrugged. "You should at least try to see your child. Juliette. A beautiful name. A name Elaine chose from the great tragedy, I think."

"What would you have done in my place? With the old man like he was . . . "

"I would have married her." Paul tugged at the ties of his robe. "I tried to, you know. After. I went to her and asked her. But she would not have me."

"I did not know you loved her."

"Of course not. How could you know?" Paul's eyes brimmed with tears. "My big brother." He waved his hand around the room. "Well, you have it all now. Everything you thought was worth more than Elaine." He leaned close and put his arm on the desktop. His fist was clenched. "To you life is like a library full of first-edition classics. Bound in leather. Gilt edges on the pages. Autographed by the authors. Only you are too busy to open the book and read the story. Pretty things without meaning."

"I did not ask you to intrude." Andre glared at his brother and again lifted the snifter to his lips.

"No. You did not." Paul stood and raised his chin. "But, like Grandfather, you have missed the whole point, Andre. You give in just a little and think it does not matter. But it does! Add up all the times you have sold a piece of your soul, and all the times every other little man sells his, and soon all the world belongs to hell. That is what I think of what you did to Elaine."

"Hell possessed the earth long before I sold myself."

"But heaven redeems the earth one soul at a time, Andre."

"It is too late now to make it right."

"If you really believe that, then I am sorry for you." At that, Paul left his brother alone.

                 ∽

Pale streamers of pink fire streaked the twilight sky.

In the depths of the chasm, beside the clamoring stream, lantern lights gleamed like fireflies darting in the gloom.

Inspector Dunston's coat around her shoulders, Eva Weitzman shivered near the rim of the waterfall.

"Sorry we weren't here sooner," Dunston apologized. "Your postmistress—Evesham, is it?—had already called the local constabulary about a suspicious hanger-on. After the affair with that Kevin Miller chap, we'd put the wind up with the locals, so they got right on to the Yard . . . and I was already on my way today to meet you. But it almost wasn't good enough, eh? Near run thing. Can't help but think you might've scampered clear, saved yourself, like. You must be tougher than you look."

"No," Eva countered, "not tough at all. But Elisa and Lori . . . after all the others? This evil . . . this plague . . . has to be stopped, no matter—" she shuddered—"before it spreads. Before more innocent lives are destroyed."

"Inspector!" bellowed a voice from the blackness of the ravine. "Found him, right enough. Blighter ain't dead . . . but his back's broke. Hafta carry him out the long way."

"You go on, then," Dunston barked in reply. "I'll escort the lady to her cottage."

                 ∽

It was a day for rejoicing. A large brown envelope with a Greek postmark—crammed full of Jacob Kalner's letters and the record of his journey—arrived for Lori.

Jacob had survived. He and those who traveled with him were alive and well and would soon arrive in the Promised Land by some secret route he dared not reveal on paper.

Tears of joy flowed freely. Prayers of thanksgiving were in every mouth. The sovereign God of Jacob had brought them through every danger.

Lori spent the afternoon reading each cherished missal again and again, sharing the record of Jacob's adventure with the marveling members of her family.

It was late afternoon before Eva slipped out of the house and climbed the ladder into the hayloft of the stone barn. Golden light filtered through the high windows as Eva settled in to read her one letter again. Only one, and yet for Eva it was everything.

Eva dearest,

I have tried to write you many times. Murphy loaned me a dictionary, but it is no help to me. I can't seem to put the right words in the right order to tell you what a dope I've been. Or how I felt about you from the first time I saw you.

You see, I'm not much good with words. Only with cameras.

On this gloomy gray day in France I try to picture you. Images come to my mind. Pictures are something I can get my brain around.

I was in Tahiti filming four years ago, and I thought then that I had never seen anything so beautiful as a South Pacific morning. My camera could not capture the colors or contain the peace I felt in that place. Is it enough for me to say that what I feel for you is something like what I felt when I was there?

You are:

Pale, translucent blue stillness, then . . .

A turtle's back, dimpling the slumbering face of the sea.

Lazy waves roll in,

Like lengthy messages from Japan,

Written cobalt on azure,

Punctuated by curly white exclamation points,

and deliver themselves.

Without you I am a portrait entitled

"Lone Man on Beach with Coffee Cup."

Eva. My dearest only one. Though I am not good with words, what I mean to say is, I have been waiting for you. Only you, always.

Mac

Epilogue

Rain fell on the hills that cradled Jerusalem. Rivulets of water turned to torrents that cascaded down the dry ravines and filled the empty pools of the desert wadis.

It was night in the city. The shutters of Rabbi Shlomo Lebowitz were closed against cold weather. Still, dampness seeped in through the cracks of the thick stone walls. The rain found its way through a hole in the roof and dripped a melody into the tin pot on the rabbi's floor.

He stretched his hands out to the warmth of the Primus stove and listened to the drumming rhythm above him.

"The dancing of an angel, Lord?" he mused aloud.

As if in reply, a drip landed on his cheek and coursed down onto his thick gray beard. "Too bad. I would have liked some company tonight."

It had been over two months since he'd received Etta's last letter, written September first, from Warsaw. Since then there had been no word. Loneliness had settled into the void left by the absence of hope in the old rabbi's heart.

In a ritual practiced a hundred times before, he gazed down at the photographs of his family laid out on his tiny table. His cat, Psalms, rubbed against his leg. As he held each photograph up, he repeated each name like a prayer. "Etta. Aaron. Rachel. David. Samuel. Yacov."

They are only pictures, he reminded himself at last after kissing each picture and setting it down. He must not hope too much for a miracle. He looked into Etta's eyes and wondered what she was seeing now. Was her vision filled with some winter scene in Poland? Or was she somewhere far away from this world . . . beyond the grief of the war that kept her from him?

He picked up the wedding picture of Etta and Aaron. "If I had known . . . it is good that I could not see the future. It is better to live one day at a time with the blessing of the Eternal than to see the end of blessings." Rabbi Lebowitz smiled as he remembered the music and celebration of that night so long ago.

There in the group was the younger image of himself beside his wife, who was also named Rachel. For a long time he gazed at the photograph of his wife. "A handsome couple, were we not, my angel?" He touched her face with his fingertip. "It is good we did not know how soon you would leave this earth. The mixing of joy and grief would have broken our hearts if we had known." And again he said, "*Nu*, it is better not to see tomorrow."

Psalms purred and he stooped to pet the cat. Then he turned his attention back to the image of his wife and lost himself in memories.

"My Rachel." He caressed the name. "You are in heaven. *Nu*. Maybe you can look down and see our Etta and Aaron and the little ones." He frowned and looked up. "What is it like? Can you fly to Poland and find them? Do you hear them speak to one another? hear the children laugh? I envy you. You know I have never heard their voices? The children, I mean. Sometimes I think I hear them when I am sleeping. They are laughing, light and clear, like water running over rocks in a stream. It is a good dream, and I hate to wake up."

Tears came to his eyes. "Or maybe you are all together already? Not in Warsaw." He raised his head at the tapping on the roof. "Have they gone home to be with you? And have you all come to dance above me tonight?" He rested his head in his hands. "I would like such a visit, Lord. To be with my family. To dance with them again as we did that night of Etta and Aaron's wedding."

Rabbi Lebowitz lapsed into silence—a silence broken only by the dripping of water in the tin pot. "Lord?" He lowered his head. "Just a little miracle is all I ask. If they are still alive, bring them here for me. Show them how to escape! And tell them I am still here in Jerusalem, waiting for them to come home."

෴

The sharp prow of the fishing trawler rose and fell in cadence with the rhythmic beat of the diesel engine. The Mediterranean was mercifully calm tonight. Even so, nearly half of the passengers onboard the *Ave Maria* were seasick. The air belowdecks was rank with the sour odor of vomit and diesel fumes.

Captain Samuel Orde and Lucy made their way to the bow of the trawler. The cold wind and stinging salt spray against their faces were a welcome relief. As Lucy shuddered from the chill, Orde put his arm around her and gripped the slick rail for support. His keen eyes scanned the midnight darkness for some sign of the British and German ships that prowled these waters.

The refugees onboard the *Ave Maria* had been fortunate in their journey. Twice they had spotted the plumes of great naval ships on the far horizons of the sea, but the little trawler had slipped away undetected. Now, only hours away from the end of a long and desperate flight, Orde prayed that the tiny vessel might run the final blockade of British gunboats patrolling the coast. It seemed strange to contemplate that they must escape both Nazi *and* British ships to win their freedom. Either navy would gladly blow a shipload of Jewish refugees out of the water with never a pause to ask questions.

Lucy leaned her head against Orde's chest, as if she sensed his apprehension. "We are so close now, and not one of us lost in all the weeks since we left Warsaw. We are almost home."

"Hmmmm," he replied, sweeping his eyes over the star-dusted skies to where the darkness marked the rim of the world. "The coast is thick with patrols. It was true before the war. It is doubly true now."

"Spoken like a military man." She brushed his cheek with her fingertips and tucked herself closer against him. "The Lord would not bring us so far only to let us die within sight of our goal."

Her faith made him smile. He kissed his wife's forehead and turned his eyes back to the horizon. He believed that her words were true, and yet this was the hour for vigilance. Alfie, Jacob, Peter, and the others had become the sons of his heart, his own dear family. He would not relax until they all stood together on safe and solid ground . . . and until Lucy held her baby—*their* baby—in her arms again.

As if drawn by the drama of these final hours, Alfie stumbled to find Lucy and Orde at the bow. Jacob and Peter followed on his heels, silent with apprehension. They, too, felt the peril of these last few miles.

Alfie cleared his throat and stroked the head of Werner-kitten, who was tucked into the boy's shirt. "Werner don't like the ocean," Alfie explained. "I told him about crossing the Red Sea and God opening up the water so we could get through, but he still isn't happy."

"Everyone is sick," Jacob said.

"Except us," Peter added. Then, "How much longer, Captain?"

Orde raised a hand to a point where the constellation Orion rose over the black horizon. "Keep your eyes there, boys. You'll see it soon enough. A light. No bigger than a star from this distance, but shining from the darkness. That will mark the place we land."

Heads pivoted to stare hard at the lowest star in Orion's Belt. Were they as close as that?

"Any sign of gunboats? patrols?" Jacob asked. He was a soldier at heart, just like Orde. He had come to believe in the angels that Alfie spoke of, yet still he watched.

"Nothing yet," Orde replied quietly.

Alfie was smiling. The starlight illuminated his broad face with joy. Or perhaps it was his joy that lit the night. "There it is." Alfie pointed as a single beam of light winked on and off. "Look, Captain! Lucy! Jacob! Peter! Look, Werner! Just like they said. . . ."

"I didn't see it," chided Peter.

"Me either," added Jacob.

"Oh yes!" Alfie insisted. "Look!" He pointed again toward where the shoreline certainly lay. "Me and Werner can see it. They are there! Right there where they are supposed to be! Can't you see?"

The group exchanged looks. There was still nothing but the stars and the darkness. And then, right where Alfie had pointed, a bright light indeed gleamed—just for an instant.

"There it is! Look!" they shouted and clung to one another at the miracle of their beacon.

Alfie pulled little Werner from the protected covering of his shirt and held the cat high over his head. "Look, Werner. Just like you always said it would be. Werner! It's the Promised Land!"

Digging Deeper into *London Refrain*

Do you long to make a difference? to know your specific purpose on this earth? to be respected as "a person of honor"?

So do many of the characters in *London Refrain*:

Journalists John Murphy and Josephine Marlow are determined to write stories that will open people's eyes to the truth of what is happening all across Europe.

The young Rachel Lubetkin "saves a life"—sacrificing her own chance for freedom in the process—by giving her precious British passport to Eva Weitzman, a stranger.

Horst von Bockman has had one life purpose: to do his duty for his country. Yet after seeing the brutality of the SS, he struggles with his conscience and his fear of what will happen to him and his family if he speaks out against the Nazis. *Can I still fight with "honor and courage"* (p. 188) *even if I no longer believe in the "cause" I'm fighting for?* he wonders.

In the dark fall of 1939, it seems all hopes for the Polish people are fading. Without France, England, or America joining the battle against the Nazis, the country of Poland is being dismembered. And yet the Polish people's spirit remains strong.

Josie Marlow experiences the people's courage and their unrelenting faith on the front lines of battle, even in the face of impending death and horror—including the senseless murder of the aristocratic Alexander Riznow. She longs to make a difference somehow. To turn the tide of the war. To right, even in a small way, the wrongs she sees all around her. In a transparent moment, Josie tells Charlie Morris, her London Associated Press chief:

"I don't want to just die without making things better by having lived. Isn't this the time . . . such a time . . . when the world needs people who measure convictions against God's love and then act on the best impulse they have? In Warsaw, up to the end, I saw people who lived and died just that way. . . . And suddenly I saw how small and blind my own soul had been. What difference have I made? It seems to me I must be alive for some reason I don't know yet." (p. 184)

Dear reader, do you feel the same way sometimes? No doubt you have myriad life questions. We prayed for you as we wrote this book—that you will find, or continue to sharpen, your "life's purpose." And we will continue to pray as we receive your letters and hear your soul cries. Following are some questions designed to take you deeper into the answers to these questions. You may wish to delve into them on your own or share them with a friend or a discussion group.

We hope *London Refrain* will encourage you in your search for answers to your daily dilemmas and life situations. But most of all, we pray that you will "discover the Truth through fiction." For we are convinced that if you seek diligently, you will find the One who holds all the answers to the universe (1 Chronicles 28:9).

Bodie & Brock Thoene

SEEK...

Prologue

1. Have you lost a loved one through death, as Shimon has lost both of his parents? How do you "remember" that person?

   _____

   _____

2. If you could write your own obituary, what would you say? What would you want others to know about you? What gives your life meaning and purpose (Moshe's life was multifaceted—as an archaeologist, scholar, and also an Old City defender)? Would others say you had "a truly honorable life" (p. xii)? Why or why not?

   _____

   _____

3. Have you written the story of your life anywhere? Each of us has wisdom to share, life lessons we've learned that can be of help to the next generation. Why not jot a few notes for those who will follow after you? Even a few lines a day will get you on your way!

   _____

   _____

Chapters 1–2

4. Imagine you are Eva Weitzman—or any of the individuals standing outside the British Embassy. Your city has just been bombed, and you don't know when the planes might return with a fresh load of bombs. Would you be shouting, like Eva? Or weary and resigned, like the older couple (see p. 4)? What thoughts would be going through your mind?

   _____

   _____

5. When have you worried about or prayed for someone who was far away from you (as Lori worried and prayed for Jacob)? Who was it, and what was the situation?

   _____

   _____

6. "You're the one man who has spoken the truth" (John Murphy).
   "A lone voice crying in the wilderness, I fear" (Winston Chur-
   chill, p. 5).
   Have you ever felt like "a lone voice crying in the wilderness"?
   Explain.

   _____

   _____

7. "The policy of appeasement is always fatal. Always. History teaches
   us. History is the schoolmaster. America cannot negotiate with evil
   men and expect to remain unscathed" (Winston Churchill, p. 8).
   Do you agree with Churchill's statement? Why or why not? Give
   historical backing for your answer.

   _____

   _____

   Chapters 3–5
8. "*So this is what death looks like*, Rachel thought, unafraid. A still-life
   painting of uneaten bread and a cabbage. Three children and a
   mother who would never come home from market" (p. 19).
   Later Rachel collapses in her mother's arms when she learns that
   her best friend, Mikka, has died in the bombing (see p. 108).
   Describe when you realized what death really means.

   _____

   _____

9. If you were a parent and knew that declaring war against evil in
   another country (such as fighting Hitler and what he stood for in
   1939) meant that your children would have to fight—and possibly
   die—would you vote to go to war? Or would you vacillate, as
   France and England did? Explain your answer.

   _____

   _____

10. Eva prayed for a miracle—and she received one (the precious Brit-
    ish passport!) from a stranger (Rachel Lubetkin). But then she
    weeps. "So many will not escape this place. And I? Why should I
    be so lucky?" (p. 25). Have you ever been on the receiving end of a
    miracle? and wondered why, as Eva did? When?

    _____

    _____

11. "I chose life. . . . But not life for myself," Rachel says (p. 31). If you were given the chance to leave family and live, or to stay with your family and most likely die, which would you choose?

_____

_____

Chapters 6–8

12. "All things work together for the good of those who love God and are called according to His purpose. . . . I am having difficulty believing such a promise. . . . Sometimes it is very hard to believe God is hearing my prayers at all" (Lori, p. 44).

   Is it hard or easy for you to believe in God's promises? Have you ever wondered if God even hears your prayers? If so, when? (Perhaps that time is right now.)

   Be encouraged with these words from Mark, one of Jesus' disciples:

   "Have faith in God," Jesus answered. "I tell you the truth, if anyone says to this mountain, 'Go, throw yourself into the sea,' and does not doubt in his heart but believes that what he says will happen, it will be done for him. Therefore I tell you, whatever you ask for in prayer, believe that you have received it, and it will be yours."
   —Mark 11:22-24

_____

_____

13. If you were Herr Niemann, the director of Jewish Education, and Rabbi Lubetkin, how would you choose which children would live . . . and which children would die? (See p. 48.) What criteria would you use? How would you explain your rationale to the parents of the children left behind? the children taken to the cathedral?

_____

_____

14. If you had to say good-bye to your best friend (as Mikka and Rachel must say good-bye—see p. 58), knowing you would never see her (or him) again, what parting words would you share with that friend?

_____

_____

Chapters 9–11

15. "I trust Captain Orde . . . and Alfie says, 'Trust God'" (p. 65). Do
you tend to trust more in a person you can see and touch (as Jacob
does) or in God (as Alfie does)? Why? Give an example from your
own life.

_____

_____

16. If a fellow traveler you'd met on a short journey were to describe
you, as Richard Lewinski describes Mac McGrath, what would that
person say? How would you describe yourself? the positives? the
negatives?

_____

_____

It's fascinating that the brilliant Richard Lewinski himself—"the
most important person to have escaped from Poland" (p. 72)—is
so misjudged by many because of his appearance. How different
would the world be if we all followed this wise admonition from
ages past?

> "Do not consider his appearance or his height. . . . The Lord does not
> look at the things man looks at. Man looks at the outward appear-
> ance, but the Lord looks at the heart."
> —1 Samuel 16:7

_____

_____

17. Have you ever stepped out of your comfort zone and become
friends with someone who is from a "different world" (as Mac and
Eva are from different worlds)? What, if any, obstacles did you
need to overcome to do so? What rewards have you received as a
result?

_____

_____

Chapters 12–15

18. Do you believe that every person has a place on earth? or that
some, like Alfie Halder, are "too useless to live," as the Nazis
believed (see p. 82)?

What do you think it would be like to live in:

a world devoid of human beings with physical or mental disabilities? a society where there were no elderly? a culture where
those of Jewish heritage were marked for genocide? a nation
that separated children from parents, dictated schooling, rewarded betrayal of fathers and mothers by sons and daughters,
condoned and practiced euthanasia and abortion? a government that arrested, imprisoned, and executed those who spoke
out against legalized murder? (p. 17)

Explain your answer based on personal experience and/or current events.

_____

_____

19. "So few protested what the Hitler Youth did to German Jewish
children. . . . May the God of love and mercy keep you safe from
those little Nazi boys who grew into monsters, nourished by the
bread of hatred" (Lori p. 87).
    Does being around hatred and evil constantly mean that *you* are
"fated" to become evil? What factors play into making children
who they are, at their core, as adults? Do you think that "not acting" (sitting back and watching) is as bad as participating in
active evil against another person (see also p. 159)? Why or why
not?

_____

_____

20. Josie Marlow was angry when she tried to comfort and care for the
injured women at the Cathedral of St. John (see p. 91). Horst von
Bockman was angry when he came upon the village where the SS
had tortured and crucified three men (see pp. 98). Why did they
feel that way?
    Have you ever been angry because you felt helpless? What was
the situation, and what—if anything—could you, or did you, do
about it? Looking back now, would you do anything differently? If
so, what?

_____

_____

21. If you could slip only *one* request of God into a chink in Jerusalem's Holy Wall, what would that request be? (See p. 103.)

_____

_____

22. "It is in the fire we will meet Messiah face-to-face. He will walk
with us even there, if it is written that we must also be thrown into
the flames" (Aaron Lubetkin p. 105).

How do you respond when you're suffering? With anger? With
resignation? With the thought *Life is not fair*? With sadness? With
the knowledge that pain is part of life? How has your response to
suffering affected your relationship (or lack of relationship) with
God? and with others?

> *When you pass through the waters, I will be with you; and when you
> pass through the rivers, they will not sweep over you. When you walk
> through the fire, you will not be burned; the flames will not set you
> ablaze. For I am the LORD, your God, the Holy One of Israel, your
> Savior.*
> —Isaiah 43:2-3

_____

_____

Chapters 16–18

23. Elaine Snow was blamed for being part of the conspiracy to kill
Hitler when she was merely delivering Jewish passports. (See chapter 16.) Have you ever been blamed for something you haven't
done? Or has something good you've tried to do been turned
around on you? What happened? How did you respond?

_____

_____

24. Mac McGrath felt caught between Josie Marlow and Eva
Weitzman—duty or love (see p. 133). Have you ever been caught
between love and doing "the right thing"? Or have you ever been
in love with someone (like Mac is with Eva) and not said anything
(see p. 142)? What happened?

_____

_____

25. When you hear of atrocities going on in other countries, do they seem like "fiction rather than fact?" (see p. 145). What was your response to the events of September 11, 2001? Did the fact that they happened on American soil impact your thinking in any way?

    Imagine living in a country where each day you wondered when a loved one would be the victim of a bomb in a restaurant or train station . . . or when you'd be hauled off to prison for sharing your faith. What parts of your life would change? How would you view those who suffered in other countries differently?

    _____

    _____

Chapters 19–20

26. "Mac had recorded the landslide toward war with the dedication of a man who believed he had a mission: 'Just show 'em the facts on film. They'll rise up with one voice and put a stop to this!'

    The foolish idealism with which he had first pursued his goal embarrassed him now" (p. 150).

    Can you relate to Mac's experience in any way? If so, how? In what ways has your "mission" in life changed as a result?

    _____

    _____

27. Eva Weitzman feels personally responsible to help the Lubetkin family. "How could she explain that her own life seemed somehow intertwined with the lives of the Lubetkin children?" (see p. 156). Has your life ever seemed "somehow intertwined" with someone you've met only briefly? Has someone's face come frequently to mind, as Sophia, the murdered Polish woman, haunted Horst von Bockman's thoughts (see p. 163)? If so, what kind of impact has that experience had on you?

    _____

    _____

28. "Like Christ Himself it seems the girl has offered her life in exchange for yours. Quite a gift you've been given. A close-up object lesson on how salvation works. . . . You're alive and free. She may not be alive. If she is, she is not free. What will you do with the gift she gave you, Eva?" (Father Brocky to Eva Weitzman, p. 157).

    If someone gave their life in exchange for you, how would you respond? Would you be shocked? grateful? disbelieving? humbled? awed? How would this "gift" change your future thoughts and actions?

This is just what Christ—Jesus, the promised Messiah, Yeshua of Nazareth—offers you. A priceless, eternal gift. His life in exchange for yours.

> "Our Lord came as a Jew to take the sins of all men upon Himself that we might be clean and whole before the Father in heaven."
> —Father Brocky (p. 157)

> "I believe He came to take my place and buy my life by offering His own."
> —Eva Weitzman (p. 157).

Chapters 21–23

29. "No one in America cares. . . . They're all too oblivious to believe what is happening over here. Easier to believe lies of evil men than to stand up and confront evil with the truth. . . . It is only a matter of time before apathy will devour you from inside your own borders" (Lori Kalner, p. 169).

If someone said this to you today, how would you respond? How much do you care about the truth? In what ways can you *actively* show you care about the truth?

"No way to let slogans substitute for actions. If only Christians couldn't preach on and on . . . ! Only way we'd have to tell other people about the love of God would be to show it, to live it. Give a cup of cool water to someone who is thirsty. Comfort some kid. It's not a church or a religion; it's a way of life. It's a different kind of war. It never ends" (Charlie Morris, the London Associated Press chief, p. 183).

---

30. "For the first time—ever—it occurred to me how much like Mama I am. And I am not going to Wales as a daughter to comfort my mother, but as a woman to comfort a woman who has lost her beloved. As I wait to hear news from Jacob—or about Jacob—I

think I may know my own mother better at this moment than I have ever known her in my life" (Lori Kalner p. 176).

In what circumstances have you received insight into someone? How did it make you see that person differently from that point on?

---

31. What would you say to someone like Konrad, who says, "If God is interested at all, I don't believe human motives fit anywhere into His agenda" (p. 181)? Or to Josie Marlow, who wonders, "Was she foolish to hope that somewhere in the horror of war God still existed, still reached out, still changed the course of human events for the sake of righteousness and the value of human life?" (p. 181)?

Chapters 24–26

32. "Whenever God is going to do something mighty, Satan attacks Christians and Jews in the most horrific way. And yet Darkness is, in the end, always defeated by the light of only one candle" (Lori Kalner p. 194).

Do you agree with this statement? Why or why not?

"What men and governments will not accomplish without love and mercy as their creed, the merciful Savior through His church may be capable of" (Father Brocky see p.157).

What can you accomplish with love and mercy this week?

---

33. The terrorist Kevin Miller was very close to killing Lori, Elisa, and Eva when he collapsed and later died of pneumonia. Have you ever been saved by a "near miss" when you could have been severely injured or killed? What happened? How did this change your thinking about your life purpose?

---

34. When Eva's grief had grown too heavy for her to bear, Helen stepped in and said, "It's no good at all to carry such a load alone"

(p. 220). When you have been grieving, who or what has helped you "carry" the load?

If you are in a place to help another who is hurting, let this motivate you:

> *Carry each other's burdens, and in this way you will fulfill the law of Christ.*
> —Galatians 6:2

If you are in need of encouragement, read Helen's soothing words again:

> "There will come a great day when Jesus will wipe every tear. Yes, every tear! But that day is not now. Not yet. And so . . . we must weep together. For those whom we loved. For the lost world we once knew. For the dark road we must walk until at last we reach the light. And then the True Light will embrace us. . . . And Jesus will wipe away even the tears we shed tonight." (p. 221)

_____

_____

Chapters 27–29

35. Josie Marlow, a widow at twenty-seven, longs for what she used to have with her husband, Danny (see p. 224). If you knew that a loved one would die within a year, how would you live "ordinary life" differently than you do now?

_____

_____

36. An angry Katrina shouts at her husband, "You value their good opinion of you more than you value your own opinion of what is true and good!" (p. 228). What about you? Do you value what you think of yourself more than what others think of you? Or do you value what others think of you above what you think of yourself? Explain.

_____

_____

Chapters 30–31

37. Imagine you are a member of the Judenrat committee. As you are handing out cups of tea to the prisoners, you spot a loved one

among the condemned (see p. 229). What would you do, if you couldn't speak or embrace, to say "I love you" and "good-bye"?

_____

_____

38. When Andre Chardon returns to Paris, he longs for company so he doesn't have to think about his memories. When you long for company, to whom do you reach out? Why this person?

_____

_____

39. "To you life is like a library full of first-edition classics. Bound in leather. Gilt edges on the pages. Autographed by the authors. Only you are too busy to open the book and read the story. . . . You have missed the whole point. You give in just a little and think it does not matter. But it does! Add up all the times you have sold a piece of your soul. . . . But heaven redeems the earth one soul at a time" (Paul Chardon to his brother, Andre, p. 259).

    Do you recognize yourself in any of these words? If so, which ones, and why? Do you believe, as Andre says, "It is too late now to make it right" (p. 260)? Why or why not?

_____

_____

Epilogue

40. What keeps you believing and hoping—as Rabbi Lebowitz does— even when you don't see the fulfillment of your dreams and longings?

    "Keep your eyes there. . . . You'll see it soon enough. A light. No bigger than a star from this distance, but shining from the darkness"
    —Samuel Orde (p. 265).

_____

_____

41. Have you, like Jacob Kalner, "come to believe in the angels that Alfie spoke of"? (p. 266). Do you believe God is watching over you? sending His angels to guide your path? Why or why not?

_____

_____

42. "Look!" [Alfie] pointed again toward where the shoreline certainly
lay. "Me and Werner can see it. They are there! Right there where
they are supposed to be! Can't you see?" (p. 266).

    Even in times of darkness, will you choose to believe, like Alfie,
that the bright light of heaven, the "Promised Land," is waiting for
you if you trust Jesus?

_____

_____

About the Authors

Bodie and Brock Thoene (pronounced *Tay-nee*) have written over 45 works of historical fiction. That these best sellers have sold more than 10 million copies and won eight ECPA Gold Medallion Awards affirms what millions of readers have already discovered—the Thoenes are not only master stylists but experts at capturing readers' minds and hearts.

In their timeless classic series about Israel (The Zion Chronicles, The Zion Covenant, and The Zion Legacy), the Thoenes' love for both story and research shines.

With The Shiloh Legacy series and *Shiloh Autumn*—poignant portrayals of the American depression—and The Galway Chronicles, which dramatically tell of the 1840s famine in Ireland, as well as the twelve Legends of the West, the Thoenes have made their mark in modern history.

In the A.D. Chronicles, their most recent series, they step seamlessly into the world of Yerushalyim and Rome, in the days when Yeshua walked the earth and transformed lives with His touch.

Bodie began her writing career as a teen journalist for her local newspaper. Eventually her byline appeared in prestigious periodicals such as *U.S. News and World Report*, *The American West*, and *The Saturday Evening Post*. She also worked for John Wayne's Batjac Productions (she's best known as author of *The Fall Guy*) and ABC Circle Films as a writer and researcher. John Wayne described her as "a writer with talent that captures the people and the times!" She has degrees in journalism and communications.

Brock has often been described by Bodie as "an essential half of this writing team." With degrees in both history and education, Brock has, in his role as researcher and story-line consultant, added the vital dimension of historical accuracy. Due to such careful research, The Zion Covenant and The Zion Chronicles series are recognized by the American Library Association, as well as Zionist libraries around the world, as classic historical novels and are used to teach history in college classrooms.

Bodie and Brock have four grown children—Rachel, Jake, Luke, and Ellie—and five grandchildren. Their sons, Jake and Luke, are carrying on the Thoene family talent as the next generation of writers, and Luke produces the Thoene audiobooks. Bodie and Brock divide their time between London and Nevada.

For more information visit:
www.thoenebooks.com
www.TheOneAudio.com

suspense with a mission

TITLES BY

Jake Thoene

"The Christian Tom Clancy"
Dale Hurd, *CBN Newswatch*

Shaiton's Fire

In this first book in the techno-thriller series by Jake Thoene, the bombing of a subway train is only the beginning of a master plan that Steve Alstead and Chapter 16 have to stop . . . before it's too late.
ISBN 0-8423-5361-5 SOFTCOVER
US $12.99

Firefly Blue

In this action-packed sequel to Shaiton's Fire, Chapter 16 is called in when barrels of cyanide are stolen during a truckjacking. Experience heart-stopping action as you read this gripping story that could have been ripped from today's headlines.
ISBN 0-8423-5362-3 SOFTCOVER
US $12.99

Fuel the Fire

In this third book in the series, Special Agent Steve Alstead and Chapter 16, the FBI's counterterrorism unit, must stop the scheme of an al Qaeda splinter cell . . . while America's future hangs in the balance.
ISBN 0-8423-5363-1 SOFTCOVER
US $12.99

for more information on other great Tyndale fiction,
visit www.tyndalefiction.com